ChangelingPress.com

Doolittle/ Charming Duet

A Dixie Reapers Bad Boys Romance

Harley Wylde

Doolittle/ Charming Duet
A Dixie Reapers Bad Boys Romance
Harley Wylde

ISBN: 978-1-60521-852-6

Publisher:
Changeling Press LLC
315 N. Centre St.
Martinsburg, WV 25404
ChangelingPress.com

Printed in the U.S.A.

Editor: Crystal Esau
Cover Artist: Bryan Keller

The individual stories in this anthology have been previously released in E-Book format.

Table of Contents

Doolittle (Devil's Fury MC 11)
Harley Wylde

Minnie -- The Reckless Kings told me it was pointless to pine after Satyr. I kept offering myself to him, hoping he'd see me as something more. I was a fool. All that man will ever see when he looks at me is a club girl. I'll always be trash in his eyes. So when the President offers me a chance at a new life, I grab on with both hands. It might mean living with yet another club -- the Devil's Fury -- but once I meet Doolittle, my entire world turns upside down. I'd thought myself in love with Satyr, but I was so very wrong. Doesn't matter. Same situation, different man. I might be starting my life over, but Doolittle knows what I am, what I've been… and he'll never want someone like me as his old lady.

Doolittle -- Beast asked a favor and I gladly agreed. I have no problem with a woman who wants a fresh start. Before I even met Minnie, I'd offered to let her work at my clinic. I don't know what I expected. But the stunning woman who shows up leaves me tripping over myself. I've never met anyone like her before, and the instant connection between us is startling. Just one problem. Well, three. The first is Meredith. The girl won't take no for an answer and is determined I'll be hers. The second is that Minnie feels unworthy of being mine. I'll just have to prove her wrong. The third I never saw coming, and it just might change everything.

Prologue

Minnie
Three Months Ago

I stood on the porch of the Reckless Kings' clubhouse and breathed in the night air. Changes had arrived, along with Forge bringing home a wife. Whisper had taken one look at the club girls and seen women in need of help. She'd ensured they got whatever they needed to start their lives over. Since then, every one of them had moved on. Except me. The only thing I wanted she couldn't give me. Satyr.

I'd been watching that man with stars in my eyes for over a year now. He was the only one who ever touched me, even though I didn't think he realized it. Brick would let me sit on his lap if Satyr wasn't around, just so it would look like I was occupied. Didn't fool the brothers. They all knew I was over the moon for Satyr and had eyes only for him.

Tonight things were different. He'd arrived around his usual time, then he'd walked right past me and gone up to one of the new girls. I hadn't fooled myself into thinking the man never touched anyone but me. Seeing it was a different story. The times I was here, Satyr had always spent his time with me. The nights I wasn't around or left early, I had no control over what he did. But this… this was different. It had felt like he'd ripped my heart out and stomped on it. Even worse, the other men had watched it happen and looked at me with pity.

Right about now, Satyr was probably screwing the new girl, if not all of them. And I stood out here, wondering what the hell I would do now. I could go back in and wait to see if he noticed me. Then again, I could go home and order a pizza, curl up with my favorite book, and pretend tonight didn't happen.

I felt a hand land on my shoulder, and I looked up at Copper. He gave me a soft smile and tipped his head toward the door. "You heading back in?"

Before I'd met Satyr, I'd slept with Copper a time or two. It had been nice, but… I shook my head. "I think I'm going home."

He sighed and backed up, letting me go. "Right. Satyr's girl."

"No, I'm not. He's proven that tonight."

"I have no idea why you seem to think he has a magic dick, but I've kept my distance, knowing you only wanted to be with him. I just thought maybe things had changed. The guy is an asshole. He might be my brother, and I'll have his back in a fight, but when it comes to women, the guy has a heart of stone. I'm sorry if seeing him like that hurt you."

"I know, Copper, and I'm sorry. It's not you. I promise."

He waved me off. "No worries. I'd enjoyed our time together and thought maybe I'd have a shot now. I think we both know you weren't made for this life, Minnie. Being a club whore isn't what you really want. Beast has looked the other way, letting you hold out for Satyr, but sooner or later you're going to have to admit he'll never love you."

"Ouch," I muttered.

"Sorry, Minnie. Just telling it like I see it. Hell, everyone knows but you."

"You're right." I faced the parking lot again, knowing it was time to leave. "I'm just a piece of ass to him. It's all I'll ever be. But, Copper, don't pretend you're any different. I could go inside and give you what you want. We'd probably both enjoy it. Then tomorrow you'd be balls deep in someone else. If you even waited that long."

"Minnie, the clubhouse isn't the place for you to find true love. You've met the old ladies here, and even a few from other clubs. Did you notice anything about them?"

"What?" I asked, feeling tired and just worn out by life.

"None of them are, or were ever, club whores. You came here willingly, spread your legs for us, and not one brother in that room will ever forget it. It's shitty, but it's just the way things are. No one wants a club whore for an old lady. Never have, and never will."

Since the only man I'd ever wanted was Satyr, I guessed it didn't much matter. The guys in town wanted one thing from me. The men here were the same. I'd either have to embrace the changes, or… I didn't know what else I could do.

"I'll see you later, Copper." I stepped off the porch and went to my SUV. My life sucked ass, and I didn't know what to do to change it. I wasn't like the girls Whisper had helped. I had a job, even if I hated it. Had an apartment, even if it was crappy. I wasn't trying to take care of kids or running from anyone. I'd just made bad choices, and now I had to live with the consequences. Whatever those might be.

If I came back here, I'd have to become a club whore for real. No holding out for Satyr. No special treatment. Could I do that? Did I want to?

I rubbed my forehead, feeling a headache building. Maybe instead of ordering pizza, I'd stop and get some wine. I needed alcohol more than food right about now. If wine didn't make things better, then I was screwed.

Chapter One

Minnie

I should have left the Reckless Kings long ago. If not back before Whisper came here and shook things up, then definitely after my talk with Copper a few months ago. Instead, I'd decided to stick it out. I'd been with Satyr a few times, but he mostly went to the new girls. I'd known Satyr would never see me as more than a convenience. The others had tried to tell me, and I'd seen their pitying looks on multiple occasions. I'd ignored all of them, holding out the hope that one day, Satyr would look at me and realize I was more than just a club whore.

The nights he hadn't wanted me, I'd had no choice but to be with someone else. Brick wasn't always around. Since his grandson came to live here, there were nights he didn't come to the clubhouse. Most of the guys gave me a wide berth, but that wasn't always the case. Aside from Satyr, only Copper wanted my attention. The others knew I didn't really want them, and they left me alone. For whatever reason, Copper seemed to like me. Not enough to make me his, but it didn't stop him from using me when he could. By being at the clubhouse, I'd given my consent to partying with the members.

The only reason I even came to the Reckless Kings was because of that infuriating man -- Satyr. But tonight, I'd had enough. Satyr had walked past me, immediately started pawing one of the new girls, and after he'd fucked her in front of everyone, he'd moved on his new favorite -- Kelly. She hadn't seemed to mind sharing him and hadn't batted an eye. The fact he'd ignored me all night had been more than I could handle.

In the last three months, I'd been with Satyr a handful of times. I'd been coming here less and less. If it weren't for Brick requesting my presence tonight, I probably wouldn't have come. When he'd asked me to join him for a drink, I hadn't been able to say no.

Brick reached out and grabbed my hand. "I know this isn't how you wanted things to end. We were all hoping Satyr would pull his head out of his ass."

"You've all been warning me for a while now. Everyone knew he'd never want me as more than easy pussy. It was stupid for me to think he might change his mind."

"Minnie, he's my brother and I have to side with him, but... I think he's missing out on something special with you. It's been clear from the beginning you're different from most of the women who come here." Brick patted my hand. "Which is why Beast would like to run an idea by you. Head on back to his office. He's expecting you."

I stood and went down the back hall and knocked on the President's door. I'd wondered why he was here on a party night. Ever since he'd claimed Lyssa, he'd started heading home when things heated up at the clubhouse. I couldn't blame him. His wife was wonderful.

"Come in," he barked.

I opened the door and stepped inside, leaving it open so no one would get the wrong idea. He sighed and rubbed at his eyes.

"Brick said you wanted to see me," I said.

He nodded. "I know things haven't worked out well for you here. You plan on staying in town?"

I shrugged a shoulder. "I have a job and an apartment, but... I really don't want to see Satyr around town if I can avoid it. There's nothing holding me here. My job isn't exactly fabulous."

"I heard you have some experience with animals," he said.

"The human variety or the furred type?" I asked.

He smirked. "Probably both, but I meant the kind with feathers, fur, or scales."

"I do. I worked in the kennels at a boarding place during high school. I mostly dealt with dogs and cats though."

"There's someone with the Devil's Fury arriving here tonight. Goes by the name of Doolittle. He's bringing a puppy for the kids. Someone tossed it into a sack and tried to drown it." I wasn't sure what that had to do with me. Was he asking me to pet sit whenever he went out of town? I must have looked as confused as I felt because he smiled and leaned forward, bracing his elbows on his desk. "The Devil's Fury are down in Georgia. Doolittle isn't just one of their patched members, but he's also a veterinarian. Owns a local practice. I mentioned your situation to him, and he'd like to help."

"Help how?" I asked.

"Meet with him and hear him out. He'd like to hire you to work in the kennels at his clinic, but also to help with the animals he takes home. He has an entire sunroom filled with all sorts of critters that need attention. Sound like something that might interest you?"

I nodded. "It does. Not sure trading one club for another is the smartest idea though."

"You wouldn't be a club whore there, Minnie. It's a fresh start for you. No one in town will know your past, except the Devil's Fury officers and Doolittle. None of them are going to say a damn word to anyone. Even though some of their other members have been here a time or two, I know you didn't spend time with them. I doubt they'd remember seeing you here. Just think about it."

"What time is he getting here?" I asked, fingering my lacy tank top. "Think I have time to go home and change?"

"Doolittle isn't leaving until the morning. Go change and come back here within the next hour or two. He should be here by then and have the puppy unloaded at my house. I offered him the guest home for the night. Just ask whoever's on the gate to point the way. I'll make sure they know you're permitted to go over there."

"Thank you, Beast. This has to be the nicest thing anyone's ever done for me," I said.

He waved me off. "You're a good kid, Minnie. Satyr yanked you around, and I let it go on too long. I knew you weren't interested in anyone else here. Should have sent you home long before now."

"I'm a grown woman, Beast. I made my own choices, and now I get to live with them. But I'd really love a fresh start, even if it's down in Georgia." It would be nice to not have the locals sneer at me, knowing I spread my legs here at the clubhouse. It shouldn't matter. It was my life, and I should be able to do what I wanted, as long as it wasn't illegal and didn't hurt other people. Sadly, that wasn't the case in a small town like this one.

"I realize that, Minnie. Doesn't make me feel any less like an asshole. If you decide you want to move to the Devil's Fury territory, their President has already agreed to letting you use one of the small apartments until you can save up for a place of your own." Beast leaned back in his chair. "Now get out of here. I don't want to see you back in the clubhouse unless it's by invitation of an old lady."

I gave him a nod and left his office. I hadn't really gotten to know the new girls, so I didn't bother telling them bye. But Brick was another matter. I gave him a hug and a kiss on the cheek.

"If I'd been smart, I'd have fallen for you," I said.

He winked. "I'm too old and set in my ways for someone like you. There's a guy out there who will worship the ground you walk on. Just keep looking."

I hugged him again. "I hope you find your woman, Brick. Anyone would be lucky to have you. Even if your daughter did come in and turn this place on its head."

He grinned. "She definitely did. Can't say I'm disappointed in how it all turned out. As much as I'll miss seeing you around here, I'm glad you won't be mooning after Satyr anymore. Get out of here, girl. It's time you find a bit of happiness."

I walked out, refusing to look back. Brick and Beast were both right. I had a chance to make a big change in my life, and I needed to take it. I only hoped Doolittle really did want to hire me. Even if the job didn't pay much, as long as the Devil's Fury gave me plenty of time to build a little nest egg, I'd still accept the offer. If I stayed here, things would remain the same. It wouldn't matter if I never came to the clubhouse again. The town had already labeled me a harlot, and yes, I'd had more than one person call me that to my face.

When I got back to my apartment, I looked around and realized I hadn't accumulated much over the years. Everything but the furniture would fit in my car. If the apartment I'd be using at the Devil's Fury compound was intended for guests, it likely came furnished and had the basics covered for the bathroom and kitchen like towels and cookware. It wouldn't be hard to have everything packed and ready to go by morning.

I stripped off my clothes and started the shower. If I was going to bother changing my outfit, I needed to wash off the scent of the clubhouse too. Even if I hadn't done more than hug Brick a few times, the stench of smoke and sex clung to me. When steam billowed from around the curtain, I stepped into the tub and did a quick wash of my hair, then let the conditioner sit while I scrubbed the rest of me. By the time I'd finished, and dried my hair, more than an hour had passed. I hoped it wasn't going to be too late to speak with Doolittle.

I grabbed a pair of jeans from my closet, and a heather gray V-neck shirt. I wanted to look casual, yet nice enough to be considered for employment at a vet clinic. Looking through the shoes at the bottom of my closet, I opted for my charcoal-colored Converse. Every time I'd gone to the clubhouse, I'd left my hair down. I fingered the long strands and decided to pull it back. I snatched a hair tie off the dresser and pulled the heavy length up off my neck, then dashed out the door.

The gates to the Reckless Kings compound opened as I drove up. I stopped just inside the gate and leaned out to speak with the newest Prospect, Bronsen. "Can you tell me how to get to the guest house? I'm supposed to meet with Doolittle."

Bronsen hunkered down and braced his arms on the door of my small SUV. "Follow the road to the right. You can see Beast's big ass house from here. Go past it and look for a gray Chevy Silverado. That's what Doolittle drove here."

"Thanks."

He backed away and I followed his directions,

finding the house easily enough. I parked next to the truck and checked my reflection in the mirror, making sure I didn't have flyaway strands of hair sticking up every which way. Snapping the visor shut, I took a breath to steady my nerves, and got out.

My door had barely shut when two paws landed in the middle of my chest, and I was knocked off my feet. My ass met the concrete driveway and I winced, knowing it would bruise. The fluffy giant grinned a doggy smile at me. "Well, hello to you too. If that's how you greet everyone, you may need obedience training."

"Sorry about Goliath. He thinks he's the size of a loaf of bread," a deep voice said from nearby.

I craned my neck back and saw Doolittle standing on the porch. Even though I hadn't met him before, he definitely wasn't one of the Reckless Kings. Far as I knew, only one Devil's Fury member had come to visit. "That's a perfect name for him."

I gave the giant floof a shove so I could stand up. Dusting off my pants, I approached the house, trying to get a better glimpse of my possible boss. I went up the steps and nearly tripped over my feet when my gaze met his. *Holy hell! Beast wants me to work with this guy*?

I stared, and then did the most embarrassing thing ever. I blurted out the first thing that popped into my head. "You're gorgeous."

My cheeks burned and my eyes widened. I could feel my heart racing and I wondered if it was too late to get back in the car and pretend this never happened. Doolittle chuckled and shoved his hands into his jean pockets.

"I'm always happy to accept compliments from beautiful women."

My face felt like I'd spiked a fever of a million degrees. He thought I was beautiful? Sure, men had told me that plenty of times. Usually right before they tried getting in my pants. Doolittle only winked then tipped his head toward the front door.

"Why don't we go in and discuss the job? I can go over the day-to-day details of what you'll be doing, what it pays, and all that fun stuff. Then if you haven't eaten dinner yet, maybe you can stick around and share some pizza with me. Although, I should warn you I placed the order right before you got here, so if supreme isn't to your liking, you're out of luck."

"Pizza sounds great, and I eat pretty much anything." I glanced behind him. "Did your old lady come with you? She won't mind if I stay to eat?"

"Don't have one."

I could have sworn I'd heard someone mention a woman in his life. This wasn't the first time Doolittle had come to visit the Reckless Kings, and while I hadn't had a chance to meet him before now, the bikers at the clubhouse gossiped as bad as little old women. The man had been mentioned on several occasions.

"Sorry. I thought someone said…" I shook my head. "Never mind."

"They like to yank my chain. Grizzly has an adopted daughter named Meredith. Her sperm donor was a member who's long gone. Twister. She's followed me around since she was a teenager."

I folded my arms across my stomach and rubbed my toe on the boards of the porch. "She going to be pissed if I come work for you?"

The last thing I needed was to upset Grizzly, and if his daughter got mad about me working for Doolittle, I could only imagine the shitstorm it would create. As badly as I wanted a fresh start, I wasn't sure

I wanted to go to battle with the ex-President's daughter.

"Meredith is a sweet kid. I like her, as a friend. She doesn't get a say in who works for me, or who ends up in my bed." He pinched the bridge of his nose. "Jesus fucking Christ. This is why I don't have an old lady. I can't talk to women for shit. I didn't mean that I expect *you* to warm my bed. The job has no strings attached."

He walked over to the door and pushed it open. I took a step closer, then another, until I crossed the threshold. Even if he'd put his foot in his mouth, I still wanted to hear what he had to say. And I'd never admit the thought of being in the man's bed made my stomach all fluttery. It looked like I hadn't been as in love with Satyr as I'd thought. If I'd been as head over heels for him as I'd claimed, I wouldn't be feeling this way around Doolittle, would I?

Or had seeing Satyr with the other women done more damage to my heart than I'd realized? Even though I'd stuck around, I had to wonder if some part of me hadn't given up on him before now. Every time I'd seen him with the other women, it had felt like he'd taken a hammer straight to my heart. The worst part was that he either hadn't noticed or just hadn't cared.

Boss. Doolittle is going to be your boss. Don't fuck this up by thinking about the man naked!

"So, what would I be doing for your clinic and at your house? Beast mentioned you keep animals there too."

Doolittle motioned toward the couch. "Let's sit and I'll outline everything. If there's anything you aren't willing to do, let me know and we'll figure it out. I understand you want a fresh start, and I'm happy to help make that happen."

I looked away, staring at the far wall a moment. "Is your club going to look at me like…"

"Like you're a whore?" he asked softly.

I nodded. "If things aren't going to be different from here, I'm not sure moving to Georgia will be the least bit helpful. I'm tired of people either walking right up to me in town and calling me names, or the way men look at me. They think I'll bend over if they buy me a drink or a meal."

"Not sure men aren't going to look. I wasn't kidding when I said you're beautiful," Doolittle said.

"It's not the looking so much as *how* they do it. They know why I came to the clubhouse. Since I'm offering myself up to any biker, then I'm free game, right? Because I'm just trash. Only thing I'm good for is a quick fuck."

Doolittle reached over and took my hand. "Stop. I don't see you that way, and my club won't either. The only brothers who are going to know the circumstances of where you came from are me, the Pres, the VP, Treasurer, and the Sergeant at Arms. We don't have a Secretary right now. Although, the Pres is the son-in-law of the old President. It's possible he'll tell Grizzly."

"And you said Meredith is Grizzly's adopted daughter? Does that mean he'll tell her?" I asked.

"No. It's none of her business, or anyone else's. I don't think Grizzly would ever do that. He's all about protecting women and kids."

"All right." I tried to relax again. "Tell me about the job."

Doolittle flashed me a grin and went into the details of what I'd be doing, the hours, and finally how much it would pay. The nine dollars per hour wasn't as great as I'd hoped for, but it was better than making minimum wage. It would still take a while to save up enough to get a place of my own, and I'd likely need a second job at some point.

But I knew I'd be foolish to pass up his offer. Once we'd come to an agreement, I spent the next hour having dinner with him and learning more about the Devil's Fury. If a small voice at the back of my mind whispered I was making a mistake, that was for me to know and no one else. And I hoped like hell it was wrong.

Chapter Two

Doolittle

When the club had mentioned a woman wanted a fresh start, and I'd offered up a job helping with the animals, I'd never imagined she'd have eyes so blue I'd get lost in them. And curves for days… Having Minnie not only underfoot at work, but in my home too, would prove to be challenging. Or rather, keeping my hands to myself would be the issue. I'd met plenty of women who interested me over the years. Not a damn one had made me feel like the earth had tilted under my feet. Until Minnie.

She'd said she didn't have much to pack, which was why I found myself at her apartment bearing gifts. Or more accurately a truck bed of empty boxes, a cup of coffee, and some muffins from the bakery. And I felt nervous as fuck. Christ! It was like being back in high school and wanting to ask my crush on a date, except I wasn't asking Minnie out. Nope. I wouldn't go there. She would be my employee and nothing else.

That's right, asshole. Keep telling yourself that. I had it bad after just one glance, and I fucking knew it. Hell, the moment she'd blurted out the words *"You're gorgeous"* I'd known I wanted her. I could tell she hadn't meant to say it, but I'd found it cute as hell. Especially when her cheeks flushed.

I got out of the truck and scanned the area, noting the drug deal going down at the edge of the building. A few women stumbled home in short skirts and heels, looking a little worn and ragged. What the hell kind of place had she been living in? No matter what it took, I'd make sure Minnie never stayed in a place like this again. Was she even safe here?

Beast had told me where to find Minnie. Bastard

had grinned when I'd asked, like he'd known my reasons weren't entirely altruistic. Fucker. I climbed the steps and found apartment 2B and knocked on the door. I heard her steps draw close and two locks twisted before the door partially opened, a chain still across the top. I bit my lip so I wouldn't tell her exactly how pointless that bit of metal would be if someone really wanted in her apartment.

"Morning, Minnie. Want some coffee and muffins?" I asked.

She shut the door, I heard the slide of the chain, then she yanked the door all the way open. "Why are you here so early?"

I held up the coffee and bakery sack. "Breakfast. I also have boxes and tape in my truck. Thought I'd help you pack so you could follow me home."

She ran a hand through her hair, and I realized she hadn't been up long. The long tresses were a crazy mess with a few strands sticking up. Fucking adorable. Her tank didn't cover much, and I saw her nipples poking through the thin material. The shorts looked more like underwear and when she turned to walk off, I about swallowed my fucking tongue. *Holy shit*! The woman had an ass I'd love to worship, and that little scrap of fabric didn't do much but cling to her like a second skin. It even left a little of her cheeks hanging out at the bottom.

She was killing me. I'd die before I made it home, but what a way to go.

I kicked the door shut and carried the food to the kitchen counter. I kept my back to her as I set everything down. Her apartment was small, all open spaces, except for two doors. I assumed one was the bathroom and the other her bedroom. The kitchen ran the length of the left wall and the living room took up the right side of the room. Despite how shabby the place looked, she'd kept it clean. I could even smell the cleanser she'd last used.

"I should grab the boxes and tape. Both coffees are the same, so grab whichever one you want. I got two blueberry muffins and two chocolate chip. I'm fine eating either so take whatever."

I turned and nearly collided with her. Woman walked as quiet as a cat, or I was still distracted as hell by how sexy she looked first thing in the morning. *Don't look. Don't look.* And my gaze dropped to her breasts. The tank was sheer enough there wasn't much point in her wearing it. I curled my fingers into my palms, making sure I didn't touch her to see if she felt as soft as she looked.

"I should change," she mumbled, her cheeks turning pink.

"Don't do it on my account." I closed my eyes and groaned. "Just forget I said that. Please. I'm going to grab the boxes and see if I left my brain in the truck too."

I heard her snicker then felt her arm brush against me. I opened my eyes and my breath caught as her breasts pressed against me. When she pulled back, I saw a cup of coffee in her hand. I swallowed hard and hoped like hell she didn't realize my cock was doing its best to escape my jeans. Today would have been a good day to *not* tuck my shirt in. I got so used to doing it when I worked at the clinic, it just carried over into my days off.

"If I didn't think it would be a bad idea, I'd just go ahead and flash you. Get it out of the way." Her eyebrows rose. "You're not the first guy to stare at the girls. Won't be the last. In your defense, I did answer the door barely dressed."

"Please don't. Seriously. If you flash me, I'll never be able to forget the sight of your breasts, which will make me want to touch them. Then I'll want to do more than that. Pretty soon I'd be sporting an erection every time you were in the same room as me."

Her gaze dropped and her lips twitched. "Looks like you're having that issue already."

"I meant what I said last night, Minnie. The job at the clinic and my house isn't contingent on you being in my bed. Sex isn't part of the deal at all. Okay?"

She nodded. "All right."

Her expression seemed to close off and I hesitated. I'd thought she'd be happy I wasn't trying to get her into my bed. She'd had enough of that shit already from Satyr. From what Beast said, the guy had been jerking her around for a damn year or more. How had the bastard given her up? I didn't understand how he could have Minnie and even look at another woman.

I knew I'd said the right thing. At least, the morally correct one. So why did she seem almost disappointed? I knew I damn sure was, but that was my issue to deal with.

"Is that not what you wanted to hear?" I asked.

"It's nothing," she said. "You're right. We need to keep things simple. You're my boss, after all. That would have crossed a line."

Right. I turned and walked out before I said something stupid. Again.

I got the boxes and tape, carried them up to her apartment, and spent the next hour helping her pack everything. She'd changed into a pair of jeans that molded to her, and an old Poison shirt that looked like it had seen better days. Or better decades.

Once she was all packed and ready, she loaded

everything into the back of her SUV. Someone who'd lived here as long as Minnie had should own more things. From what I'd seen of her closet, she'd tossed the bulk of her clothes into a pile she said were donations, and packed three pair of jeans, a handful of shirts, and one dress. I'd eyed the clothes she'd discarded and realized they were the things she'd likely worn to the clubhouse.

I'd also discreetly checked her sizes and ordered a few things online while she checked the place over again, making sure she hadn't missed anything. With a half dozen shirts similar to what she'd worn last night, a few more jeans, and two dresses in my shopping cart, I submitted the order, having it all shipped to my house. I hadn't wanted to go too crazy. As it was, she'd probably read me the riot act over buying her clothes. She seemed to like standing on her own two feet, which I admired.

Even though she'd accepted the club's offer of a place to stay, and agreed to work in my clinic and house, I'd seen the glint in her eyes. She'd be saving up and moving out soon enough. Although, with what I'd offered to pay, I didn't think she'd be moving anytime soon. No fucking way I'd let her end up in another apartment of this quality. She deserved better.

"I'm assuming Goliath wasn't the puppy you were leaving with Beast. Where is he?" she asked. "Do we need to pick him up at the compound?"

"No, it seems one of the Reckless Kings decided he needed a dog."

Her eyebrows arched. "Who?"

"Copper. Said he had enough space for the big lug, and the two got along really well. Goliath seemed happy to go with him. I left the things I'd brought along for the trip. Dog bed, two bones, a stuffed toy, and his food and bowls. Already made a recommendation for a vet in the area and asked my office to transfer the records over."

She smiled. "I'm glad he's going to a good home. Copper will probably spoil him rotten."

"Good to know."

She leaned her hip against her car. "Can I ask you something personal?"

"Depends on how personal. There were lines you didn't want to cross."

She rolled her eyes. "Get your mind out of the gutter. *Boss.* It's about your road name. Doolittle. I figured it was because of the character who can talk to animals. Until I looked it up and it's not spelled the same."

"That would be Steel's doing," I said. "There was a general called Doolittle. You're right about the spelling being different. The main reason I got my name was because of the animals, but Steel suggested the altered spelling, like the general's, since I'm also a biker and not afraid to get my hands dirty. I'll do whatever it takes to protect the club and those I love. Even if it means marching straight into war."

"Does that mean I can't call you Dr. Dolittle?"

If she weren't technically my employee, I'd tell her to call me whatever she wanted. Fuck it. I wouldn't be able to hide my attraction to her anyway. If a little flirting was going to be an issue, I needed to know now. "Minnie, you can call me whatever you want."

She bit her lip. "Whatever you say, Doc. I need to drop my keys off with the front office, put the trash in the dumpster, then we can hit the road."

"I'm not letting you do either of those things alone." I folded my arms when she tilted her chin at a defiant angle. "It's not negotiable, Minnie. I saw a drug deal happening when I pulled up, and two hookers coming in from a night of work. I fucking hate that you've been living here."

"I've been doing just fine."

I moved in closer, pulling her against me. "Really? You're doing fine? You sure about that, sweetheart?"

Her cheeks pinked up nicely and she glanced away. "Maybe not entirely fine. But I haven't needed any help, Doolittle."

"Never said you did. Doesn't mean I'm going to let you do this alone though. Just because you can doesn't mean you should. I want you safe, you hear me?"

She nodded. The look she cast up at me had me wanting to toss her over my shoulder and carry her off like a damn caveman. I'd laughed at a few of my brothers when they'd fallen, thinking they were moving too fast. Now I knew exactly how they'd felt. If I hadn't already offered her a job, I'd be luring her home for other reasons. Like putting my name across her back and my kid in her belly.

I released her and grabbed the sack of trash she'd left on the ground nearby. "Come on. Show me where this goes, then we'll leave your keys with the manager. The sooner we put this place behind us, the better I'll feel."

I tried to hide my surprise when she took my hand. Hopefully I succeeded better at that than I had in hiding my hard cock. Damn thing still hadn't softened enough and having her hand in mine only made things worse. I didn't know what the hell to do about her. Logically, I knew I should keep my distance. Be her boss. Her friend. And leave all thoughts behind of ever getting her into my bed.

But since when had anyone at the Devil's Fury thought logically when it came to their women? Why the fuck should I be the first? I'd heard my brothers say how they took one look at their women and just knew… I hadn't understood until now. The moment I'd met Minnie, I'd felt this pull. Like there was no other woman in the world, and I'd wanted to grab hold of her and never let go.

I tossed the bag of trash into the dumpster then went with Minnie to leave the keys and break her rental agreement. The slimy bastard behind the desk tried to get another hundred out of her.

"No one said anything about paying a fee," she said, her brow furrowed.

"Well, I'm sure we could work out other arrangements." The man eyed her tits and licked his lips. I didn't miss the way he shifted in his seat.

"How about you and I come to one instead?" I asked, leaning across the desk and yanking him over it and onto the floor. He sprawled at my feet, and I gave him a hard kick to the ribs before doing my best to put my fist through his face. Twice. I went to pound on him some more when I felt Minnie's small hand on my bicep.

"He's not worth it, Doolittle."

I glanced at her before spitting on the motherfucker whining like a little bitch. "You listen real fucking good, asshole. She's not some damn whore, and she's sure the fuck not spreading her legs or sucking your cock for some supposed fee to get out of this shitty apartment complex. If she weren't here right now, telling me to go easy on you, I'd make sure you were pissing blood for the next week."

He groaned and squeezed his eyes shut. "Sorry."

"Yeah, you're damn right you are. Piece of shit!"

I kicked him again, just because I could, then took Minnie's hand and led her away. My rage hadn't settled even when we reached the cars. I pinned her against the side of her SUV and pressed my forehead to hers.

Minnie slid her hands up my chest to my shoulders. "Thank you for protecting me."

"Sweetheart, I wanted to do far more to that prick. If he pulled that shit with me standing there, what would he have done if you'd been alone?" She leaned into me, and I wrapped an arm around her waist, hugging her tight. "Anyone ever treats you like that again, you come tell me. I'll make sure they learn a lesson they'll never forget."

She brushed a quick kiss against my lips before trying to pull away. I refused to let her go, needing to know why she'd just done that, after saying we needed to keep things uncomplicated. Kissing me, even that small peck, sure the fuck seemed like more than a boss and employee relationship.

"No one's ever done that for me before," she said. "I know Beast called your club and is helping me that way, but I've dealt with men like that apartment manager all my teen and adult life. You're the first man to ever take up for me. It means a lot."

"No offense, but I think you've been hanging out with shitty men if that's the case. Including the Reckless Kings. Beast may have stepped up for you now, but where the fuck was he the past year while Satyr was yanking your strings?"

"That was my own doing. I'm the one who kept thinking Satyr would see me as more than a club whore. I was stupid and should have walked a long time ago."

"Loving someone is never stupid, Minnie. Not

even when they don't love you back. It took guts to stick it out and try to win him over. Especially a guy with a name like Satyr. I mean, wasn't that a big enough clue he put his dick in anything that held still long enough?" I grinned to soften the blow. "His loss is my gain. Well, mine and all the animals. They're going to love you."

She eyed her SUV. "How long is the trip to the Devil's Fury compound?"

"About six hours. Little more depending on number of stops and how fast you want to drive. Why?"

"I'm nervous about meeting all of them and seeing my new place. I know I need to make this change, and I'm eager to get started on my new job. But..."

"Change is always scary," I said.

"Could we stay somewhere overnight? Maybe halfway there? I think I need a night away from this place before I jump into my new life with both feet. Or do you need to get back right away?"

Technically, yeah. I did need to be back. I wasn't scheduled at the clinic tomorrow, but the animals at home would need to be tended. I pulled out my phone and messaged Meredith.

Can you feed and water everyone for another night? Things are taking a little longer than expected.

I saw the little dots that showed she was typing then her response popped up. *Sure thing. Drive safe! Can't wait for you to be home.*

Well, fuck my life. If everyone hadn't kept teasing me about Meredith liking me, or trying to push the two of us together, then maybe she wouldn't still have a crush on me. I knew that's all it was. At least, I hoped so. She might look at me with lust every now and then, but I'd never seen that soft sappy look someone gets when they're head over heels in love. Didn't mean shit wouldn't hit the fan when Meredith realized I was bringing a woman home. Unless Grizzly had already told her. I just hoped like fuck he'd kept his mouth shut about Minnie's past. I'd assured her no one would say anything, but the more I thought about Meredith and how tenacious she could be, I hoped I hadn't lied to Minnie.

"We'll stop on the other side of Atlanta. It's a little more than halfway." I tucked her hair behind her ear. "Give me your phone. I'll program in my number. You need to stop anywhere between here and there, you call me. Wish like fucking hell you didn't have to drive your SUV down there. I'd prefer to let you ride in the truck next to me."

"It's fine, Doolittle. I'll be okay driving that far. And yes, I'll call if I need any breaks. Promise."

I kissed her forehead before I could think better of it and backed up so she could get into her car. Once she'd buckled and locked the doors, I got into my truck and led the way down south into Georgia.

Chapter Three

Minnie

Why the hell had I asked to stay at a hotel overnight with him? Well, I knew why. Didn't mean I should have done it. The man was irresistible. I hadn't lied about being nervous though. It really did scare the crap out of me to move into an unknown town, and into a compound of bikers I either didn't know at all or had only met in passing once or twice.

The pinched look on Doolittle's face told me something hadn't gone according to plan. I'd waited in the parking lot while he checked in. Seeing one keycard in his hand wasn't a big surprise. Had he thought I'd intended to have my own room? Because I hadn't. We could share a room easily enough, especially since most hotels and motels had rooms with two beds.

I rolled down my window and looked up at him. "Why do you look like a bear with a thorn in its paw?"

His brow smoothed and he gave me a slight smile. "Sorry. They had a room available, but there's apparently a few weddings happening this weekend. We only got this one because of a last-minute cancellation."

"I'm confused. Is that a bad thing? Does it cost too much? I'm all right driving straight through if that's better for us."

"It's not the cost, Minnie." He sighed and hunkered down, making himself eye level with me. "The room only has one bed. It's a king size, but I didn't want you to think I was trying to get in your pants."

I snorted. "It's not like I'm a virgin, Doolittle. Besides, even if my fresh start begins in your town, I was still technically a club whore last night."

He growled and his jaw tensed. His touch wasn't gentle when he reached out and gripped my jaw. "Listen well, little one. I won't lie and say I don't want you, because I do. More than I've ever wanted anyone. But it has *nothing* to do with your status at the Reckless Kings. Understood? You don't bring that shit up around me again."

"I'm sorry, Doolittle." I reached up and covered his hand with mine. I'd never had someone get so upset over me badmouthing myself before. Although, I'd only told the truth. Maybe I hadn't made the right decision with the Reckless Kings, but I couldn't change my past. It was a piece of what made me… well, *me*.

"You packed an overnight bag, right?" he asked.

"Yeah. It's in the backseat."

"Grab it and let's go." He went to his truck and pulled a duffle from the front floorboard, then waited patiently while I got my bag, my purse, my phone, and made sure I had my tablet. I locked my SUV and followed him inside the hotel.

We took the elevator to the third floor, and he led the way to our room. His phone started ringing and he paused to check the screen, then silenced it. I had to admit, the fact he'd ignored it made me wonder who was calling. Not that it was any of my business. Nope. He was my boss and nothing more. If some woman was going to blow up his phone, it didn't matter to me at all.

Shit. He'd said we'd be sharing a king size bed. Plenty of space for us to keep to our sides, except… I knew I tended to move around a lot in my sleep. What if I groped him? Even worse. What if I *talked* in my sleep and he found out exactly how bad I wanted him? I'd woken this morning with my panties soaked and my nipples hard, with Doolittle's name on my lips.

No, the worst thing would be waking up to find out I'd been masturbating to thoughts of Doolittle and calling out his name. That would be embarrassing as hell. I'd never be able to look him in the eye again.

On the plus side, my body and brain clearly got the message Satyr was a dick. Knowing he didn't have a hold over me anymore did make me feel free. Doolittle unlocked our room and pushed the door open then motioned for me to enter first. Sunlight filtered through the curtains so I could see the room well. Part of me had hoped there'd been a mix-up or miscommunication and I'd see two beds. But nope, Doolittle hadn't lied and neither had the desk clerk. Only one bed in the room. The sight of it, and the thought of sharing it with Doolittle, both terrified and excited me. It looked smaller than I'd pictured a king would be. I set my bag and purse on the dresser before I walked over to the window.

"Our room actually overlooks a little park," I said. "I've always gotten rooms with a view of the next building. This is nice."

Doolittle came up behind me, the heat of his body making me want to lean back into him. I refrained. Barely. His phone started ringing again and he cursed, silencing it once more. Whoever was calling really wanted to speak to him. Did he not want to talk to them while I was around?

"If you want to take that, I can step out and find the ice machine or something," I offered.

"That what you think? I'm avoiding the call because of you?"

I shrugged a shoulder. "They seem persistent."

It rang again and he cursed as he silenced it a third time. "It's Meredith, and she's pissing me off."

Meredith? He'd said she was watching the animals at his house while he was gone. I also remembered him saying she had a crush on him. Something told me it was more than that. Someone didn't call this many times in a row unless it was an emergency, or they were obsessed. Neither option sounded good.

I turned to face him. "What if it's about the animals? One of them could be hurt."

He smiled softly and cupped my cheek. "Such a sweetheart. Already worrying about the crew and you haven't even met them yet."

Hard not to worry about them. I'd always liked animals more than people. Less chance of getting hurt. If an animal bit you, they were usually scared. People were just outright assholes a lot of the time.

He pulled up his contacts and sent a message to Meredith, not bothering to hide the screen. I wanted to be good and not peek, but curiosity got the better of me. I had a feeling his words weren't going to make the woman the least bit happy.

We're settling into the hotel and figuring out dinner. Is there an emergency with the animals?

"Did she know you were staying at a hotel with me tonight?" I asked.

"I don't think I brought it up. Why?" His phone started ringing again and he grumbled as he answered the call. "Is one of the animals sick?"

I couldn't hear the other side of the conversation, but Doolittle looked about ready to launch his phone across the room. I wondered if maybe Meredith was being extra clingy because she knew he was with me. This seemed like a lot more than some schoolgirl crush. Of course, I had no idea how old she was. Meredith could very well be older than me. It was possible he was every bit as blind to Meredith as Satyr was to me. Did the woman love him? If so, she wasn't going to like me being in his house, even if it was just to work.

"Meredith, if this isn't about the animals, then I need to go. I told you that I'd see you when I got back. Stop calling. You're blowing up my damn phone because you're feeling insecure."

I winced. Not the right thing to say to a woman, especially one showing obsessive behavior. Doolittle ended the call. Before he could put the phone away, she'd started calling him again.

"I don't think that worked," I said.

"Nope, but I know what will. Give me a second and we'll see if there's a restaurant guide or something in one of the drawers." He pulled up Grizzly in his contacts and put the call on speaker.

"Doolittle, you shouldn't --" He gave me a glare that silenced me.

The call connected. "Hello."

"Griz, it's Doolittle. I need a favor."

"Something wrong?" Grizzly asked.

Doolittle held my gaze a moment. "You know I went to the Reckless Kings to drop off a puppy and talk to Minnie. I'm bringing her back with me. But your daughter is being a pain in my damn ass. She's called more than four times. I don't know why her infatuation has turned into an obsession, but you need to get her under control."

He showed me the screen and Meredith's name flashed on the screen. She was calling *again*? Jesus. He had a right to be concerned. If there wasn't an emergency, then her behavior was beyond crazy. Had she thought one day Doolittle would fall for her, the way I'd stupidly thought Satyr would ever give me a chance? My heart hurt for her if that was the case.

Doolittle had made it clear to me he didn't think of her as more than a friend. From what I'd gathered, he'd said the same to both her and at least some of the members of his club.

"You know she's in love with you," Grizzly said. "Why can't you take her on a date and see how things go? The two of you get along."

Meredith's name flashed on the screen again as she called for a sixth time. The woman was persistent. She must want Doolittle awfully bad to keep calling, even after he told her not to. I think if he'd spoken to me in that tone, I'd have given him a wide berth for a bit. Clearly she'd made him angry. If she couldn't tell, then someone needed to clue her in.

"Not the point, Griz. Your daughter is out of control. Since I placed this call, she's tried reaching me twice more. And I already spoke to her. There's no emergency."

"Doolittle, she doesn't mean any harm. You know that."

I inched a little closer and looked at the phone before gazing up at Doolittle. He tipped his head to the side then gave me a nod.

"Um, Grizzly? This is Minnie. I know I'm a complete stranger to you, and I don't have the entire story of what's going on. But I had feelings for one of the Reckless Kings. He didn't feel the same way. It was a painful lesson. More embarrassing than anything really. My point is that Meredith is probably feeling threatened that Doolittle is bringing me home with him. She's trying to hold onto him, and speaking from experience, the harder she chases him the worse it's going to be later."

He snorted. "No offense, Minnie, but you're right. You don't know anything about the situation. I appreciate you trying to help, but this isn't any of your business."

I stepped back. "You're right. I'm sorry."

I looked around the room, wondering where I could run to. It seemed I kept making stupid choices. I hadn't even arrived at the Devil's Fury compound, and I'd already made a bad impression with one of the brothers. If this didn't work out, I had nowhere to go. I couldn't afford to piss them off. No matter how much I wanted to help, or how attracted I felt to Doolittle, I needed to keep quiet. Just do my job and keep to myself. If I did that, then maybe I could save up enough to get my own place sooner rather than later. I had a feeling I wasn't going to want to stick around the club.

"Grizzly, that was a shitty thing to say." Doolittle glowered at the phone. "I'm not dating Meredith. In all the years she's been with the Devil's Fury, not once have I ever wanted to ask her out. There's no attraction on my end. Not even a little. If anything, she's more like my baby sister. That's not going to change just because you and everyone else seems to want it to. I think you owe Minnie an apology, and you sure the fuck owe me one."

The man sighed. "I'm sorry if I've been pushing so hard. I just want to see her happy. She's been through so much, Doolittle."

"That's no excuse, Griz. Every old lady with the Devil's Fury has a shitty past. Each of your adopted kids has been through a fuck ton of crap. It doesn't condone Meredith's behavior or give her a free pass. She's been with us for years. Years! I'm sorry, but I'm putting my foot down. It's time for all of you to quit giving her hope that I'll ever claim her as my old lady. It's never happening. All y'all are doing is setting her up for more heartbreak." Doolittle reached out and grabbed my hand as I went to pass him. He laced our fingers together so I couldn't escape, and I stood awkwardly listening to his conversation. "I'd appreciate it if you'd talk to your daughter. I know you like spoiling those girls and giving them everything they've ever wanted, but I'm not a prize to hand over to Meredith."

"I'll have a chat with her. When are you coming home?"

"Tomorrow." Doolittle squeezed my fingers. "Minnie needed a night away from the Reckless Kings before jumping into her new life. I didn't see the harm in the delay."

"So you have my daughter watching your zoo so you can spend the night with the whore?" Grizzly asked.

I felt the blood drain from my face, and I yanked on my hand, trying to break free from Doolittle. It seemed word had already spread, and I hadn't even made it to the Devil's Fury compound yet. Coming with him had been a mistake. I'd never get away from that label. It didn't matter that I'd moved to another state. As long as I remained in the company of bikers, they would know who I was and what I'd been. None of them would ever allow me to become something more.

"I don't know what the hell has gotten into you, Grizzly, but you've gone too fucking far. I've never known you to treat a woman this way. Whatever is going on, you need to handle it. I won't stand around and let you or anyone else disrespect Minnie." Doolittle ended the call without giving the man a chance to respond.

Tears burned my eyes. "I shouldn't have come

with you."

Doolittle tossed his phone onto the bed and tipped my chin up. His touch was so gentle. So… kind. It broke me. I couldn't stop crying and leaned into him, sobbing as if my heart had been smashed to bits. And perhaps it had. If I'd never seen Satyr, never been tempted to go to the clubhouse to visit him, then I wouldn't be here now. I'd still be considered respectable back home and wouldn't have needed to leave.

The Devil's Fury might have offered me a place to land, but the idea of a fresh start had been slaughtered with Grizzly's words. If he felt that way, then others probably did too. Doolittle said the club kept pushing Grizzly's daughter at him, and I knew they'd see my presence as a threat. The moment Meredith let her displeasure be known, every last person there would turn against me.

Doolittle dried my tears and smoothed my hair back. I looked up at him, wondering why I couldn't have met a guy like him before now. I'd thought good men no longer existed. Before I could process what he was doing, he leaned down and captured my lips in a kiss. I sucked in a breath, and he took advantage, his tongue sweeping into my mouth. I clung to him, worried my knees would give out at any moment.

Doolittle put his arms around me and held me closer, my body pressed tight to his. I couldn't hold back a whimper as he took control, bending me to his will. I felt like I was going up in flames, and all I could think was that I wanted more. What would it hurt to grab hold of something I wanted just this once? I knew it wouldn't last. Doolittle would go back to his life, and I'd start mine over tomorrow. But for tonight…

"I want you, Minnie. Say yes. Please tell me you

feel whatever this is between us."

"I want you too," I admitted.

"Thank fucking Christ," he muttered, reaching for the hem of my shirt. I let him pull it off and toss it aside. He cupped my breasts, stroking my nipples through my bra. "So damn beautiful, Minnie."

"I'm not anything special."

"I disagree." He reached behind me and popped the clasp on my bra, then slid the garment down my arms. I unfastened my jeans and shimmied out of them, leaving me only in my panties.

As Doolittle reached for the last bit of my clothing, I had a moment of panic and reached down to still his hands. "Wait."

"If you've changed your mind, it's all right."

I shook my head. "It's not that. I do want you, more than anything. But I… Beast always made the men use condoms. I still think I should get tested. I'd have done it before I left, but it all happened so suddenly."

"Who were you with?" he asked, his gaze turning dark for a moment.

"Satyr and Copper. But Satyr has been with the new girls the last few months. And those are just the women I know about. Who knows where Copper has put his dick? Condoms break or go bad. I don't want to risk your health, Doolittle."

"It's my choice if I want to take that chance, Minnie, but knowing you want to protect me just proves that you aren't the whore they keep calling you. I've known plenty of those women. None of them are anything like you." He ran his hands down my arms, his touch light and teasing. "Did any of the men in your life ever worry about your pleasure? Or did they only take what they wanted?"

My cheeks burned. "I've found bikers don't much care if the club whores enjoy themselves. We're there to serve a purpose and nothing more."

"Bastards," he said, frowning at me. "Let me show you how it *should* be between a man and a woman. I want to make you scream my name, claw up my back, and beg me for more."

I licked my lips and gave him a nod. "All right, if you're certain. But you should use a condom, just in case."

I didn't get a chance to say anything else, like he should use one anyhow since I wasn't on birth control. I had been, until the prescription ran out. There hadn't been time to schedule an appointment to get a refill, and since my yearly exam was due, they weren't going to call it in without seeing me first. Before I could get the words out, his lips were on mine again.

His hands skimmed down my sides to my panties and I felt him push them over my hips. It didn't seem fair that he'd bared me completely and he hadn't removed a single piece of clothing. I pushed at his cut, hoping he'd take the hint, but he grabbed my hands and held them at the small of my back.

His mouth dominated mine and my pussy grew slick with need. My nipples hardened and pressed against him. No one had ever made me feel like this before. Not even Satyr. I had a feeling he was about to ruin me completely. After tonight, I'd never be able to settle for a selfish lover ever again.

Chapter Four

Doolittle

I knew exactly what I was doing, and I hoped like hell she didn't hate me for it later. While I knew there was a good chance if she'd been with Satyr, she could very well have caught something, I had no fucking intention of using a damn condom. Not with Minnie. She may not know it yet, but she was mine. The moment I'd seen her, smelled her sweet scent, touched her soft skin, I'd known.

Yeah, it was careless and the gamble could come back to bite me in the ass later. It wasn't like I'd never been with any of the club whores at the Devil's Fury. While I'd wrapped my dick every time, that little bit of latex was never a guarantee. The damn things broke too often. It hadn't happened to me, but I knew others had dealt with the issue.

I toppled her to the bed and shrugged off my cut, tossing it onto a chair. I yanked my shirt over my head and toed off my boots. By the time I'd unfastened my pants, I knew I needed another taste of her. I leaned over her body, pressing her down into the mattress, as I kissed the hell out of her. She grabbed at my shoulders and moaned as I nibbled her bottom lip.

Working my way down her body, I paid extra attention to her breasts. She had the prettiest nipples and I took my time sucking and licking them. Minnie tasted every bit as wonderful as I knew she would. I couldn't wait to fuck her pussy with my tongue and have her come on my face.

I leaned back and looked down her body, admiring the view. There wasn't a single inch of her I didn't want to kiss and touch. I'd gone to bed last night with my cock in my hand and images of Minnie in my head. Yeah, I'd yanked one out picturing her just like this.

Kneeling at the foot of the bed, I shoved her thighs wide and groaned at how pretty and pink she was. Her pussy was already wet and swollen. Eager for my cock. I leaned in and licked her, gathering her sweet taste before going back for more. When I sucked her clit into my mouth, she shrieked and her thighs clamped down on me. My beautiful girl came so hard she soaked me and the bed, and I didn't fucking care. I loved every damn minute of it.

"Need you inside me," she said, reaching down to run her fingers through my hair. "Please, Doolittle."

"My name is Zachary." I moved up over her, shoving my jeans down enough to free my cock. "When I'm inside you, I don't want the name Doolittle on your lips. You say my real name."

Without giving her a chance to say anything, I thrust into her and damn near came on the spot. She felt like warm, wet silk around me. I reached up and pinned her hands over her head, wrapping my fingers around her wrists. Using the other hand to brace myself, I stroked in and out of her, each one a little harder than the previous.

Minnie wrapped her legs around my waist, letting me slide in deeper. "Fucking killing me, Minnie. Feel so damn good."

"I'm close," she said. "Don't stop. Please, Zachary."

Hearing my name was enough to set me off. I fucked her harder, driving into her as I came. Yeah, I was an asshole, filling her with my cum. But I'd done it on purpose. I wanted Minnie with me, by my side, in my bed. And if I had to knock her up to accomplish it, then that's what I'd do. Even if she was on birth control, there was still a chance it would fail. I might be an animal doctor and not a human one, but even I knew there were plenty of cases where women got pregnant while on the pill, having an IUD, or being on the shot.

I kissed her and changed the angle of my hips, brushing against her clit on the next stroke. It was enough to make her come, her pussy clenching down on my cock. I released her hands, and she gripped my shoulders, her nails biting into me.

"I'm ordering room service because we aren't leaving the hotel," I said before kissing her again. "After I've fed you, we're doing this again. And again. We'll be exhausted in the morning, but I want you to know exactly how beautiful you are, how wonderful."

"Doolittle…"

I growled and nipped at her. "That's not what we agreed you'd call me."

"Zachary," she said softly. "You know this can't go anywhere. We can have tonight, and that's all. Your club will never accept me. You heard Grizzly. There will be others who think the same way."

I stood and finished removing my clothes. "Turn over."

She gave me an apprehensive look as she did as I'd commanded. The way she obeyed without question had my dick getting hard again already. Minnie rolled to her stomach, and I yanked her back and lifted her onto her knees. With her ass in the air, I smacked each cheek, leaving a pink handprint on each side. She squeaked and tried to scramble away, but I pinned her with my body before thrusting into her again.

"Never disobey me, Minnie."

She whimpered as I took her rougher than I'd intended. The way she pressed back into me, arching her back, let me know I wasn't hurting her. No, the little minx was enjoying herself. I worked a hand under her hips and found her clit, rubbing it with small tight circles. She cried out my name, her release squirting around my cock. My body rocked against hers faster and I filled her with my cum a second time.

"You haven't been using protection," she murmured.

"No, I haven't." I pulled out and lifted her into my arms. I settled her on the bed with her head on the pillows and stretched out next to her. She curled against me, tears slipping down her cheeks. "Why are you crying?"

"I told you that I didn't know if I was clean. You… What if…"

I tipped her chin up and pressed my lips to hers in a soft kiss. "It was my decision, Minnie. Are you on birth control?"

Her eyes went wide and she stopped breathing. I saw panic flash in her eyes and had my answer. The thought of her swollen with my child made me want to beat on my chest like a caveman.

"I…"

"It's okay. Let's rest a moment then we can order some food." I held her close, hoping I hadn't made a mistake. I knew some of the others had knocked up their women to make sure they stayed. What if it backfired with Minnie? I didn't even know if she wanted children. Yeah, I'd been a complete and total ass. And I already knew I wouldn't be using a condom at any point tonight, or ever. Not with her.

Jesus. Steel kept telling me I was different from the others. It seemed he was dead fucking wrong, because I wanted Minnie and I was going to make her mine. Didn't matter what anyone said. If she resisted,

I'd wear her down.

"Why couldn't I have met you sooner?" she murmured, her finger tracing a pattern on my chest. "I didn't know men like you existed."

"Assholes who take what they want?" I asked.

She poked at me. "No. You're a good guy, Zachary, and you know it. The men I've known, the ones I've been with, they aren't anything like you."

I squeezed her hip and tugged her closer. "Rule number one. No talk of other men while we're in bed. For that matter, no talk of other men around me at all. Understood?"

"Not even a little." I felt her smile against me. "You almost sound jealous, but that's ridiculous. We don't know each other. Starting tomorrow, things will be different. I'll be your employee and nothing more."

I covered her body with mine and pinned her to the bed. "That what you think?"

Her brow furrowed and she stared up at me. I could almost see the thoughts flitting through her mind. I'd confused the hell out of her. She'd said she wasn't used to men like me, and I believed her. How any of those assholes at the Reckless Kings could have let her slip through their fingers was beyond me. Minnie was stunning, so fucking responsive, and I couldn't seem to get enough of her. Not just for sex. I might have only known her for about a day, but she fascinated me. And sure, we hadn't had as much of a chance to talk as I'd have liked, but what I'd heard so far, I certainly liked. Just being with her made me feel… different. More alive.

"Do you really think now that I've been inside you, tasted you, that I would ever let you walk away?" I asked.

Her eyes widened. "What are you saying?"

"You're mine, Minnie. Whatever it takes to convince you of that, I'll do it. But tonight isn't a one-time thing. Don't make me be a complete dick. You know damn well there are ways to keep you by my side."

Her lips parted and she let out a soft cry. "Did you… did you *try* to get me pregnant?"

"No. Yes." I hesitated. "Maybe."

She beat on me with her fist. "Why would you do that? What's wrong with you? You can't just go around trying to knock someone up! What the hell, Doolittle?"

I growled and put more weight against her. "That's not what you call me."

"Right now it is because you're an asshole biker just like all the others. Is that what this is about? Proving you *aren't* different? Because congratulations. You've succeeded."

I closed my eyes and put my face in the crook of her neck. *Fuck*! The woman had me tied in knots. The fact Meredith was *still* calling had me wanting to beat the hell out of someone. And now Minnie was calling me on my shit.

"I'm sorry." I lifted my head and held her gaze. "Hearing what Grizzly said about you, even thinking anyone would ever dare say that to you, it pissed me off and made me a little irrational. Even worse, you believed him. It's not that everyone else thinks you're just a club whore, Minnie, it's that *you* believe it too."

"So… you're what? Going to claim me to prove me and everyone else wrong? Do you hear how insane that sounds?" she asked.

"The only crazy thing is that I've been alive for over thirty years, and not once have I ever felt the way I did the moment I met you. You got out of your car, and I couldn't look away. I wanted to kiss you the second you were close enough to touch." I ran my nose down the length of hers before kissing her. "The men in my club all fall hard and fast. I never understood… until now."

"They'll never let us be together," she said. "You know it as well as I do."

"You seem so certain of that."

She sighed. "You heard Grizzly. What do you think the rest of your club will say? Especially if Meredith loses her shit? The girl is crazy about you, emphasis on crazy apparently, and your club sounds like they dote on her. You may not know what I'm walking into, but I do. It's not going to be sunshine and roses for me. They're going to do their best to run me out of there."

"I won't let them. Minnie, I've never felt this way before. If I'm going to have to fight the club, then so be it. You're worth it."

Her eyes misted with tears, and I could see her struggling to hold them back. It gutted me that she wasn't used to people being kind to her. She was so sweet. How could anyone ever hurt her on purpose? If Satyr hadn't done me a favor by pushing her away, I'd hit the bastard next time I saw him.

I wanted everyone to know she was mine, but it seemed she didn't want the same thing. Or rather, she did, but she was too scared. After everything she'd been through, I couldn't blame her.

"What about this… Around other people, we act like we're just boss and employee. Maybe friends. At night, you're mine. Whatever stolen moments I can have with you, I'll take. I'm not giving up, Minnie. I refuse."

"This is going to be really hard, Zachary. You

know that, right?"

"Nothing worth having ever comes easy." I pushed my cock against her pussy, easing inside her. "Except you, my pretty Minnie. You come so *so* easily."

She bit her lip and arched her hips, taking me in deeper. "Horrible pun, but you aren't wrong. It's never happened before. It's like you have a magic cock."

I grinned and thrust into her with slow, steady strokes. "Magic cock?"

Minnie moaned and I felt her pussy clench me tighter. She was already close. It wouldn't take much to make her orgasm. And I fucking loved it! I held her gaze, watching her expressions. The moment she started to come, her cheeks flushed and her eyes partially closed. Minnie tossed her head back and gave the sexiest cry as her pussy milked my cock. I filled her up, sliding in and out of her until every last drop of cum had been wrung from my balls.

"This is nuts," she murmured.

"Might be. Doesn't mean I'm backing down. There's only one other thing I've ever wanted near this bad. Well, two. Being part of the Devil's Fury and becoming a vet. I already accomplished both of those tasks. But I think getting you to fall in love with me will be the hardest thing I've ever done."

She leaned up and pressed her lips to mine. "Not as difficult as you think. I'm already partway there."

"Me too, pretty girl. Me too."

I'd always laughed at those love at first sight movies. It had seemed like utter garbage. Then Minnie came into my life. I might not be all the way in love with her, but I was definitely heading that way. Instant lust was certainly a thing. I'd seen it often enough. Even felt it a few times. This wasn't that. What I felt for Minnie was different. Scary. Thrilling. And I knew that having her in my life would change everything.

Fuck anyone who tried to get between us!

If the club tried to keep us apart, I'd come out swinging.

Meredith wouldn't back down? I'd have to stop being so damn nice and get real with her. Even if it made her cry and broke her heart.

Anyone else tried to take Minnie away, and I'd show them why I was part of the Devil's Fury. I might be considered one of the weaker links, but I wouldn't back down from this fight. Minnie was worth… everything.

Chapter Five

Minnie
One Week Later

The way Doolittle kept eyeing me at the clinic, it was no wonder the other workers gossiped. I might not hear everything they were saying, but the way they looked at me and stopped whispering when I got closer, said plenty. I'd even heard one of them call me a slut. I could have told Doolittle, but what was the point? He couldn't fire everyone who didn't like me.

It didn't help he did things like corner me when he thought no one was watching. Like now. I'd walked past and he'd grabbed my arm, hauling me into his office and shutting the door. The second I heard the lock click, I knew he was up to no good.

"Doolittle, you're going to get me in trouble."

He flashed me a smile. "As your boss, I can guarantee you won't be punished. Unless you want to be."

My cheeks warmed at his suggestion and I bit my lip. When he said things like that, how could I possibly refuse him? I couldn't lie and say I didn't want him. My panties were already wet. I shifted, rubbing my thighs together. He caught the movement and kissed me, pressing me back against the wall.

"Someone will hear," I murmured.

"Then you'll have to be quiet."

He dragged me over to his desk, swiped all his papers onto the floor, then bent me over the surface. The cool air hit my ass cheeks as he yanked my pants and panties down. One touch of his fingers against my pussy, and I knew I was going to give him whatever he wanted. Mostly because I wanted it too, no matter how much I protested.

He parted the lips of my pussy and rubbed my clit. I ground my teeth together and shut my eyes, willing myself not to make a sound, but it was damn hard. All I wanted to do was beg for more, scream his name, and let everyone know how amazing he made me feel.

"I have ten minutes until my next appointment," he murmured, as I heard the rustle of his clothing. Then I felt his cock pressing into me. "Sorry, sweetheart. This will be quick."

Like I cared? He thrust into me and I nearly saw stars. I squeezed his cock and heard him groan. Doolittle gripped my hips and hammered into me, every stroke deeper than the one before, until I knew I'd taken every inch of him. I grabbed hold of the edge of the desk and buried my face against my arm, knowing I wouldn't remain silent for long.

He changed his angle and hit that special spot inside me, and that's all it took. Two strokes and I was coming so damn hard. He growled and slammed into me faster, chasing his own orgasm. When he came, I felt the heat of his release. The man had a tendency to avoid condoms. Right about now, it would have been nice not to have a mess to clean up.

He pulled out and grabbed two tissues out of the box on the corner of the desk, pressing them between my legs. I used them to wipe myself clean but knew more would be trickling out over the next fifteen minutes or so. It happened every time, and I ended up with a sticky mess in my panties the rest of the workday. The way he smirked as I righted my clothes said he damn well knew it, and enjoyed the fact I was covered in his cum.

I stood facing him and Doolittle wrapped his arms around me, kissing the side of my neck, my jaw, then my lips. "Wish I could close everything down and spend the day with you."

"That's not going to happen, Zachary. You have patients to tend to, and I need to leave soon to care for the animals at home."

He rubbed his beard against my neck. "I love when you call my place home."

It's how I thought of it, even if I didn't live there. He drew back and yanked at my top, lifting it to my chin. He yanked the cups of my bra down and leaned forward to suck and lick my nipples. Moaning, I held him close.

"No fair. Now I want you again," I said.

"Later. When I get home, we'll rinse off in the shower, then I'm fucking you until neither of us can stand. One of these days, you're going to stay in my bed all night. I can never get enough of you, Minnie."

I kissed him to refrain from admitting I felt the same. I had a sinking feeling that my heart would end up broke again. He'd kept our relationship a secret from everyone, and while I understood to some extent, it still hurt. I felt like his dirty little secret.

"Get back to work, Doc. I'll see you later."

He swatted my ass on my way to the door, and I hoped like hell all this wasn't going to blow up in our faces at some point. I wanted him. Needed him. And despite how new things were between us, I was almost all the way in love with him already. But I felt like I wasn't getting *all* of Doolittle, and that scared the shit out of me. Loving a man who wasn't fully committed would only end in disaster.

* * *

Two Weeks Later

My hair kept falling out of my ponytail. Or

rather, the cute little marmoset Doolittle had in his house kept yanking the hair tie out and throwing it across the room. It liked to groom me then snuggled in my hair while it rode around on my shoulder. The adorable little guy was only a temporary resident while Doolittle arranged for him to move to a wildlife sanctuary. I'd miss him when he left.

I pulled another tie from my pocket and pulled my hair back again. The moment the little guy reached for it, I plucked him off my shoulder and returned him to his cage. He fussed at me, and I had a feeling he'd make a bigger mess for me to clean up.

Two of the rabbits went racing across the floor and I smiled as I watched them. I loved being here. Working at the clinic was nice, but it was Doolittle's house where I felt most at home. The place was completely crazy, and I loved every second of it.

I'd already cleaned the cages and given everyone fresh food and water. Technically, I could go home now. Well, back to the little apartment the Devil's Fury had given me. Instead, I sat in the middle of the floor and waited for the animals to come visit.

A ferret scampered closer and hopped around me before darting off again. One of the rabbits got into my lap, wanting cuddles. I stroked its ears and watched the other furry babies. Even creatures that typically wouldn't get along didn't dare fight in Doolittle's house. A kitten came closer and flopped onto its side next to me. I reached over to grab its paw, running my fingers over the soft little toes.

Being here made me feel at peace. The animals didn't judge me. All they cared about was getting some attention and being cared for. If only people were the same way. The Devil's Fury hadn't been cruel since I'd been here, but no one had gone out of their way to befriend me either. I had a feeling Meredith had something to do with it. The girl had taken one look at me and sneered.

I'd tried to talk to one of the old ladies when I'd run across her the first week I was here. The conversation had been stilted at best, and I'd known she'd wanted to get away without being too rude about it. So I hadn't bothered trying to talk to anyone since then. What was the point? I wasn't going to force myself on people who didn't want me.

A door slamming caught my attention and I tensed, straining to hear who might have arrived. I wasn't expecting Doolittle this early. He kept the house unlocked so anyone could have walked in. I glanced around at the animals, hoping it wasn't anyone who would hurt them.

I should have known it would be Meredith. She burst into the room, glaring daggers at me.

"You need to leave," she said.

"I was just visiting with everyone before I left."

Meredith folded her arms over her chest. I still didn't know how old she was, but she acted like she was maybe eighteen or nineteen. Grizzly had mentioned a trauma she'd suffered, and I could understand the club wanting to coddle her, but I didn't think they were doing her any favors. If anything, they were making her into a brat who would pitch a fit if she didn't get her way. Or rather, if she didn't get Doolittle.

"I meant you need to leave the club. How long are you going to hang on Doolittle? It's pathetic. Do you think he really wants you? He'll never offer you anything real. Everyone knows what you are."

I swallowed, refusing to let the spoiled club princess make me cry. I moved the animals so I could stand and I dusted myself off. "I think it's up to Doolittle when I leave."

"What the hell does that mean?" she demanded.

"He asked me to come here, Meredith. I work for his clinic a few days a week and here at the house every day, helping him care for all the animals. Having a place to stay was part of the agreement. I'm sorry if you don't like me being here."

"He's not going to ask you stay forever. You know that, right?" she asked.

I wasn't about to tell her he already had. It wasn't my job to break her heart and disillusion her. I knew Doolittle had told her multiple times he wasn't interested in her that way, and yet she persisted.

"I'm sorry it hurts you to see me in his house." I took a breath and blew it out. "Mostly, I'm sorry that everyone here has given you the impression you can have something just because you want it. He's told me stories about you. The times you've spent together, and how you followed him when you were younger. What happened to that girl, Meredith? Because the sweet girl he remembers isn't the same woman standing in front of me."

Her jaw dropped and she took a step back. "What? How dare you…"

I shook my head. "No. How dare *them*! This club might have saved you, given you a safe place to finish growing up, but since then they haven't done you any favors. They cater to you. Give you what you want because they feel sorry for the life you had before. It's turning you into a selfish, spoiled woman."

"I think you've said enough," a man said from the doorway. I hadn't met him yet, but his cut said *Hot Shot*. "The club needs to discuss how long you'll be here, Minnie. But if I were you, I'd start packing. You aren't part of the Devil's Fury, and you don't get to speak to her that way."

My throat burned with unshed tears, and I tipped my chin up. Looked like I'd already outstayed my welcome. I'd known it would happen. The moment I'd seen how Meredith clung to Doolittle, I'd realized I wouldn't be able to live with the Devil's Fury for long. I pushed past the two of them and left Doolittle's house for what I figured would be the last time.

When I got in my SUV, I couldn't hold back anymore. The tears fell down my cheeks as I drove to the apartment I'd been using. Hot Shot had said I should pack. The funny thing was that I'd known this day was coming, so I'd never *un*packed. I'd been living out of boxes and my suitcase since I'd arrived. Well, not entirely. Doolittle had purchased a few things for me, and I'd hung those in the closet.

I walked into the apartment and looked around. I hadn't been working enough to save much of anything. Doolittle fed me whether I worked at the clinic or his house, so I hadn't needed to spend my money on food. He also topped off my gas tank every few days, so that hadn't been an issue either.

I went to the kitchen and opened the drawer under the microwave. Taking out the envelope, I counted the cash I'd been saving. I'd only managed to earn a little under four hundred dollars. The money in my account brought the total to almost seven hundred. I knew it wouldn't be anywhere near enough to get a place to stay. And if the Devil's Fury said I couldn't be here anymore, it would mean I couldn't work for Doolittle in his house.

"I need another job," I mumbled to myself.

If I'd been smart, I'd have lined something up already. I'd just hoped I'd have more time. Doolittle had seemed so sure he could win the club over. My cheeks warmed when I thought of all the stolen moments we'd had. Not a day had gone by that he hadn't managed to either take me to bed or up against a wall. Ever since that night at the hotel, things had changed between us.

Someone knocked on my door and I swallowed hard, wondering if I was about to be evicted without notice. I opened it and stared at the man on the other side. Steel. I knew he was like a father to Doolittle and the few interactions I'd had with the man had been pleasant enough.

"How long do I have?" I asked.

His lips turned down as he stared at me. "For what?"

"To pack and be gone."

He sighed and motioned to the apartment. "Mind if we come in?"

"We?" I glanced behind him and noticed a woman heading our way. Since she had on a cut, I figured she was his old lady. Doolittle had talked about her a little. What was her name? Something with an R.

I took a step back and let them inside, then shut the door. They stood awkwardly in the living room, and I waved a hand at the worn-down couch. Rachel! That was the woman's name. She rolled her eyes and shoved Steel until they'd both taken a seat.

"I'm afraid I'm a little confused," I said.

"You're not the only one," Steel muttered. "Why did you think I was here to throw you out?"

I licked my lips and pondered how much I should say. Then again, he was a patched member of the club, so someone would tell him eventually anyway. "Meredith came by Doolittle's while I was there. She wasn't very nice, and I might have said a few things. Hot Shot heard me and said I should start packing."

"Christ." Steel ran a hand down his beard. "First off, that little shit doesn't run this club. Badger does. Second, I have a feeling you didn't tell Meredith anything she didn't need to hear. And third, if anyone thinks Doolittle is letting you leave, they're fucking blind as shit."

"Doolittle comes to visit us often," Rachel said. "We've heard quite a bit about you. We also know Meredith has been driving him insane ever since she turned eighteen. The club keeps shoving her in his direction, but they need to stop."

"I might have called her spoiled." I sighed. "And I said the club hadn't done her any favors because she thought she could have whatever she wanted."

Rachel laughed. "Oh my God. No wonder Doolittle likes you. No one around here will say a word about Meredith, but we all know she's getting out of hand. She's super sweet, most of the time. When it comes to Doolittle, she goes a little… crazy."

"Girl needs to open her eyes," Steel said. "Doolittle has never looked at her the way he stares at you. That boy is half in love with you already. Question is how you feel about him."

"Does it matter?" I asked. "The club will never let us be together. I've told him that. He doesn't listen very well."

"And I'm sure he finds way to distract you," Rachel said.

My cheeks warmed and I nodded. "He does. Every single day."

Steel groaned. "More than I needed to know. I think of that boy as a son. Last thing I want to hear about is his sex life. That being said, are the two of you being careful?"

I paled. "The tests came back already. I'm clean."

Steel's brow furrowed and he glanced at Rachel. She shrugged her shoulders and the biker turned back to me. "Not what I meant, but congratulations."

"Then what… Oh."

"Yeah. Oh," he said. "That kid knocks you up then it changes things. No one in this club is going to make him give up his kid."

Was that why he'd been so insistent on not using protection? Had he been trying to get me pregnant? The room spun a little and I stumbled, falling on my ass. It made sense. The man didn't pass up a chance to get me naked. I'd thought it was romantic. Could I have been wrong about his motives?

Rachel got up and knelt in front of me. "Honey, when was your last period? Is it possible you're pregnant already?"

"I… I, um…" Was it possible? I tried counting the days. My period was never regular. There were times it came early or even a week late. "I don't know."

"Would you like to take a test and find out?" Rachel asked.

"No. Not right now."

If I didn't know for sure whether or not there was a baby, then Doolittle wouldn't either. I wasn't about to let him use a baby as leverage against the club. Steel was right. They wouldn't keep Doolittle from his kid. Didn't mean they wouldn't still kick my ass to the curb. How many times had I heard the guys at the Reckless Kings say if they knocked up a club whore they'd just keep the kid?

"Doolittle has gotten himself into one big mess," Steel said.

"It's not entirely his fault." Rachel stood and faced her man. "You know as well as I do everyone is shoving Meredith at him. He's made it clear, so many times, that he doesn't think of her that way.

"Something is up with Grizzly. Not sure what. He's not acting like himself." Steel stood. "I'll do what I can, Minnie. I can't promise to be successful in reining the club in, but I'll try. If I can figure out what's wrong with Meredith's dad then it might help."

"I'll try talking to some of the old ladies," Rachel said. "I think Adalia will listen to me. She might be Meredith's adopted sister, but I don't think she agrees with how things have been handled so far. Just because she fell for Badger when she was a teenager doesn't mean things will work the same way with Doolittle and Meredith."

"Try Farrah," Steel said. "If you can win her over, then we'll have Demon on our side too. Maybe Shella and Glory too. I think those two would be sympathetic."

"I'm on it," Rachel said. "You hang tight, Minnie. We won't let this happen without a fight. It's clear that Doolittle cares about you. That boy deserves some happiness, and if he thinks he can have that with you, then I'm in your corner."

"I appreciate it." I glanced between the two of them. "Um, about the possible pregnancy… can we keep that between us right now? I'm never regular so it's probably a false alarm. If I say something and it turns out not to be true…"

Rachel nodded. "Then it would only upset everyone more and make you look like a liar. Don't worry. Our lips are sealed until you know for sure."

"Come on. Time to do some damage control," Steel said, herding Rachel to the door.

After they left, I made myself a sandwich. Even though I never really ate here, Doolittle made sure my kitchen was stocked with a few things. Mostly drinks, but I also had bread, peanut butter, and jelly. I leaned against the kitchen counter while I ate and wondered what the hell I was going to do. Even if Steel stopped them from tossing me out right now, it didn't mean I was in the clear for good.

Placing a hand over my belly, I had to wonder if there was a kid in there already. If not, I had a feeling Doolittle would make sure it happened sooner rather than later. The thought of bringing a baby into this world scared me to death. I didn't know much about raising kids. What if I screwed up and scarred them for life? Maybe the Reckless Kings had the right idea, wanting to hand off any kids to the brother who fathered them. Granted, some of the club whores had already been mothers. Good ones. But women like me? I wasn't so sure I needed to have a baby.

My gaze kept drifting to the door, and I realized I was waiting for someone else to stop by. Like Hot Shot. Something told me he'd be downright gleeful over throwing my ass out of the gates. I'd already heard the whispers whenever I left the apartment. Beast might have asked Badger to keep things quiet, but the entire club knew I'd been a whore for the Reckless Kings. And they took every opportunity to make sure I knew I wasn't worth a damn thing.

Most of them. It seemed Steel didn't feel the same way. If he could see me as something more than a convenient piece of ass, then maybe others would too. I only wished they'd give me a chance. All I'd wanted was a fresh start. A new life where people didn't call me names, spit at me, or sneer as I walked by. Instead, it was more of the same, except from the people I'd thought would keep me safe.

"Just proves you can't trust anyone," I said looking around the apartment. I'd bounced around to so many places I was starting to wonder if I'd ever have a home. I should have had my shit figured out by now, but I didn't.

I grabbed my keys and decided to go for a drive. Maybe I needed to clear my head. With some luck, when I got back things wouldn't look as dismal as they did right now.

Chapter Six

Doolittle

I'd had an emergency surgery at the clinic and hadn't been able to reach Minnie. As much as I hoped she was still at my house, my gut said she'd already left. I knew she stayed after cleaning and feeding to play with the animals, but when I didn't come home at my usual time she'd likely headed out. I tried calling again. It rang six times and went to voicemail, or rather an inbox she'd never set up. If that woman got it into her head that I wasn't home because I was out on a date with someone, I wouldn't be held responsible for my actions. She already seemed to have one foot out the door. I knew she doubted her place in my life, and me having to hide her hadn't made it any easier to convince her.

I pulled the truck up to the gates and stopped when I realized Minnie's SUV was in front of me, and the Prospect seemed to be arguing with her. What the fuck was going on? I opened the door and before my foot hit the ground, I heard his words and saw red.

"Minnie, I was told you can't come back in. You need to turn around."

"But… my things are in there!" I could hear the hint of panic in her voice. I also noticed something moving around the inside of her car. Had she taken one of the animals for a ride somewhere?

I got out and walked over, trying not to take a swing at the guy right off. If he'd been told not to let her back in, then he was just following orders. I'd like to know who barred her from the compound, so I could put my fist through their damn face.

"What the ever loving fuck is going on?" I demanded.

"Doolittle," Minnie said softly, hope lighting up her eyes when she saw me.

"I was told Minnie isn't allowed inside anymore." Tal shifted from foot to foot. I could tell he didn't like the situation either. Far as I knew, he didn't have an issue with Minnie. He'd always been respectful with her.

"Whose orders are you following?" I asked.

He rubbed the back of his neck. "Well, Meredith said..."

I held up a hand. "Hold the fuck up. Are you telling me that you're keeping Minnie from her God damn home because Grizzly's kid said so? Not a brother. Not an officer. But Meredith. Since when the fuck does Meredith run shit around here?"

"Never," Demon said from the other side of the gate. "Let her in. Now."

I moved closer to Minnie, hunkering down so I could look through the open window. "You okay?"

"Yeah. I just needed some air and wanted to take a ride. I should have known better. When Hot Shot told me I needed to plan on packing, and then I got back and Tal wouldn't let me in, I thought they'd kicked me out."

I pinched the bridge of my nose and counted to ten. Then twenty. Nope. Not working. "You're going to explain that. Drive straight to my house. I also want to know where you got... is that a damn goat?"

She gave me a shy smile. "It's just a baby."

I chuckled and shook my head. I couldn't exactly get mad at her for bringing home an animal, not when I had a damn zoo at my place. Granted, I did try to rehome the ones I took in. I had a feeling Minnie planned to keep this one. Looked like a pygmy goat so at least it wouldn't be huge when it was fully grown.

We'd also discuss the safety issues of her putting it in the front seat of her SUV, even if she put a collar and leash on it.

The gates opened and Minnie pulled through. Demon and I shared a look before I got into my truck. He stopped me as I started to drive past him. I rolled down the window.

"We need to talk. Obviously, there's some shit going on where your girl is concerned. Farrah and I will stop by in about fifteen minutes. Should give you some time to talk to Minnie." He paused. "We may bring a few others with us. You do have some people in your corner, even if it doesn't feel like it."

"Thanks, Demon."

I rolled up the window and followed behind Minnie. She pulled into the driveway and I parked next to her. When I got out, she hadn't even opened her door yet. I helped her from the car then walked around to the other side. The second the passenger door opened, the little goat jumped out and I saw Minnie had fastened the end of the leash through the seatbelt. I unfastened it and let the goat wander the yard a moment while Minnie seemed to pull herself together.

"Come on, sweetheart. Time to have that talk."

She took the leash from me and led the goat into the house, not even bothering to ask if she could. Of course, if she'd asked, I'd have told her it was fine. There was a reason I didn't have carpet anywhere in my home. The flooring in every single room had been selected with easy cleanup in mind. After one too many accidents, I'd ripped up the old floors. The main living areas all had vinyl that looked like wood flooring, and the kitchen, bathrooms, and sunroom all had tile.

She led the goat into the kitchen and gave it some water before sitting at the table. I eyed the little critter wondering what she'd planned to feed it. While I'd had goats in the past, I didn't have any right now. There was a small barn out back and fencing suitable for livestock. One look at the way she stared at the little goat, and I knew she wasn't going to let me put it out there. Not long term at any rate.

"Start talking," I said, taking a seat next to her.

"I came by to work like I always do in the afternoons. Before I leave, you know I like to visit with the animals. Play with them or get cuddles."

"I know. They enjoy that time as much as you do."

She smiled a little, then it fell from her face. "Meredith stopped by. She said…"

"Whatever it is, you can tell me," I said, reaching for her hand. The little goat came over and rubbed its head against her leg before settling down at her feet.

"Meredith said my time here was limited because you wouldn't ask me to stay forever. Her tone and the hostile way she glared at me didn't seem like the girl you've talked about. So I may have… said… a few things."

I squeezed her hand. "I need to know everything."

"I told her the club hadn't done her any favors by giving her everything she wanted. I asked what had changed because she didn't seem like the girl you'd described to me. Our conversation pretty much ended there. Hot Shot came in and had overheard me. He told me I should go ahead and start packing."

"Hot Shot doesn't get to say who stays and who goes. As for what you said to Meredith, you weren't wrong. You spoke the truth, and I know you. There's no way you were aggressive when you were talking to her. I bet you had a nice, sweet tone, just like you use with the animals."

Her eyes went wide. "Did you just compare Meredith to your zoo?"

I snorted then laughed. I hadn't done it intentionally, but yeah, it seemed I'd done that very thing. At the moment, the girl was acting like a rabid honey badger, so the analogy wasn't far off.

The front door opened, startling the little goat. It gave a bleat and pressed closer to Minnie's legs. Demon came in with Farrah, Steel and Rachel were behind him, and perhaps the most surprising was Adalia bringing up the rear.

"Where are all of your kids?" I asked.

"The ones who aren't in school are with Colorado." Steel pulled out a chair for Rachel, Demon did the same for Farrah, and I gave my seat up for Adalia. Once the ladies were all comfortable, Demon didn't waste any time diving in.

"Steel and Rachel have made me aware of the issues you're having with Meredith, as well as an altercation earlier that resulted in Hot Shot running his fucking mouth and telling Minnie she needed to leave," Demon said.

"He didn't *exactly* say that," Minnie said.

"It was implied," Steel said. "And I know it scared you. I could see the panic in your eyes when we showed up at your apartment. You were wondering where you'd go and how you'd survive because I know damn well you haven't been here long enough to save up the kind of money you'd need to move out. Besides, we know how Doolittle feels about you. It's time the rest of the club gets their heads out of their asses."

"You know how I feel?" I asked, staring at him and Demon.

"We aren't blind," Steel said. "Not to mention about every other word out of your mouth has to do with Minnie. If everyone else hasn't figured it out yet, then they're dumber than I thought."

Adalia sighed and folded her hands on top of the table. "There's something you should all know. It can't leave this room! Badger is aware of the situation, as am I and my adopted siblings. There's a reason Meredith is acting out, and why my dad is pushing her toward Doolittle."

"I figured something was up with Grizzly. He snapped at Minnie and called her a whore," I said. "Pissed me the fuck off. I hung up on him."

Adalia smiled but I noticed it held a tinge of sadness to it. "Dad isn't getting any younger. The lifestyle he's led with the drinking, smoking off and on over the years, and his poor diet have taken their toll. I finally forced him to go see the doctor. The news isn't as bad as it could be, but it's not great either."

"What's wrong with Griz?" Demon asked.

"For the moment, the doctors are trying to manage his health issues with medication. High blood pressure and heart disease. They told him to change his lifestyle, definitely change his diet, and they're trying some meds. If he doesn't follow their instructions, then he'll most likely need surgery at some point." She dropped her gaze. "Or he could have a heart attack or stroke and die. I'm not sure who it scared more. Him or us."

"Shit," Steel muttered. "The stubborn bastard needs to tell the club. Not only can we watch for any signs that something is about to happen, but we can hold him accountable too. Especially on the diet. Next time I see him scarfing down a cheeseburger at the clubhouse, I'm going to kick the shit out of him."

"It's why Meredith is acting out, and it's why Badger and my dad are letting her. Neither one knows what to do with her. Dad wants to see her settled in case anything happens to him. The others aren't old enough yet, but he's going to make sure they've got a place to go." Adalia held each of our gazes a moment. "I'm not saying it makes any of this right. Meredith is acting like a spoiled brat and needs to be taken in hand. I don't think my dad or Badger will be able to get the job done."

"Anyone in the club interested in Meredith as more than a friend?" Minnie asked. "Like I told Grizzly before, I know my situation is different, but I was so hung up on Satyr I wouldn't have noticed anyone else. Once I met Doolittle, I realized I was head over heels in lust with Satyr but had never loved him. Maybe we could try something similar with Meredith?"

I tried to think back over all the times I'd seen the club interact with Meredith in the past few months. At nineteen, she hadn't been of legal age long enough for any of us to really think about her that way. I also didn't want to throw a brother under the proverbial bus. Switching her focus to someone else who didn't want her, wouldn't do any of us any good. We'd just be right back in this situation later.

"My dad sent Mariah here. I know Grizzly won't arrange for Meredith to be with someone like that. I was just thinking we could arrange for her to take a trip? Maybe visit the Dixie Reapers or one of the other clubs?" Farrah looked at Adalia. "There has to be someone who's interested in her. If they aren't here, then maybe one of the other clubs? We've had enough visitors since Meredith came here."

"Dad wants her to be happy. At the same time, if she's not with a member of *this* club, then he'll likely push for her to be with an officer. Only ones I know of who are single are Charming and Cobra at the Devil's Boneyard; Prospero with the Reckless Kings; Bear, Knox, and Slider with the Hades Abyss in Missouri; Pretty Boy, Wizard, and Boomer with their Mississippi chapter, and… I think that's all?"

"No offense to Meredith, but she's not Prospero's type. I don't see him going for any sort of deal that ends up with him claiming her," Minnie said.

"Forget the Devil's Boneyard," Demon said. "Neither of those men are going to take her."

"So that leaves Hades Abyss," Adalia said. "Farrah, the Dixie Reapers have ties to the Hades Abyss. Think they'd take Meredith? Or at least arrange for a visit so she could meet other people?"

"I think we're all forgetting something here," Steel said. "While this is all well and good, I don't see Meredith going along with it. Neither will Grizzly or Badger for that matter. I think they want her to remain here."

Minnie reached over to take my hand and the look in her eyes said I wasn't going to like what she said next. I gave a slight shake of my head, hoping she'd listen and keep quiet. There was no fucking way I was letting her leave. Hell, I'd call up Outlaw right now, or reach out to Shield with the Reckless Kings, and have one of them work a little keyboard magic. If I had to make Minnie mine without her knowledge, so be it.

"I appreciate everything the Devil's Fury did for me," Minnie said. "But me being here is just causing trouble."

Demon looked at me, eyebrows raised. "You

going to let her finish that train of thought? Because I know what I'd do if Farrah uttered such complete bullshit."

Minnie gasped and her fingers tightened on mine. She glanced at me, and the hopeless look damn near gutted me. I knew she didn't really want to leave. The way she gave in to me, her soft cries every time I was balls deep inside her, and all the times she watched me when she thought I didn't notice told me plenty. She felt just as strongly for me as I did her. And I wasn't letting her go.

"Anyone talked to Outlaw?" I asked. "How does he feel about all this?"

Demon smiled. "Why don't I step outside a moment and find out?"

I gave him a nod, and knew he'd be asking more than that. Demon understood I wanted to keep Minnie. While he might not like club whores, he'd apparently made an exception for a reformed one. In all honesty, his support had shocked the hell out of me. If anyone at the club had fought against me to keep Minnie, I'd thought it would be him. The one person I'd thought would have my back was Grizzly, and he'd been the furthest thing from supportive.

"You know you can't just pawn her off like an unwanted puppy, right?" Minnie asked. "This is her home. Her family. Meredith counts on all of you. If she's struggling with the news of Grizzly's health, then she needs your support now more than ever."

I moved closer and placed my hand on Minnie's shoulder. "Sweetheart, we'll always be here for her. None of us are saying we won't. Doesn't mean I'm going to give her what she wants."

"I feel bad already," she said, looking up at me. "You said you were her friend. She needs that friendship right now."

"I see why you like her," Adalia said. "She's sweet. Stupid, but sweet."

Minnie gasped and stared at Adalia. "Stupid?"

"Do you want Doolittle?" Adalia asked. "And be honest. Do you want to stay here with him? Maybe be his old lady one day?"

"Well, I..." She wouldn't look at me, but I saw the way her cheeks flushed. She might not admit it, but that's exactly what she wanted.

"If you don't want him, this is all pointless," Adalia said. "If you *do,* then it's time to fight. I love my sisters. All of them. Doesn't mean I agree with everything they say or do. Same for Badger and my dad. There are times I want to hit them with a two by four because they're stubborn jackasses."

Demon came back into the room. He gave me a nod and I knew the issue with Minnie had been handled, even if the club wouldn't like it. I damn well knew none of them would vote her in, except the two men already in this room with me. So I'd done things the underhanded way. Badger would likely hand my ass to me, but since Demon had technically made the call, the Sergeant-at-Arms would be on the chopping block.

"I called Slash and Savage, but neither were available. If I can talk to them, along with their women, it would put every officer except the President on your side. With all of us being the voice of reason, maybe we can get Badger to pull his head out of his ass." Demon folded his arms. "And if not, then I'm more than happy to take a swing at him. If he's going to be a dick, then he deserves to be knocked around a little."

My phone chimed and I pulled up the message from Outlaw. *Called Shield. He's handling your little problem. Give him thirty minutes.*

I responded with a quick *thanks,* not expecting him to type anything else. What I saw next made me smile.

He's backdating the marriage certificate to the night before you left the Reckless Kings. If anyone goes digging, Minnie will have been your wife the last two weeks.

Only one problem. I needed to talk to Minnie in private, or she'd blow the thing out of the water. I tugged on her arm until she stood and led her from the room, going far enough I didn't think anyone would hear us.

"What's wrong?" she asked.

"Got something to tell you. Not sure how you'll react."

Chapter Seven

Minnie

When a man says you won't like his next words, and you've fallen for that guy, then it makes your stomach feel like it's free falling while you wait. Not in a good way. This wasn't a thrilling ride on a roller coaster. It was more like plummeting off a cliff with no chance of survival. The way he'd been fighting to keep me, I didn't think he was going to send me away. Then again, what the hell did I know about men? I'd blindly waited for Satyr, and he hadn't been the first mistake I'd made in my life.

Still… If Doolittle wasn't breaking up with me, assuming you could call what we had an actual relationship, then why did he think I wouldn't like what he had to say?

"Just tell me," I said. "Please, Zachary. I can't handle the suspense right now."

He cupped my cheek and kissed me softly, drawing me closer. "In about thirty minutes, or less, if anyone goes snooping, they'll find a marriage certificate."

A marriage certificate. Why was that going to make me angry? Who got married? Oh, God. What the hell was going on?

"I don't understand," I said.

"Shield is hacking into the Tennessee Department of Vital Records." He gave me an intense stare, like he was willing me to understand something.

"Vital Rec…" I stared. No. He couldn't mean what I thought he did. Could he? Things like that just didn't happen. Not in real life. Sure, I knew Shield was called a hacker around the club. But it hadn't occurred to me exactly what type of work he did for the Reckless

Kings, and apparently the Devil's Fury when a favor was called in. "We're married?"

He nodded. "Paperwork will show we got married before you left the Reckless Kings' territory. You were technically no longer a club whore after your talk with Beast. And a few hours later, you became my wife. If you deviate from that story, this whole thing will blow up in our faces."

"You'll be in trouble," I said. "And Demon... Shield."

"Outlaw too," he said. "He's the one who called Shield after Demon spoke to him. His hands don't work that great after an incident with the Dixie Reapers a while back. He doesn't regret it though."

"So I'm your wife. They won't find it odd I don't have a wedding ring? Or we've been living in separate homes? Wouldn't you have stood up for me long before now? I mean, I know you've not let them run roughshod over me, but you haven't come forward before now to claim me as yours."

"Let me handle it," he said. "You're mine, Minnie. Now and forever."

It seemed so surreal. I wanted to ask why he hadn't just done that from the beginning if he'd been so certain he wanted me to be his. Except I was a little afraid of the answer. Doubt still filled me. Why had he done this now of all times? Steel and Rachel had promised they wouldn't say anything about my possibly missed period. Had they lied? Did Doolittle know and that's why he'd taken this step?

Whatever the reason, I had a choice to make. Embrace this big change, or... Well, go along kicking and screaming.

"Guess that means I better start acting like it," I said.

He smiled. "Yeah. You can start by kissing your husband. I wanted to come home and spend time with you. Instead, I drove up to the gate and had to deal with all this bullshit."

"Kissing you is one of my favorite things to do," I murmured before going up on tiptoe to do exactly that. He held me closer, our bodies pressed together. I didn't know what sort of fallout would happen from me being his wife, but I'd never been happier. Assuming he'd married me for the right reasons. I was too damn chicken to ask if he knew I could be pregnant. Then again, he'd not used protection even once. The odds weren't in my favor.

The front door opened, and I heard voices right before everything went silent. And that's when all hell broke loose.

"What the fucking hell is going on?" a man's voice boomed.

I flinched and would have pulled away if Doolittle hadn't held on even tighter. I glanced toward the doorway and saw a man staring at us. They'd said the other two men couldn't make it. Had one changed their mind? I eyed the man's cut. *Badger*. Shit. This was so very bad. He hadn't been invited, and the way he glared at me, I had no doubt he'd have flayed the skin from my body with that look if he'd had the ability.

"Badger. Didn't realize you were coming," Doolittle said.

"All my officers were either here already or received a summons. Seemed a little odd everyone should be at your house. Can't think of a single reason you'd need the officers here, unless you're up to something. Hot Shot stopped by earlier to tell me about your girl there overstepping her bounds and going off on Meredith. You hear me? The daughter of our ex-

President. And your little whore decided to put her in her place." Badger's face started to turn purple, and I wondered if he was about to have a stroke.

Doolittle tensed and pushed me behind him. I held onto his cut, worried what he might do. The men from the kitchen decided to join the conversation, each one filing into the living room. I noticed Demon put himself between Doolittle and Badger. I hoped he could defuse the situation, but something told me it was about to go from bad to worse.

"She's not a whore, you asshole! She's my wife!" Doolittle yelled at the President.

Badger's nostrils flared, his lips thinned, and his eyes narrowed. My stomach flipped and my hands shook as I watched him shove Demon out of the way and come closer. Was he going to hit Doolittle? Or worse… me? I didn't know the man. He hadn't said more than a few words to me the entire time I'd been here.

"Everyone in Church. Now," Badger said, his voice having dropped low. If anything, it sounded even scarier than when he'd been yelling.

"I'm not leaving Minnie behind," Doolittle said. "Right now, I'm not sure I'd trust you to keep her safe."

"That's strike one," Badger said. "Keep it up and we won't just be discussing your lack of judgment where women are concerned. We'll also be taking a vote to see if you keep your patch."

No. No, no, no. I'd never let that happen! It didn't matter what I felt for Doolittle, or how badly I wanted a life with him. I'd never allow him to be tossed from the club because of me. I glanced at Steel, hoping he'd understand. He gave me a little nod and I breathed slightly easier.

"If we're discussing Doolittle and Minnie, then let her come along," Steel said. "Wouldn't be the first time a woman was allowed into Church. She deserves to hear what's said about her."

"Fine." Badger stared at every patched member before looking at the women. His gaze softened a little when he spotted Adalia. "Ladies, go home. Doolittle, bring Minnie to the clubhouse. Demon, send out a message that everyone needs to have their ass in Church in the next ten minutes. I don't give a shit where they are or what they're doing. This is more important."

Badger stormed out and I swayed, not sure my legs would hold me much longer. In all my time at the Reckless Kings, not once had Beast or Hawk ever scared me the way Badger did. I didn't know what I'd expected. After hearing they were letting me come here for a fresh start, I'd thought maybe they were kind. Since meeting them, and being called names, I had to wonder what Beast had gotten me into.

"Take Minnie in your truck," Steel said. "She doesn't look like she could hold onto you on the back of a bike right now."

Doolittle pulled me into his arms and hugged me before leading me outside. He helped me into his truck before getting in and heading for the clubhouse. I saw the ladies all pile into what I assume was Adalia's SUV since she was driving, and the men followed us on their bikes.

"Zachary." He wouldn't even look at me, but I saw his hands tighten on the steering wheel. I knew he was listening. "You can't let them take your patch. Not over me."

"Minnie, I swear to Christ if you start uttering that bullshit about not being worth it, I'm going to pull this truck over and spank your ass until it's red, then I'm going to fuck you into submission. Now isn't the time."

I took a breath and let it out, deciding maybe he was right. No matter what I said, he wasn't in the frame of mind to be logical about the situation. He was angry and lashing out. But I knew I'd do what I had to. Not just for me. Doolittle couldn't lose this club, or his home. It would devastate him, assuming he survived whatever process the club used when someone got kicked out. I wasn't sure I wanted to know the details.

When we arrived at the clubhouse, I saw a line of bikes out front. The men who had been following us parked and went inside. I saw Hot Shot standing on the porch, smirking in my direction. I didn't know why he disliked me so much. I'd not spoken to him in all the time I'd been here. My only interaction with him had been earlier, when he'd heard me talking to Meredith.

Doolittle shut off the truck engine and got out. I didn't wait for him to help me down. I just opened the door and jumped out. What hurt the most was the fact Doolittle walked ahead of me and didn't even look my way. I didn't know why he was so pissed at me. He relied on this club. They weren't just his friends; they were his family. I'd never ask him to give that up! He had to know I was trying to do what was best for him. I couldn't be selfish and hold on if it was going to mean he'd experience the pain of losing everyone he knew and loved.

I followed him up the steps and Hot Shot stepped in my way.

"Told you that you needed to pack. The minutes are counting down, whore."

I sighed, feeling a little defeated and a whole lot

tired. "Your club is very unoriginal. If I tried to count how many times someone here had called me that, I'd need more than my fingers and toes. I'd probably need more than the entire Devil's Fury has to offer. Let me pass. I'm supposed to go inside."

His gaze narrowed but he stepped aside. I went into the clubhouse and saw Steel waiting near the hallway. He motioned for me to come closer then turned when I was nearly there. I followed him into Church and spotted Doolittle at the table, in what I assumed was his regular seat. I didn't know what to do or where to go. After a quick look around, I saw all the chairs were taken once Steel and Hot Shot took their places, so I leaned against the wall.

Badger slammed his fist onto the table. "Church is in session. It seems Doolittle has been keeping secrets. So here's what we're going to do. We're going to take a vote right this minute. All in favor of Doolittle claiming Minnie as his old lady, raise your hands. Except Doolittle. Your vote doesn't fucking count."

Steel and Demon raised their hands. Then I saw two others put their hands up. Four. Out of the entire club, only four had voted for me to stay with Doolittle. It felt like my heart was breaking into a million pieces.

"And everyone against?" Badger asked. He raised his hand, along with nearly everyone else at the table. Except the four who'd been kind enough to side with Doolittle. I did notice a slight hesitation with two of the men. One was the VP.

"There we have it. I don't give a shit if you married her or not. She can't be your old lady, which means she's not allowed to stay at the compound. I want her the fuck out of here immediately," Badger said. "If you want to go with her, just say the word. We'll vote on your patch too."

"No!" I shoved away from the wall. "Please. Don't make him go through that."

"I didn't ask for your fucking opinion," Badger said.

"I… I'll go. All of you are Doolittle's family. I could never ask him to leave all of you." I glanced at the man in question and saw his jaw had tensed to the point I worried his teeth might crack. He also refused to look at me. That hurt more than anything else. "I'll have my things in my car, and I'll be gone by end of the day. I only request that you let Doolittle stay."

I heard someone mutter a quiet *fuck* and a few others shared a look. My throat burned and ached as I fought not to cry. With as much dignity as I could muster, I walked out and didn't glance back even once. No matter how much I wanted to. I walked to the apartment I'd been using and started closing up my boxes and throwing the few things in the closet into a bag. When I'd finished, I hauled it all out to my SUV and loaded it into the back.

The tears fell down my cheeks unchecked once I got behind the wheel and realized this was it. I hadn't even had the opportunity to tell Doolittle goodbye. Staying in town was pointless. I couldn't work with him, not after this. Seeing him at the clinic would be too painful, and I'd be tempted to throw myself into his arms.

As I pulled through the gates for the last time, I turned my car away from town and decided to drive until it didn't hurt so much anymore. I'd either go numb or run out of gas. Although, as bad as I hurt, I was betting on needing fuel before I stopped crying.

I hadn't even realized where I was going until I'd left the state of Georgia behind and entered Florida. My phone pinged with a text message. Then another.

After the fourth, I decided to pull over and read them. I found a gas station where I could get something to drink and figure out my next move.

After I got a bottle of water, I checked my phone. Two texts from Shield and two from Beast. I read Shield's first.

What the hell just happened? Outlaw said you'd left.

I scrolled to the next.

You're legally married to Doolittle! You're officially Minnie Morgan, wife of Dr. Zachary Morgan. Why are you leaving town?

I laughed because I couldn't help it. Morgan. I hadn't even known his last name, but I was technically married to the guy. Even at the clinic, everyone called him Doolittle. Actually, they called him Dr. Doolittle, which always made me snicker. When did my life become so fucked up? I pulled up Beast's messages next. I wasn't even going to ask how he knew I'd left town.

Where are you? This isn't how things were supposed to go.

I snorted. No shit. So much for my second chance.

Shield hacked the GPS on your phone. I'm sending you directions to the Devil's Boneyard. Charming has agreed to take you in. No fucking arguments, Minnie!

With a sigh, I accessed the directions and plugged them into the map on my phone. Looked like I was about to rely on yet another club to save my ass. When was I going to learn? How many times did I have to get hurt before I realized bikers were assholes and couldn't be trusted? If I had more money saved, I would have said a big fuck you to all of them and kept going. But I couldn't do that. I knew damn well I didn't have a way to provide any sort of shelter other than my car. The money I had wouldn't last long, especially with the cost of food these days.

Looked like I was going to the Devil's Boneyard to speak to Charming. I remembered him being mentioned at Doolittle's as a single officer who might be an option for Meredith.

"Out of the frying pan and into the fire," I muttered as I got back on the road. "Minnie, this is the last one. No more clubs after this. You either sink or swim."

And now I was talking to myself. I glanced at my passenger seat and wished I could have taken the goat with me. I hoped someone had let it out of Doolittle's house. If not, he'd likely have some chewed furniture and a big mess to clean up. We'd all run off without a second thought to the poor thing. My fingers itched to send him a message to check on the little guy, but I didn't dare. Besides, I was probably the last person he wanted to talk to right now.

A clean break. That's what we both needed.

Maybe if I kept lying to myself, I'd start to believe the shit I was thinking. Because even a clean break wasn't going to erase Doolittle from my memories. Not now, and not ever.

Chapter Eight

Doolittle

What the fuck just happened? I couldn't look at my brothers. I sure the fuck couldn't watch Minnie walk away. As much as I wanted to get up and run after her, I wouldn't. At least, not yet. There was something I needed to say to my brothers. Minnie was right. They were my family. Or they were supposed to be. Right now, they weren't acting like it.

I slowly stood, staring at the table. One glance at any of them, and I'd completely lose my shit. I braced my fists on the table and took a breath. Then another. If I didn't, I was going to start swinging.

"I've been part of this club in one way or another for nearly half my life. I've helped wherever I could without question. Not once have I ever shied away from getting my hands dirty, even though Steel has done his best to remind me I have a legitimate life outside the club with my veterinary practice. I've been there for each and every one of you, every fucking time you've needed me."

"Doolittle..."

I held up a hand, not letting Steel finish his sentence. "No. I appreciate you, Outlaw, Demon, and Dragon siding with me. It means a lot. But what I learned today is that the rest of you fuckers are a bunch of backstabbing bastards. I've never asked you for anything. *Never*. My wife just walked out the door because she didn't want me to have to choose my family over her. Do you have any idea how fucked up that is?"

"We didn't know," Slash said. "This is the first I've heard of you being married."

"Does it matter?" I asked. "I *chose* Minnie. I've

walked on eggshells for the last two weeks because precious Meredith couldn't be hurt. Grizzly and the rest of you have never told the girl no, and now I'm paying the price for it. You want my patch? Fucking take it. I won't put up a fight."

"No one wants you to go..."

I glared at Dagger. "Shut up. Just shut the fuck up. All of you. I'm done. This isn't family. It's not the brotherhood I thought I was part of. And, Griz, I know what's going on. Adalia told me. I'm sorry for your health issues, and I understand you wanting your girls taken care of. Doesn't mean you get to push everyone around like pieces on a damn chessboard. I know Badger is being a fucking dick because he's worried about Adalia, even though she seemed to be handling things just fine when she stopped by earlier."

"What's he talking about?" Slash asked. "What's going on with you, Grizzly?"

The old man sighed and ran a hand through his hair. "Heart failure and high blood pressure. The doctor has me on a diet, said I need to exercise, and I have to take pills to help manage the issue. I'm not invincible after all."

"If he follows the doctor's instructions, he should be okay," Badger said. "If not, then he'll need surgery. Even then, he could still outlive a lot of us. Old bastard is too stubborn to die. Not as long as his girls need him. And, Griz, May will be waiting on the other side when it's your time. No need to rush the trip there."

"We aren't taking your patch," Slash said. "And if I'd known you were married before I headed into Church, I'd have voted for you to claim Minnie as your old lady. What I want to know is why Dragon, Outlaw, and Demon sided with you. Everyone knows how Steel feels. It was no surprise to see his hand go up in favor of you keeping your woman."

"Liliana is Grizzly's adopted daughter too, even though people tend to forget. I knew the shit with Grizzly was why Meredith had lost her damn mind. The way she's always chased after Doolittle, it made sense that she'd want to run Minnie off." Dragon folded his arms. "You're with one of his daughters. Why the fuck didn't you figure this out, Slash?"

"Because no one told me a God damn thing!" Slash glared at Grizzly, Badger, and Dragon. "Does Shella even know?"

"No," Grizzly admitted. "I asked the girls not to tell her. She tends to be… sensitive."

"You're telling her. Today," Slash said.

Grizzly gave a nod. "I will. Everyone bring the girls by for dinner. We'll have a big family meal and discuss what's going on."

"I can't look at any of you right now," I said. "I need to go find Minnie and try to fix this shit. You may have all voted for her to leave, but I'm not letting my wife walk away."

"Did any of you stop to consider he's been spending time with Minnie for two weeks now? You damn well know every single one of us with an old lady lost our heads around the women we care about," Steel said.

"What are you saying?" Badger asked, his voice softer than before, having lost its hard edge.

"Really? None of you can figure it out?" Steel asked.

"Son of a bitch," Slash muttered. "Is she pregnant?"

The world tilted under my feet and my vision went black for a moment. Shit. Was Minnie carrying my baby already? I'd been trying like hell to knock her up, but I hadn't known her more than two weeks. If she'd gone too much longer without a period, I'd have started to wonder.

"All of you just threw out my pregnant wife?" I asked, my voice barely louder than a whisper.

"Not certain she's carrying your kid already," Steel said. "But when Rachel asked her this afternoon, she didn't seem to know for sure."

I closed my eyes then let out a roar as I brought both fists down on the table. I heard it crack as my chest heaved with my labored breaths. Straightening to my full height, I didn't spare them a glance as I left Church. Badger hadn't dismissed us, but I didn't give a fuck. I was going after Minnie so I could fix this mess. She already had a good twenty-minute head start.

The way she'd left, she'd had every intention of packing up and leaving. Which meant she'd gone to the apartment. I got into the truck and drove straight there, hoping to see her along the way. She would have walked from the clubhouse. The apartments were nearby, and I arrived in less than two minutes. My heart dropped like a stone when I noticed her SUV was gone and the apartment lights were out.

She couldn't have moved that fast, could she? I rushed inside and realized quick enough that all her things were gone. "No. She's not gone. She can't be."

I looked around, hoping for a note. Anything to tell me where she'd gone. The only things left behind were the items that had been here already. I got back in the truck and thought for a moment. Whoever was at the gate might know where she went. I didn't think it was likely she'd confided in them, but I had to hope. The thought of her being gone was more than I could handle.

When I reached the gates, I saw Garrick standing

guard. I pulled over and got out. Before he even spoke, I knew she wasn't here anymore. She'd left me, thinking she was saving me. Little did she realize she meant more to me than the club did.

"She didn't go into town," Garrick said. He tossed his cigarette on the ground and put it out. "Took a right. I know it's not my place to question things in the club, but you should know she was crying. Not a little. Women had tears pouring down her face. I'm not sure how she could even see the road."

I rubbed at my chest, feeling like my heart had been ripped out. "The club voted against her. Told her to leave."

"And you let her go?" Garrick asked.

"I stayed long enough to make a point. Minnie took off because she thought I'd lose my patch if I tried to hold onto her. She said she wouldn't make me pick her over my family, and just… left."

"That woman has some balls. And a heart of gold too. Heard about the little goat she brought home. Not sure you could have found a more perfect match for yourself." Garrick shoved his hands into his pockets. "What are you going to do now?"

I glanced in the direction she'd gone. I could take off after her. Only one problem. The road she'd taken forked about three miles down. I had no idea which way she'd have turned, and from there it was anyone's guess where she'd head. Running after her might be my first choice, but it wasn't the smart one. No, I needed to find a way to track her. Maybe Outlaw… If she had her phone on, perhaps he could track her through the GPS. Unless she'd disabled it. Damnit!

"Go home and hope her goat hasn't eaten everything in the house. I kind of forgot to put it out back before we went to Church. Then I'll come up with a plan to get Minnie back."

"If you need anyone to go with you, whenever you decide to chase down your woman, let me know. I'd be happy to help. I might be new around here, and maybe I don't know everything yet, but you're a good man, Doolittle. You deserve to be happy, and I could tell Minnie was it for you."

"Thanks." I swallowed hard, wishing everyone else had realized it too. "If she comes back..."

"I'll send her straight to your house."

I nodded and went back to the truck and drove home. The little goat hadn't done as badly as I'd thought, although I'd need to either repair the couch or buy a new one. He'd ripped the fabric off part of it before yanking a cushion on the floor to sleep on. The little beast had also peed and pooped in several spots, but that was easy enough to clean up. I sank to the floor next to the goat, reaching out to scratch behind his ear.

"She left us both, little guy. Don't worry. I'll find a way to get her back."

He bleated at me then butted his head into my side. I took that to mean he was in agreement. I spent a little time with him before leading him out back and putting him in the pasture. I made sure he had access to a stall with fresh straw and clean water. Then I went about bedding down everyone else for the night. The rabbits and ferret went into their cages. The birds were covered. The lights were turned off over the reptile tanks that required heat lamps or UVB bulbs.

I closed the door behind me and realized Minnie wasn't just gone from my life here. Since she'd left town, it meant she wouldn't be at the clinic either. I pulled my phone from my pocket and sent Outlaw a text, hoping he'd either be able to help, or convince someone else to do it.

Find her. Please.

Outlaw didn't answer for at least twenty minutes. By the time he did, I'd managed to think of every horrible scenario possible. Minnie was out there alone. Possibly pregnant. What if human traffickers picked her up? What if someone ran her off the road? If she stayed somewhere cheap, anyone could break in and rob her, or worse. The police could show up tomorrow and tell me she'd been left dead in a ditch.

I've been asked to stand down.

What the fuck? I stared at Outlaw's message a moment, trying to process the words. *By who*?

Beast called Badger. He's pissed as fuck and making threats.

Fuck. This was bad. Really bad. I knew Badger wouldn't risk losing the Reckless Kings as allies. We'd relied on them too many times in the past. Not to mention it could make things awkward as hell for Savage and Demon. They might both have claimed Dixie Reaper daughters as their old ladies, but so had Ranger with the Reckless Kings. If we ended up on the wrong side of the Reckless Kings, then it would possibly make the Dixie Reapers take a step back from both of us. Or worse… They'd show up to try to take their daughters home.

Home. Minnie hadn't really had a home to speak of with the Reckless Kings, and I knew she'd handed over her keys to her scumbag landlord before we'd left. Where else would she consider home? Would she have gone there? We hadn't talked much about her past. Mostly because she liked throwing it in my face that she was a club whore for the Reckless Kings when I found her, as if it would somehow make her unworthy in my eyes.

I couldn't say I'd be eager to claim any of the club whores we had here, but if I'd fallen for one? Maybe.

A hint? Where would she consider home? I hit SEND before I could talk myself out of it. I didn't want Outlaw to get into trouble, but I also didn't want my wife running out there unprotected. She didn't even have a property cut or a wedding ring.

Sorry, Doolittle. My hands are tied.

"Motherfucker!" I nearly threw my phone across the room but refrained -- barely. There was only thing I could think to do, and I wasn't sure it was the right move. If this went badly, then Badger would have my ass.

I dialed the number for Beast and hoped like hell he'd answer. It went to voicemail, so I called back again. And again. On the fifth try, he answered. Not with a hello. No, he just barked out one line and hung the fuck up.

"Don't call here again."

I didn't know if he'd read a text or not. He'd possibly delete it before he even saw the first words. But I had to try. I needed Minnie. Wanted her by my side. Hell, I was almost certain I loved her. Don't know how it happened. We barely knew one another.

I'm sorry. I never wanted Minnie to get hurt. All I wanted was for her to be with me. She's mine. I could feel it the moment I met her. My asshole brothers refused to vote her in as my old lady. She ran but I didn't realize it until it was too late. I need her, Beast. She's my one and only. I'll do whatever it takes. Just please tell me she's safe.

I hit SEND and started pacing again. A knock on the door had me racing to the front of the house. Had Minnie come back?

I threw open the door and growled. "What the

fuck are you doing here?"

"I came to talk," Meredith said.

"I have nothing to say to you." I started to close the door then stopped. "No, I take that back. I was your friend, Meredith. From the time you arrived here, I tried to help you heal. I was your sounding board, your confidant. You repaid me by making sure the woman I love would never be allowed to stay. That's not what friends do. I can't stand to look at you right now. I need you to leave and give me space."

Before she could reply I shut the door and twisted the lock. I stared at it, wondering when I'd last bothered to shut the world out. I'd always left the door open so my brothers could stop by whenever they wanted. It wasn't unusual for me to come home and find one of the old ladies in the back room playing with the animals, and if not them, then their kids.

Things had changed today. I no longer saw my club in the same light, and right now, I wasn't sure I could count on them. If anything happened to Minnie, I'd never forgive them for what they'd done. Not even Grizzly. He might have been scared and trying to protect his daughter, but he'd gone about it in a really fucked up way.

Another knock on the door had me cursing. I threw it open ready to tear into Meredith. Except it wasn't her.

"Can I come in?" Badger asked.

I took a step back. "It's technically your house. You're the President of the club. Everything here is yours, right? The land. The houses. Our laws. Us."

He winced and rubbed the back of his neck. "I deserved that. I know I can be an asshole sometimes."

I cleared my throat and folded my arms over my chest.

"All right. Most of the time," he amended. "But I really do want what's best for the club. When Beast asked about Minnie coming here, I didn't see the harm. It never occurred to me she'd latch onto you. Everyone knows Meredith has been after you since she turned eighteen. Even before that, she had a major crush on you."

"What exactly was the plan?" I asked. "Wear me down until I agreed to claim a woman I've never thought of in a romantic way? Or wait until I found someone I could love and then throw a bomb at my relationship? Oh. That's right. You already did the second one."

"I guess none of us understood why you'd want someone like Minnie when Meredith was throwing herself at you." Badger shook his head. "I still don't get it. You know what those women are capable of. They've tried to trap some of us in the past. Caused all kinds of trouble. Damn near got an old lady killed. Beast might have vouched for her, said she wanted to start over, but the fact remains she was a club whore."

"None of you took the time to get to know Minnie. Do you know how many of the Reckless Kings she's been with? Two. Copper and Satyr. The others never touched her because they knew she wasn't really a club whore. She was only there because she wanted Satyr. Thought herself in love with him. I know Beast told you why she'd been at their clubhouse. That's not news to you, Badger. So what? Because she spread her legs for the guy and wasn't his old lady it makes her trash? You really want to go there?"

"Beast isn't going to tell us where Minnie is, but I'm pretty sure he knows. On the upside, that means she's okay. I have no idea how to convince him to tell you where he's stashed her, or where she ran to. I'm not sure which it is."

I stared at my phone, still clutched in my hand. "You think she'd have called him?"

"No. He called her. Outlaw reached out to Shield after you left Church to let him know what happened. I wish he'd waited until I'd had a chance to talk to Beast about it. Now their club is pissed as fuck at us. Me specifically." Badger shoved his hands into his pockets. "I think Shield somehow tracked Minnie, or Beast called her and she told him her location. Either way, you know they'll find a way to watch over her."

"I know you're trying to help. It's just too little too late. I needed you, all of you, and the club let me down."

"I talked to the others after you left. We understand we need to regain your trust, and we'll do whatever it takes. Short of letting Outlaw use his skills to track Minnie. If we do that, Beast is going to find out." Badger came closer and placed a hand on my shoulder. "I don't always have all the answers, and I'm going to fuck up sometimes. I might be the President of this club now, but I'm still human. This club is my family. But my woman is the daughter of Grizzly and the sister of Meredith. I should have taken a step back and let someone else handle things since it hit so close to home. But I didn't, and I'm sorry."

"I understand you were in a tough spot." I ran my hands down my face. "I get it, Badger. I do. Now think for a minute. If you'd been with Adalia for two weeks, not using protection, had married her, then had the club run her the hell out of here… how would you be feeling right now? What if everyone had voted against you making her your old lady? Told her to leave. Been downright hateful to her every second she'd been here?"

"We have a lot to atone for," he said softly. "To you and to Minnie. Meredith left here and went crying to Grizzly. They're having a long overdue talk. We'll get your woman back, and when we do, we'll all apologize. Do whatever it takes to make her feel welcome. Anything."

"If only y'all could have done that from the beginning." Yeah, I could admit I was bitter. Angry. Ready to hit something, or someone. "Did we learn anything from this?"

Badger gave a nod. "If I hadn't given in to Grizzly and had told the club what was going on, things wouldn't have escalated the way they did. Or as quickly. More of us could have held Griz accountable for his actions and could have wrangled Meredith a bit better. Or at all. Guess we thought you'd always been there for her, knew she loved you, so we didn't realize how crazy things had gotten. No more secrets. But you kept one too. Why didn't you say you were married?"

I sighed and went to sit down. I suddenly felt so fucking tired, even though I knew I wouldn't sleep. "Before I made it home, Meredith started calling constantly. I didn't answer her first few calls and Minnie pointed out something could be wrong. So I took the next one. She wanted to know when I'd be back, kept going on about how much she missed me. I'd been gone one night, Badger. One."

"She found out you were bringing Minnie back," he said.

"Yeah. Then I had Grizzly on speaker when I told him what Meredith was doing. Told him I was staying overnight with Minnie so she could take a moment to breathe before starting her new life. He was so nasty and mean, knowing she could hear him."

"You knew, before you got here, you'd be facing

problems." Badger sat down and leaned back, looking like he'd aged a decade in the last hour.

"I wanted the club to have a chance to get to know Minnie. I'd thought maybe I'd gotten through to Grizzly, or that he'd come around quickly. I told y'all again and again that I wanted Meredith to back off, that I wasn't interested. No one listened to me. And it's not recent. I've been trying to convince everyone for over a year that I didn't see her that way."

"Some of your brothers did listen," Badger said. "Steel may have a family now, but it didn't change how he feels about you. I think you were always a son to him. Still are. Which meant Rachel was on your side too. When you said you didn't want Meredith, they didn't push like everyone else."

"Farrah wanted to ship Meredith off to another club, like Venom did with Mariah. I had to admit, I was tempted to say it was a great idea. Then I thought about Grizzly. He's already dealing with heart problems. Last thing we need to do is send one of his adopted kids away."

The doorbell rang this time and I groaned, dropping my head into my hands. I wasn't in the mood for company and everyone wanted to stop and talk. Yet no one had a damn solution for how to get Minnie back.

"I'll get it," Badger said, getting up to answer the door. He returned a moment later with Meredith. I narrowed my gaze at her then noticed Garrick standing behind her. "I know you don't want to talk to Meredith right now, but just listen to what she has to say."

Girl seemed ready to bolt. One look from Garrick planted her feet firmly in place. Huh. I hadn't seen that one coming. He'd said he'd do anything to help. It looked like he'd found a way to do exactly that. I felt Badger's presence behind me and knew he planned to listen to whatever she had to say.

"I know I caused trouble for you and acted like a brat," Meredith said, glancing at Garrick again. "I only thought of myself and what I wanted. When you said you weren't interested, I should have backed off. I didn't even give Minnie a chance."

Garrick cleared his throat, staring her down. Meredith shifted from foot to foot, wringing her hands in front of her. She didn't say anything, and he poked her, causing her to jump and yelp.

"All right! I'll say it. I'm the reason Minnie had such a hard time at the Devil's Fury. I spread rumors about her to some of the old ladies, the Prospects, and a few members, like Hot Shot. Told them all she'd fucked everyone at the Reckless Kings and had sunk her claws into you the first chance she had." She pressed her lips together. "I… I told the women who work for you that she was some whore you'd brought home. It's why they didn't befriend her."

"Why?" I asked. "Why would you do that to Minnie? To me?"

"I was jealous," she whispered. "I wanted you. Not once had you ever looked at me like I was more than a kid."

Badger growled and I had a feeling he'd be having some choice words with Meredith later. She'd played on his affection for Adalia, and I knew he wouldn't let that slide.

I closed my eyes and reminded myself not to yell at her. I wanted to. No, I wanted to wrap my fingers around her throat and give her a good shake. "Minnie might be pregnant. You didn't just run my wife out of here. She could very well have my kid growing inside her."

Meredith sobbed and tears slipped down her cheeks. "I didn't know! No one said anything about you being married. I thought she was like the others. I swear, Doolittle. I would have never worked so hard to keep her from you if I'd known."

"It shouldn't have mattered," Badger said. "You knew he didn't want you. He might have said as much to the rest of us, but I hadn't realized he'd already confronted you about your infatuation with him. Do you have any idea what you've done? Not only to Doolittle and Minnie, but to the entire fucking club?"

"I didn't mean to!" Meredith swiped at the tears on her cheeks.

"Just go. Please. I can't…" I swallowed hard and stared at the floor. So much trouble and drama, and all because a nineteen-year-old girl hadn't gotten what she wanted. And yeah, I considered Meredith a girl. She hadn't grown up enough to be a woman.

Garrick hung back and I acknowledged what he'd done. "Thank you for trying to fix things."

He nodded. "I had a talk with her when she came near the gate. Grizzly had already given it a go. He'd left out a few things. Mainly you being married and Minnie possibly being pregnant. She didn't realize she was breaking up a marriage and destroying a kid's life."

"I appreciate it. You got through to her when no one else could. When it comes time for you to patch in, you'll have my vote." I smiled faintly. "Long as you don't fuck up between now and then."

Badger and Garrick both left, but the Pres gave me a look on his way out the door. I knew he felt like shit for how things went down. Sooner or later, we'd have to mend things between us. Right now, the wound was too fucking raw.

After I was alone, I made a pot of coffee. I didn't see the point in lying down. No fucking way I'd sleep while I worried about Minnie. If Outlaw wouldn't help, and the Reckless Kings were keeping quiet, then I'd just have to figure out where Minnie went on my own. Somehow.

Chapter Nine

Minnie

I'd been with the Devil's Boneyard for a week now. They were kind to take me in, give me a place to stay, and none of them had made me feel like trash. There hadn't been any vacant places for me to use during my stay, but Stripes had opened his home to me. I had my own bedroom and bathroom. Stripes made sure my favorite snacks and drinks were stocked. He'd been so nice to me.

"Morning, *zaichik.*" Stripes ran his hand down my hair as he passed me, heading for the coffee pot. "Do you have plans for the day?"

"I need to find a job so I can save some money. Otherwise, I'll never be able to provide for myself." *Or my baby.* I hadn't told the Devil's Boneyard I was pregnant. I'd only found out three days ago. My period was not only late, but my breasts had become more tender than usual, and seemed a bit larger. I'd taken a home test, then a second. Both came back positive.

"You could go to work with me," he said, his Russian accent heavy first thing in the morning.

"At the strip club?" I asked with some amusement. "I don't know how to dance on a pole."

He scowled. "Not funny, *zaichik*. You help me in the office. None of those men are putting their hands on you, or watching you dance naked."

"I guess it wouldn't hurt. But I meant what I said about needing to save money."

"I'll pay you ten dollars an hour if you clean up my office." He took a swallow of coffee. "But it's a disaster."

I didn't doubt it. I'd seen his organizational skills at work around the house. As in, he didn't have any.

I'd spent the first few days putting the kitchen into some sort of order. Then I'd tackled the hall closet. Stripes had been thrilled. The man was a big softy, and said while I was here, it would be like having a daughter. Apparently, when he called me *zaichik,* it was a term of endearment. I had to admit it made me feel a little warm and fuzzy. I'd not had a dad growing up.

"Can I start today?" I asked.

"*Nyet*. We'll go in tomorrow. Today, we're going to talk."

Well, that sounded rather ominous. I couldn't think of a single conversation that started that way and ended on a positive note. I got up to make a cup of tea. While the water boiled, I busied myself with checking the refrigerator to see if we needed dinner items. Stripes got up and shut the fridge door, trapping me between him and the appliance.

"No avoiding this," he said. "Get your tea and sit."

"All right." The kettle whistled and I poured a mugful before dunking a tea bag. I carried the mug to the table and took a seat. "What's the bad news?"

He chuckled, swallowing more coffee. "Why is it bad news? I'm simply waiting for the truth."

My stomach knotted and I looked everywhere but at Stripes. Did he know about the baby? Had he seen the test sticks in the trash?

"Little birdy says your Doolittle is looking for you," Stripes said. "He's not sleeping. Not eating. The Devil's Fury are worried and asking the clubs they know to keep an eye out for you, Minnie Morgan."

"He didn't come after me, Stripes. He wouldn't even look at me. If he's searching now, it's only because he feels guilty."

"*Zaichik,* I think you ran too far too fast. Your Doolittle didn't give up on you. I hear he yelled at his club, said they'd betrayed him. Your animal doctor was furious." Stripes pushed his cup away. "I'll not tell you what to do. You're an adult. But, *zaichik,* I think you should consider calling him. Let him know you're safe. Set his mind at ease, yes?"

I sighed and twisted my mug in a circle. "Maybe I can send a text message. It doesn't mean I want to see him. The Devil's Fury made it clear what they thought of me. I won't put Doolittle through that again. He shouldn't have been in that position to begin with, but I couldn't tell him no. I'd never met anyone like him before."

"I know. Do you think perhaps he felt the same about you? Did you give him a chance at all? Or did you always have one foot out the door?" Stripes asked.

"You weren't there," I said softly. "The way they talked about me. Badger yelled and told me to leave immediately. Only four of them voted to let me stay as Doolittle's old lady. Badger didn't care that we were married. None of them did."

Stripes reached over and placed his hand on mine. "Your heart hurts now. It's understandable. One day, it won't hurt so much. Perhaps sooner than you think, if you reach out and speak to your Doolittle. Give him a chance to decide if he's willing to fight for you. Because, *zaichik,* if I had a woman like you, I'd go to war for her. I suspect your Doolittle is the same."

"It's only been a week, Stripes. I doubt things changed that much while I was gone."

"You won't know if you don't ask. Text him, Minnie. Tell him you're all right. At least give him that much. Open up the communication between the two of you. Maybe things aren't the way they seem. It sounds like the man is suffering over your loss." His gaze dropped to my belly. "Both of you."

I gasped and placed my hand over my mouth. "How did you..."

"Doolittle has sent out a request to all clubs, asking for information about his wife and baby. If you didn't tell him, he figured it out. Doesn't sound to me like a man who doesn't want you around."

I set my phone on the table and opened up my text messages. I'd had countless phone calls, voicemails, and texts from Doolittle since I left. I hadn't been able to listen to them or read any of them. It was too painful. I didn't bother skimming them now. I just typed out a simple message and hit send.

I'm okay.

Stripes snorted. "That's it? The man is searching for you across multiple states, and he gets two words? I now remember why I'm single."

"Since he hasn't bothered to read it, I think it's sufficient."

"Tell him something else. Anything. Give the man a crumb, Minnie."

I sighed and started typing again. *I'm safe, have a place to stay, and I'm not going hungry. I even have a job I start tomorrow. You don't have to worry about me.*

"Satisfied?" I asked.

Stripes grunted then stood and rinsed his mug. "What you had with Doolittle... it's not something that comes along often. You understand, yes? It's precious and should be treated as such. I know you think he threw you away. His actions now say otherwise. I think you need to hear the entire story, from his side of things. He's just a man, Minnie. Flawed. No one is perfect. Not even you."

"You think I should tell him where I am?" I

asked.

"Not yet. Soon." He pointed to my phone, which had jingled with incoming messages. Each from Doolittle.

Thank God! I've been so worried, Minnie. Please come home. Things will be different. I promise.

The pain was still too fresh for me to go racing back to him. If I did, would he think it would always be so easy to win me back when things went wrong? I didn't want that. I wanted him to learn something from this. The entire club needed to. How many other women had they judged?

"Come, *zaichik*. The ladies are having lunch at the clubhouse. Potluck. Everyone is invited. But first we scrub the place and make it look nice, yes?"

"I can do that." I smiled. "It will be nice to visit with everyone. It's like a big, happy family here."

Stripes nodded. "These lunches are for us single men too. The old ladies don't like knowing we're alone, fending for ourselves. Often, they will make casseroles and take them to the clubhouse to ensure we have a nice meal. It's nice to be thought of, even though I know they're busy tending their families."

"Then let's go clean and get things set up. I may not be able to eat breakfast right now, but by lunch I'll be starving. Should I make something too?"

"*Nyet*. You're a guest, *zaichik*."

"I don't feel right going emptyhanded."

"The cleaning is plenty. Come. We'll get it finished so you can rest before we eat. The little one will tire you out more."

I rolled my eyes. "All right, papa bear. I'm barely pregnant. I don't think I'll get tired until after I've started showing. Right now you can't even tell there's a baby in there."

Sadness flashed in his eyes a brief moment, and I wondered what I'd said. I studied the older Russian man. The easy way he'd accepted me into his home, his kindness and understanding… but mostly the way he treated me like a daughter. I hoped I was wrong, but I needed to know.

"Stripes, where's your daughter?" I asked softly.

His expression shuttered. "I don't know what you're talking about."

I reached out and grabbed his arm. "Please. You're helping me and I want to help you too. The way you act around me. None of this is new for you. You have a daughter, don't you?"

"There are things best left in the past," Stripes said.

"In the past? Or in Russia?" I asked.

He glowered and stormed off, only to return a moment later with a worn photo in his hand. "You want to push and prod? Want to know why I don't wish to speak of it? Here."

He thrust the picture at me, and I grabbed it, looking down at the sweetest little girl. She looked like Stripes and couldn't have been more than three years old in the picture. "What happened to her?"

"She died," he said. "I got someone pregnant when I was fifteen. Our parents were going to force us to wed. The girl found a way to end the pregnancy. I'd never thought to have a child after that. It was a small town. News traveled fast, and fathers didn't want me near their daughters. I knew then I'd never marry, so I spent time with other types of women. The kind you didn't marry."

My brow furrowed. "But… this little girl…"

"Is different. I was older. Thought I knew the world, that I could beat it. Survive Russia. I was wrong. I didn't know until after I'd fled to the US that I'd left a child behind. Her mother was..." He raked a hand through his hair. "A prostitute. Beautiful woman. I cared for her. Snuck her food when I could. We grew close, or so I'd thought."

I moved closer, placing my hand on his back and leaning into him. "Talk to me, Stripes. It's not good to keep all this bottled up. Does the club even know?"

"*Nyet*. And they never will. This remains between us, *zaichik*."

I nodded. It wasn't my place to go running to his President anyway. If he wanted his brothers to know about his daughter, he'd tell them. I waited patiently as he seemed to struggle with his thoughts and memories.

"I come here when I was much younger. Grown man, yet still child." His accent got heavier the more he spoke, and I could tell this was hard for him. "I live here two years before I find out the woman I'd been caring for had a child. My child. She sold my daughter when she was three years old. That picture is all I have."

My heart ached for him. Sold? How could anyone sell their own child? It was horrible. I knew monsters lived in the world, but... I could never do that to my baby! "Did you find out who bought her?"

He nodded, his expression changing to one of pure agony. "I have friends with questionable backgrounds. They looked into it. My daughter, Oksana, was sold to a collector. You understand? Her life would have been very unpleasant. They found records of her death before she'd turned six years old."

"I'm so sorry." Tears streaked my cheeks. "I shouldn't have brought up something so painful for you. I didn't think..."

I handed the picture back to him. He took it,

staring for a long moment, before taking out his wallet and placing the picture inside. He stroked his finger down the little girl's chubby cheek. "Had I known, I would have stayed. Would have gotten them both out. It's my fault my little one is gone."

And everything clicked into place. Stripes wasn't a carefree bachelor because he enjoyed that lifestyle. He felt unworthy of falling in love, having a family. "You think you abandoned your daughter, left her to die, so now you don't deserve to have anyone in your life other than the Devil's Boneyard."

He smiled faintly. "You're very smart, *zaichik*. See much that others don't. This never leaves this room. Understood?"

"Yes, Stripes. I understand." I looked up at him wistfully. "Your daughter would have been very lucky to have you in her life. I didn't have a dad growing up. My mom wasn't all that fantastic, but she did the best she could I suppose. Being here with you this past week has given me a taste of what it would have been like if my dad had cared that I existed."

Stripes pressed a kiss to my forehead and hugged me. "It was his loss. You're a strong, beautiful woman, *zaichik*. He should have been proud to have a daughter like you."

"Come on. Let's get the clubhouse cleaned so you can show me how a club is supposed to act around one another. The Reckless Kings only have a handful of old ladies, so they're still mostly bachelors. And the Devil's Fury…" I winced.

Stripes grunted. "Boys playing at being men. They need to be taught a lesson."

"I just need to forget them. Make a plan and move on with my life." I pressed a hand to my belly.

"*Zaichik,* I won't tell you what to do, but I will

say this. Losing my daughter, never getting to meet her, it damaged something inside me. No matter your anger at Doolittle and his club, if our roles were reversed, I would want to know my woman was pregnant. Do what you feel is best. Just keep in mind one day your son or daughter may ask for their papa." He studied me before giving a slight nod and leading me outside.

The Devil's Boneyard had loaned us one of the club trucks. Mostly because Stripes didn't fit in my small SUV without looking like I'd stuffed him in there. He didn't like riding his motorcycle and leaving me to drive alone whenever we went somewhere. The man really was a big teddy bear. I hated that he hadn't had a chance to know his daughter. He'd have been an amazing dad. Unlike mine.

Stripes parked outside the clubhouse and we went inside. My nose wrinkled at the smell of stale beer and sex. Not too long ago, I wouldn't have batted an eye at any of this. I went down the hall and searched for a closet. If this clubhouse was anything like the Reckless Kings, they'd have some supplies stashed. I ran across one of the Prospects, Carlos, and saw he already had everything we'd need.

"You here to help?" he asked, his brow pinching and his lips tipping down. "I've never seen them bring one of their women here for something like this."

"One of their women?" I asked, curious about his phrasing.

"You're with Stripes, right?"

I wasn't sure how to respond at first. "Um. I'm staying with him temporarily. I'm not his old lady or anything."

"Right." He pushed past me and went into the main part of the clubhouse.

I followed along, snagging a spray bottle and some cleaning cloths. I decided to start on the tables and chairs. After the first swipe of a tabletop, I was wishing I had gloves. I would ask what the hell they did in here, but I most certainly didn't want to know. Not even a little. I gagged, wondering if the clubhouse at the Reckless Kings was this dirty. How many times had I sat at their tables? Eaten there for that matter.

My stomach flipped and flopped. I stopped, focusing on my breathing. My mouth filled with saliva, and I knew I wasn't going to make it. I rushed outside and leaned over the railing. I sputtered as I threw up into the bushes. I felt a large hand on my back, rubbing up and down in soothing strokes.

"Perhaps I should not have brought you, *zaichik*."

"I'm fine." I whimpered before throwing up again. Maybe fine wasn't the best word to use. When I'd finished, I wiped my mouth and winced, wanting nothing more than to brush my teeth. "But I wouldn't say no to some mouthwash."

Stripes smiled and led me inside and down the hall. He pushed open the bathroom door and ushered me into the room. Someone had put a cube organizer along one wall. Stripes pulled out a drawer and took out a travel sized bottle of mouthwash then handed it to me. I wasn't going to ask why the club kept this stuff around. I had a feeling some of the other drawers contained condoms. At least, I hoped these men were using protection.

I gargled and swished three times before I felt a little better. Stripes took my arm and led me back into the clubhouse, then straight out the front door. I glanced behind us and saw Carlos frowning at me. I'd met each of the Prospects since being here, but it seemed no one had told them my role in this place.

Hell, I didn't even know it. Other than guest. Except guests usually had a set amount of time they planned to stay.

"I thought we needed to clean," I said.

"You're not in any condition to be wiping down the filth in there. I'll take you home and bring my bike back over so I can still help. If you wish to bake something or prepare a dish for the potluck, you're welcome to use anything you need in the kitchen. I would prefer you rest."

"You know that won't happen," I said.

"Remember it's not only yourself you need to worry about," he said. "If you need me, you call."

I agreed and watched him leave. Hurrying into the kitchen, I washed my hands before searching through the ingredients Stripes had stocked. After settling on chocolate chip cookies and cornbread, I got to work. I didn't know how much I'd need of both, and I wanted to be prepared. The Devil's Fury hadn't given me a chance to be part of their community. I wanted to experience everything I could today. Seeing the Devil's Boneyard in action on a family day would help me make a few decisions about my life. Namely, would I ever tell Doolittle where I was, and where would I go from here.

Chapter Ten

Doolittle

I'd immersed myself in work at the clinic and concentrated on the animals I took care of at home. Spending less time than usual with the club meant I'd been able to focus my energy into finding homes for some of the temporary guests in my home. Not that I would ever toss them out, but this wasn't their last stop. The marmoset had gone to its new home at a local wildlife park. One of the bunnies had made a little girl a little less sad after she lost her grandmother. I placed three kittens and two puppies that I still had at the clinic, and even found a home for one of the lizards.

The staff at work had been quiet and reserved. I'd noticed the glances they cast my way and heard the whispers about Minnie vanishing without so much as a goodbye. They thought they were being sneaky, but they weren't. I heard them. Every damn time. And until today, they hadn't crossed a line. Well, not by much.

"I heard she was a prostitute," my receptionist whispered to one of my techs. "Do you think she went back to the streets? No wonder he had her working in the kennels out back."

"You don't think he was paying her for more than that, do you?" the tech whispered back.

"First of all," I said, interrupting them, "Minnie was never a prostitute. She's not a whore, slut, or any other name you want to call her. She was a hard worker, and if you're wondering if she was also in my bed, the answer is yes."

They gasped and looked at one another in horror. I ground my teeth together, reminding myself I couldn't hit women. Or shouldn't at any rate.

"Where the fuck else would you expect my wife to sleep?" I glared at the two of them and stormed off to my office. Looked like I'd be hiring new staff. As much as I hated to be shorthanded, I wouldn't have those two around. Not after today.

I called them into my office one at a time and let them know they were fired. I handed each a letter of termination, outlining why they were no longer employed, and told them when to expect their final paychecks. That task completed, I called in the other two workers, wanting to know if I needed to clean house all the way.

"Are they… fired?" Cindy asked, her eyes going wide.

"They are. You should both be aware the woman everyone likes disparaging isn't a prostitute, or whatever other ridiculous rumors are going around. Minnie is my wife," I said.

Cindy's jaw dropped, but Sara didn't seem the least bit surprised. She remained calm and cool, almost looking bored with the conversation.

"She's not going to be here for a while. I'm afraid we've had a miscommunication, and I now understand a bit more why she reacted the way she did. I'm sure she heard the other two whispering about her. The people I call family weren't much better." I eyed the two of them. "Are we going to have a problem?"

"Not at all, Dr. Doolittle," Sara said. "I'm sorry if I wasn't more welcoming to your wife. I didn't realize the two of you were married, but I could tell you were a couple. Which meant that regardless of her working in the kennels, which she seemed to enjoy, she was also higher ranking than me."

I blinked and stared at my vet tech. I'd

underestimated her. So had Minnie, it seemed. I had a feeling Sara would be a good friend for her, if I ever discovered where she'd run off to.

"What can we do to help?" Cindy asked.

"When Minnie returns, if she wants to work, I'll let her manage the front desk. I don't want her working in the kennels in her condition. But that means we need a kennel worker and another vet tech, and one of you will have to help with the phones and appointments for the moment."

"You could hire a temp to handle the phones and appointments," Sara suggested. "As for the kennel worker, my cousin is in high school. Only seventeen, but he wouldn't mind earning some cash to pad his college fund. I think he could handle the kennels."

"Tell him to stop by after school. I'll conduct an interview and tour, see if he's interested in sticking around until he's graduated."

"How experienced do you want the tech to be?" Cindy asked.

"Why?" I narrowed my gaze. "Have someone in mind?"

"A friend of mine is a single mom. Recently divorced. She's a fully licensed vet tech, but she was only able to work six months before she went out on maternity leave, then decided to stay home with her son. She could really use a job."

"See if she can come by tomorrow. Find a break in the schedule and tell her to be here if she wants an interview. I'll see how much knowledge she's retained and decide if she's a good fit. I can always hire her on a trial basis and see how it goes."

Once they were out of my office, I took a second to just breathe. It felt like time was slipping by too fast. Minnie had been gone a week and I was no closer to finding her. No one would tell me what they knew, if anything. Even worse, thanks to Beast, none of the hackers would help me. The asshole still hadn't responded to my text. A faint knock on the door had me wanting to yell at whoever needed me now. Until I saw Elena standing in the open doorway. Outlaw's wife was a sweetheart and looked like she had something on her mind.

"Come in and have a seat. Everything okay?" I asked.

"Yes and no. Outlaw isn't supposed to be looking for Minnie, and he's not. At least, he said he wasn't directly trying to find her. If anyone asks, he said he'll tell them he just wanted to know more about where she came from." Elena chewed her lip and slid a file across the desk to me. "I don't think even Minnie is aware of what's in that file, Doolittle. Tread carefully. If she comes back, and you decide to share any of that with her, it's..."

My interest piqued, I flipped open the file and started reading. Although, it confused the hell out of me at first. "This doesn't look like it's about Minnie."

"Read all of it," Elena said. "And just... be prepared. There are some pictures. The kind that make our club do things like march into hell to save the innocent. Minnie's history, and that of her family, isn't pretty. It's downright horrifying."

"On your way out, would you tell the girls to cancel the rest of the appointments for today? And flip the closed sign for me. I don't think I can concentrate on work now that I have this, but I appreciate you bringing it here. Even if it doesn't lead me to Minnie, it might help me understand her better."

Elena left and soon the building became silent, except for the sounds of the dogs and cats in the kennels. I scanned each page of the file, feeling sick the further back into her family history I went. Did Minnie know any of this? Elena seemed to think she may not be aware of where she came from, or her mother for that matter.

Ivanna Carter. Age 18. The picture showed a scarred and battered young woman, already noticeably pregnant. Reading the notes in the margins, and the other things Outlaw had compiled took a bit of time, and a lot of unravelling. It didn't fit together smoothly, mostly because Ivanna hadn't come to this country legally. Not in the strictest sense. It looked like she'd been rescued, given a different name, and hurried out of Russia before anyone was the wiser.

Minnie Carter. Seemed my woman really was named Minnie. The last name matched Ivanna's, and yet, I didn't see a marriage license or any sort of proof of marriage for Ivanna. Was that her maiden name? It didn't seem likely, having immigrated from Belarus.

I pulled out a pad and pen, making my own notes and trying to get everything into some sort of order that made sense. I found the pictures of Minnie's mom, the ones Elena had warned me about. The kid had been abused since she was just a toddler, and it hadn't stopped until she'd left Belarus. Only… Ivanna Carter wasn't her real name, and she hadn't been born in Belarus. *Oksana Bogrov.* She'd been sold when she was three and hadn't managed to escape unscathed. Poor girl had been sold twice more before landing in her final ring of hell overseas.

The reports Outlaw compiled had tracked down Oksana's mother. A prostitute who'd had a rough life. One cut short in a rather brutal way not long after she sold her daughter. Good riddance, in my opinion. What sort of person sold their own child? No word on who Oksana's father might be, but then, he was likely just one of her customers. Could have been anyone off the street. The woman hadn't exactly been a high-class hooker pulling in large bills.

From the accounts Outlaw had tracked down, someone in the home of her last buyer had secured passage for himself and Oksana out of Belarus, under new names. The man had been a lower-level employee, but apparently saw more than he should have. *Grigory Carter*. How had anyone believed that man's surname was Carter? Fucking idiots, unless he'd greased some palms in immigration. It was possible. He was listed as the husband of Ivanna Carter, except there was no marriage record anywhere in Belarus or Russia.

After that, Grigory disappeared a few years later, leaving Ivanna on her own with a daughter. Minnie. If I was reading all this right, then Minnie had never known her father. Even if she remembered Grigory, it was doubtful he'd been her sperm donor. No, that honor most likely went to Yakov Dulstev. The asshole rapist who'd purchased Oksana last. For one thing, Minnie didn't look like Grigory. I could see a bit of her mother in her. My money was on her looks coming from her dad.

Minnie was alone, except for me and the Devil's Fury. The obituary for her mother showed the woman had died several years back. So if she didn't have family to turn to, where would the Reckless Kings have sent her? I doubted she went back to their compound. Not if she wanted to get as far from Satyr as possible. No, they'd have sent her somewhere else.

I pulled up a map of the southern US on the computer. The nearest clubs to us, who would be allies with the Reckless Kings, were the Devil's Boneyard, Dixie Reapers, and possibly the Mississippi chapter of

Hades Abyss. I stared at the wall, thinking. Garrick said she'd turned right, heading away from town. That meant she'd been traveling south. It was possible she'd cut over into Alabama, or she could have gone down into Florida and headed for the Devil's Boneyard.

It was time to call in a few favors. Men I'd helped in the past, who had no ties to the club. And unless people went digging, they wouldn't find a connection to me either. I didn't want to text or email, so I placed two calls. One to the nearest contact to the Dixie Reapers' compound, and one closer to the Devil's Boneyard. The men agreed to keep an eye on both clubs and watch for my wife. I'd had to describe Minnie and not chance sending a picture. My phone hadn't been out of my possession so I wasn't worried about it being bugged. Didn't mean one of the hackers wouldn't be able to access any messages I sent.

If I didn't use club resources to find her, then Beast couldn't come after the club. At least, that was my hope. If Badger got pissed at me, I'd handle it. The fucker owed me. Toeing the line, following his rules, helping where I could hadn't gotten me anywhere. Right now, I needed to bring my wife home where she belonged. Then I wanted to discover what she knew about her past. Even if she didn't have blood relations she'd want to associate with, because I highly doubted she wanted to track down the man who'd raped her mother, she still had me and my brothers. Now that the dust had settled, and they'd pulled their heads out of their asses, they'd welcome Minnie. Make her feel like she belonged.

"At least they fucking better," I mumbled. I'd been the easy-going, laid-back brother long enough. What had it gotten me? Nothing. With the exception of a select few, everyone had made sure Minnie felt unwelcome. They'd run her out of the compound, voted against me claiming her, and shown they didn't have my back when I needed them to the most. I hadn't forgiven them yet. It would come in time. For now, the wound was too fresh.

With nothing but time on my hands, I decided to do a bit of digging on my own. I might not have the skills of Outlaw and the others but running a Google search on someone seemed easy enough. I wanted to know everything I could about Yakov Dulstev. The odds of him knowing about Minnie or coming for her after all these years were slim to none. I just wanted to be armed with as much knowledge as possible. If I told Minnie about her family history, I wanted as many facts as I could gather.

I found a picture of Yakov and there was no doubt in my mind Minnie was either his daughter, or a relation of some sort. It said the man had two brothers. If he'd shared Oksana with them, any of the men could have been her father. Once I went down that rabbit hole, it was hard to stop. I checked out everything I could on the entire Dulstev family, not liking a single thing I learned.

Whatever hardships Minnie had faced, her mother had done the best for her that she could. She'd made sure Minnie wasn't born in Belarus and was kept away from the poisonous Dulstev family. It wouldn't have surprised me if the men would have used young Minnie as a business transaction and sold her to the highest bidder, just like they'd purchased Oksana.

I gathered my notes, and the file Outlaw had prepared. It was time to go home and take care of all the creatures who depended on me. I wanted to talk to someone about all this shit, but who? Outlaw had sent Elena to me, which meant he hadn't wanted anyone to see him with the file. I didn't know why sending Elena was any safer. It wasn't like she would have gotten something like that from anyone other than him. No one else in the club had those skills, and Elena didn't exactly have connections.

Making one stop on my way home, I grabbed a large coffee and a kolache. I ate in the truck and downed the coffee before I reached the compound. As I pulled through the gates, I saw Smuggler getting on his bike and hesitated. I'd have called us friends before the vote in Church. We'd hung out numerous times, just the two of us. I also knew he'd spent a few years in the Army. It wasn't a horrible idea to bounce a few concepts around. I'd call Steel, but I didn't want to get him into trouble. He had a family to consider.

Rolling down the window, I shouted Smuggler's name. He glanced my way and gave me a chin lift before walking his bike closer. "What's up, Doolittle?"

"Can you come by the house in about an hour? I need to take care of everyone first, but I want to run a few ideas past you. I'll have pizza delivered."

He grimaced. "Make it Chinese and you have a deal. Don't think I can handle a greasy pizza right now."

"Deal. Text me what you want, and I'll get it ordered. And, Smuggler, keep this quiet for now."

"This is about Minnie, isn't it?"

I nodded. "Beast may have said Outlaw couldn't go digging into her location. He didn't say anything about us figuring out her past. I learned some things I'm not even sure my wife knows about herself."

"I'll be there. For what it's worth, if I'd known Minnie was your wife, I never would have voted against her. Truthfully, I'd never spoken to her before, and you hadn't talked to me about her. All I had to go on was all the whispering going on."

"I understand. One more vote wouldn't have made a difference. I'd have needed more than half to vote her in as my old lady. But I appreciate the honesty." I rolled up the window and drove home.

It was going to be a long ass night. I only hoped that by morning, I'd be one step closer to finding my wife. It didn't matter she'd never spent the entire night here. She belonged in my bed, in my home… by my side. I wouldn't stop searching until I'd found her. Then I'd tell her what she meant to me.

Chapter Eleven

Minnie

The potluck for lunch had ended up lasting until dinner. Since most of the food had been consumed, the club had ordered a massive stack of pizzas and breadsticks. Mostly at the kids' insistence. The adorable little monsters had taken over the place. Some of the older ones were on their phones. A few who looked to be in middle school were playing board games. The youngest of the bunch had puzzles and toys.

Stripes sprawled in the seat next to mine, refusing to budge from my side. He'd been so sweet to me, and the old ladies had welcomed me with open arms. Even knowing my past, not a single one had judged me. I had to wonder if part of it had to do with the giant Russian. Everyone seemed to love him.

Charming entered the clubhouse, looking a bit harried. I'd noticed he'd been here earlier, vanished for a while, then returned before disappearing again. Stripes had made a comment about the President acting a little strange the past six months. He looked like he hadn't been sleeping well, if the dark circles under his eyes were any indication.

The man headed straight for us, taking the seat across from Stripes. "We may have a problem."

"What kind?" Stripes asked, looking every bit as relaxed as he'd been before.

"Someone's been checking out the compound. Subtle, but they're definitely looking for something." He paused. "Or someone."

"Do you think Doolittle suspects I'm here?" I asked. "Would he have sent someone to look for me?"

The tension in Charming seemed to drain, which

I found interesting. Clearly, he hadn't thought the person was here for me. So who else had someone searching for them? The club seemed completely at ease, unless someone wasn't here? None of them appeared worried anyone would come knocking on their door.

"Yeah, it's probably Doolittle. No idea how he'd have found you though." Charming sighed. "Since you've been in here since lunch earlier, I don't think he's spotted you. If he had, he'd have left already. Instead, he's found a way to drive past the compound multiple times in the last few hours. First time he had boxes in the bed of his truck. Another he had garbage bags of crap back there. It's always something, probably trying to keep suspicion low."

Stripes patted my thigh. "Text your Doolittle. See if he slips up and gives anything away."

I pulled out my phone and stared at it for a second. I didn't have any idea what I'd say to him. Then I recalled my conversation with Stripes earlier. About how much he wished he'd known he had a daughter, had been a part of her life. As I'd watched the Devil's Boneyard today, I'd realized I could never keep Doolittle from his child.

There's something I need to tell you. I hit send before I could chicken out.

He didn't respond right away, and I started chewing on my thumb. Stripes reached over and tugged my hand from my mouth. I scooted my chair closer and leaned against him, wishing I'd had someone like him for a dad when I was growing up.

Doolittle finally answered. *Like your location? Because I'll come pick you up right now.*

I snorted. Nice try. *No. I'm not ready. Being around your club…* How did I tell him that his family didn't make me feel safe? The people here did. They accepted me, made me feel like I was a part of their little circle.

What about the club? Doolittle asked.

I don't feel safe there. It was like having a target on my back. I took a breath and knew this was a good moment to tell him. *I don't know if they'd welcome our baby or try to take it from me, then shove me out the door again.*

There! I'd said it. A minute went by. Then another. I looked at Stripes, who was slowly sipping on a beer. Charming stared at the phone in my hand almost like he expected it to explode or something. After five minutes and no response, I set the phone down.

"I guess that was answer enough," I said. "If he was looking for me, I don't think he is now."

Charming picked up the phone and read the messages, his eyebrows climbing nearly to his hairline. "Damn, Minnie. You were out for blood."

"What? What did I do?"

"You basically said his family would throw you away and take your kid away. Those are the people who have his back. The ones who stand by him through anything. They said blood is thicker than water, but the bond of the brotherhood is even tighter than DNA." Charming handed the phone back. "You just insulted him and everyone at his club."

I glanced up at Stripes. "I wasn't trying to do that, but he needs to understand. It was scary. No one liked me, not until my last day there. I did meet a few nice people then. The rest of the time they called me names, threatened to have me thrown out. Then Badger *did* toss me off the property. Told me to leave immediately, so I did. Is it wrong to think he could do that again? Or worse, do it after the baby is born and refuse to let me take my child with me?"

"When did Badger and his crew become assholes?" Charming asked. "Something weird is going on over there. And I don't fucking like it. Apparently, Beast doesn't either since he asked if you could crash here for a bit. Although, I'm starting to think Stripes may not let you leave. The two of you seem cozy."

My cheeks burned and I tried to pull away, but Stripes put his arm around me. "My *zaichik* is like a daughter to me. I would be honored for her to stay."

"Daughter, huh?" Charming almost turned a little green.

What the hell was going on with him? Did Stripes notice something was off? I didn't know the man and even I could tell he wasn't acting normal. Stripes squeezed me to him as he stared at his President. Yeah, he'd caught it too. Did it have something to do with his sudden relief when I said the man who kept driving past might be searching for me?

I leaned forward, about to ask him the same thing I'd asked Stripes earlier. Until my phone chimed with an incoming text. I opened it and saw Doolittle had finally responded.

First, I'd never let anyone take your child from you. Second, the club has come to the realization they were wrong. No one is going to throw you out of the compound, Minnie. Please come home. I miss you.

Stripes shook his head. "He misses you. Not one word of love. Hold out longer, *zaichik*. That one hasn't quite learned his lesson yet."

"What about the person checking out the compound? If he sees me, and he *was* sent by Doolittle, then it will only be a matter of time before the Devil's Fury are at the gates." I chewed my lower lip, stopping when I tasted the tang of my blood. "I don't want to cause trouble for all of you. You've been so kind to me, and Stripes is like the dad I never had. It seems like a crappy way to repay you, letting them storm the gates."

Charming smiled a little. "You need to decide which it is, Minnie. Either his club hates you and will throw you out on your ass the first chance they get, or they're coming to take you home. Can't be both. Take tonight to think long and hard about what you want. You're carrying his baby. If you want him to be part of the kid's life, you need to be at their compound, or at least living in their town."

"I know. You're right. I guess everything in my head is just a jumbled mess."

I decided to text Doolittle again, at least not leave him hanging.

I miss you too. I need some time to figure things out. I'm confused, scared, and I have no idea what's considered the right thing in this situation. You have your club standing behind you. Who do I have?

He responded immediately. *Me.*

I had to admit it gave me a warm fuzzy feeling. I'd fallen for Doolittle almost immediately. With him, I'd found a connection I'd never had before. It had gutted me, leaving him behind, but it's what I'd thought was the best thing to do. Badger had made it clear I wasn't welcome. What had changed?

My phone buzzed with another message, and when I read it, my heart nearly stopped.

I know who your mother was. Her real name, not the one she started using while she was pregnant with you.

What was he talking about? *My mother was Ivanna Carter.*

I'd seen her documents when I'd cleaned out her

things after her death. Why would he say that wasn't her real name? Who else would she have been? And why would she have needed to assume a new identity? The room started to spin a little and I realized I wasn't breathing. I sucked in some air and stared at my phone, willing him to respond again.

Ivanna Carter immigrated from Belarus while she was pregnant with you. A picture was attached. When I saw it, I stared hard before sliding my gaze to Stripes and back to the picture. Was it my imagination, or did she look like the man sitting next to me? Why hadn't I ever noticed that before? Then again, my memories of my mother weren't exactly something I liked dwelling on. She had never been a warm and caring person. But if my hunch was right…

Doolittle sent another text. *Her real name was Oksana Bogrov and she was from Russia.*

"Oh, God. Oh…" Tears burned my eyes and nose as I looked from my phone to Stripes again. I was right. The younger version of my mother looked like Stripes because that was his daughter. The one he'd thought died. Knowing she'd been sold at a young age, I could only imagine the horrors she'd faced. No wonder she'd never been the sort to give hugs or say she loved me. "Instead of a daughter, how do you feel about a granddaughter?"

His brows bunched and his nose wrinkled a little. "I don't understand."

"Oksana," I said softly. "Would her last name have been Bogrov?"

He sucked in a breath and gave a sharp nod. "How do you know this?"

His accent had thickened again. I threw my arms around him, hugging him tight and whispered in his ear. "My mother's real name was Oksana Bogrov. She changed her name when she immigrated to the US. I think you're my grandfather."

Stripes made a choking sound, his strong arms banding around me. Someone let out a shrill whistle and the entire room went silent.

"What's going on?" Charming asked.

"It's time," I said to Stripes. "They need to know. Please. I can't… I don't want to go back to being no one. To not having a family."

He cupped my cheek and pressed a kiss to my forehead. "Never, *zaichik*. You will never be without family again."

"Damnit! I said tell us what's going on," Charming demanded.

I leaned against my newfound grandfather while he explained about the daughter he'd lost, the one he'd never met. The club seemed stunned, and I could imagine this had been a complete shock. Stripes said he'd never mentioned his daughter to anyone here. How he'd lived with this secret for so long I would never understand.

I shared what Doolittle had told me, and Charming immediately put Shade to work, looking into Oksana Bogrov. When he'd found the information, he slid the papers to Charming and Stripes. Oksana really was Stripes' daughter. She hadn't died as he'd believed but been sold yet again. And her prostitute mother had died shortly after getting paid.

"Mom passed a few years ago," I told Stripes. "She'd always had health problems. Now I have to wonder if it was because of everything she suffered in Russia and Belarus. Cancer is what took her out. I wish you'd had the chance to meet her. Maybe the two of you could have healed one another. And if I'd known you sooner, I never would have gone to the Reckless

Kings and been a --"

Stripes silenced me. "You are never to be ashamed of your past, *zaichik*. Minnie. My mother, her name was Marina. If I'd known your mother when she was small, she'd have learned about her grandmother. Perhaps she'd have given you that name. You do not seem like a Minnie to me. That is a cartoon mouse, and you are too strong for such a name."

"Wouldn't be hard to change her name," Shade said. "If that's what she wants."

"Marina," I murmured. "Marina Morgan."

Stripes glowered a moment. "Marina Petrov Morgan. You will also carry my family name, as you're my blood."

I wasn't the only one gaining a family. Stripes had a new connection. While he'd never get to meet his daughter, we'd managed to find one another. It was a miracle! One I'd never take for granted.

"I like it. But I can still be Minnie to those who want to use that name. It's the only one I've had all these years. Minnie Carter."

"I'll get on it," Shade said. "Anything with Minnie Carter will be changed to Marina Petrov. All the records with your married name will also be adjusted. Congratulations on finding one another. Just proves fate works in mysterious ways. If you hadn't been running from your past with the Reckless Kings, if Badger hadn't then tossed you out of the Devil's Fury, you may have never crossed paths with Stripes."

Stripes leaned in closer. "My name is Mikhail Petrov. But you may call me *dedushka* if you wish. It is how a grandfather would be called in Russia, and you are of Russian blood."

"I need to get home for the night," Charming said, standing suddenly. "If anyone needs me, text. I don't want any calls tonight."

He rushed off without another word. "Anyone else find his behavior strange?"

Stripes grunted. "Something is going on with our President, but I don't yet know what it is. All will come out eventually."

"Hopefully it happens before it bites us on the ass," Shade muttered. "I've been good so far, not poking into things. Not sure I can hold out much longer. Marina, for now, I'll change your address to Stripes' home and get the DMV to send over a driver's license. If for some reason you aren't here anymore when it arrives, we can forward it to you. It will be a little extra work, but it's no problem hacking into their systems. They'll never realize you didn't already have a license here."

The man took off and I shook my head. When the men at the Devil's Boneyard made a decision, they didn't seem to waste any time handling their business. If only Doolittle had been the same way. Hiding me away, keeping our relationship a secret, hadn't really worked in our favor. I should have fought him on it. At the time, I'd understood. He hadn't wanted to shove our relationship in Meredith's face. I'd agreed we should ease everyone into it. I'd been wrong. If I did go back to him, I hoped things would be different this time.

Now that I had family, at least I'd have a place to land if my life went to shit again. I had no doubt that Stripes would welcome me back with open arms. I wasn't the only one who'd yearned for a family. He'd lost his daughter, only to get her back, in a way, through me. We just hadn't realized we were actually related.

Shade was right. Fate did work in mysterious

ways.

My phone buzzed again, and I realized I'd never responded to Doolittle after he'd dropped that bomb on me.

Minnie, are you all right? Maybe I shouldn't have told you that in a text.

I smiled. No, his timing had been perfect. *I'm fine. Knowing who my mother really was, helped me more than you realize. It gave me the family I've always wanted. If you want to come get me, figure out who my grandfather is. I'll be staying at his house.*

Stripes read the message and gave a slow chuckle. "Smart. He'll work tirelessly to find you, and when he does, I'll try hard not to break his nose for making you cry. But no promises, *zaichik*."

I kissed his cheek. I had a feeling he wouldn't hold back, not even a little. "Come on, *dedushka*. Let's go home. I'm getting a little tired."

Home. For the first time as far back as I could remember, I finally had one. Even when my mother had been alive, we'd bounced from apartment to apartment. Now I had a place where I belonged. If Doolittle's club ever accepted me, I'd be Devil's Fury by marriage. But it seemed I was part of the Devil's Boneyard by blood. No wonder I'd been attracted to bikers. It was in my DNA.

Chapter Twelve

Doolittle

What the absolute fuck? I read the message a dozen times. She knew who her grandfather was? All from the true name of her mother? That meant it was someone she'd already known. Or was it someone she'd recently met?

"I hate puzzles," I muttered.

Minnie's little goat butted its head against me. I'd taken pity on the creature and let it into the house each night. I'd put it in a large dog crate when I went to sleep so it wouldn't destroy anything, but at least it was warmer in here than in the barn.

I called Outlaw, hoping he could help. When he didn't answer, I tried texting Elena. She responded within a few minutes.

His hands are hurting really bad tonight, Doolittle. I'm sorry, but he can't help you. I took his phone so he wouldn't even be tempted if anyone called or texted.

As much as I hated it, I understood. Elena made sure she took good care of Outlaw, while he tried to protect the rest of us. Which meant I wouldn't be getting help from him tonight and possibly not tomorrow. I wasn't waiting though. Now that I had a clue on where Minnie might be, I wasn't about to let the trail go cold.

I hesitated only a moment before calling Wire at the Dixie Reapers.

"It's late. What the fuck do you want?" Wire said.

"Well, hello to you too. That's how normal people answer the phone, you know?"

"Fuck off."

"Wait!" I didn't want him to hang up. Or get

pissed. "I need help."

"I'm not telling you where your wife is, so don't bother asking."

Motherfucker. Did everyone know her location except my damn club? This was absolute bullshit. "I wasn't asking where she is. Not exactly. She texted me with a clue but it's not something I can solve without hacking skills."

"So… you don't want her location, you just want the answer to whatever she texted so you can figure it out yourself."

"Right." I held my breath, hoping that meant he'd agree.

"Fine. What have you got?"

"Minnie's mother was listed as Ivanna Carter, but that wasn't her real name. If I text you some images of what I've got so far, can you see what you can find? When Minnie heard her mother's true name, she seemed to suddenly know who her grandfather was. She told me if I wanted to come get her, she would be staying with him."

"Holy shit," Wire muttered. "That's… Damn. All right, text me what you have. I'll send back a bit of info, but I'm not making it easy on you. You want that woman, you're going to have to work for it."

"She's worth the effort," I said.

Wire hung up and I went to get my notes. I snapped a few pictures of what I had and sent it over. The messages showed delivered and read, which meant I had nothing to do but sit around and wait. Wire might be the best at what he did and would possibly have an answer pretty fast. Didn't mean he'd send it to me right away. I wouldn't put it past him to teach me a lesson and drag his damn feet.

I scratched the goat behind his ear. "You need a

name. Doesn't seem right for me to name you though. Minnie brought you home. She should have the honors. Just need to find her first."

He bleated at me, then bumped my leg with his head again. An old bloodhound I'd brought home from the clinic wandered into the room and settled at my feet with a groan. He'd been tied up to the front door two days ago, no note or anything. I had a camera system set up. Identifying the person hadn't been doable. They'd worn a hoodie and hid their face. Other than the fact they were white, I had nothing else to go on, which pissed me off. I'd have gladly taken the dog if they'd properly surrendered it. The only blessing was that they hadn't just released him or dropped him at the nearest shelter, which would have put him to sleep because of his age.

"You need a name too," I told the dog. It broke my heart he'd already had one, but his piece of shit owner hadn't bothered to even tell me what it was. The old guy didn't have a lot of life left in him. It seemed cruel to change his name. "I think we're going to need more supplies."

Most of the women I knew tended to shop when they were stressed or restless. I did the same, except I hit up the pet stores, both in town and online. Or in this case, Amazon, since I could search for items with two-day delivery. I restocked the dog and cat toys, ordered some treats and bully sticks, then switched to the pet store app to place an order for same day delivery.

"All right, old man. We're getting three new dog beds today." I'd also ordered a large gravity water dish that would hold a gallon of water. The bowl wasn't going to work with the goat, the old bloodhound, and my usual crew running around. Since the lizards went through a lot of bulbs, I'd ordered a few of those too.

I looked at the time and grumbled under my breath. An hour had passed and still no word from Wire. Either he hadn't found what I needed, or the bastard didn't want to send it over yet. The house was already clean, the animals cared for, which meant I didn't have a damn thing to do to occupy my time. Watching TV wasn't going to work. I couldn't have read a book if I tried.

The phone rang and I jumped, answering it quickly. "Wire?"

It was silent on the other end, and I checked the screen, wincing when I saw Badger's name.

"Why the hell would Wire be calling you?" he asked.

"Um. I asked him to find some information on Minnie's family. He said straight up he wouldn't tell me where she was, and I didn't even ask him. All I want is her family history."

"Fine. That's not why I called. Grizzly and I had a long talk, then we pulled Meredith in to discuss a few things with her. She knows she was out of control, and as much as she wants to be here with Grizzly, we all think it's best if she takes a little time off."

"You're sending her away?" I asked.

"Yes and no. She's going on an extended vacation. She wants to travel. We're sending her to New Orleans first. The Broken Bastards agreed to keep an eye on her. She won't be staying with them though."

"And from there?" I asked.

"She'll check out Texas. One of the Hades Abyss guys is familiar with a club there. The Wicked Mayhem. One of their guys will make sure she stays safe. Then she's heading to Oklahoma. Outlaw has friends there who will also protect her."

"How long is this trip?" I asked.

"She agreed to take two months off to get her head on straight, process the fact Grizzly is getting up there and has health issues, and hopefully we'll have our sweet Meredith back when she returns."

"Thanks for letting me know. Hopefully I can find Minnie before then. She might settle in better without Meredith around at first. I think the two can work out their issues, eventually."

"Why is Wire searching for Minnie's family?" Badger asked. "And don't lie to me."

"I discovered Minnie's mother went by another name before she immigrated. I texted it to Minnie, hoping it would spark a conversation between us. Instead, it triggered something for her. She now knows who her grandfather is and said she'll be staying with him. If I want her to come home, she said to figure it out and come get her."

Badger chuckled. "Your woman is smart. She wants you to prove you'll work to find her, which means you'll put in the same effort to keep her."

"You seem calmer about it all. We good?" I asked.

"Yeah. Sorry I had my head up my ass. We all did. Grizzly dropping that bomb on the club put things into perspective for them, and for me. Slash is still pissed as fuck that we kept him and Shella out of the loop. Grizzly is working hard to repair the damage done to their relationship."

"You really think the old man is going to croak that easily?" I asked. "He's been to hell and back."

"No. He's determined to do what's necessary to be here longer. We both know that doesn't always mean shit though. If it's his time, then that's it. We need to prepare ourselves for when it happens. Blades isn't getting any younger either but finding Meiling and China has helped. I've noticed he's slowing down though."

"Hell, Badger. None of us are as young as we once were. I'm still one of the younger patched members, but even you have more silver in your hair these days."

"We need more new blood if we want this club to keep going after we've passed on. There was a time when we had as many as five Prospects. Now we only have two or three, if any."

"We'll figure it out." My phone chimed and I saw an incoming text from Wire. Then another. "I've gotta go. Wire messaged me."

"Find your woman and bring her home," Badger said. "We'll clean up the clubhouse and have a party, welcome her the way we should have in the beginning. We all owe her an apology."

I hung up and read Wire's messages. He'd sent a picture of Oksana and her mother, along with the men who'd bought Oksana. She'd changed hands three times before immigrating. He hadn't really told me much of anything useful. Except one thing. Oksana's birthplace in Russia and a note.

Mikhail Petrov was a known acquaintance of Oksana's mother.

Who the fuck was Mikhail Petrov? Something told me he was Oksana's father, but that didn't help me any right now. If that was the grandfather Minnie mentioned, it meant he wasn't in Russia anymore. Would he have immigrated under that same name? And when?

Another text came through with Petrov's immigration date and original location. Nothing else.

Looked like I would be trying to follow the man's trail on my own. At least I wasn't entirely useless on the computer.

It took hours for me to figure out how to use Petrov's immigration information to start following his trail. My eyes burned, I'd consumed two pots of coffee, and the sun had risen by the time I'd found mention of the man in the southern US. Then he vanished. No mention anywhere after the early two-thousands.

I rubbed my eyes and cracked my back and neck. There was no way he'd disappeared into thin air. Only reason for a man to not use his name anymore, and still be living, was if he changed his identity.

"Or joined a club," I muttered. I felt fucking stupid. Why hadn't I drawn that conclusion earlier? That had to be it. Mikhail Petrov was either with the Devil's Boneyard or Dixie Reapers. I knew of at least one Russian in both. Grimm was far too young to be the father of Oksana. That only left…

"Motherfucker!" I threw my pen against the wall and stood so fast my chair crashed to the floor. The goat startled and ran from the room, leaving a trail of pellets in his wake. "Awesome. I literally scared the shit out of him."

I groaned and rubbed my hands over my face, knowing I'd need to clean the mess up before I did anything else. I got to work, then started more coffee while I showered. If I was going after Minnie, I wanted to look my best. Or as good as it was going to get since I hadn't been sleeping.

I sent a quick text to the two contacts I'd had watching the Boneyard and Reapers, letting them know I'd found my wife. I promised the debt was clear and thanked them before grabbing my keys and shooting off a message to Badger.

Leaving town to get Minnie. I know where she is.

Fuck. The clinic. I'd have to stop by there first and post a note we were closed for a family emergency and would reopen in a few days. I'd also have to let the workers know so they wouldn't bother coming to work. Which meant I'd have to pay them for their time off since this was my mess. I seriously needed another vet. There had been two of us in the clinic for a while. Then the other one got a better offer in a big city and took off.

I messaged Garrick when I got to the clinic. *Call the newspaper and place an ad for a veterinarian for the clinic. Keep it simple. Tell them to send resumes to my email or to the clinic's address.*

After I went to my office and called my employees, then printed a sign for the door, I made quick work of cancelling the day's appointments so I could get on the road. Now that I knew where Minnie was, I couldn't wait to go get her.

As badly as I wanted to speed all the way down into Florida, I did my best to keep it within five miles of the speed limit. The last thing I needed was a ticket. I stopped for food and drinks, and once to take a piss. Otherwise, I stayed focused on my destination.

"I'm coming for you, Minnie. I hope you're ready to see me," I said, cranking the radio and pressing the pedal a little harder.

When I reached the Devil's Boneyard compound, the truck skidded to a stop outside the gates. The Prospect eyed me and approached. I rolled down the window and grinned when I saw the glare he gave me. Yep. Minnie was here, and it looked like she'd made some friends.

"I'm here for my wife," I said.

"You don't have clearance. I'll have to check with

Charming before I let you in," he said.

"You do that. I'll just sit here and wait. Blocking the entrance."

He scowled and pulled out his phone, walking off so he could talk without me hearing him. I still caught the word *asshole* and knew he meant me. Good. Minnie had another club ready to protect her, even if they were guarding her against me.

"Charming says you can come in. He wants you to wait at the clubhouse in your vehicle. Someone will come get you."

I nodded and pulled through when the gates opened. I parked at the end of the bikes outside the clubhouse and scanned the area, hoping for a glimpse of Minnie. When I saw her, everything in my world felt right again. And she looked so fucking happy. She'd thrown her head back to laugh at something one of the women next to her said. They were walking my way and hadn't seen me yet, which meant she probably wasn't the one they'd sent to get me. Did she know I was here yet?

A motorcycle was coming up fast behind them. He didn't even slow as he passed the ladies. I'd been right. Stripes was the Russian I'd been looking for. He came to a stop, looking all kinds of pissed. The man got off his bike and came up to my window. Before I even could say so much as a hello, he reached through and grabbed my shirt, yanking me closer. His fist collided with my nose, then my jaw before he released me.

"You hurt my *zaichik*. Do it again and I'll break more than your nose."

My eyes had teared up and I pinched my nose, knowing what I was about to do would hurt like a bitch. With a quick snap, I reset it best I could, and let out a few curses. I worked my jaw back and forth, then reached for the handle of the door and got out.

"You hear me, Doolittle?" he asked, his accent heavier than I'd remembered from past interactions with him.

"*Dedushka*! Was that necessary?" Minnie asked, rushing to my side.

"Yes," Stripes said.

Minnie rolled her eyes, but I saw the smile on her lips. She liked that he'd taken up for her, and I had to admit, I admired him for it. I should have stood up for her like that long ago. I'd tried to tread carefully so no one would get hurt. Instead, the woman I'd come to love had paid the price for my idiocy.

"You found me," she murmured, looking up at me.

"Yeah. Wasn't easy. Wire only gave the name of your grandfather and his immigration date and location. I'm shit at computers compared to him or Outlaw. Took me all fucking night to figure out it was Stripes."

"We're family now," Stripes said. "Doesn't mean I won't cut you into pieces if you hurt my *zaichik* again."

"Got it. And for what it's worth, I'm glad she found you." I held out my hand and he grudgingly shook it. "Minnie means everything to me. If I can't keep her safe, then I know you will."

"Marina," he said, glancing at my wife. "She goes by Marina now."

She smiled at him and leaned into me. I wrapped my arms around her. "It will take me a bit to remember that, but I'll try. I take it Marina is a family name?"

Stripes nodded. "Take care of her. Or I'll break you."

"*Dedushka*, you can stop now," Minnie scolded.

Yeah. I didn't think I'd ever remember to call her Marina. To me, she'd always be Minnie.

"Come inside. We'll have a drink and talk," Stripes said.

"Inside the clubhouse?" I asked, eyeing the building. I knew Minnie might have been a club whore for the Reckless Kings, but surely Stripes didn't let her hang out with the ones here.

"The clubhouse has been shut down for now. Family only while your wife is here," one of her new friends said. "I'm Grey. My husband is Samurai."

The other one waggled her fingers at me. "And I'm Alora. I'm with Rooster."

"She also writes dirty books," Minnie whispered. "I have six signed copies to take home with me, and she promised to send her next one to me."

My heart ached. She'd found the connection she'd wanted, but she'd had to leave my club for it to happen. What if she didn't want to go back to the Devil's Fury? I wouldn't blame her. My club had treated her like trash, and these people had welcomed her like she was part of their family. Technically, she was since Stripes was her grandfather. The man didn't look old enough, but if he'd fathered Oksana, he had to be in his fifties or sixties.

Minnie took my hand and led me inside. She pushed me onto a chair then rushed off, only to return with two handfuls of paper towels. One set was wet and one was dry. She dabbed at the blood on my face then handed me the dry set. I pressed it to my nose, hoping the bleeding had already stopped.

"Want a beer?" she asked.

"Uh. I've had about four pots of coffee in the last fifteen hours and haven't slept. I'm not sure alcohol is a good idea right now." I gave her a sheepish smile.

"Once I had the clues I needed to find you, I didn't want to stop. I've missed you. So damn much."

"I missed you too." She kissed my cheek. "If you're tired, we can go to *dedushka*'s house and you can rest. We're staying tonight, right?"

"I didn't bother to pack a bag. I just jumped in the truck and drove straight here. I did tell everyone the clinic would be closed a few days."

"Then you sleep and I can get you some clothes. I'm not ready to leave, Doolittle. I know you have responsibilities at home, but I just found my family. I don't want to give up Stripes just yet."

The old Russian gave Minnie a warm smile. "*Zaichik*, I will always be here for you."

"Come on, Doolittle. You're dead on your feet," Minnie said, pulling on my arm.

"All right, but I'd rather lie down with you in my arms." Stripes growled and I smirked at him. "Rest easy, Grandpa. I'm too tired to do anything but sleep while I hold her. I just need her close to me."

His expression softened as he looked at his granddaughter. "Write down your sizes. I'll have someone pick up two changes of clothes. My *zaichik* isn't leaving until she feels secure returning home with you. Try leaving with her before that, and I have plenty of places to hide your body."

Minnie patted his arm. "He's going to behave. If you'll help me make sure he stays on his feet long enough to get in the truck, I'll drive him to the house."

Minnie looped her arm around my waist, and Stripes gripped my arm, a little tighter than necessary, but I got the point. He'd found his granddaughter and he'd do whatever it took to keep her safe and happy. Good thing we both had the same goal.

Chapter Thirteen

Minnie

Sleeping in Doolittle's arms had been… wonderful. I'd taken a nap with him after I'd gotten him to Stripes' home. But last night had been the first time he'd held me overnight, except for the one night we had at the hotel when I'd first left the Reckless Kings. It was the only time I'd actually felt like his wife.

I padded into the kitchen, rubbing the sleep from my eyes, coming to a stop when I saw both Doolittle and Stripes at the table. They were across from one another, having a staring contest while drinking coffee. What the hell?

"Are you both five?" I asked.

Stripes didn't look away from Doolittle. "He wants to take you away. Today."

I walked up behind Doolittle, placing my hands on his shoulders. "*Dedushka,* you knew whenever he came here that I'd eventually be leaving with him. I'm so glad I found you, and I love you, but I can't stay forever."

My grandfather dropped his gaze to the table. "Why not?"

I sighed. "Because Doolittle is part of the Devil's Fury. It's not that far of a trip. They're just across the state line in Georgia. It's only a few hours."

"You could come with us," Doolittle said. "Minnie might like having a few Devil's Boneyard at her back when she faces the Devil's Fury again. They weren't very nice to her last time. While they're all sorry, I know she'll be anxious seeing them again."

Stripes leaned back in his chair. "Is not bad idea."

My lips twitched. I'd learned to read his emotions based off how strong his accent became, or how broken his English was. There were times you almost couldn't tell he hadn't been born here. Other times, it was like he'd arrived only days ago.

"Who do you think would go with us?" I asked. "What about Shade? He doesn't have a family here who would need him. And he can do his computer thing from anywhere."

"Outlaw would probably enjoy visiting with him," Doolittle said.

"Maybe Rebel or Gator?" I asked.

"Perhaps," Stripes said.

"Badger won't mind some company." Doolittle set his phone on the table. "I can call and set it up right now. Just say the word."

Striped grunted. "You have two vehicles here. My *zaichik* arrived with all her belongings in her SUV. And you drove a truck instead of riding your bike."

"Your point?" Doolittle asked.

"I want to drive my *zaichik*. Show the Devil's Fury if they hurt her, there will be consequences. She's not alone anymore."

"He doesn't fit in my car very well," I said, trying not to laugh at the image of him scrunched up in the SUV.

"I can't drive two vehicles. And if Stripes drives my truck, how is he getting home?" Doolittle asked.

"We'll take a Devil's Boneyard truck," Stripes said. "You drive your vehicle. I'll get someone to drive Marina's SUV. They can ride back with me when the visit is over."

"Then it's settled. I'll call Badger and set it set up." He eyed Stripes. "Would you like to stay at our house? I have to warn you, there are tons of animals running around. Including a goat your granddaughter brought home in her SUV."

"*Nyet*. I'll give you space. Find a place for me and my brothers to stay. But I will visit with my *zaichik* as often as I can before returning home."

"Then it sounds like we're all set," Doolittle said. "I'll finish my coffee and get started on the arrangements, then I'll help my wife pack. I'd like to be back home before dinner. I'll most likely need to open the clinic tomorrow. If you plan to stay a few days, you can have Minnie all to yourself while I'm at work."

I frowned at him. "Who's taking care of the animals?"

"I sort of forgot to set anything up when I was leaving town. After I woke from my nap that first day, I put in a few calls. One of the Prospects is taking care of the ones at the house, and my new kennel worker is handling the clinic."

"You replaced me?" I asked, folding my arms. "I don't even have a job anymore?"

"Sweetheart, you don't need to work unless you want to. I also fired the receptionist and one of the vet techs. I'd thought, if you did want to still work with me, you could maybe answer the phones and set up appointments." He pressed a hand to my stomach. "Not sure I want you handling a lot of animals and cleaning up after them. For one, you shouldn't change the litter boxes while you're pregnant."

"All right. We can discuss it later. Do whatever you need to. I'll start packing."

He took my hand and kissed the back of it. "Actually, why don't you go hang out with your new friends for a little bit? I'll pack your things. You seemed close with Grey and Alora. I'm sure there are others here too."

I smiled and leaned down to kiss him, ignoring Stripes' not-so-subtle gagging noises. "I'll go change and have breakfast with them."

When I got to my room, I sent out a group text before grabbing some clothes and getting in the shower. Even if they couldn't all meet with me, I knew most would. Doolittle was right. I'd become good friends with the ladies here, and I would miss them. Maybe we could come back to visit after the baby was born.

By the time I'd gotten cleaned up and dressed, I checked my phone to see everyone could make it except Clarity and Charisma, who offered to watch the younger kids who weren't in school today. I got the keys to my SUV and headed into town. Alora had shown me this amazing breakfast café, and it had become our go-to place in the short time I'd been here.

Grey managed to beat me to the café and had already gotten a large table for all of us. I joined her and placed my drink order with the server when he stopped by.

"I can't believe you're leaving already," Grey said.

"It's time, but Stripes and a few others are going too. He wants to drive me there, make sure the Devil's Fury understand I have the protection of the Devil's Boneyard. If they fuck up and hurt me, there will be hell to pay."

Grey grinned. "Why does that not surprise me?"

Alora plopped down in the chair next to me while Josie and Meg sat across from us. Only a few more ladies and we'd all be present. I eyed their cuts, envying the fact they had property cuts and I didn't. Would I get one now? The club had voted for me *not* to be Doolittle's old lady. Had they taken another vote? I hadn't asked him yet. Truthfully, I was a little worried about his answer. Even though he said it was safe to come home, I wasn't convinced. Those people had been so hateful!

"I wish Clarity and Charisma could have come too," I said.

"I'm sure you'll see them again soon. You aren't going to be living all that far away," Alora said.

Jordan, Darby, Nikki, and Janessa came in together and claimed the remaining seats. I was going to miss these ladies so much! Not once had they made me feel unwelcome or unworthy of being in their presence. Even knowing my past, they'd never called me names.

"You know, my brother is with the Devil's Fury," Jordan said.

"Which one is your brother?" I asked.

"Dingo." She grinned. "If he steps out of line again, tell him how much his niece would love to come visit. I adore my daughter, but she's hell on wheels. Even Cinder will back down from Lanie."

Meg snorted. "No. He doesn't back down. He runs as fast as he can. If he sees her coming, he reverses direction and hides before she spots him. It's rather humorous considering the man has had a gun held to his head before."

I blinked and tried to process that. "Little Lanie? She's what? Maybe twelve? Why do the men find her so scary?"

"Besides the fact she's a girl, she's also the product of Jordan and Havoc. She inherited a little of both personalities. When that girl gets bigger, it wouldn't surprise me if she either tries to patch in joins the Marines," Janessa said. "She's badass like her mom."

"Is it wrong to admit I'm scared?" I asked. "The Devil's Fury weren't kind to me before. Just because Doolittle says things have changed, it doesn't make it true. What if they haven't?"

"One way to find out," Jordan said, setting her phone on the table and pulling up her contacts. I saw the name *Jameson* on the screen as she hit send and put the call on speaker.

"Morning, Jordan," a man said when he answered.

"Hey, Dingo. You're on speaker. I'm with all the old ladies except Clarity and Charisma, and Minnie is here too. Got a question for you."

"What?" he asked, sounding apprehensive.

"Did y'all remove the sticks from your asses yet? Or is my girl coming home to a viper's nest?" Jordan asked, giving me a wink.

"Your girl?"

Jordan nodded, even though he couldn't see it. "Yep. Minnie is Devil's Boneyard by blood. That makes her one of mine. Which means if you fuck up again, I'm not just going to come visit, I'm going to put my foot up your ass."

He sighed. "I know we all fucked up. In our defense, we didn't have all the information either. No one said she was married to Doolittle, and we had no idea Grizzly was having health issues. That made Meredith act out, and Badger gave her a free pass. Minnie, if you can hear me, I'm so damn sorry for what went down. I'd have voted for you to be his old lady if I'd known all the facts."

"Thank you, Dingo. Still not feeling all that great about returning," I admitted.

I heard an *oof* from him. "This is Meiling. My man is an idiot. If you don't believe me, ask his sister.

And he's not the only one. I already yelled at him and my dad. Then I tore into Meredith."

"She wasn't entirely to blame," I said.

"You're sweet," Meiling said. "But she needs to be held accountable for her actions. And she is. Grizzly arranged for her to travel the next two months. She left this morning. I'd like a second chance if that's okay with you. And I promise to keep an open mind and hear your side of things. It's what we all should have done to begin with."

"I appreciate that, but I'm sorry to hear she was sent away. That's her home. More so than it was mine." I glanced at the ladies around me. "I've found where I belong so I understand."

"We'll have a welcome home party when you get here," Meiling said. "Just thought you should know so you aren't taken by surprise. I know I'd hate walking into that unprepared."

Jordan took over the conversation and I leaned closer to Alora, dropping my voice. "What do you think? Should I run while Doolittle isn't watching?"

She snickered. "No. You'll be fine. If they give you any shit, just call us. Even Charming has a soft spot for you."

"How can you tell? The man is always running home for some reason."

"Don't think we haven't noticed," Alora said. "He won't let anyone in his house either. Shuts the door before we can get a peek inside. I think he's hiding someone in there, or something. Maybe he got a pet and it's a teacup yorkie so he's embarrassed. Eventually, he'll have to tell us what's going on."

Jordan ended her call. "Charming? Trust me, if he doesn't come clean soon, Havoc isn't above breaking down the door to get to the bottom of things.

As the Sergeant-at-Arms, he doesn't like the idea of Charming putting the club in danger. Not knowing what's going on *inside* the compound is about to drive my man bonkers."

"Are you sure it's not your kids doing that?" Meg asked.

"Shut it." Jordan glared.

"I don't know about y'all, but I'm starving and thankful to be away from the house," Nikki said. "Let's eat and have some fun before Doolittle drags our new sister away. You may not be a Devil's Boneyard old lady, but you're blood. Come visit us anytime."

I spent the next hour enjoying my time with the ladies of the Devil's Boneyard, then went back to Stripes' house. Doolittle had already packed my things and loaded them into my SUV. I noticed his truck, my car, and the club truck were all running, which meant they were ready to leave immediately. My stomach knotted and I hoped I was doing the right thing. Not only for me, but for the baby too. I still needed to make an appointment, just in case the tests had been wrong. I didn't think it was likely.

I got into the Boneyard truck with Stripes and gave Doolittle a wave as he pulled out in front of us. Stripes took the middle, with Rebel and Gator both riding in my car. Shade had backed out, claiming he had something that needed his immediate attention. I tried not to smile at how small the guys made the vehicle seem.

"Why didn't one of them take their motorcycle?" I asked.

"No point in only one bike going. This will be fine, *zaichik*. The priority is you, not our means of transportation."

"Thank you for going with me. I know Doolittle

says things are different, and I spoke with Dingo and Meiling today, but I can't help feeling like I'm walking into a hornet's nest. Everyone was so warm and welcoming at your club. Why couldn't I have experienced that with the Devil's Fury?"

Stripes patted my knee. "All things happen for a reason. We may not know what it is, but that doesn't make it pointless."

"Will you teach me Russian?" I asked. "Obviously not right now, and I'm sure it's difficult to learn, but maybe a little at a time over phone calls?"

"I'd like that. It's good for you to know your heritage and where you came from. I only wish I could have given you better bloodlines. Your grandmother, she had a hard life. I will never forgive her for what she did to Oksana, or to me, but she grew up in a hard world where she had to fight to survive. That's all she was doing. Trying to live."

"Instead, I think that's what got her killed," I said.

"Very possible."

"Why didn't you hold it against me? The fact I was a club whore?" I asked. "I know your own club doesn't think very fondly of those women."

"This world is a dark and horrid place at times. Women tend to be softer than men. That's not a bad thing. You can only be beaten so many times before you decide to fight back. Your grandmother used her body and her cunning to survive in Russia. Your mother…" He sighed. "I don't know enough about her to say, but being sold as a child, the things she suffered… It's a miracle she managed to stay alive long enough to raise such a pretty, smart young girl such as yourself."

"That didn't really answer my question," I said.

He grinned. "Good. Never let your Doolittle get away with anything either. You, my *zaichik*, had to grow up fast. I've spoken to Beast and know your story. Or parts of it. You thought yourself in love and went down the wrong path. And yet, if you hadn't, we may have never met. How can I look down on your choices when they gave me a family?"

"The Devil's Fury weren't so understanding. They called me a whore every chance they had."

He took my hand and held it tight. "They will not dare now that you're my blood. No one who insult you will keep their tongues in their heads. Man, woman, child… well, maybe not child. But man or woman insults you, I will tear their tongues from their mouths."

I winced. "That's a little bloodthirsty, *dedushka*."

He shrugged. "I'm Russian. Did you expect flowers and poetry? I protect those I love, at any cost, my *zaichik*. These hands have been bloodied many times and will be covered again at some point. It's the way of our world. Your Doolittle is not so innocent either."

"I know." I looked at the truck ahead of us. "He made me feel safe. Special. Even though we were hiding our relationship, the times we were together, he gave me all his attention. If he'd been home the day everything snowballed, he might have been able to stop it sooner. I don't think he'd have allowed either of them to say something like that to me."

"And yet he didn't stand up to his President, did he?" Stripes asked.

"No. I mean, he did. Sort of. At the house, he got angry and told Badger I was his wife. Then in Church… he didn't fight for me. He just sat there. After I left, he must have said something though. Otherwise, why would they have changed their minds about me?"

I squeezed his hand. "Dingo said they weren't given all the facts. He said if he'd known Doolittle and I were married, or that Meredith was lashing out because of Grizzly's health issues, he never would have voted against us. It makes me think there must be others who feel the same way."

"For their sake, I hope so."

"Don't you mean for my sake?" I asked.

"*Nyet*. For theirs. If they wish to remain breathing, they will speak to you with civility. We may be guests, but you're my granddaughter. They need to know I will do anything for you, that I'm not afraid of them."

"Jordan said if Dingo didn't act right to let her know and she'd send her daughter to visit."

Stripes threw his head back and laughed. "Little Lanie will set everyone straight. That one is going places."

By the time we pulled up to the gates of the Devil's Fury, I wasn't quite as anxious. Stripes had set me at ease. He parked in front of the clubhouse and kissed my forehead. "Be brave, *zaichik*. Show them what a Petrov is made of, yes?"

I nodded and got out. Doolittle took my hand and led me inside with Stripes, Gator, and Rebel at our backs. The place had been scrubbed clean. Someone had put balloons and streamers everywhere. A banner hung on the back wall, most likely painted by the children. *Welcome Home Minnie*. Food filled one table and another had drinks and a large sheet cake.

Badger came forward with a bag clutched in his hand. "Doolittle, I have something for your wife."

I held out my hand, but Badger shook his head. Instead, he removed a black leather cut from the sack and held it up so I could read the back. *Property of Doolittle.* Tears misted my eyes and I reached for it, slipping the leather over my shoulders. It fit perfectly.

"I'm sorry we were such assholes before, Minnie. Welcome to the family."

Stripes stepped up beside me. "That's the best you can do?"

"*Dedushka,* stop." I focused on the President of the Devil's Fury. "I appreciate the apology, but it shouldn't have been necessary."

Stripes glowered at Badger and the President just stared him down. He took a step closer and hugged me, not once looking away from Stripes. When he backed up, others came to welcome me home. It was a bit overwhelming, and still felt incredibly awkward. Mostly because I'd known how they felt before. It still seemed like the change happened too fast. I was waiting on it all to unravel.

Hot Shot stopped in front of me. "I was over the line before. As both Doolittle's wife and part of the Devil's Boneyard by blood, you had every right to say what you did to Meredith. I was trying to protect her."

"Sometimes when we want to guard those we love so they can't get hurt, that's when we cause the most pain," I said. "Do you think if she'd acted like that outside these gates the person would have just taken it? Or would they have retaliated?"

"You make a good point." Hot Shot smiled a little. "I really am sorry for my part in all this. I'm not expecting to be friends anytime soon, or ever. But if you need anything, let me know. I want to make amends."

"We are Russian, Marina. If they wish to apologize, they need to show you with actions. Not words," Stripes mumbled.

"Technically, I'm American," I said.

Meiling and another woman slowly made their way over to me. I hadn't met the second lady. She held her hand out when she got close enough.

"I'm Zoe. I'm with Dagger and Guardian."

I blinked. Two men? "I can't even handle one guy. How are you managing two?"

Meiling smiled. "We've often asked her the same thing. Double the laundry. Double the cooking."

Zoe gave us an innocent look. "Double the orgasms."

I burst out laughing and knew I liked her. I had no idea how she'd felt about me before, since we hadn't had a chance to meet, but I could see us becoming friends. Meiling gave me a tentative hug.

"I hope you'll give all of us another chance."

"That's all I'd wanted to begin with. A fresh start," I said.

She winced and nodded. "I know. We all behaved horribly. Next time, I'll make sure I do my own research and listen to both sides. I let Meredith ramble on, and when I saw Badger didn't seem to like you, I thought..."

"I was a bad person?" I asked.

"Something like that." She paused. "Badger gets... moody, for lack of a better word, whenever there's something going on that will impact Adalia. He's overly protective of her, and by extension, her adopted sisters. He's not a bad guy. I know his behavior with you says otherwise, but he was doing what he thought was best for Adalia, Meredith, and the other girls Grizzly has taken in over the years. But he should have considered Doolittle's feelings too."

Meiling left, along with Zoe. I made sure Stripes met Rachel, since she'd been the first to try and make me feel welcome. By the time the party wound down, we'd stuffed ourselves with food and cake, and I had to admit I was wiped out. Not just physically, but I'd been emotionally drained.

"Your grandfather and the other Devil's Boneyard members will be staying in the apartments. I thought Stripes could use the one you were staying in previously, and his brothers could take the one next to his," Doolittle said. "Someone will show them the way. As for you, it's time to go home. Besides, you have a goat to name."

I smiled. "You didn't name him?"

"Nope. You brought him home, that makes him your responsibility. Um. He kind of ate part of the couch. I haven't had a chance to replace it yet. And we have a new dog. Or rather, an old dog who needed a new home. He doesn't have a name either because his asshole owner left him tied to the clinic door without a note."

I leaned into him. "You really are a big softie, aren't you?"

"Only when it comes to animals, women, and children."

"That's more than half the planet," I said.

He shrugged and led me out to the truck. I hoped someone would take my SUV to the house because all my belongings were in there. Right now, I was too worn out to care. If it wasn't at the house in the morning, I'd mention it to Doolittle.

Chapter Fourteen

Doolittle

Finally! I had my woman in my bed, and she had her property cut. No more hiding from the club. I'd started the shower for Minnie, thinking she might want to relax and wash away the stress from the day. It hadn't been until she'd undressed that I realized all her things were in her car. A quick text to Tal had ensured her vehicle and things would be delivered. When I heard him pull up, I went outside and started hauling in her boxes and bags.

I cleared out a drawer for her and put bras, panties, and socks in there. Then realized she'd need more space. The closet wasn't all that large, even though she had room to hang some dresses. This was something I could have fixed before I'd brought her home, but I hadn't been thinking about what would happen when she got here. I'd been too focused on finding her.

I took everything back out of the dresser and decided to buy new furniture. It would be a good bonding experience for the two of us, and I hoped it would make Minnie feel more like this was her home.

Stripping out of my clothes, I went into the bathroom and joined her in the shower. I smoothed her hair back and leaned down to kiss her. I'd only intended to take a small taste. I hadn't counted on losing control.

Lifting her, I pressed her back to the wall and nudged her legs around my waist. My lips devoured hers and I felt her nipples harden against my chest. I'd missed her. Not just sex with her, even though it had definitely been too long since I'd last been inside her, but just holding her, talking to her. Having her in my home…

"I need you, Minnie. It's been hell since you've been gone."

She curled her fingers around the back of my neck. "I never wanted to leave you, Zachary. I only did what I thought was best for you. This place, these people, it's your home. You belong here, and I didn't feel like I was welcome. I don't know the details of what they would have done if they'd stripped your patch and colors from you, but I know the survival rate is low. That alone tells me it's a brutal process. There was no way I could let you go through with that. And before you ask why I know something like that, the guys at the Reckless Kings might not have said much to me, but I listened. When they thought no one was paying attention, I picked up a few things."

"I love you, Minnie. Wherever you are, that's home."

A tear slipped down her cheek. "Really? You love me?"

I kissed her again. "How could I not? You're one of the bravest and kindest women I know. Do you have any idea how incredible you are?"

"Make love to me, Zachary. Please."

"I can think of nothing I'd like more. Want to move to the bedroom?"

"No. Yes. No."

I chuckled and licked the side of her neck before biting down. "Which is it?"

"Both! I want you here and now, but I want you again in the bedroom."

"How wet are you, Minnie? You ready for me?" I asked, dragging my beard along the soft skin on her shoulder.

"Yes. So ready."

"I better check." I gave her another nip as I adjusted my hold on her so I could work my hand down over her hip and the curve of her ass. I stroked her pussy, lightly rubbing her hard little clit. She moaned and trembled in my arms. "Did you pleasure yourself while you were gone? Did you touch your pussy and think of me?"

"Oh, God! Zachary, I..."

I slid a finger inside her, stroking it in and out slowly. "Did you?"

"Yes! In the shower, where no one could hear me."

"Tell me about it," I murmured, working her pussy with my finger and rubbing her clit every fifth stroke.

"Zachary... Please. I can't... I need you!"

"Then you better tell me all the naughty thoughts you had. Otherwise, I'll leave you aching and not give you what you want."

"I leaned back against the shower wall and braced my feet. I pinched my nipples before spreading my legs."

I added a second finger and pumped them in and out faster. "Good girl. Keep going. Tell me more."

"I rubbed my clit and closed my eyes, picturing you there with me."

"What was I doing?"

She shuddered as her pussy clenched down on me. I could tell she was close. It wouldn't take much to make her come.

"You were fucking me against the shower wall. Your cock filled me up, stretching me open. I imagined you pounding into me." She gasped. "And then I'd come. Sometimes it wasn't enough and I'd do it again."

I growled and pulled my fingers free. In one

stroke, I filled her pussy. I drove my cock into her, my hips jerking as I took what I wanted, what I'd needed since she'd been gone. I didn't make love to her gently. I fucked her.

"Yes! Zachary, don't stop."

"Never." I felt her coming and it was enough to trigger my own orgasm. With a roar, I pumped my cum into her, not stopping until every drop had been drained from me. "You have no idea how badly I want to punish you for running away. I gave the club a piece of my mind and went after you, but it was too late. You'd left the compound and wouldn't tell me where you were. It drove me fucking insane, worrying about you."

"Punish me?"

Hmm. She sounded intrigued by the idea. "Do you think you've earned a punishment, Minnie? You were a bad girl, taking off the way you did. Not giving me a chance to come to your defense."

"I'm yours, Zachary. Do what you want with me."

"Oh, sweetheart. You should have never uttered those words. You're in for a long night." I shut off the water and didn't even bother drying us off. I carried Minnie to the bedroom and tossed her onto the bed. I came down on top of her, forcing her thighs apart. "We're only getting started."

I reached up and gathered her wrists in one hand, pinning them over her head. Bracing my weight with my other hand, I slid into her wet pussy. If I'd had a chance to plan this, I'd have been more prepared. Seeing her tied to my bed would have been the highlight of my night. More than once I'd fantasized about it. Having her completely at my mercy, taking everything I had to give her, and begging me for more.

No more stolen moments. She was mine and we had all the time in the world.

I thrust in and out, long deep strokes, that brushed my body against her clit. She screamed as she came, but I wasn't finished with her. My cock was so damn hard. There wouldn't be a need for longer recovery time tonight. I'd been waiting too long to have her in my arms again. I made her come three times before I pulled out and flipped her over.

"Zachary, what are you..."

I brought my hand down on her ass hard enough to leave a handprint. She yelped and stared at me over her shoulder with wide eyes. I smacked the other side before spreading her open. I drove my cock into her pussy again, taking her like some savage beast.

"You won't leave me again, will you?"

"N-No. I won't."

"Good. Do you know what I'll do if you run off?" I asked. She shook her head and I felt her body tremble. She was so damn perfect for me, taking my soft side, my wild side. It was like she'd been made just for me. "I'll tie you to this bed and fuck you until you can't come anymore. Then I'll let you rest a little before I start over. I will spank your ass until you can't sit. I'll fuck your pussy until you're overflowing with my cum. Make you swallow my cock again and again."

Jesus. Just the thought of having her submit to me like that unleashed something inside me. I roared out my release as I nearly fucked her into the mattress, my hips slapping against her until my cock jerked and my cum filled her up.

"I think..." She panted for breath. "I think you like that idea. Do I need to be extra naughty so you have a reason to do all those things?"

I grunted and rolled off her.

"Or can I just ask you nicely?" She smiled and leaned in to kiss me. "I don't want to run from you again. Technically, I was running from your club, because Badger told me to."

"Never again. You're my wife. My old lady. And if anyone tries to take you from me or sends you away, I will gut the bastard and then feed him to the pigs."

"We don't have pigs," she whispered, cuddling close.

"Then I guess I need to get some."

Minnie laughed, her body shaking against me. "You're terrible, but I love you. There's nowhere I want to be but right here with you, Zachary."

"Love you too." I pulled the covers over us. "Get some sleep. I can't promise I won't wake you up in the middle of the night for another round. We have a lot of making up to do."

"Not sure I'll wake up," she murmured.

"Oh, you will. It just might happen after I'm balls deep inside you."

When she didn't respond, I looked down and saw she'd fallen asleep. I smiled and held her close, vowing that I'd never let her go. Now that I had Minnie back, I'd do whatever it took to keep her happy and safe. Even if it meant protecting her from my own damn club.

I heard my phone go off where I'd left it in my jeans pocket. No fucking way I would get out of bed right now. Whoever it was would have to wait. The ringer shut off only to start back up again. They called four times back-to-back before I hauled my ass out of bed and answered.

"What the fuck do you want?" I asked, not even bothering to check the display.

"Is Minnie with you?" a man asked.

I yanked the phone away and realized I didn't recognize the number. But I did know that area code. It had to be someone in the Reckless Kings. "Who wants to know?"

"It's Satyr."

"Look here, you piece of shit. You strung her along, then abandoned her for a shiny new toy. Don't call looking for her again."

"I know I fucked up. I can admit it, okay? I'm not ready to settle down, and Minnie is the forever kind. Heard you married her so I guess you know that already."

"Then why are you asking if she's here?"

"I just wanted to make sure she's all right. Do you love her? Are you going to be faithful to her?"

I pinched the bridge of my nose then started cussing since it hurt like a bitch. "None of that is any of your fucking business. Minnie is mine. Not yours. She was *never* yours. Why? Because you threw her away like a dumbass. Your loss is my gain."

"Just tell her… let her know I'm sorry for how I acted. I knew she liked me. It was a shit thing to do, giving her hope for a year that maybe I'd pick her. When those new girls arrived, I saw my chance to push her away. I didn't realize she'd skip town, or immediately hook up with someone else. Guess I should have seen it coming. Either way. I only want her to be happy."

"She is. Now don't call here again." I hung up and faced the bed only to realize Minnie was awake. I grimaced. "Any chance you missed that entire conversation?"

"Nope. And I'm guessing it was Satyr, based off what you said. What did he want?"

"To make sure you're happy, and to say he's

sorry. The guy is an asshole, Minnie. He knew you liked him and fucked those other women to make you leave. If he were here right now, I'd put my fist through his damn face."

She held her hand out to me. "But he's not, and in the end, he did us a favor. If he hadn't acted the way he did, I might not have left the Reckless Kings and ended up here with you or found my grandfather. Stripes said all things happen for a reason, and he's right."

I got back in bed, pulling her closer to me. "Doesn't change the fact he's a dick. I meant what I said. That fucker better never call here again."

"He won't. Now let's get some sleep. Someone promised to wake me up in the most delightful way. Can't do that if I'm awake."

I kissed her then tightened my hold on her. Minnie was my life. My everything. And I'd almost lost her. "Never letting you out of my sight."

"That's going to be awkward at times, but all right." She sighed. "Just keep giving me orgasms and I won't mind."

I smiled and promised myself I'd give her more orgasms than she could handle. Right after she rested.

Epilogue

Minnie
Three Months Later

"Doolittle, you're a doctor. Act like it!" I glared at him.

"Nope. Totally different. I treat animals. You're a human, and my wife. Sorry, but this is freaking me the fuck out. Why did they take one look at the damn machine and bolt out of here?"

"I don't know," I said softly. "I'm scared and I need you to be strong for me right now. I can't do this on my own. What if it's bad news? What if something is wrong with the baby?"

"Should have come in sooner," he mumbled.

He wasn't wrong. And I'd tried. I really had. The first appointment had been canceled by the doctor when he got called out for a delivery. I hadn't even made it out of the house. The second I'd had to change when I ended up being sick with a stomach virus. The third we'd rescheduled due to Doolittle having an emergency surgery. So now several months had passed and I was seeing the OBGYN for the first time during my pregnancy. Well, a different one.

The moment Doolittle realized my doctor was a guy, he'd gone all caveman on me. He'd insisted I find a female doctor. He didn't care if the other OBGYN was gay or not. He said no man was looking at my pussy except him. Which meant the first doctor I'd set an appointment with hadn't had a chance to do an exam. As irritating as it had been to find another doctor, I'd kind of loved him for it. The alpha bullshit annoyed some women, but I liked that he wanted to protect me. Even if it was from a male doctor seeing my girl parts.

A doctor came in with the frazzled tech behind her.

"Let's take a look, shall we?" the doctor said, giving me a smile that seemed a bit forced.

"Just tell me. Whatever it is, I can handle it. Well, maybe not, but Doolittle will keep me from falling apart in your office. We need to know what's wrong."

"Nothing is wrong, Mrs. Morgan. I'm sorry if we gave that impression. Your pregnancy is just..." The woman cleared her throat. "Have you noticed you started showing earlier than most women?"

I glanced at my baby bump. "Well, yeah. But I eat all the time. I'm constantly hungry."

The doctor nodded. "That's to be expected. I'm not sure how to tell you. You're not having just one baby."

"Twins?" Doolittle asked. "I don't think they run in the family on my side."

"Uh, no," the doctor said. She moved the wand around on my stomach then turned the screen. She pointed to three little blobs. "You're having triplets. Were fertility drugs involved at any point?"

"Nope," I said, staring at the three blobs. "You're saying I have to push out three babies, all on the same day."

"Well... yes." The doctor looked from me to Doolittle. "Since you hadn't mentioned the possibility when we scheduled the appointment, I wasn't certain if you were aware you had multiples."

"I could ask my grandfather if he knows about triplets running in the family on his side. I'm not sure if he'd know about my grandmother's family." I glanced at Doolittle, who looked a little pale and had gone slack-jawed as he stared at the screen. "No triplets on your side?"

He shook his head. "Uh uh. I, um… We can ask Shade to look into your dad, except…"

"We don't know for certain who it was." I sighed and saw the pinched expression on the doctor's face. "The man my mom married wasn't my biological father. I didn't find out until they'd both passed away, and the information was never shared with anyone we know. My dad could have been anyone."

"Technically, Grigori didn't die that we know of. He just ran off," Doolittle said. "Maybe we could find him and see what he knows."

"Shade and Outlaw already tried," I said. "I asked them shortly after I found *dedushka*. Grigori might have run off, but he didn't stay gone by choice. At least, I don't think so. The people he and my mom ran from in Belarus tracked him down. They killed him."

"Oh my," the doctor murmured, watching us with wide eyes. "That word you used. It's Russian, right?"

I nodded. "Yes, my grandparents and mother were all born in Russia."

"Your life sounds… fascinating," the doctor said. "Since you don't know all your family medical history, we'll keep a close watch during your pregnancy. As of right now, the babies seem fine. It's too soon to find out the sexes, but we can check again later. Do you have any questions for me?"

"I think we're still buzzing from the news of triplets," Doolittle said, smiling a bit. "Can we call if we think of anything later?"

"Of course, or just keep a list and we can discuss everything at the next appointment. I'll call in a prescription for prenatal vitamins. You'll need something stronger than the over-the-counter ones. If you notice any changes in your body or appetite that seem concerning, don't hesitate to call."

After the doctor left, Doolittle helped me dress and we left the clinic.

"Triplets," I murmured. "I think we need more space."

"We'll figure it out, Minnie. Maybe we can add on to the house. I could also add a second building out back for the animals we aren't keeping as part of the family. We have some time. Let's call Stripes and give him the news. I have a feeling he'll be as stunned as we are."

That didn't even begin to cover my grandfather's reaction. Or anyone else's. Although, when Silver found out, he started laughing and saying something about super sperm. Until Romeo had smacked him upside the head.

* * *

Four Months Later

I stared at the printouts from the doctor. Doolittle had missed the appointment, but Stripes had been in town and gone with me. "We should stop by his office and show him."

My grandfather looked entirely too gleeful. "Yes. Let's tell him he's having two daughters and a son, so he can start worrying *now* about all the boys sniffing at his precious girls."

"You're enjoying this too much."

"*Zaichik,* he now gets to understand how I felt. Even if I didn't know you were my blood at first, you were like a daughter to me. The moment I saw you, I felt like you were mine. I had to listen to you cry over him and hear how his club mistreated you. Now he'll get to go through it, twice. Possibly at the same time."

I sighed. "Come on, *dedushka*. I'll set the pictures down, then you give him the news, since you're so damn giddy about it."

I entered the clinic and breezed by reception and into the back with Stripes on my heels. I went into Doolittle's office and calmly placed the sonogram pictures on his desk in front of him.

"What am I looking at?" he asked, squinting. "Humans aren't the same as animals."

Stripes chuckled. "Men are always like animals when it comes to women, as you'll soon find out."

Doolittle looked at him. "What the hell does that even mean?"

"It means we're having two daughters and a son," I said.

Stripes gave a booming laugh. "Yes! And now you will see what it's like when your little girls cry because a boy has broken their hearts. My *zaichik* was broken when she came to me. You hurt her. The Devil's Fury caused her much pain. And now the universe is getting even."

Doolittle paled. "No. Girls? Two of them?"

I nodded. "Yes. Two girls and a boy. *Dedushka* has some ideas for a boy's name, if we'd like to give his grandson a piece of his Russian heritage. As for girls..."

Doolittle stood and came to me, wrapping me up his arms. "What is it, Minnie? You know I can't deny you anything. We'll name the babies whatever you want."

"Oksana," I said softly. "I want to give one of our daughter's my mother's true name. I wish I'd known about her past and all she'd suffered. Maybe I could have made things better for her. Been kinder to her. More understanding."

Doolittle kissed the top of my head and hugged me harder. "Oksana it is. Any idea for the other girl?"

I shook my head.

He looked at my grandfather and smiled. "I know Mikhail is your real name, Stripes. What about calling her Mikhaila?"

Stripes rocked back on his heels and I noticed his eyes got suspiciously bright. "I would be honored."

"You said you had an idea for a boy name?" Doolittle asked him.

"My father's name was Nikolay. I think he'd be pleased to have it passed to his great grandchild." Stripes looked at me. "If it's all right with my *zaichik*."

I nodded. "I think it's perfect. So we have our children's names. Oksana, Mikhaila, and Nikolay. Of course, that means you'll have to teach them Russian, *dedushka*. They can't very well have Russian names and not know any of the language."

"Consider it done," Stripes said.

"Well, I'm not getting any more work done today," Doolittle said. "Not after finding out I have two daughters and a son. How about I hand off everything to the new doctor for the afternoon and we all go get some lunch to celebrate?"

"That sounds amazing. I'm starving," I said, patting my rounded stomach.

Doolittle cupped my cheeks in his hands and kissed me softly. "You're beautiful and amazing. Thank you for gifting me with three children, with your love, and for giving me a second chance when I nearly screwed it all up."

"I didn't have a choice." I smiled up at him. "You're my one and only, Doolittle. Now, feed me! Otherwise, I won't be held responsible for my actions."

Stripes laughed as he led me back out to the new

SUV Doolittle had bought me. Once he'd found out we were having triplets, he insisted I trade in my smaller one for something with third row seating.

My life wasn't perfect. It was messy, and at times painful. But I'd been blessed with Stripes and Doolittle, and so many others. Perfection was overrated. What I had was so much better.

Charming (Devil's Boneyard MC 11)
Harley Wylde

Dakota -- Having a half-brother who's an infamous assassin isn't all it's cracked up to be. At twenty-five, he's still micromanaging my life. The moment Specter tells me about an arranged marriage to one of his associates I do what any sane woman would... I run. Never counted on meeting a biker I can't seem to forget, nor did I plan on our two days together to have lasting consequences. When bad men find me, there's only one person I want. Charming. I'm just not certain I'll get a warm reception.

Charming -- Dakota is different from anyone I've ever known, and it's not because of who her brother is. It's simply her. Some sixth sense keeps telling me she's in trouble. When she calls and asks for help, I know I'll do anything for her. The men after her have no idea she's mine, or that she's carrying my kid, but they will soon enough. I won't rest until they're six feet under.

Prologue

Dakota

"I'm sorry. I just hallucinated." I glared at my phone before putting it on speaker. "Repeat that, please?"

My big brother sighed. "I've arranged a marriage for you, Dakota. It's a good match. He'll keep you safe. Take good care of you."

"Did I fall into a wormhole? Accidentally time travel?"

"What?" he asked, sounding bewildered.

"Specter, you realize we're not in the Middle Ages, right? You can't marry me off to some guy sight unseen. The world doesn't work that way anymore."

"Technically…"

I growled and flipped off my phone, wishing he could see the gesture. "You listen well, big brother. I am *not* marrying some guy you've picked out for me. You can't do this to me!"

"You're my only weakness, Kota. It's only a matter of time before you end up with a target on you. Do you have any idea what it would do to me if I lost you? Like I lost…" He went silent, and I knew he was thinking about his daughter. The one they'd tortured, raped, and murdered.

"I love you, Specter. You know I do. But I can't live like this. I have a life! Friends. A job."

"I'm sorry, Dakota. Someone will be there in a few hours to pick you up. You'll meet your intended by morning and be married shortly after. I swear I would never pick someone who would hurt you. The guy is someone I trust."

I screamed and ended the call, throwing my phone against the wall. I hated when he did shit like this! Usually, I went along with it, at least for a little while. Not happening this time. I wouldn't marry some guy just because Specter wanted me to. Nope. Nope. Nope.

I started throwing my stuff into a bag. I eyed my busted phone and realized this was it. My only chance to escape. I packed as quickly as I could, loaded my car, and put my apartment key in the manager's drop box. Then I got the hell out of town as fast as I could.

Even though I didn't have a destination in mind, I hit the highway and decided to see where life took me. When I ran out of gas, I'd make a decision. Either stay wherever I'd landed, or drive a little farther. Whatever the case, I wouldn't sit on my ass and wait for my brother to manage my life. He'd gone too far this time. Spend a month with some bikers? Sure. Get sent on an extended vacation to some unknown private island? Not a problem. But this? Hell to the fucking no.

"Sorry, big brother. I'm not playing your games this time." I pressed the accelerator a little harder. There was a good chance he had other trackers on me besides my phone. I'd found one in the heel of my shoes before. He'd realize where I was and could still send someone to get me. I only hoped my running away would send him a message. I wasn't some pawn on a chessboard or a toy he could play with.

It was one thing to worry about me, and another to micromanage my life. He hadn't even asked me about getting married! Maybe if he'd let me meet the guy, get to know him a little, I might have felt differently. But this was positively insane.

I cranked the radio and sang along to Halestorm's *Better Sorry Than Safe*. She might be talking about a romantic sort of relationship, but the need to flee seemed pretty perfect for my current situation. I belted it out and poured my heart into the lyrics. I could be running headlong into danger. Or this could be the start of a new adventure. I'd never know if I'd stayed behind and waited like a good little girl for big brother's hired men to come pick me up.

I was done playing it safe. It was time to live a little…

Chapter One

Dakota
One Month Later

Sighing, I thought about my brother. I'd gotten a new phone with a different number. I didn't delude myself into thinking he couldn't reach me. He had people who could track me down, give him my number, or do pretty much anything else he asked. And yet he hadn't… I had to wonder why.

What are you up to, Specter?

"Stop daydreaming, Dakota," my boss barked from farther down the bar.

I gave him a salute, grabbed the pitcher of beer and mugs, then carried them over to one of my tables. The guys were obnoxious, with way too many grabby hands. I'd already tried moving away multiple times, but it did little good. They latched onto me just the same. Glaring didn't help either. At one inch shy of being five feet tall, I wasn't exactly intimidating. Not even to drunk guys who looked barely twenty-one. In fact, I'd wondered if their IDs were fake, but the boss had let them order alcohol.

Not my circus, not my monkeys. If the big guy wanted to get in trouble for serving minors, that was all on him.

"Can I get you anything else?" I asked.

"How about your number?" one of them asked, leering at me.

"Nah, we don't need her number. Why don't you give us a round of blowjobs?" All of them laughed. I knew the boss wouldn't take kindly to me dumping a pitcher of beer over their heads, but it was tempting. My hand tightened on the handle as I slowly counted to ten silently, hoping to cool my temper.

Before I could even respond, a tall man with scruff along his jaw and a leather cut over his shoulders slammed the guy's head into the table. "Apologize."

I hadn't even seen him! Where the hell had he come from? I glanced around and saw several people staring in our direction. The guy pinned to the table didn't seem so tough now. I got a closer look at the man who'd come to my rescue.

My heart skipped a beat, and I wanted to check my chin for drool. Handsome men were a dime a dozen. Even big sexy ones. But something about this one checked all the boxes for me. I'd never really dated much or had a genuine kiss before. I didn't count the lackluster ones I'd received in the past. Some guys needed to learn to use less tongue. No woman wanted to be slobbered on like a dog was licking them.

So why did one look at this guy make me want to press my lips to his?

I started to fan myself and stopped. *You're being ridiculous! He's a stranger.*

While that was true, I knew his type. Seeing a guy like him get all protective had always been my kryptonite. Well, unless the guy was my brother. Specter just annoyed the crap out of me. But his friends trying to keep me safe? Biggest turn on ever. Not that I'd ever have told him that. And his buddies had never, not even once, tried to hit on me.

I eyed the man again, wondering if he was one of the bikers who knew my brother. He'd helped more than one club over the years. If this guy knew Specter, I shouldn't be lusting after him. Being with him would only end in trouble. The type that left me with an overprotective brother threatening to kill the poor guy, or worse, Specter would try to marry me to the man.

Sexy or not, I didn't want to ride off into the sunset with someone I didn't know.

"S-sorry," the guy stammered. "We were just giving her a hard time."

I barely contained my snort. Sure. Let's go with that. The asshole had been groping me and making lewd suggestions since he got here. I didn't understand why the men always thought the servers were up for grabs. It wasn't like you bought a beer and got a complimentary blowjob or something.

"I've been watching the lot of you. If so much as one more finger lands on my girl, I'll rip your Goddamn hands off and shove them up your asses." He growled and put more weight on the guy. "Understood?"

He got a jerky nod from the guys at the table before he backed off.

His? I arched an eyebrow as I watched the hunky man. Since he was saving my ass, I wasn't about to call him out on his brutish behavior. Not in front of these guys, anyway. Besides, my savior was hot. More than hot. Scorching.

Marriage material? No. But… It didn't mean I couldn't be tempted to take him home for the night. Being the baby sister of an assassin meant my options had been limited over the years. Well, truthfully, it was worse. I'd had none.

"Come on, beautiful," he said, holding his hand out to me.

I glanced at the patches and stitching on his cut. The one that said *President* gave me a slight pause. I didn't remember my brother mentioning this club, but what if this guy figured out who I was? Could I risk it?

I saw his name… *Charming*. I bit my lip so I wouldn't laugh. This guy was anything but Prince

Charming. More like Captain Caveman. The almost cute-sounding name put me at ease.

He led me over to the bar and I realized he'd been sitting in the shadows, probably for some time since he had two empty mugs by his spot and one that was still half full. How I hadn't noticed him, I wasn't sure. The bartender would have been serving him, though, so it wasn't like I'd passed by him all that often. My tables were in his line of sight, but far enough I'd have never spotted him in the shadows.

"Thanks for the assist," I said.

"No problem. I don't like seeing men treat women like that."

I leaned against the bar and studied him. "Really? According to my brother, men like you are nothing more than beer-guzzling machines who screw anything that's female."

My brother might not have said those exact words, but close enough. I'd been shipped off to a club for protection a while back. I hadn't observed them much. The clubhouse had been off-limits. Everyone had been nice enough while still maintaining their distance. It had been clear I was an obligation and nothing more. Which was one reason I hadn't stayed long.

"Sounds like your brother needs an education." He took a swallow of his drink. "How many bikers has he known?"

I shrugged a shoulder. "To hear him tell it? A few. He helped some guys not too long ago. Devil's Fury? I got sent to them for about a month before I got the hell out of there. I knew what my brother was up to. Not sure the club realized it, though. Big brother hoped one of them would claim me."

Telling him that much was a gamble. If he knew

them, he might figure out who I was. And I seriously didn't want a guy attempting to get into my pants simply because I was related to the infamous Specter. It had happened too many times, and I'd shut down every single one. I might want a hunky man in my bed, but not on those terms.

His gaze was assessing and intense. "You have a problem getting claimed by someone like me?"

How cute. Even big tough guys could get sensitive if they felt they weren't accepted. The way his jaw tightened slightly told me enough. More than one person had told him he wasn't good enough at some point or another.

"No. But I don't want to be some sort of trophy either. Or a way to get in my brother's good graces. I want a man who likes me and not my family connections." There. The truth and vague enough, if he hadn't figured out my identity yet, there was a chance he never would. At least, not anytime soon.

He leaned back a little, taking me in from head to toe. "Any guy who doesn't want to spend time with you is fucking stupid. For the record, I'm not dumb."

I smiled and moved closer, brushing against him. He hadn't even asked what connections I had. I was liking this guy more and more. Others would have been trying to figure out who I was related to and wondering how they could use me for their own personal gain. Not this one. Nope, he was just a red-blooded man wanting to have some fun. That I could deal with.

"I get off in twenty minutes. Care to prove you're different?" *Oh my God.* Had I really just said that? And all flirty like? I'd never been like this before. Usually, men either infuriated me, or had me stammering like an idiot.

"I've got all night. Might be persuaded to stay longer."

I brushed my lips against his and knew I was playing with fire. "Challenge accepted."

He grinned as I got back to work.

I kept waiting for him to ask who my brother was. It never happened. Even though I sweet-talked my boss into letting me serve Charming and spoke to him a handful of times while I waited on orders for my tables. If Charming wondered about my mysterious brother, he was keeping it to himself. I didn't think he realized who I was. Most didn't. Thanks to Specter's job, I had a tendency to change my hairstyle and color. He'd even tried talking me into a nose job once. I'd punched him and told him to leave me the hell out of his fucked-up world.

By the time I got off work, Charming was about the only man left in the bar. I clocked out, pocketed my tips, and grabbed my things. Since I didn't live far, I'd walked to work. I eyed him as he stood, wondering if he'd had too many beers to safely ride his bike. When we stepped out onto the sidewalk, he yanked me closer and slammed his mouth down on my mine.

I leaned into him, not caring that people could see us. All that mattered right then was the way he made me feel. Alive! I'd kissed guys before, but it had never been like this. I melted against him, dropping my things as I wound my arms around him. He held me tighter, and I felt the hard length of his cock pressing into me.

Gasping, I took a step back. My cheeks burned when I realized I was a few seconds from stripping off my clothes in public.

"My apartment isn't far," I said.

"You invite strange men home often?"

I shook my head. "Never. But something tells me you're trustworthy."

"Then show me your place, sweetheart." He bent down to retrieve my items and started walking. Thankfully, he was heading in the right direction, since he hadn't bothered asking for my address. I raced to catch up and hooked my arm through his, leading him to my small apartment.

I stopped in front of the house someone had turned into four efficiencies and unlatched the gate. Charming followed me up the walkway to the front porch. After I unlocked the door, I pushed it open and ushered him inside.

"Home sweet home," I said. "Or nearly. My door is the one on the right."

I let us in, and he set my things down on the little bistro table I kept inside the apartment. The space was tiny, but clean. I'd scrubbed it with lemon cleanser the night before, and the air still held a hint of the citrus scent.

"For someone who has an overprotective brother, you sure live simply," he said.

"I'm on the run," I said. "I realize he means well, but he drives me crazy. So when I found out he planned to marry me off to an associate, I decided I'd had enough."

"He's friends with men like me, arranged a marriage for you, thinks you need protection… sounds like your brother leads a dangerous life."

Even as he said the words, he seemed to only be making an observation and not going on a fishing expedition. He hadn't asked for my brother's name. Hadn't tried digging into my personal life more. It was a refreshing change.

"You have no idea," I muttered. "He's

technically my half-brother. We have the same dad, but different moms. I'm younger by *a lot* of years."

Actually, I was closer to my niece's age. Or would be if she were still alive. She'd been such a sweet girl. I missed her all the time, and I knew Specter did too. He hadn't been the same since her death. And I'd now given him way more information than I should have. I seriously needed to keep my mouth shut about my family.

Charming smiled a little. "That right? Lots younger, huh? Since you work in a bar, I'm guessing you're legal."

"I'm twenty-five," I said. "And yes, I'm aware that's a little old for my brother to be dictating my life still. He thinks I'm helpless."

Shut up, Dakota! I needed to smack myself because I was being stupid.

He rubbed at his jaw, his fingers rasping against the shadow of whisker there. "Damn. I knew you were young, but I didn't... Um. I'm a lot older than you. That a problem?"

Now that he'd mentioned it, I noticed what I thought were lighter blond strands in his hair actually had a hint of silver to them. I didn't care. He was still the sexiest man I'd ever seen. As long as he didn't want me to call him daddy, then I was still down for a night of fun. It wasn't like the man was proposing. He'd said he might be persuaded to stick around longer, which told me he wasn't local. A night or two of hot sex? I'd be stupid to pass up the chance. It might not come along again soon -- or ever.

I moved closer and cupped his cock, sliding my palm up and down the hard length. "I'm not asking you for a happily ever after. You seem well-equipped to handle what I need right now."

He fisted my hair and yanked my head back. "Oh, I'm more than *up* for whatever you want, sweetheart. Just making sure you weren't going to bail on me."

"Nope. I want this --" I said, giving his cock a squeeze, "-- buried deep inside me. Think you can make me scream your name, Charming?"

He hesitated only a moment, and I saw something flicker in his eyes. "For tonight, I'm not Charming. You're not some club whore I'll forget before I've even pulled out. Call me Halden."

I knew it was a big deal he'd shared his name with me. Not one member of the Devil's Fury had done the same while I'd stayed with them. I reached up to cup his cheek and went on tiptoe to kiss him. This man… He wasn't anything like I'd expected. I thought he'd be like the other bikers I'd met. The Devil's Fury weren't bad men. They were… a little rough around the edges.

I understood now why this man was called Charming.

"Halden," I whispered. "Thank you for trusting me with your name."

"What do you usually do when you get home?" he asked.

I wrinkled my nose. "Shower, so I don't smell like the bar."

He rubbed my lower lip with his thumb. "Want company? I could be quite handy reaching those hard-to-get places."

"I bet you are." I kissed him. "Think we're both wearing too many clothes. Race you to the bathroom?"

I drew back and started stripping off my clothes as I rushed across the apartment. I ran inside the bathroom and started the shower, hoping like hell we actually fit in there together. It was a relatively tiny stall.

I stepped under the spray and groaned when I turned to face Charming. The man had removed all his clothes, and if I'd thought he looked good before? Now my mouth was watering. What had he said about being too old for me? The guy had abs for days, and just enough hair on his chest that I wanted to pet him. His cock… Jesus. To say the man was packing some heat below the belt was an understatement.

He smirked and tapped his chin. "Think you have a little drool right about here."

I narrowed my eyes at him, then reached out and yanked him into the shower. Or rather, I yanked… and he stepped in on his own, because there was no damn way I was moving him unless he let me.

He pressed against me and my back met the tiled wall. I hissed in a breath at how cold it felt. Charming shut the shower door, and I'd been right… there wasn't enough room for both of us in here. I wasn't about to kick him out, though. I rather liked him being this close.

Charming put a pump of shampoo into his hands and worked it into my hair. His fingers felt incredible, digging into my scalp and easing the tension from working at the bar. He rinsed my hair before conditioning it. I wanted to ask how he knew so much about a woman's hair. Most of the men I'd known might put some effort into their beards, but for the hair on their heads, they used generic shampoo. But decided I didn't want to know. At his age, it wasn't likely he'd never had a serious relationship. Unlike me.

Thanks to my brother, no one would dare touch me. At least, not anyone I'd been interested in. I'd had to take my own virginity with a decent-size vibrator. It had also been my only companion in bed until it stopped working. When I'd gone to buy a new one, I'd gone a teensy bit overboard. Now I owned three dildos, four different vibrators, and even a vibrating anal plug. I hadn't worked up the courage to use the last one yet.

While my conditioner set, he soaped my body. His hands were just rough enough that his palms sliding over my nipples made me shiver -- in a good way. He took his time exploring my body. By the time he'd washed me and helped me rinse, I was one big, needy, aching mess.

"Ready to get dirty again?" he asked.

"I haven't washed you yet."

He kissed me, then nibbled the side of my neck. "Later. Right now, I need to be inside you. I swear I'll make it better next time."

"Next time?" I closed my eyes as my voice squeaked like a little mouse. *Great. Now he's going to think you're some virginal young girl.* Of course, he wouldn't entirely be wrong. I'd never been with anyone before. Just my toys.

I felt his fingers stroke my pussy, and I gasped, my eyes going wide. I stared at him as he sank a finger inside me, pumping it in and out.

"Already so wet for me," he murmured. "You have no idea what a turn-on that is. You want me as much as I want you."

I nodded, unable to speak.

He added a second finger, working me slowly, stretching me. I whimpered and shifted, wanting more. Charming pulled his fingers free and lifted me. I wrapped my legs around his waist and felt his cock press against my pussy. Soon, he was sliding in a little at a time. When I'd taken all of him, I finally took a breath.

"You feel fucking amazing," he said. "Hold on tight, sweetheart. This first time is going to be fast and hard."

I gripped his shoulders as he pumped into me. His hips smacked against me as he took what he wanted. As pleasure sparked along my nerve endings, some distant part of my brain realized we hadn't discussed the important things -- like STDs and birth control. Then he shifted the angle on his next stroke, and I saw stars. After that, nothing mattered but how incredible it felt to have him inside me.

Charming pounded into me and I came so hard I could barely catch my breath. He roared out his release, filling me with his cum. His chest heaved, and he pressed his forehead to mine.

"Damn. That was…" He gave his head a slight shake. "Never in all my life have I felt anything like that."

And that was the beginning of the end for me. It wouldn't matter if he stayed a day, a week, or a year. He'd already taken a piece of my heart, and I knew I wouldn't get it back.

Chapter Two

Charming

Normally, I'd feel a burning need to escape if I fell asleep with a woman after sex. This time was different. I'd made Dakota scream my name all night and into the morning. According to the clock, we'd only been asleep about three hours, and yet I'd gladly go for another round with her.

The morning light filtered through the blinds, bathing her in a soft glow. If she'd seemed like a pixie last night, this morning she was an angel. I smiled, remembering everything we'd done. Then again, I didn't think she had a halo on top of her head. More like horns. She'd been a wild cat, and I had the claw marks to prove it.

I hadn't given my club an exact day I'd return. It had been so long since I'd had a vacation, I'd decided to make this trip both work and pleasure. I'd signed an agreement with some businessmen who wanted to expand their territory, then I'd found Dakota at the bar last night. She had seemed like the perfect ending to my day, and now I was ready to spend the day with her too. Assuming she was up for it.

I ran my fingers through her hair, smoothing it back from her face. She looked far younger than twenty-five at the moment. Her tiny stature didn't help matters any. I felt like a damn giant beside her, and it wasn't like I was a big bastard. I considered myself average height.

"You're staring," she mumbled without even opening her eyes.

"Can't help it. I'm enjoying the view."

She smiled a little. "I can see why they call you Charming. Are you heading out today?"

"Thought I'd stick around a little longer. Unless you're tossing me out."

She opened her eyes and reached out to place her hand on my cheek. "I enjoy having you around. I don't have to work until later this afternoon. I won't have a lot of time today, but I'd like to spend it with you."

"I'll stay and walk you home from your shift."

"Better watch it. I'll get used to having you around. Might make me cry when you go home."

I leaned in and kissed her. "I'll make sure you have my number. Call me anytime, pretty girl."

"So what do big, bad bikers do on their days off?"

"Thought you stayed with the Devil's Fury?"

She nodded. "I did. They didn't exactly ask me to hang out. I was more of a chore for them than anything else. As soon as I could leave without them incurring my brother's wrath, I hit the road. I try not to stay where I'm not wanted."

"Can't imagine anyone not wanting to have you around. They were all fucking idiots. But their loss is my gain. At least for now."

She rolled her eyes. "Don't worry, big guy. I get it. You aren't in this for the long haul. We're only having a bit of fun, and I'm okay with that."

"I'm not used to women like you. Most want to grab hold and never let go. You'd be surprised by the lengths some of them have gone to in order to snag themselves a biker."

"Guess I'm not like all the other women you know."

"Thank fuck!"

"You hungry?" she asked. "I think I have some pancake mix in the kitchen, or we could go out to eat. There's a café nearby, or I'm fine with fast food."

"How is it such a beautiful woman who isn't overly picky, is still single?" I asked. "Because you seem a little too good to be true."

"I told you. No one wants me just for me. They all want a piece of my brother, or to be related to him. I can't ever trust the guys who ask me out don't have an ulterior motive. Makes dating a little difficult, much less marriage or a long-term relationship."

"I get it. Women like being with the President of the Devil's Boneyard. They throw themselves at my feet, but it wouldn't matter who wore the title. They want the patch, not the man."

She kissed me, then rubbed her nose against mine. "Then they're stupid because you're pretty wonderful. You came charging to my defense last night, made me come so much my pussy still hurts a little, and you say the sweetest things sometimes."

I slid my hands between her legs and stroked my fingers over her slit. "Exactly how sore?"

"Why? Are you ready for more?" she asked.

I took her hand and placed it on my cock. "What do you think?"

"Oh, my." She slid her hand up and down my shaft, and my cock twitched in her grasp. "Whatever shall I do with this?"

"Let's start with your fantasies. Everyone has them. What are some of yours?"

Her cheeks turned pink. "Nothing we're going to do."

"Hit me with it."

"All right. But remember, it's a fantasy. I'm not sure I'd want to actually try these. I've wondered about having sex with more than one man." Nope. Not happening. I didn't like to share. "And the thought of someone watching me have sex is thrilling."

"Now that I might be able to do. Sort of."

She tightened her grip on the next tug of my cock. "How?"

"I have a laptop with me. Brought the truck instead of my bike. It's right outside the bar. We could record ourselves and do a little role playing. Pretend there's a live audience watching on the other end. Like a webcam show."

Her eyebrows rose. "But it will really just be us?"

I nodded. "I'll pull up the recording app on my computer, it will let us see what the supposed audience sees. I can even give you orders like people are watching us. It will sort of check off one of your boxes of things to try."

"I like that idea."

I got up and pulled on my jeans, then went out to the truck to retrieve my bag. I hauled it back to Dakota's apartment and locked the door behind me. Picking up the little table by the door, I carried it closer to the bed and set up the laptop. It only took a moment to set it to record.

"Crawl to me," I said, stepping up to the side of the bed. The camera on the laptop had an excellent shot of my profile, and the mischievous look on Dakota's face.

When she reached me, she licked the head of my cock. I gripped the shaft and painted her lips with precum. She moaned before sucking the head into her mouth. I threaded my fingers through her hair and controlled her motions.

"That's it. Show them how good you suck my cock. Your little nipples are getting hard, aren't they? Does my baby get turned on having a dick in her mouth?"

She moaned again, the vibrations going down

my shaft and making my balls draw up. *Shit!* She was going to make me come if she kept doing that. I pulled free and reached down to cup her breast, giving it a slight squeeze. Dakota went up on her knees, placing her hands on my chest. I'd been right. Her nipples were rock hard.

"Such a naughty girl. You like being used?" I pinched one nipple, then the other. "Want to be my sex doll?"

"Yes! Please, I want that. I want it all."

"Where are the toys? Sexy thing like you must have some. I'm going to have you screaming and begging before I give you my cock. I want to see you soak this bed."

She pointed to the small dresser nearby, and I opened the top drawer, seeing a rather impressive collection of toys taking up one side. I pulled out a small rocket vibrator, a larger dick shaped one, a dildo, and a wireless toy that looked like it would be a lot of fun, especially later when she had to work. I wondered if she'd be able to serve drinks while coming.

I shifted a few things around and saw a double dildo and anal vibrator. She'd mentioned wanting to be fucked by more than one man. This might help me tick that item off her list too. I decided we'd try it. I didn't know if she'd ever used it before.

I held up the double dildo. "Use this one often?"

Her cheeks turned pink. "Never, actually. I bought that and the vibrating anal plug because they sounded fun and exciting. I've been too chicken to try them."

"Get yourself warmed up while I clean these off," I said, not wanting to take a chance with her getting an infection.

I washed each toy and checked out the wireless

one. I'd have to download the app to my phone, and she'd need to be within so many feet of me for it to work, but I still wanted to try it later. I carried the pocket rocket, the dick-shaped vibrator, and both dildos back to the bed.

Dakota lay on her back with her knees spread and her fingers working her clit. I hoped she wouldn't be too pissed if I didn't delete this video. Something told me I'd be using it to jerk off for months to come. Way better than using my imagination or my memory.

"You ready to show your adoring fans how much you love cock?" I asked.

She nodded, seeming eager as she eyed the toys in my hands. "Lube is in the bathroom."

I went back to grab it. I grabbed the wireless toy too and quickly downloaded the app. I'd figure it out as I went, but I had a feeling we'd be using it both now and later. Returning to the bed, I poured some of the lube on my fingers and spread her ass cheeks. Her breath caught and her eyes went wide as I rubbed the lube against her tight little hole before working one finger inside her. I took my time stretching her. After she was taking two fingers, I lubed the double penetration dildo.

I climbed onto the bed and held it front of me, both cocks facing up. "Come sit on your toy, pretty girl. Fill that ass and pussy up."

She crawled backward toward me and I noticed she trembled a little. I helped her work the toys inside her and she slowly sank onto both cocks. She cried out as they filled her completely, tossing her head back.

I turned on the little pocket rocket and pressed it against her clit. Dakota went wild! She bucked and thrashed, rising and lowering on the cocks as she chased her orgasm.

"That's it. Let them see those tits bounce. Such a good girl taking two cocks."

"Charming, I need… need…"

I rubbed her clit faster, and she came, her release coating the toy and my hand. Her strokes stuttered, and she lost rhythm. Made me wish I had two dicks so I could fuck her the same way. I thrust the toy into her, using long, deep strokes. She came twice more before I eased the double dildo from her body and tossed it aside. It bounced on the mattress not too far away.

"I'm tempted to use the vibrating anal plug. I'd slide that into your ass while I fuck your pussy, good and hard. I bet you'd like that, wouldn't you?"

She nodded. "I'd love it."

Since she'd admitted she hadn't played back there, I didn't want to end up hurting her. "Next time. Hands and knees."

She scrambled to obey, and I pressed my cock against her ass, sliding it up and down. I spread her cheeks and pushed inside. Dakota cried out, her body tensing a moment.

I grabbed the wireless toy and slid it in, the smaller part fitting inside her pussy with the wider side pressing against her clit. I fumbled with my phone until I heard the toy whir to life. Dakota whimpered and her arms shook. I upped the vibration, and fuck me if she didn't come right then. While she rode the waves of pleasure, I stroked in and out of her ass. The way she squeezed me, I knew I wouldn't last long.

I came as she bucked against me. My chest heaved as I struggled to catch my breath. I felt her trembling under me and reached over to change the rhythm of the wireless toy. She moaned and rocked back. The woman was going to kill me, but what a way to go. I was getting too old to keep up with her, but fuck me if I wouldn't try.

"You're fucking amazing," I said, kissing her neck and her shoulder. I eased out of her. I curved my body over hers, my chest to her back, and used the wireless toy to make her scream several more times.

She collapsed onto the bed and laced her fingers with mine. "I think you ruined me for other men. No one will ever be able to measure up to that."

Part of me thrilled at her words. But the practical side wanted to tell her she'd find someone. Our paths were about to head in different directions, and the last thing I wanted was for her to miss me. Although, if I were being honest with myself, I had a feeling I'd be thinking about Dakota for a while. I'd never met anyone like her before.

"Rest for a minute, then we'll clean up and go get some food. My treat so pick anyplace you want. You'll need your energy later."

"For work?" she asked.

"During your shift."

She gasped and sat up. "Are you crazy?"

"Yep. I want to see how composed you can be while coming in a crowded bar."

She scowled, but it quickly changed to a smile. "Sounds like fun. As long as I don't get fired."

"You won't. If your boss says anything, I'll have a little chat with him."

"Not sure what I'll do when you leave. I won't have anyone standing up for me or giving me so many orgasms I've lost count."

I had an idea. One I hoped didn't backfire. I didn't want her to cling to the idea we'd see each other again. While I did plan to leave her my number, I knew it wasn't likely we'd be together after this.

"Download the toy app to your phone before I

leave. I'll program in a few favorites. Use them and think of me."

She kissed me. "Deal. Now shower and food. I'm starving."

She wasn't the only one. But I wasn't certain it was only food I craved. My life just got fucking complicated. This pint-sized woman was wrapping me around her finger, and she didn't even realize it. Maybe I should worry more about me acting like a lovesick calf instead of her. I was getting addicted.

* * *

Dakota
Six Weeks Later

Why? Just why? I rubbed my stomach and groaned. Crackers didn't help. Ginger didn't help. Everything those bastards said would fight morning sickness had been an epic failure. The doctor didn't have any other recommendations for me. Because of some allergies I had to certain medications, I'd always been limited when it came to prescriptions. Which meant most of what I ate came right back up. I wasn't gaining the weight I should be.

I pushed the cart of groceries through the store, making my selections carefully. I not only needed to watch my money, but I knew half of what I bought would only come right back up. Saltines and chicken noodle soup were already in the cart. I'd added some fruit and a bag of mixed greens for a salad, then chose a low-fat dressing. Ever since finding out Charming had left me a parting gift, I'd done my best to eat better.

Within three weeks of Charming leaving town, I'd known I was pregnant. I'd missed my period by nearly a week and then taken three home tests. I hadn't needed the doctor to confirm anything, but she had anyway. Next week, I'd get to hear the heartbeat. I couldn't wait! And it wouldn't be long before my first ultrasound. I'd chosen my doctor with care, not wanting anything to happen to my baby.

I paid for my items and pushed the cart out the door. Scanning the parking lot, I couldn't help but feel as if someone were watching me. I'd felt the same sensation for days now. Not once had I caught anyone openly staring at me or seeming out of place. My brother had made me paranoid. But a little voice in my head always whispered, *what if you aren't*, and that's what made me overly cautious.

I got to my car and put my things into the trunk before checking out my surroundings again. I seemed to be the only person within view. It didn't mean someone wasn't in a vehicle and I didn't see them. Still… I fisted my keys and got into the car, hitting the locks right away. The entire drive home, I monitored my rearview, waiting to see if anyone followed me.

Once or twice, I thought I saw the same Mercedes I'd spotted down the street from my apartment two days ago. Then it would disappear, and I'd wonder if I'd only been imagining it. By the time I got home and unloaded my car, my nerves were shot. My hands shook and my heart raced. I peeped out the window and looked up and down the block. Nothing appeared out of place.

"You're overreacting, Dakota. No one is out to get you."

And yet… I couldn't shake the feeling I'd lied to myself.

I put the groceries away and made a salad with a cup of soup on the side, then put the leftovers away for later. After I ate, I nibbled a few crackers, hoping my food would stay down. Sometimes I lucked out. Others, I hugged the toilet until I had nothing left in my stomach.

The boss had left me off the schedule today and tomorrow, saying I needed more rest. He'd been reluctant to keep me on in the past few weeks. I hadn't told him about the baby, but I couldn't hide my fatigue or nausea. More than once I'd been sent home because of my stomach bug. Little did he realize that bug would be with me another eighteen years -- or more. Not all kids moved out right away these days.

The food stayed down, which I was immensely thankful for, and I went back to the window. I gasped when the same Mercedes was back, this time closer to the bar. It wasn't a coincidence. Couldn't be. The men inside wore suits. Even though I couldn't make out a lot of details, I'd be willing to bet those were custom-made, which meant they definitely weren't from around here.

I fisted my hands at my sides and contemplated what I should do.

"Can't stay," I muttered. And I damn sure wouldn't call Specter. That left me with only one option. Charming.

I started packing the essentials and hoped the landlord would understand. I wrote a quick note and shoved it under his door, along with my keys. Piling my things by the front door, I pulled out my phone and called my boss. There was a chance he wouldn't help, but I hoped like hell he would step up and get me out of this jam. Or at least gain me a head start.

"Dakota, what the hell do you want? I'm busy."

"I need to leave town. There're two men outside the bar, parked in a newer Mercedes. Can you stall them? I just need a head start," I said.

I heard a bottle crash and winced. Great. That better not have been his top shelf liquor, or he'd be pissed. Well, *more* pissed.

"Jesus," he muttered. "This have anything to do with the brother you're trying to avoid?"

No one in town knew who my brother was. I'd talked about him before, just not by name or job title. It wasn't a good conversation starter -- *Hey, my brother is an assassin, what's yours do for a living?* But everyone knew I'd run from him because his need to protect me was a bit smothering.

"Yeah. He didn't send them, but I think they want to use me to get to him. I'm pregnant. I can't let them catch me."

I heard him cursing under his breath. "I'll see what I can do. Take care of yourself, kid. You be careful out there. If you ever make it back this way, you can have your job back."

"Thank you." For a man who barked orders at me every shift, he really wasn't a bad guy.

I ended the call and waited. It didn't take long for him to step outside and walk up to the car. From what I could see, it looked like he was picking a fight. The driver got out, and I made my move. I got into my car and sped off, glancing in my rearview every few seconds to make sure they weren't following. It wasn't until I'd gotten on the interstate and put a good twenty miles behind me before I relaxed a little.

When I stopped for gas, I noticed my hands were still shaking. I took a few calming breaths before I went inside. The clerk looked to be near my age, and he gave me the once-over as I went to get a bottle of water and a package of peanut butter crackers. I set them down on the counter and pulled out some cash.

"I need twenty in gas on pump two," I said. He

rang everything up, and I paid. Before I left, I decided he could possibly help with one other thing. Or know someone who could. "If I'm looking for a particular motorcycle club, is there anyone who might be able to point me in the right direction?"

"Bar down the street. It's open twenty-four-seven. Few guys in there might know."

I thanked him and went out to fill my tank. When I'd finished, I searched for the bar. The place looked empty except for a truck and three motorcycles in the lot. I braced myself and went inside. The interior was dark and full of smoke. I waved my hand in front of my face.

Three bikers sat at the bar. None were wearing club colors, and I started to wonder if I'd stopped for no reason. Deciding I wouldn't find out if I didn't ask, I made my way over to them. The oldest looked at me, his brow furrowed.

"Honey, you look lost."

"I am. A bit. I'm trying to find someone, and I'm not sure where to start."

The guy straightened a little. "Who you lookin' for?"

"The President of the Devil's Boneyard. The club is in Florida, but I'm not entirely sure where."

One man let out a low whistle. "Girl, you don't want to get messed up with them."

My lips twisted a little and I placed a hand over my belly. "Too late."

The elder guy's eyebrows rose. "I see. I don't know the exact town they're out of, but I can get you in the right general area. You can ask someone once you're there."

He dragged a napkin over and pulled out a pen from his shirt pocket. He wrote down some directions and handed it over. I skimmed them and gave him a nod. "I appreciate it."

"You be careful," he said. "When you get there, stop at a place called Buxton's Bar & Grill. Ask for Sammy. She can tell you where to go from there."

I gave him a wave and headed back out to my car. Now that I had a destination, I felt a little better about the situation. The next time I stopped, I could have sworn I saw the Mercedes parked nearby. After zigging and zagging around the area, I felt certain it either wasn't them or I'd lost them, and I hit the highway. No matter what, I didn't want to stop again. Not until I needed directions to find Charming.

By the time I found Buxton's and had my next set of instructions, I was bone weary and ready for a rest. Thankfully, the town I needed wasn't much farther. I found a motel, checked in, and knew I needed a nap before I did anything else. Not long. Enough I wouldn't feel like I might fall over at any moment.

Although I had noticed no one following me since the stop right before Buxton's, I still didn't feel safe. I wasn't sure what I expected Charming to do, but if he had a setup for his club similar to the Devil's Fury, maybe he'd have a place I could crash for a few days while I figured things out.

Then again, what if he didn't want his club to know about me? I hadn't had the luxury of thinking things through and coming up with a solid plan. If this ended up being a dead end, then I'd have to figure something else out. At least I'd put a little distance between me and the two men. Or I hoped I had.

I set an alarm on my phone for one hour, then stretched out on top of the covers and shut my eyes. I must have fallen asleep immediately, but it felt like I'd only blinked before the chimes went off, letting me know I needed to get up. My eyes felt like I had gritty sand in them, and my head hurt. The growling of my stomach got me moving.

I got off the bed and pulled out a fresh set of clothes, then rinsed off in the shower before making the dreaded call to Charming. If he didn't answer, I'd leave a message, and I'd give him until morning to call me back. After that, I'd move on and come up with a different plan. It didn't escape my notice I'd have been closer to the Devil's Fury. The lackluster greeting they'd given me before hadn't made me too eager to reach out to them, but at least I knew they were safe. Of course, there was the risk they'd call Specter.

I took a breath, held it a moment, then blew it out. My hands shook a little as I pulled up Charming's name in my cell phone and pressed the green call button.

Please let him answer!

Chapter Three

Charming

"Are you sure no one knows where she is?" I asked Badger. I'd been keeping tabs on Dakota through Shade, making sure she was all right. But he got a ping this morning showing she'd turned in her apartment keys and left. It seemed sudden, and now I was worried.

"Look, she stayed for a bit, took off, and we didn't exactly keep in touch. Why are you asking? If you'd made a big enough impression, she'd have given you her number," Badger said.

I didn't want to admit what I'd done. Not to him, and I sure the fuck didn't want Specter finding out. While I'd had every intention of it being a one-night stand, after one taste, I'd known I wanted more. But he was right. I'd left my number, and she hadn't called, nor had she given me a way to reach her. Maybe this was all one-sided.

I hadn't realized at the time who she was. It wasn't until I'd been home a few days before the pieces all clicked together in my head. Overprotective brother. Went to the Devil's Fury for protection. People wanted her only for her connections. My little sweetheart was the baby sister of one of the most feared assassins in the world.

"None of your fucking business. I just need to find her."

I hadn't stopped thinking about her since I'd come back home. Not once in my life had a woman ever wormed her way past my defenses until now. I'd wanted to hold on to her, even before I realized who she was. Dragging her into my world hadn't been the best of ideas. At least, not when I'd thought she lived a somewhat normal life. Sure, she'd hinted she had connections to dangerous people. Didn't mean any of that nastiness ever touched her.

I'd been giving her space, hoping she'd come to me on her own. By nature, I wasn't an overly patient man. Not when I really wanted something. Then Shade had given me the heads-up. It looked like she'd abruptly left town. Something was going on, and I didn't like the thought of her being in trouble. Why the fuck hadn't she called me? I'd made sure she had my number.

"No one here has seen Dakota since she left after her short visit. I asked Outlaw to track down her last known address. It was a dead end, which you know, since that's the entire reason you're searching for her. Honestly, you've seen her since any of us have. None of us will be much help. We didn't keep in contact with her."

"Shade has found nothing on her either. She couldn't have vanished." Not without some assistance. What if someone hurt her? Or worse… she'd died. With a guy like Specter in her life, plenty of people would use her as a pawn to get to him. I didn't like the thought of her out there alone, with no protection. The fact she hadn't reached out bothered me. Here I was thinking about her non-stop, and now I had to wonder if I'd only been a bit of fun for her. It fucking sucked, especially since I knew damn well I'd done the same thing to many women over the years.

I felt like a fucking teen girl. My club would give me shit for months if they knew. I ended the call and ran my hands through my hair. I didn't understand why I felt this driving need to find Dakota. I wouldn't rest until I knew she was at least safely tucked away somewhere. Even if she'd started over again and put me in her rearview, all that mattered was her. I wanted her to be happy.

Fucking hell. I groaned and shut my eyes. I did *not* fall in love with a woman in twenty-four hours. That shit didn't happen. I didn't care what any of my brothers said. I didn't believe in love at first sight, or any of that other nonsense.

I texted Shade, hoping he'd found something else. Anything.

Where the fuck is she?

Instead of a text, he called me.

"Pres, no offense, but chill the fuck out. I'm doing the best I can. I even have Wire and Lavender helping, and I spoke with Outlaw. None of us can find her. The woman hasn't used any credit cards. If she has a cell phone, it's one of those pay as you go types. Which means no contract. Without a number, there's not much I can do."

"I don't like this," I muttered.

"We could call Specter," Shade said. "Just one problem. He's already reached out to Wire. He can't find her either. Although, from what I've gathered, she hasn't been in contact with him in over a month."

My gut clenched. Shit. If her big brother didn't know where she was, then what the hell had happened to her? Not calling me was one thing. Why the hell hadn't she called her brother?

"He's concerned," Shade said. "One of his recent marks had Mafia connections. He's heard those men are searching for Dakota. They're going to hurt her, Charming. They'll make Specter pay, by using her."

"Find her. I don't give a shit what it costs."

"Pres, I need to know. Why are you trying so hard to find Dakota? What's really going on?" he asked.

"I met her almost two months ago. We spent a little time together, and I'm worried about her. Don't make a huge deal out of it."

"Fine. I'll keep digging."

Shade hung up, and I pocketed my phone. I didn't want the club asking me too many questions about Dakota. The less they knew, the better. It wasn't like the woman would ever be my old lady. At my age, I'd decided I'd never have one. I wanted to focus on the club, like Cinder had done until he'd claimed Meg. I already had too many people dependent on me. Even worse, I'd do anything to protect them, and everyone knew it. They all could be used against me at some point, and the last thing I needed was to add a woman of my own to that mix.

I pulled a beer from the fridge and sat at the kitchen table. Maybe I needed to get laid. I hadn't been with a woman since Dakota. Not that I didn't have offers. The girls at the clubhouse would fight each other for a chance to get into my bed. They all wanted the bragging rights of having been with the President of the Devil's Boneyard. There was a time I'd enjoyed that sort of attention.

Not so much these days.

"I'm getting too old for this shit," I muttered to myself. I wasn't ancient by any means, but I'd already seen fifty come and go. I wasn't exactly getting younger as the years passed. One day, I'd have to find my replacement. Just as Cinder had chosen me when he'd been ready to step down.

My phone rang, and I pulled it out, frowning at the number. It was local, but not one I recognized.

"Hello," I said as it connected.

"Halden." The soft voice on the other end made me pause.

"Dakota. I've been searching for you," I said, then wanted to smack myself. Way to sound desperate!

"I need your help. I didn't know where else to go. Not my brother. If I called him, he'd have me married off before sunset. Can you meet me somewhere?"

I looked at my phone again. "Are you in town?"

"Yeah. There's a diner nearby. Can you be there in about fifteen minutes?"

"I can and I will." I hesitated. "Dakota, is everything all right?"

"Not even close. I'd prefer to tell you in person."

"I'm on my way." I ended the call and grabbed my keys, then hauled ass outside to my bike. I didn't bother telling my club anything. As I approached the gate, Hunter threw it open, and I raced through. Now that I knew where Dakota was, it felt urgent that I reach her.

I parked outside the diner and went in, scanning the room for her. I spotted her in the back corner and smiled as I made my way to her table. She looked beautiful. I knew often our memories made things shinier than they'd been in real life. Not the case with her. She might be thinner, and clearly hadn't been sleeping well, but to me, she was still stunning.

"It's good to see you," I said.

She rolled her lips into her mouth and gave a quick nod. I took a seat and noticed her hands twisting on top of the table. I reached over and covered them with mine, hoping to set her at ease.

"I didn't know where else to go," she said.

"What's wrong? You seemed happy when I left. Did your brother find you?" I knew that couldn't be it since Shade had told me Specter hadn't heard from her in a month or longer. But I wasn't quite ready for her to realize I was aware of the fact.

She shook her head. "Worse. I noticed men around town who didn't look like they belonged. Thought I saw them again on my way here. I'm pretty sure they're after me, even though I don't know why."

"How did you find me?" I asked. "I left a phone number but not an address. Why the hell didn't you call? I'd have come to get you."

She smiled a little. "I knew your club was in Florida. Stopped along the way and asked if anyone knew where you were located. Got directions from a woman named Sammy a few towns over. I got a room at a nearby motel since I wasn't sure you'd take my call. As to why I didn't call before coming here... I guess part of me was scared you'd have forgotten me. At least by waiting until now, I'd have escaped those men."

"Dakota, I left you my number for a reason. I'd wanted you to use it."

"I know we only had a quick fling. You stayed for two days. It wasn't a relationship or anything."

I squeezed her hands. "Sweetheart, if I'd only thought of you as a quick release, I'd have never told you my name or left you a way to contact me."

She sighed and nodded. "All right, but you may change your mind when you hear the rest of what I have to say. I wasn't sure if I should tell you. Then those men showed up and I've been running the past day. Feels longer."

"Whatever it is, we can work it out. You're safe, and that's all I need to know. I've been worried about you."

"You're too sweet," she mumbled. "And I'm so sorry. I swear I didn't do it on purpose."

"Do what?" My brow furrowed. "What's going

on, Dakota?"

"I'm pregnant," she said, her cheeks turning pink. "It's yours, in case you're wondering. And before you ask, I'm certain. Because…"

She wouldn't meet my gaze, and I reached out to tip up her chin. My heart was pounding, but it wasn't from fear. The exact opposite. "Because why?"

"You're the only man I've ever been with," she admitted in a near whisper. "I'd only used toys before. I was on birth control, but it failed. Since we hadn't had the safe sex discussion, I got tested after you left. I'm clean. And I didn't tell you about my lack of experience because I worried you'd change your mind about spending the night with me."

"Sorry, sweetheart. I should have covered all that." It felt a little like the world was spinning. Pregnant? She was carrying my kid? Shit. I'd never thought I'd have a family. Wasn't sure I'd wanted one. Until those words left her lips. "I'm taking you home with me."

She shook her head. "I don't want to bring those men to your doorstep. I'd come here, thinking I could stay somewhere at the compound, but now that I've seen you again… I can't put you in danger."

I almost smiled. It was cute that she worried I couldn't handle those men. Some might be offended, but I knew her heart was in the right place. She wanted to protect me. Except it was *my* job to take care of *her*. Especially now that I knew she was pregnant with my child. Yep, I was close to going all caveman on her. I'd laughed at my brothers when they did that to their women, and already I wanted to toss her over my shoulder and run.

"We'll ditch anything they might track. Your car and phone. We can hide your car a few towns over. I'll rent a spot at one of those long-term rental places. I'll use a fake name and pay cash, so there won't be a paper trail. Or I'll get someone else to do it."

"Are you doing all this because of the baby?" she asked.

"No. I told you I'd tried to find you. I had this feeling in my gut that something was wrong. I shouldn't admit it, but I've kept tabs on you. Just making sure you're all right. Got a hit this morning you'd suddenly left town. It worried me." I laced our fingers together. "I'll take you to my house after dark. I don't want the club to know you're there. Safer for everyone that way."

"So you're going to hide me away in your house?" she asked.

"For now. They already know I wanted to find you. At least a few did, as well as two other clubs. Dakota, I wanted you here with me even before I knew about the baby. For what it's worth, I'm so fucking happy to see you, and excited as hell we're having a kid. "There's something else you need to know. Your brother asked a hacker with the Dixie Reapers to track you down."

She paled and tried to pull her hand away, but I wouldn't let her. "You know who I am then."

I nodded. "I do. I didn't when we first met. It wasn't until I'd been home for a few days that I put the pieces together. If you think I left you my number to gain a connection to the infamous Specter, you're wrong."

"Why aren't you angry? Most men in your position would be furious if some woman showed up pregnant."

"I might not know a lot about you, but you're not the type to lie about something like this. If you say the baby is mine, then I believe you. And it's not like we can turn back the clock and undo it all. I wouldn't want to." I shifted in my seat. "Look, it's not all manly and shit to admit this, but I've thought about you every day since I left. You were more than a piece of ass to me, Dakota. You and me having a baby? That's pretty fucking awesome."

The tension eased from her shoulders, and she gave me a brief nod. "You meant more to me too. When I saw those men after me, it wasn't my brother I wanted to call. It was you. I had this feeling if I could make it here, then you'd keep me safe. I didn't want to chance me being wrong and calling ahead of time. I couldn't have handled your rejection right then."

"I will always protect you. Both of you. I promise." I lifted her hand and kissed her fingers. "Me hiding you from my club doesn't mean I'm not proud to have you by my side. It's strictly a safety issue right now. But enough talk of evil men. Have you eaten?"

She shook her head. "I was too scared to show my face for long. I might have ditched those men, but I have a feeling they're going to find me again. I don't know how they located me to begin with, or if they just happened upon me. I doubt that's it, though. There wouldn't be a reason for them to have come to that town except to hunt me down."

"We'll order some food, then go to the motel and get your things. You all right to drive to the storage place? It's about an hour and a half from here. I want to put enough distance between us and that car in case they're tracking it."

"I'll be okay."

I reached out and cupped her cheek, taking a good look at her. She might say she was fine, but she wasn't. There were dark circles under her eyes, and I could see how exhausted she was. As much as I didn't want my club knowing shit about what was going on, I'd need help getting her into the compound, anyway.

My brothers would gossip like little old ladies. But the Prospects... They were too intent on proving themselves. My brothers would be furious later. I only hoped they'd understand why I was doing this. As much as I loved my club, and I trusted each brother to have my back, this was entirely different. It wasn't my life on the line but my woman's and kid's. That changed everything.

I sent off a text to Carlos.

Meet me at the diner with a truck in about thirty minutes and have someone pick up my bike.

I got a thumbs-up emoji back, which nearly had me rolling my eyes. I hated when they did that shit. At least I knew we'd have some help. I needed to swear him to secrecy. I wouldn't risk Dakota for anything, especially now that I knew she carried my kid.

"I'll have someone drive your car. They're bringing a club truck with them. We'll follow in that and give them a lift back. Someone with the club will pick up my bike."

I flagged down a waitress, and we ordered some food and drinks. As much as I wanted to hear everything she'd been through since I left, I didn't want to tire her out even more. Dakota looked like she was barely upright. When she stood and went to the bathroom, I eyed her stomach. Still flat. But we'd only been together not quite two months ago. I couldn't remember when the ladies at the compound started to show, but I knew it wasn't this early.

Whatever it took, I'd keep my little family safe. I didn't like lying to my club, not even by omission. They'd give me hell about it later. For now, Dakota and the baby were my priority. If I didn't want the men after her to realize she was staying with me, then I needed as few people as possible to know her current location. That included my brothers.

Everyone in the diner knew who I was. I didn't know how to keep them silent, except one way… The town might be wary of my club, but there was one woman whose word was law in this place. While Dakota started eating, I got up and went to find Midge. She was older than dirt and respected by everyone in town. They were also scared of the old dragon. I'd had a few dealings with her over the years and knew she was exactly what I needed right now.

She was sipping coffee at the bar, and I took the spot next to her.

"Pretty thing," she said. "Little young for you, isn't she?"

"Need your help."

She nodded. "Figured. That girl looks two seconds from bolting, if she can stay awake that long."

"Bad people are after her. I need to keep her safe and hidden, which means I don't need anyone running their mouths about me having a meal with her right now, or about her leaving with me. For that matter, I need everyone in this damn town to pretend she never came here. Can you make that happen?"

She snorted. "Of course, I can. Leave it to me, Charming. You take care of the girl. I know people have given you shit over the years. The entire club. None of you are what I'd call bad per se, even if you don't walk the straight and narrow. I know about the good your club does."

"We try to keep the scales balanced," I said. "Besides, I can't stand it when men hurt innocent women and kids."

"I know. Get back to your girl. Leave the town to me. I'll put a bug in their ears, make them feel like heroes for keeping her location a secret."

I patted her shoulder and went back to Dakota. If she was curious about my conversation with Midge, she didn't ask. Then again, with a brother like Specter, she'd probably learned early on not to ask questions.

Chapter Four

Dakota

I'd been around men like Charming most of my life, courtesy of Specter. While my big brother tried to keep me out of things, we'd spent enough time together that I knew guys like him didn't always handle things legally. I'd always tried to obey the law. Look where it had gotten me. Some creeps who wanted to hurt my brother were after me, and now not only was I in danger, but so was my baby… and Charming. The moment I'd realized those men meant to hurt me, I'd not wanted to reach out to anyone except the biker who'd wrecked me for any other man.

We might have only spent two days together, but he'd made an impression. And not just because he'd knocked me up. I was as much to blame for that one. Even though I'd been on birth control, I'd taken some antibiotics not too many days before his visit thanks to a nasty sinus infection. The drugs had worked, and I'd been back to normal in less than a week. They'd also made my birth control pills useless.

The doctor assured me she'd mentioned that could happen, but I'd apparently been too cotton-headed to understand what she was saying. I'd wanted the pills, some sleep, and to feel normal again. I'd gotten my wish.

I pressed a hand to my stomach as Charming spoke to the old lady at the bar once more. I waited by the door, scanning the street now and then, hoping like hell I didn't see those men again. He came back over to me, taking my hand in his.

"Midge is going to have a little chat with everyone here. Make sure they don't tell anyone you're in town. These people know and trust her. If they'll listen to anyone, it would be Midge. Carlos is nearly here, so we'll wait out front for him."

We stepped outside, and I tipped my head back to look up at him. "Who's Carlos?"

"One of my prospects. He wants to patch in, and if he keeps this secret, it will go a long way toward earning his way into the club. Not sure everyone else will see it that way, but I'll deal with that later. Right now, I just want to get your car far away from here and safely get you into my house."

"I don't like people being in danger because I'm here," I said.

"Hey. You're mine, okay? The baby you're carrying? It's a part of the Devil's Boneyard through blood. I'm glad you called and came here to find me."

"I'm yours?" I asked. What the hell did that mean?

"We can discuss it later. Carlos is here." He jerked his chin toward a dark truck parking beside his bike. The guy who got out looked my age or younger. Charming stepped away to speak with him, but I saw the guy casting me glances. I didn't know what Charming said to him, but Carlos gave a quick nod of acceptance and held out his hands. Charming gave him my keys. He retrieved my bag from the back before the guy drove off in my car.

A second man got out of the passenger side and Charming tossed him another set of keys. The man started up the Harley and gave me a slight nod before backing out of the space.

"When did you get my keys?" I asked, peering into my purse.

"It's easy to pick your pocket, or in this case, your purse. You were too distracted inside."

I wouldn't ask how he'd gained that skill set.

Something told me it was better for me not to know. If he was anything like my brother, his moral compass was a little different from the average person's. Didn't make him bad.

"Now what?" I asked.

"We follow him. He has cash to cover the rental space, and he has a fake ID he can use to secure a spot for your car. We'll pick him up a few blocks from the place, in case there are cameras pointed toward the location. As much as Carlos didn't want to do it, he's going to remove his cut and make sure none of the writing is visible until he's back with us. He'll also make sure his face is never on camera."

"You've thought of everything," I said.

"Not quite. I'm making it up as I go right now. Once we get home, I can work on a plan. I also need to know more about the men who are after you."

I got into the truck and buckled. "Can I ask you something?"

He nodded.

"If you asked people about me, won't that be traceable? What if the men find out and come here, anyway?"

"Shade is good at covering his tracks. And if he missed anything, Wire and Lavender will handle it. Trust me. No one is going to risk putting you in danger. They don't want your brother paying them a visit."

"Can't say that I blame them. Most people don't enjoy finding him on their doorstep."

Charming smiled. "Everything will be fine. You'll see."

He gave me a quick kiss before he walked around to get in on the driver's side. By the time we were on the road, I'd realized something. He hadn't freaked over the baby. Had been searching for me. And then he'd called me his. Charming didn't have any plan to release me. When all this was over, he wanted me to stay. No, it was more than that. Something told me he wouldn't be giving me a choice. Whether or not I liked it, I'd be a permanent resident here.

Maybe I should have wanted to run as far and fast as I could, but it gave me a warm, tingly feeling inside. Other than Specter, no one had ever really wanted me. Even my mother had constantly called me a mistake. While I might not have liked my sperm donor, at least he'd given me a connection to Specter. Once my big brother found out I existed, he'd made it a point to make sure I was taken care of. Whether it was money to help pay the bills or dropping in for short visits. Specter had been a larger part of my life than either of my parents.

"What if I'm a bad mother?" I asked.

"Why would you be bad at it?"

"My mom wasn't all that great. Specter's dad knocked her up on accident. She didn't want me, but she tried to shake him down for money. He paid her a large sum to not abort me. Too bad he wanted nothing to do with me."

"Their loss. You're smart, sweet, and thoughtful. Those two days we were together, I saw more kindness than I witness regularly. You gave a homeless woman a coat, helped some kids buy their mom a present, and made sure a veteran got the help he needed."

I shrugged. "That's all little stuff."

"Not to the people you helped." He reached over and took my hand. "I knew then you were better than me. It would have been best for me to give you a wide berth. Instead, I'd wanted you for myself, even if it was only for a day or two."

"It doesn't hurt to be nice to someone. I'd watched women yank their kids across the street to pass the homeless woman. They treated her like she was trash. The coat wasn't anything fancy, but it would keep her warm on the cooler nights, and maybe bring a smile to her face for a little while."

"To you, it wasn't a big deal. But I bet if you went back and spoke with her, you'd find out that coat meant a lot to her. The fact you talked to her and treated her like a human being was more than she received from most people. Don't belittle the things you do, Dakota."

No one had ever made me feel the way Charming did. The things he said, the way he treated me… I hadn't realized until now how little I heard that the things I did mattered. Even with Specter, he thought it was cute when I gave a homeless person money. Not once had he ever said that act of kindness made any difference.

I loved my brother. I didn't see him as often as I'd like. Once he'd gotten it into his head that I needed a man in my life, I'd started holding him at arm's length. It seemed better for my sanity. Not speaking to him for the last several months had been hard for me. Even when he was off on a job, he made time to call me at least once a week, sometimes more. I knew he didn't understand my reluctance to let him plan out my life. To his way of thinking, he was keeping me safe and making sure I'd be taken care of.

I wondered what he'd think about Charming wanting to keep me. Had the two ever met in person? Charming was closer to my brother's age than mine. Would it matter to Specter? Or would he be happy I wouldn't be on my own anymore? I hadn't even told him about the baby.

We drove through the town where I'd stopped at Buxton's to ask for directions and didn't pull over until we'd gone two more towns over. Charming pulled the truck into a parking space in front of a baby boutique. I pressed my fingers to the window and peered at the little outfits. I hadn't bought a single thing for my child yet. It bothered me, but I'd wanted to wait until I knew if I was having a boy or girl. Now I wondered if I shouldn't start gathering neutral items over the next few months. It wasn't like I needed pink or blue towels.

"I don't want you going in there right now," Charming said. "I see the way you're eyeing those baby clothes, and I promise to take you shopping soon. Might be online until those fuckers are caught. When we get to my house, you tell me which room you want to set up as a nursery and we'll get started on it."

"Really? You'll let me decorate a nursery at your place?" I asked.

He reached over and took my hand. "Told you. You're mine. Both of you. We'll discuss it more later. Right now, just know you aren't in this alone, Dakota."

"Thank you, Halden."

He smiled. "None of that once Carlos gets in the truck. Around anyone else, I'm Charming. When it's only you and me, that's different. You're my woman and you can call me whatever you want in private."

"Your club..." I nibbled my lower lip a moment while I gathered my thoughts. "Is it like the Devil's Fury?"

"In what way?" he asked.

"The girls at the clubhouse. When you aren't home, are you going to be with them?"

His gaze softened, and he cupped my cheek. "Sweetheart, there's no one I want except you. Since I left, I haven't touched another woman. Hadn't been with anyone before you in quite a while, either. I'm clean, and I was then too. Should have told you. Guess I lost my head around you."

"Not all men like you are faithful, though, are they?" I asked.

"In my club? Yes. The Devil's Fury, Dixie Reapers, Hades Abyss, and Reckless Kings are all the same. Once they find a woman, they commit to her. There are clubs where things that happen in the clubhouse don't count. If a man wants to fuck around with the club whores, then go home to his woman, that's his right."

I winced. "I'm glad you aren't like that."

"Being faithful to you is important to me. It doesn't make me a man to chase anything in a skirt. The fact I have a dick doesn't give me the right to fuck other women when I have you in my bed at home. Sorry to say those guys are just assholes looking for a reason to not fully commit to a woman. Five years from now, I'll still want only you. Ten years. Twenty years. Won't matter. You're the only one I want, Dakota."

I leaned across the console and kissed him softly. "Thank you. That puts me at ease. I watched some of those biker shows after you left. I didn't like thinking of you being like that. It bothered me a lot."

"When I say you're my woman, it means you're my equal in the house. With the club, that's another matter. I'm the President, and with that comes a certain amount of respect and expectations." He leaned in and pressed his forehead to mine. "I'm in charge of everything at the Devil's Boneyard, Dakota, which means outside our home, what I say goes, even for you. If you disrespect me in front of the club, I'll have to take action whether or not I want to. Understood?"

"I think so."

He kissed me, gripping the back of my neck to hold me in place. His mouth ravaged mine. A tap on the window jolted us apart, and he glared over my shoulder. I turned my head and saw the man he'd called Carlos waiting outside the truck with a grin on his face. Charming rolled down the window.

"Get in, fucker. You're riding in the back seat and remember what I said. Not one damn word to anyone about Dakota."

He nodded and climbed in back. Once he was buckled in, Charming pulled out onto the street and circled back the way we'd come.

"So… is she your old lady?" Carlos asked.

I remembered that term from the shows I'd watched. I glanced at Charming to judge his reaction. He was staring at me instead of focusing on the road and I shrieked a little.

"Road! The road!"

Charming winked. "I've got you. As to Carlos' question… Technically, the club has to vote old ladies in. We bend the rules from time to time, though. So yes, you're my old lady. Soon as I know you're safe again, you'll also be my wife."

My eyes went wide, and I wondered if the man was completely insane. "Wife?"

He nodded. "Told you. You're both mine."

"Both?" Carlos asked, leaning forward.

"I'm pregnant," I whispered.

Carlos whistled. "Damn, Pres. When you have a secret, you go big, don't you? No worries. Not saying a word to anyone. None of us will."

"Us?" I asked.

"Three Prospects know about you," Charming

said. "And now Carlos knows you're pregnant. Guess the other two should as well. Extra protection for you."

I worried at my lip again. "You said we could set up a nursery. How are we going to do that if no one knows I'm there?"

Carlos cleared his throat. "I think I can handle that part. If you want to pick out some stuff online for a pickup from any of the area's big box stores, I can take a truck and load it up, then tie a tarp over the back. You've got a garage at your place. No reason I can't back the truck in at night so we can unload it while no one's paying attention."

"Thank you." I turned in my seat to face him a little. "I'm sorry to put all of you in this position."

He waved me off. "No worries. Happy to help. And just saying, but anyone comes looking for you, I have no problems making them disappear. You and that baby will stay safe, no matter what."

For the first time in a few days, I felt like maybe I could relax a little. I was with Charming. He wasn't angry over the baby, and he had men ready to defend me. Now I needed to find the courage to call my brother.

* * *

Charming

Getting Dakota into my house had been easier than I'd thought. The Prospects had kept their word, and no one knew her location. Not even her brother. Although, I needed to fix that soon. If Specter found out she was staying with me, and I had let him keep searching, there would be hell to pay.

Carlos had picked up the things from her motel room, checked her out, and made sure no one said anything about her having ever been there. I'd asked him to find Midge and make sure she had a chat with them too. They'd listen to her before one of us. Thankfully, she seemed to be on our side.

The first night with my woman in my bed hadn't gone the way I'd thought it might. Instead, she'd fallen asleep almost immediately and only woke long enough to use the bathroom twice before crawling back under the covers. I'd left her sleeping while I made breakfast this morning. I'd need to look online for the best foods to feed a pregnant woman and alter my grocery list. The crap I usually kept on hand wouldn't cut it.

I smiled. A baby. I was going to have a baby, and Dakota was mine to keep. I felt like the luckiest bastard ever. After I plated the eggs, bacon, and toast, I went to check on her. The sound of retching in the bathroom had me quickening my pace. I rushed to her side, holding her hair back.

She whimpered and gave me the most pathetic look. I glanced around the bathroom, wondering what I could do for her. Opening the cabinet, I yanked out a washcloth and wet it, then handed it to her. She wiped her face, then her mouth.

"Morning sickness?" I asked.

She nodded. "Sometimes it lingers for hours, or even the entire day."

"If you think you can eat something, I have breakfast on the table. We can order some groceries and I'll ask Carlos to grab them for us. This morning, we have eggs, bacon, and toast."

She turned a little green and threw up again. When she'd finished, I helped her stand and waited while she brushed her teeth. Taking her hand, I led her to the kitchen and pulled out a chair for her after pushing her plate away.

"Tell me what you can eat," I said.

"Maybe the toast. If that stays down, I can try the eggs. I don't think the bacon will work, though. The grease would probably make me sick again."

"All right." I went to the sink and opened the cabinet beside it, taking down another plate. I put her toast, and mine, on there before handing it to her, then I got the butter and some jam from the fridge in case she wanted them. I made more toast for myself and added her bacon to my plate. I watched her like a hawk while she nibbled the toast. When it seemed to stay down, I nudged the plate of eggs a little closer.

"Thanks for taking care of me," she said, her cheeks turning a light pink.

"You might be the one who has to carry the baby, but it's my kid too. Why wouldn't I take care of their mother? Besides, I've been wishing for weeks that you were here, and now you are."

"Does your club realize you're this sappy and sweet?" she asked.

"No, and I'd like to keep it that way. In fact, most of them think I'm a complete asshole."

She ate a bite of egg. "I have a hard time picturing you that way. From the moment we met, you seemed to race to my rescue. How can anyone think you're not sweet and kind?"

I finished my food and shoved my plate aside, folding my arms and leaning them on the table. "I've been a dick to several of my brothers, particularly when it comes to their women. In some cases, they needed a kick in the ass, but I'm not sure they saw it that way."

"You have a lot of responsibility here, don't you? Your brothers. Their women." She glanced toward the windows, which I'd made sure no one could see inside. "And the children. I heard some when I woke up. Out of all those people, who takes care of you?"

I studied her quietly. No one had ever asked me that before. "I don't guess anyone does. My brothers have my back if shit goes sideways, but I don't think that's what you mean."

She shook her head. "No, it isn't. Don't get me wrong. I'm glad to know someone is watching out for you when something bad happens. I meant more in the way of who takes care of you if you're sick? If you're the one who needs a kick in the ass over a woman, who would do it? Do you have a best friend you can talk to when something's bothering you?"

"Do you?" I countered, feeling uncomfortable with her line of questioning. I'd had friends. Then I became President of the club. Now I had people who counted on me. Yeah, I still considered them my friends, but things were different.

"No." She sighed. "I'm sorry. I wasn't trying to poke at you. That wasn't my intention at all."

"I know." I reached over and took her hand. "Guess I got a little defensive. Truth is, with my position, I don't want the lines to blur. There can't be confusion when I'm talking to someone and need to clarify if it's me talking as their friend or their President."

"Sounds lonely," she said.

"It can be. For a while, I eased that loneliness with the women at the clubhouse. After a while, that didn't satisfy me anymore. They all want something. Usually they're hoping to become someone's old lady. I wasn't about to get trapped by any of them."

"Instead, you knocked me up and now you're stuck with me."

"No!" I winced at how harsh the word sounded. I tightened my hold on her hand. "Sweetheart, that's not anywhere near the same thing. Had I planned on starting a family? Not at my age. Then you told me you were pregnant, and suddenly I wanted a different future. One with you and our baby."

"I don't want to be a burden. You have no idea how expensive it's going to be to raise a child. I'll need to change my doctor to one who's local. Specter has me on his insurance." Her eyes widened. "Crap! He's going to see the bills and know I'm pregnant."

Well, I knew I needed to call him. Hadn't planned on it being right now. Looked like my plans had changed. *Fuck.*

I pulled out my phone and scrolled through my contacts. Every club considered an ally of the Dixie Reapers now had Casper VanHorne and Specter in their contacts. Or at least all the presidents did. I hit the call button, put it on speaker, and set the phone in the center of the table.

"Did your club find her?" Specter demanded the second the call connected. "I'm assuming Wire reached out."

"Dakota is safe, for now, but there are men looking for her. What do you know about them?" I held her gaze and saw the panic there. Reaching over, I laced our fingers together.

"I'll tell you when I arrive. I can be there by nightfall."

"Hold up, Specter. No offense, but right now, no one knows she's here. Not even my club. I want to keep it that way. We ditched her car in case they were tracking it somehow."

The line was silent, and I knew what he was about to ask.

"Why the fuck is my sister with you? If your club doesn't know about her, how did you find her?"

I winked at her and knew things could get ugly fast. First, I needed him to know she was listening. I didn't want to say anything he couldn't take back. He was her family, even if she had run from him.

"Your sister is listening to this conversation, so choose your words wisely. You might be her brother but make her cry, and I'll kick your fucking ass." I heard him suck in a breath and kept going before he had time to say anything. "As to why she's here, she called me and said she needed help. We met almost two months ago in the town where she'd been living. Gave her my number so she could keep in touch."

"You fucked my sister, didn't you? Motherfucker… those appointments she set with her female doctor. You knocked her up!" I heard a crash and had a feeling a coffee mug had met his wall. "Charming, I swear to Christ if you hurt her…"

"I'm fine," Dakota said, her voice low, but he heard her.

"Dakota, why didn't you come to me?" he asked.

"I didn't want you to marry me off to an associate. I've already picked the guy I want to spend my life with." She looked from me to the phone. "I belong to Charming, and before you hurl insults at him, you should know that you're right. I'm pregnant. You're going to be an uncle, and Charming is the father."

"Motherfucker," Specter muttered. "When I see you, Charming, we're going to have some words. You knocked up my baby sister, asshole."

I had a feeling those words would be made with his fists. Could be worse. He hadn't threatened to kill me. Since Dakota said he'd wanted to marry her off to someone, maybe he realized this wasn't necessarily a bad thing. I'd do anything to keep her safe, and I'd have my club standing at my back -- once they knew about her.

"Seems that way. And I'm fucking glad I did. Ever since I left to come home, all I've thought about is Dakota. I knew she was meant to be mine, and I wanted her here with me. Haven't told my club about her, or introduced her, because the fewer people who know her location, the better."

"Agreed," he said. "Destroy her phone. I'd send her another, but I don't want to chance them tracking it."

"I'll handle it. Until then, I think we need to keep this call short. I'll get a burner from across the state line, so it will have a different area code. You have a secured line, right?"

"Yeah. Call or text every day. I want to know she's all right."

"I need to know what we're up against. Send me everything you have on the men who are hunting her. I want this settled as quickly as possible."

Specter sighed. "Been working on this for a while now. Took them longer than I'd thought to track her the first time. Not sure they'll be quick to find her again. Either way, keep her on lockdown until I've dealt with these men. They're like a fucking hydra. You cut off one and another grows back, except in this instance, they have a shit ton of disposable men and will keep sending them until they have Dakota. They want leverage over me."

"Handle your shit, Specter. I won't have my woman and kid in danger because of who you are to them."

He grunted. "Guess this makes us family. I'll be seeing you soon."

The line went dead, and I held Dakota's gaze.

She blew out a breath and seemed to relax a little. "Well, he doesn't want to kill you, so that's a positive. But it seems like I'm not leaving the house anytime soon. How are you going to hide me from your club long term?"

"It won't be easy, but we'll figure it out." I ran a hand over my hair. The guys were used to dropping in anytime. I couldn't let that happen with Dakota in the house.

"You're going to have to tell someone other than your prospects that I'm here."

"Nope." I stood and carried my plate to the sink. "I'm not putting you in jeopardy. You or the baby."

Dakota placed her hands against my back. I hadn't heard her move and jolted a little. Turning, I pulled her against my chest and held her tight. She didn't realize that I'd give up everything for the two of them. My club. My life. I never thought a time would come that something was more important than the Devil's Boneyard. I now knew why Cinder had stepped down. It hadn't only been because of his age. Although, that had been one excuse he'd given. He'd wanted more time with Meg and his kid. Couldn't blame him. Now that I had a little one on the way, I wondered how many times I'd get called away from my family to deal with shit for the club.

"Time for some changes around here," I said.

"Like what?" she asked.

"The Dixie Reapers evolved as more of them settled down. For the most part, we have too. Just not nearly as much. I want to open more legit businesses and step back more from the illegal shit. It might pay well, but it's not worth it if it puts you and our baby in danger."

"Something tells me your club won't like that,"

she said. "Might want to ease them into things."

"We need to make a list. I don't want you to be bored, and I have no idea how long Specter will take to straighten his shit out. Books, movies, games… whatever you want. And you need more clothes. Need groceries too."

"You don't have to spend a bunch of money on me, Halden. I don't need a lot of material things. I only need you and our baby. Nothing else matters. Well, maybe my brother. Jury is still out on that one. It might take me a bit to forgive him this time. He didn't just endanger me." She covered her belly with her hand. I placed mine over hers. "I'll make a list of baby things too. We won't be able to paint the nursery because of the fumes."

"We can get those giant wall stickers," I said.

"Sounds good." She kissed me. "Get me a pad and pen. I do better handwriting things. Otherwise, I forget stuff."

"On it. Head to the living room and get comfortable."

I watched her go, admiring the view. I made sure the front door was locked, as well as the back one, before getting the things she needed. Sitting beside her on the couch, I helped her create the lists. I hoped Carlos knew what he'd gotten himself into by agreeing to get whatever we needed. I had a feeling this would take multiple trips.

Chapter Five

Dakota

It had only been five days since Charming had brought me to his house. It felt like five months. I'd never been confined inside before, not like this. There was no hope of stepping out in the sunshine. No chance of getting my own groceries and clothes. Not until my brother took care of the mess he'd created.

I couldn't believe his actions were affecting me this way. When would he learn? He'd lost his daughter brutally. Now he'd put me in the crosshairs of some nasty people. As much as I loved my brother, being part of his life wasn't easy. There were so many times I'd wished he'd retire. I knew it wouldn't stop people from coming for him, but it would lessen the volume a bit.

I leaned against the nursery room wall and watched Charming. He'd already put together a crib and a changing table. We'd decided on forest animals for the walls and I'd helped put up the giant wall stickers. I had to admit it was coming together and looking rather cute. I'd ordered curtains online last night, and Charming was currently putting a rocking chair together.

The prospects had been a tremendous help. Not only had Carlos brought a truck full of stuff over after I'd given him a list, but the others had been dropping things off too. I had more clothes than I knew what to do with, a ton of books, and Charming had bought me a tablet so I could download some games.

While all of it was thoughtful of him, it hadn't eased the boredom enough. I still wanted to leave the house. Desperately so. Charming kept leaving to head to the clubhouse and deal with… well, whatever it was he did for the club. I'd asked once, and he'd said it was club business. I hadn't bothered asking again.

"Are you leaving soon?" I asked.

"What time is it?" He glanced at me before turning back to the chair.

"You have about an hour and a half until lunch."

He grunted. "Guess I better go show my face and put some time in at the office. The longer I'm home, the better the chances of someone stopping by."

"Any news from my brother?"

He stopped putting the chair together. I saw his shoulders hunch and knew my brother still had resolved nothing. Each day that passed, I doubted more and more that this would ever be over. Whatever my brother had done this time, he might not get out of it. Or worse, he would, but not in enough time to save me and the baby.

"Never mind," I said. "They always say no news is good news. Not sure that's true this time."

Charming stood and came toward me, taking my hands in his. "I'm sorry, Dakota. I'd do anything to free you from the house, but it's not safe. Specter wants to handle this on his own. When I told him to send me the details of what was going on, he was vague as shit. That tells me one thing. He wants to take care of this himself."

"I'm starting to feel like a dirty secret," I mumbled.

"Not a dirty one."

"I get lonely when you're out of the house. I know you can't babysit me all the time. I get it, I really do. It's just… hard to be on lockdown."

"Come on, sweetheart." He led me down the hall to our bedroom and then into the connecting bathroom. "I'll run you a bath, get one of your books, and you're going to relax. Don't worry about lunch. I'll fix us something when I get home."

"Halden, all I do is relax. I'm going to go crazy! I need a purpose. A… a job."

He started the water and added some bubbles. Slowly, he stripped my clothes off and helped me into the tub. He went into the bedroom and came back with the book I'd left on the dresser, then placed a towel nearby.

"If you want something to do, then we'll talk about it when I get back. I'm sure we can come up with a few ideas."

"Doubtful." I skimmed my hands over the surface of the water. "I have little in the way of skills. I can wait tables and run a register. That's about it."

"Stress isn't good for you, Dakota. I promise this won't last forever. I'm sorry if things are a bit miserable right now."

I shook my head. "No. No, Halden. I have you. That's more than I had before all this. And if those men hadn't come for me, I might have never found the courage to call you."

He leaned in and kissed me, his lips soft against mine. "We'll get through this, sweetheart. One way or another."

His phone vibrated, and he pulled it from his pocket. He frowned at the screen and tried calling someone. I assumed it didn't go through because he growled and shoved the phone back into his pocket.

"Something wrong?" I asked.

"Phantom has decided to leave town suddenly, and he shut his phone off. I'll deal with him later."

"Guess that means you have to go," I said.

"I should." He sprawled on the floor beside the tub. "But I think I'll stay here a while longer. You need me more than the club does."

"You sure about that?"

He reached out and cupped my cheek. "Positive. Besides, I have a VP for a reason. I'll call Scratch and tell him I need some time off today."

I tried to remain quiet while he made his call, his gaze never leaving mine except to dip down to my breasts. The way his eyes darkened told me plenty. He might want me to relax in this tub, but soon enough, my heart would race and I would scream his name.

"So, you're free for the day?" I asked when he ended his call.

"I am. Whatever shall we do?" He waggled his eyebrows at me, and I couldn't stop the giggle that erupted from me. There were times he was almost silly, and I loved that about him. Especially since he said no one else got to see that side of him. It made me feel special.

"Well, after I'm all nice and clean, you could get me dirty."

"I think I like that idea." His voice went deep and husky as he reached for the soap.

He lathered his hands and went up on his knees. He massaged the soap into the column of my neck and down my shoulders. I felt my nipples tighten. He trailed his fingers down my breasts and palmed them. I moaned and shut my eyes, tipping my head back. His rough, callused hands caressed my nipples, and I pressed my thighs together.

"You're so beautiful," he said.

"You say that every time I'm naked."

He grinned. "I say it when you're dressed too, smartass. Can't help if I think my woman is the sexiest, sweetest, finest woman on earth."

"Before long, I'll be the roundest."

He leaned down and kissed me, his tongue delving between my lips. "And I can't wait."

I shifted, rubbing my legs together, trying to ease the ache that was building. Why did the man have to be so potent? One touch and I went up in flames. He slid his hand down my belly. He tapped my leg, and I parted my thighs. The first stroke of his fingers over my pussy and I knew it wouldn't take much to make me come.

Charming rubbed my clit in small, tight circles. I thrust my breasts up, wanting him to touch me everywhere. He eased a finger inside me, pumping it in and out.

"Halden! Please, I'm so close."

"I know, sweetheart. Just let go. Show me how pretty you are when you come."

His finger drove into me faster. Harder. My hips bucked, and I cried out his name. My body trembled as the orgasm faded. Charming let the water out of the tub and lifted me into his arms. He dried me off and carried me to the bedroom, placing me on the bed. I watched as he removed his clothes with quick, jerky movements. Once he was naked, I inched backward and spread my legs. My cheeks burned as he stared at me, his gaze fastening on my exposed pussy.

"You have no idea how much I want you," he said, reaching down to stroke his cock.

I sat up and crawled over to the edge of the bed. He was close enough I could reach out and touch him. The moment I wrapped my fingers around his cock, he moved even closer. I leaned over and licked his shaft before taking him into my mouth.

"Jesus fucking Christ! You're going to kill me." He groaned and fisted my hair. He controlled my motions, deciding how deep I'd take him. Sucking his cock turned me on and made me want him even more. "That's it, baby. Take every inch."

I hummed around my mouthful of cock and sucked harder. He cursed and thrust into my mouth faster. After three strokes, he abruptly pulled out and reached for me. Flipping me onto my stomach, he yanked my hips back and drove into my pussy. I screamed his name as I clawed at the bedding, my channel squeezing him tight.

"Halden! Please..."

"I've got you, sweetheart. Just hold on tight." He pumped into me, his hips slapping against my ass. It didn't take much before I was coming, my release running down my thighs. Charming ran a hand down my back before smacking my ass. "I fucking love when you come that hard."

He pulled out and lay back on the bed, tugging me over him. I knew what he wanted and straddled him, sliding down onto his cock. He gave my breasts a light squeeze as I rode him. When my movements became more frantic, he let go and licked his lips.

"Love seeing your tits bounce like that. Get yourself off. I want to watch."

His words unleashed something inside me. I went wild, slamming down on his cock over and over until I screamed out my release. I hadn't even caught my breath when he rolled us so that he pressed me into the mattress. He fucked me hard, taking what he wanted, and I felt the heat of his cum filling me up.

"I think I need another bath," I said.

He chuckled and kissed me. "Not yet. Give me twenty minutes, then I want to try something else."

"What?" I asked, almost scared to ask.

"Want to put you in front of a mirror, give you a good, hard fucking. That way, I get to see everything, even when I take you from behind." He nipped my ear. "Then I'm getting that toy of yours out. The wireless one. How many times do you think I can make you come today?"

"Oh, God. It's too much, Halden. I can't…"

He ran his nose down mine. "You can. And you know you'll love every second. You're my personal little porn star. Only dick you get is mine, but damn, sweetheart. You could put those professionals to shame."

My cheeks warmed. "Sex didn't interest me until you. Or rather, I was never tempted to be with someone. The toys were fine on their own. Then this big, sexy biker came to my rescue, and now his cock is the only one I want."

"Good answer." He kissed me hard and held me close.

Life might not be perfect right now, but at least I had Charming. He made it all worthwhile. I'd never be alone again.

* * *

Charming

I glared at the phone and answered as quick as I could. "Do you have any idea what time it is, you motherfucking asshole? If you woke up…"

I snapped my mouth shut and looked at Dakota. I'd worn her the fuck out, and now she slept soundly in our bed. Even if we hadn't had sex multiple times today, it was late enough she'd still be asleep by now. If the phone had woken her, I'd have kicked Phantom's ass.

"If I woke up who, Pres? Last I heard, you didn't have an old lady. I haven't been gone that long."

"Long enough. Next time you take off without

discussing it with me first, I'm going to kick your fucking ass. Now what the hell was so important you had to take off like that? A few lines of text and you shutting off your damn phone isn't how this works. I need details. If you're going to run off like a damn vigilante, I need to know exactly what's going on."

I listened to him for another ten minutes and ended the call. Scrubbing my hands up and down my face, I wondered why nothing could ever be easy? Someone was after my woman. Now Phantom was bringing home a woman and kids he wanted to keep. And they had trouble on their heels. I could just feel it. More shit was about to hit the club, and I hoped like hell we were ready. The worst part was not being able to tell the club about Dakota.

I skimmed the texts from Specter. The fucker was no closer to ending the mess he'd made. If I got one more excuse from his sorry ass, I'd break his damn nose when he finally showed up. For someone worried about Dakota, he didn't seem to be moving very fast. I hated not knowing what the fuck was going on. Why was she in danger? Who the hell had he pissed off, and how?

I hoped I didn't regret my next move, but I needed some answers. As much as I liked Shade, his skills weren't good enough this time. Even he would admit as much. I pulled up Wire's contact information and quietly slipped out of bed. I went into the bathroom and shut the door, not wanting to wake up Dakota.

The call connected almost immediately, and I realized it was late there too, and they had kids in the house. All I heard was a deep growl. No hello or anything.

"Sorry if I woke you, or bothered the kids, but I

need help," I said. "I know Specter contacted you about his sister."

I heard the rustle of sheets and his steps, then the squeak of a door. "What about her?"

"Specter is aware of her location. That's all I'm going to say about that. However, I need some information. I hoped you might know why she was in danger to begin with. He's given me cryptic answers to every question I've asked, and I don't like it."

Wire snorted. "No offense, Charming, but he doesn't owe you shit. Unless…"

I didn't like the sound of speculation in his voice. "Don't continue that sentence. I won't confirm or deny your suspicions. But it's important for me to know why she's in trouble. Specter doesn't seem to be any closer to making sure she's safe."

"Fine. We'll play that game for a moment, but we're circling back to why you need to know. I'm not going up against Specter. Being able to destroy lives from the comfort of my home doesn't mean I want on that asshole's bad side. You hear me?"

"I got you, Wire. Really. This is important."

"I did some digging. Didn't go too deep because I didn't want him getting suspicious. What I can tell you is that he's on the Cartel's most wanted list right now. He took out an important player, and the guy's wife disappeared around the same time. My assumption based on things I found is that Specter has her. They want her back, and since he's not playing by their rules, they want Dakota as leverage."

"Well, they can't fucking have her," I said.

"That's what I thought," he murmured. "Just her? Or am I protecting… more."

I sighed, hating that he'd uncovered the truth, but it was a risk I'd known I would take when I reached out to him. "More."

"Won't say a word to anyone. Does he know?"

"He does," I confirmed. "No one else does. Well, that's not entirely true. The prospects do, since they helped me sneak her in. But my brothers and their old ladies are in the dark."

"Right." Wire cleared his throat. "You know, Darian and Bull might want to come visit Scratch. Wouldn't hurt to send a few extra guys with them. I can plant a few seeds, see what happens."

"I appreciate it, but mostly, I appreciate your silence."

"I hope you know what you're doing," he said. "Call if you need anything. I'll keep this off the radar of my club and yours. Need to tell Lavender since she helps me most of the time. She won't say anything."

"Thanks, Wire. I'll owe you one."

I ended the call and stared at my reflection in the bathroom mirror. The motherfucking Cartel wanted my woman? Wasn't the first time we'd gone up against men like them. There were a few times I wasn't sure we'd survive. Now I had more at stake than before.

"What the fuck, Specter?" I muttered. If he didn't give the woman to them, there was no way those fuckers would back off. So why was he holding onto her?

As much as I wanted to rip into him for the stupidity of risking Dakota's life, and my child's, over some woman, I knew better. He wouldn't have kept her from those assholes for no reason. Which meant they'd either hurt her, or the dumb shit had gone and fallen for her. I hadn't heard about a woman in his life, even though I knew he'd had a daughter.

I rubbed my hand over my face and went back to bed. I didn't think I'd fall asleep anytime soon, but I could at least hold Dakota. I enjoyed having her close. Every time I left the house, some part of me feared I'd return and find her gone. I couldn't leave a Prospect with her. It would look odd for Carlos or the others to be in my house when I wasn't home, and I wanted the club to ask fewer questions. I'd already caught a few looks when I'd run off quickly.

The club would only get more curious the longer things dragged out. I'd spent more time at home this past week than I had previously. More than once, someone had come to the door and Dakota had run off to hide before I opened it. Hadn't let any of them inside, which made things worse. Something needed to give, and soon. My woman wasn't the only one losing her mind these days.

Now I had Phantom coming home with a family. A woman and kids in trouble. I didn't know how much more we could handle. Samurai had settled down, now his cousin. The club would find out soon enough I'd found a woman. We were dropping like flies. Before too long, there wouldn't be any single men left in the club. It wasn't necessarily a bad thing. Our lives were definitely changing, though.

I sent Scratch a text. Might as well keep busy since I couldn't sleep.

Call Church at noon tomorrow. Need to make some changes around here.

He didn't answer, but I hadn't expected him to. He was more than likely snoring his ass off, if he wasn't balls-deep in his woman. The two were still crazy about each other, even all these years later. I hoped one day Dakota and I would be like Jackal and Josie, Scratch and Clarity, and the others. Well, maybe not like Havoc and Jordan. They were both batshit fucking crazy. But I wanted to grow old with Dakota.

Raise a family with her.

The downside to our age difference was the fact I'd have to leave her behind at some point. When I turned seventy, she'd only be in her mid-forties. I didn't like the idea of leaving her alone. As much as I wanted to be her one and only, I hoped when my time came that she'd find someone else to love. A man who would protect her. Make her happy.

I rubbed at my chest, hating the ache building there. This was why I'd avoided settling down. It turned bad ass men into sensitive, sentimental shits. Then again, spending the next twenty or thirty years with the incredible woman in my arms would be worth any cost. If I was lucky enough to live that long.

Dakota whimpered in her sleep and twitched. I tightened my hold on her, murmuring in her ear. She relaxed and breathed out a sigh as she snuggled closer. I didn't know what the fuck she was dreaming about, but it didn't seem to be a happy one.

"You're safe," I whispered. "I've got you."

"Halden," she said softly.

Her even breathing told me she hadn't woken. I smiled, loving the fact she called for me in her sleep. Whatever it took, I would slay her dragons. Usually. In this case, the ball was in her brother's court. Unless those assholes tracked her here. If they even tried to take her from me, I'd gut every last fucking one of them. Didn't matter if I died in the process. I'd do anything for Dakota.

I kissed her forehead and tried to think of ways to keep her occupied, for however long it took for Specter to resolve his fuckup with the Cartel. I could tell she was going stir-crazy already, needing to leave the house. Even though my house wasn't near the fence line, it didn't mean someone couldn't hide in the surrounding woods and spot her with some high-powered binoculars or through a sniper's scope.

I'd stay with her every second of the day if I could. If the club knew about her, some of the old ladies would take turns visiting. Then they'd be in as much danger as Dakota. I couldn't risk it.

My phone chimed, and I checked it. Wire had sent something. I clicked on it and smiled at what I saw.

No one has any fucking clue who you really are. Even the club doesn't know your true last name. What the fuck?

There was a reason I'd assumed another identity long ago. Another lifetime, for that matter. It wasn't something I'd been very proud of, and I'd hoped it stayed buried. Looked like Wire had found out the truth about me. Should have known. Eventually, one of the hackers was bound to stumble across it.

What are you getting at? I asked. I saw the little dots and knew he would respond in a moment.

If someone dug enough, they'd hear the President of the Devil's Boneyard was Halden Roberts. Even though you keep that name pretty hidden. It's on your legal documents, which I'm guessing no one ever sees except the DMV, Vital Records Office, or IRS. No one would look at the Devil's Boneyard for Romeo Halden Strayer.

I cracked my neck. I hadn't even seen that name written out in forever. No one had known me as Romeo in over three decades. *Again, what's your point?*

The eye roll emoji was nearly enough to have me roll mine for real. What was it with everyone and those damn emojis? I sent some back to one of my brothers once, to see if I could annoy the shit out of him as much as it did to me. Hadn't worked.

Dakota Angelique Masters married one Romeo Halden Strayer today… in Las Vegas, Nevada.

Was he for fucking real? I might not have ever been told my woman's full name, which in hindsight might seem a little fucked to some people, but I knew he meant the woman lying in my bed.

What the fuck? There's a reason that name was buried!

The phone rang, and I answered quickly, not wanting Dakota to wake up. My pregnant *wife,* thanks to Wire.

"Why aren't you using your connections to keep her safe?" he asked.

"Because I don't have them anymore. I left that world first chance I got. Granted, this one is just as fucked up sometimes."

"Your father was a ranking member of the Bratva based in Los Angeles. You don't think that could be handy?" Wire asked.

"Look. If Stripes found out who my family was, he'd lose his shit. My dad isn't a nice man. Assuming someone didn't take his ass out. Even if they hadn't, he'd be in his eighties by now. I haven't seen him or spoken to him since I was seventeen. I left. Changed my name and as much of my appearance as I could, and I have never looked back."

"Your woman deserves to have your true name, and it's only my two cents worth, but I think you need to stop hiding who you are. You're not only the president of your club, but your Bratva ties could keep the wolves from your door. Not just this time, either. It could be a permanent solution to giving your club a bit of peace in the years to come."

I sighed and closed my eyes for a moment. "I know you mean well, but no good would come of me doing that. Romeo Halden Strayer needs to stay dead and buried. Besides, I'm sure my father had plenty of enemies who'd love to take a shot at me."

"Too late, seeing as how he got married in Vegas today. I'll keep watch. If anyone goes looking, I'll find out why. Worst case, your father's people search for you. Best case, the people after Dakota were sent on a wild goose chase to the other side of the country." Wire went silent a moment. "And you need to talk to Stripes and the rest of your club. They should know the truth. Your entire life right now is built on a lie. Eventually, the wall you built will crumble. You'll need their support if that happens, but it would be smarter to rip the fucking wall down on your own."

I couldn't exactly refute his logic. I'd hoped the truth would stay buried, along with Romeo Halden Strayer. Looked like I was wrong, seeing as how Wire just resurrected me.

"Fair enough." I looked at Dakota. "Thanks, Wire. I wanted to make her my wife, but I didn't dare with everything going on. I didn't want to lead anyone to her."

"I'll keep you posted. For what it's worth, I understand why you cut your ties. I also know that you'd do anything for your woman and kid, like I would for mine. Keep that in mind when it comes to possibly taking back your identity. It might not be as bad as you think. And as for Stripes, he hasn't lived in Russia in a long-ass time. I don't think this will be as big an issue for him."

I thanked him again and ended the call. If I'd thought I might sleep at some point, I'd been wrong. With all the new information, and even more worries, circling my mind, there was no fucking way I'd fall asleep. I decided to brew a pot of coffee and figure shit out. I'd already told Scratch to call Church at noon. I needed a solid plan in place by then.

Chapter Six

Dakota

I woke to an empty bed, and Charming's side was cold. Even though the blinds were closed, it still seemed dark outside. I didn't see sunlight peeking through the slats. I rubbed my eyes to clear my vision more and glanced at the bedside table clock. *4:30*. I got up and went to the bathroom, taking care of business, then splashing water on my face. Too early to be awake. However, I knew I wouldn't sleep even if I closed my eyes again.

Finding Charming was easy enough. I followed the only light in the house, straight to the kitchen. He had two notepads, a pen, and lots of balled-up paper scattered across the table, and it looked like he'd drained most of a pot of coffee. Unless he hadn't brewed a full one, which was doubtful. The man loved his coffee.

"What's wrong?" I asked, pulling out a chair beside him.

"I'm not sure where to even start."

I smiled and leaned my head against his shoulder. "The beginning is usually a good spot."

He sighed and kissed the top of my head. "It's not a pretty story. There are things you don't know about me. No one does."

"You know who my brother is. Do you really think anything you say is going to make me run the other way?"

"Guess not. You want anything to eat or drink?"

"You're stalling," I said, poking him in the ribs. "Get to it, Halden. I'm not getting any younger."

He smiled and put his arm around me. "All right, oh ancient one. The story starts when I was just a kid. My grandparents immigrated here from Russia. My grandfather was Bratva, and my father followed in his footsteps."

"So I'm with a biker who has Mafia ties. Does my brother know that?"

"Not yet," he said. "When I was seventeen, I knew I didn't want any part of that life. My father had been grooming me to join the ranks. When his actions resulted in the death of my mother, I knew enough was enough. I was only ten when she died, but in that world, I was wise beyond my years.

"He replaced her with a much younger woman, who also died about five years later. Similar circumstances. It took two years of planning and waiting. I made my move, and… died. Or rather, the man I'd been died that day. With my connections, I knew who to reach out to for a new identity."

"So your real name isn't Halden?" I asked.

"It is. Sort of. My birth name was Romeo Halden Strayer. As long as I had my father's last name, he didn't care what my mother called me. She'd always been a romantic, even when her husband cheated on her or beat her. If anyone believed in happily ever after and true love, it was her. I have no idea why, since she clearly hadn't found it."

"Unless she did, but it wasn't with your father," I said.

He tipped his head, and I could tell he'd never considered that angle. With a nod, he continued his story.

"I became Halden Roberts. It was easier to use a name I'd been familiar with, so it was more likely I'd respond if someone called out to me. I made my way across the country, working jobs that paid cash under the table. When I was nineteen, I bought my first motorcycle. Been in love with them ever since."

"And you eventually became part of the Devil's Boneyard," I said. "What does all that have to do with right now? Something triggered those memories."

"Wire," he said. "He did some digging and found out who I really am. Worse, he put Romeo Halden Strayer back on the map, and among the living."

I tensed a little. "What's that mean exactly?"

"Might as well tell you. We're married. Except Wire married us in Las Vegas and under my true name. If anyone is searching for you, they'll think you're across the country. But it also means someone from my past could discover I'm not dead. I have no idea what sort of fallout might happen from that. Not even my club knows who I was."

"And that has you up scribbling on paper, then balling it up?"

"Something like that." He held me a little tighter. "I'm not sure how they'll react to my news. How do I tell them without also admitting I'm married to you and you're living in my house? I still want to keep your location a secret, even from those I trust the most. Wire figured it out. Others might. I don't know what the fuck to do right now, Dakota."

I cuddled closer and put my hand on his thigh. "I know you're the big bad president of the Devil's Boneyard, and apparently have ties to the Russian Mafia, but it doesn't mean you have all the answers or are all powerful. You're only a man, Halden. One I care about and admire, but an everyday human just the same. It's okay to ask for help."

"I have Church at noon today. Need to make some changes around here, but Phantom is also bringing his new family home. I can maybe argue the changes are for the betterment of the club in general. We have quite a few families now, and more children could account for us taking a step back from some of the less than legal things we do."

I nodded. "You're right. All that would make sense."

"I'll table the discussion about my true identity for now. I'll tell them when the time is right. This isn't it. I'll drop some hints that I have a past I need to discuss with them, but that I need some time to figure things out first. Might hold them off and explain my odd behavior." He shook his head. "I know they have to be wondering why I keep running home."

"Maybe you should have gotten a puppy. Then you'd have the excuse of having to let a furball out of the house."

He smiled and kissed me. "I think taking on a wife and baby is enough for right now. We can discuss a dog when our kid is a little older. Not sure either of us is up for changing diapers, midnight feedings, and potty training a puppy all at the same time."

"Probably not." I wrinkled my nose. "I don't think I'm going back to sleep anytime soon. Want me to help with your lists or whatever you were writing?"

"Sure. I need some family friendly ideas for physical changes to the compound. We already added a play area and picnic pavilion. Maybe some family friendly events other than potlucks at the clubhouse?"

"All right. Never had kids before, but I'm sure I can think of a few ideas. How old are the children here?" I asked.

"They range from infant all the way to seventeen years. There's quite a few between the ages of seven and ten, then another group between twelve and seventeen, with a handful that are younger. Phantom is coming home today with a woman and three kids, so that's going to add to the numbers."

"I'll work on that list, and you focus on whatever else you were writing out. Together, we can do the work in half the time."

He kissed my cheek and pulled the two pads over, sliding one to me. He gave me his pen and got up to get another one for himself. We spent the next half hour working in silence until my stomach grumbled. As hungry as I felt, I wasn't sure I'd keep down the food.

"I'll start some toast and eggs. You seem to do okay with those," he said, getting up from the table.

"I'm not incapable of feeding us," I pointed out. "You don't have to cook for me all the time."

"Humor me. I haven't had a woman live with me. Ever. I like spoiling you a little. If you want to cook, you can make lunch while I'm at Church. Shouldn't be more than thirty minutes to an hour."

We ate and spent some time cuddling on the couch. He let me pick the movies, even though I knew he couldn't possibly want to watch the romantic comedies I preferred. Although, I did like a good scary movie now and then, as long as they were of the paranormal sort. The ones based on reality were a little too much for me. I didn't think Krampus was going to come after me anytime soon, but taking a wrong turn and ending on the lunch menu for cannibals? Maybe not likely, but it *could* happen. So I avoided those.

His phone rang, and he took the call. "Hey, Phantom. You nearly here?"

I couldn't hear the other side of the conversation and tried not to eavesdrop. It was a little hard to ignore him entirely since he was sitting beside me while he spoke to the guy.

Charming chuckled. "Already taken care of, brother. We got Li the same system Taggart likes, and Jian has the one Levi and Caleb have. The women went a little crazy on Nova's room. She has dolls, stuffed animals, art shit, puzzles and all kinds of crap in there. Your dog is about to lose her damn mind trying to figure out what the hell is going on, though."

I had a feeling he was talking about the kids coming to the compound. He'd been gone for a bit last night around dinner, saying he had a few things to handle. Since he'd brought back pasta and cheesecake, I'd assumed he'd only gone out to get food. Sounded like he'd done more than that.

"The kids are covered. Just bring your family home. Everyone is eager to meet them." He ended the call and shoved his phone back into his pocket.

"You're going to go over and greet them, aren't you? Might make them feel more welcome to meet you right away."

"That what you want?" he asked.

"Well, I'd love to go with you, but we both know that can't happen right now. You should introduce yourself to his new family. I'll be fine staying here."

He kissed me softly. "All right, sweetheart. I'll grab Scratch and head over there in a few minutes. Phantom doesn't live far, so I can walk."

"You should shower and dress first." I eyed him. "Although, I'm liking this look. I'd just prefer you don't show off your body to everyone."

He pinned me to the couch and rubbed his whiskers against my shoulder. I squealed and giggled as I pushed at him. Not that I really wanted him to go anywhere. He hadn't shaved yet, and I kind of liked the sexy five-o'clock shadow he had going right now. I wondered if I could talk him into growing a beard. I knew most of the bikers I'd met before had one. No idea why he hadn't grown one, or maybe he'd had one before and shaved it off.

"Want me to tattoo your name across my heart?" he asked, nuzzling my neck. "Because I will. Don't want anyone but you, Dakota. I'd do anything to make you happy."

"Anything?" I asked.

He leaned back to peer down at me. "Yeah. What did you have in mind?"

I licked my lips and turned my face away for a moment while I gathered my thoughts before returning my gaze to his. "I know you can't tell anyone about us right now. When you can, I'd like to have wedding rings. For both of us. I want everyone to see you're taken. I know it might not make a difference. The women at the clubhouse will probably still try to tempt you. I can't say that I blame them. But you said you'd be faithful, and I believe you."

"Rings. A tattoo. How about I do both? And soon as it's safe for everyone to know about you, I'll have a property cut made for you."

"Who makes them?" I asked.

He paused. "Actually, Midge made a few of them. The old woman at the diner? I can talk to her. See if she'll make one for you and keep it a secret. She already knows you're here."

"I'd like that." I kissed him, then bucked my hips against him. "Now go shower before we end up getting distracted by other things. You don't want to make a poor impression on the woman and kids."

He winced. "All right. If I have to. I'd rather stay here with you, though."

I shook my head and smiled. "Go, Halden. They need to meet the President of the Devil's Boneyard.

Make them feel safe. Wanted. Considering your past, you know how important that is. Treat them… the way you'd want your club to greet me. It's obvious he has feelings for her. Don't be a shithead just because you can be."

"Bossy wench," he said, growling softly. He nipped my bottom lip before kissing me, then rolled off before I could grab hold of him.

Charming left, and I heard the water running a few minutes later. I found another movie to watch and wished him well when he left the house. No matter how badly I wanted to go peek out the windows, I didn't dare. He'd kept all the blinds closed, doing his best to keep me hidden, and I'd not chance anyone spotting me. Not after everything he'd done regarding my safety.

* * *

Charming

I stood in Phantom's yard with Scratch, watching for him to pull in with the newest additions to the club. Scratch's two boys were across the street with their noses pressed to the windows of his house, waiting to see their potential playmates. I liked that the club was growing. Just wished the lot of us could figure out how to follow the rules when it came to our women. I couldn't fucking gripe too much, since I had told no one about Dakota, and I was already married to her.

I'd called Midge before I'd left and given her Dakota's size. She knew where I got the leather cuts and had an embroidery machine she used to make the patches. She promised to have it done by the end of the week. I couldn't wait to see it on my wife.

"You didn't give him too much shit about this, did you?" Scratch asked. "You know, we all fall hard and fast when we find the right woman."

"I know. And honestly, I'm glad he got them out of the hell they were in. Not too happy about the potential trouble knocking at our gates, but it is what it is."

He gave a nod toward the road. "Here they are now. Try to remember your name, Charming, and don't be a damn ogre."

I mock-punched him in the shoulder. "Asshole."

Phantom pulled to a stop in his driveway and got out. The woman and children followed, and I could see the fear the boys tried to hide. I didn't like it. No kid should ever be terrified, especially going to their new home. So I did what I needed to and manned the fuck up so I could welcome them with a smile, and hopefully set them at ease, exactly the way Dakota had wanted me to.

Phantom turned slightly, so he was partially facing his woman when he made the introductions. I remembered him saying she was deaf.

"This is the club's President and Vice President. Charming and Scratch. They helped put together a surprise for the kids."

Scratch smiled and waited for Charisma to look at him. "Welcome to the Devil's Boneyard family. I live across the street with my wife and kids. You're welcome anytime."

She frowned and looked at Phantom. He told her what Scratch had said.

"VP, I think you're going to need to trim the bush on your face or learn to sign. She couldn't read your lips," Phantom said with a smile.

Scratch ran a hand over his beard and nodded. I held out my hand and Charisma hesitantly took it. I pulled her in close for a quick hug, then stepped back.

"We're all happy to meet you. Take some time to get settled in, then we'll plan a party so you and the kids can get to know everyone."

Nearly everyone. I fucking hated the fact no one knew I had a wife or had met her yet. It sucked big-ass donkey balls, but I wouldn't risk her life. My club would never intentionally say anything. It was the fear they might mention her without realizing someone else listened that had me keeping quiet.

Scratch made his way back home, and I had a feeling those boys of his would be at Phantom's door before too long. I wanted to give Phantom time with his new family, which meant I'd keep things short during Church. I wouldn't delve into as much as I'd originally planned. Now that I'd met Charisma and seen the children, I knew he needed to focus his attention on them.

As often as I wanted to go back home and check on Dakota, I made myself walk to the house and get on my bike. I rode over to the clubhouse and decided to get a beer and work in the office a bit before Church started. The club needed to see me more than they had the last week.

I went inside and scanned the interior. A few of the club whores lingered at the edges of the room, looking bored as fuck. Beat the hell out of me why they thought anyone would want their kind of attention this early in the day. Most of the brothers didn't come to the clubhouse until closer to lunch. I went behind the bar and grabbed a cold longneck from the fridge and went to the office down the hall.

The chair creaked when I sat, and I turned on the computer. After I logged in, I pulled up the club's accounts to check the balances, then started on the paperwork. We had a few people who hadn't paid yet, and they'd need to be dealt with. I'd have Havoc pay them a visit.

Booted steps came closer, and I looked up as Cinder came in. I leaned back in my seat and waited to see what he had to say. He glanced over his shoulder, then shut the door, which put me on instant alert.

"What's wrong?" I asked, sitting up straighter.

"Should ask you that," he said. "Any reason your house is all closed up? Or why you're suddenly home more than you're at the clubhouse?"

Shit. "Why are you so interested in my house?"

Smooth. Real smooth, asshole. Not going to raise his suspicions at all. It was like I was new to this. My fingers twitched, thankfully where the fucker couldn't see them. He'd have honed in on that small tell and kept digging.

"Just seems odd is all. People are talking."

"Maybe I like my solitude? Between the shit with Samurai and now Phantom bringing home a family, there's a lot going on. I have a feeling trouble is going to follow that woman and those kids."

He nodded. "Could be. This job…"

I folded my arms and waited for him to continue.

"It can be hard, especially when you don't have someone in your life other than your brothers," Cinder said. "I was there once. For a long-ass time. Fought my attraction to Meg, thinking I didn't need her, or that she'd be better off without me. Truth is, she gave my life some balance. This club was everything to me, and I see you traveling that same path."

"Thought that was why you picked me," I said.

He leaned in, his voice dropping. "I picked you because of who you are. You think Wire was the first person to go digging into your past? And yes, I'm aware of what he found. I still have connections and get pinged whenever shit pops up on one of our brothers. That includes you."

"You've known all this time that Halden Roberts wasn't my real name?" I asked.

He nodded. "Your daddy was a piece of work. Could tell you weren't like him. However, you have his drive and commitment. You don't mind getting your hands dirty. The difference is that you do it to protect others. He did it to line his fucking pockets and gain power."

"Not sure I know what to say to that."

"When I decided you would replace me as President of this club, I put a lot of thought into it. You care about the people here. To the point, you put this club above your own happiness. I've watched you since I stepped down. The more the mantle of President settles on your shoulders, the more withdrawn you become. You don't joke with your brothers as much as you used to. Don't fuck the club whores from what I've seen, and you're more... solemn." He ran a hand down his beard. "I sometimes wonder if I made a mistake. You're changing, Charming, and not in a good way."

"I have priorities outside the club," I said. "I don't eat, breathe, and sleep all things Devil's Boneyard. Is the club important to me? Of course. Would I die for every man, woman, and child here? Yep. There's just a lot of shit weighing on me right now. As happy as I am for Phantom, I really didn't need the extra drama."

He scratched at his jaw and looked away before piercing me with his gaze again. Man might be aging, but I still wouldn't want to meet him in a dark alley. I knew he'd still kick the shit out of someone.

"You're clearly hiding something. From me and

the club. Eventually, it's going to come out. I'm guessing you have your reasons. Just remember this, Charming. We're a family here. We look out for each other. Whatever you're battling, you don't have to do it alone. If it has to do with your past, then talk to the club. They won't hold it against you. You're probably worried since you've essentially lied to them all these years, but you'd be surprised how many will understand."

He said he'd been pinged when Wire went digging into my past. How much did his people tell him? I leaned forward. "Exactly what do you know about what Wire was doing?"

He stared at me silently, not saying a word. Fucking hell. I'd be willing to bet the bastard had it all figured out. Maybe not everything. He possibly suspected Dakota was at my house, if he'd learned Romeo Strayer was married to her. The question was whether he knew who she was.

"For now, I'm going to pretend I don't know your real name. Have no knowledge of Wire accessing your information. Certainly know nothing of a *marriage* taking place." He stood and headed for the door. "But, Charming, this shit won't end well if you try tackling it on your own."

"I'm not," I admitted. "I have help, just not from within the club. Dakota…"

He faced me fully and waited.

"She's my wife. Yes, I've hidden her at the house. No, I don't want the club to see her or know of her existence right now. It's not safe. Not for her, and not for the rest of us. No one can know her location. Except now, other than me, three people do. That's three too many."

"Club hasn't seen you with anyone special. This

a marriage of convenience to save some poor damsel?" he asked.

"I met her over a month ago. And no, it's an actual marriage. This can't leave this room, Cinder. You don't know the kind of trouble coming for her. They found out where she was living, and she came to me for help. She needs to remain hidden."

"Sounds like more than three people know." He smirked. "Otherwise, she wouldn't have made it through the gates and to your house."

"Fine. The prospects know."

"I'll keep your secret. You know I'd never do anything to endanger a woman. Won't even tell Meg. Love her to death, but I know damn well she'd go running off at the mouth to the other old ladies. When you're ready, tell everyone about your wife. If you need me to help keep her safe, call me. I may be old, but I'm not dead yet."

"Thanks, Cinder."

He left, and I leaned back in the chair again, contemplating everything he'd said. I'd had no idea he'd been aware of my true identity all this time. And if he had my name flagged, what else did he have on the members of the club?

With six people being aware of Dakota and her current location, excluding myself and her brother, I worried it would only be a matter of time before the Cartel came for her. I pulled out my phone and checked for anything new from Specter. Not a damn thing. I had no idea where he was or what he was doing. I knew he loved his sister, which meant he'd want to fix this mess. Apparently not by giving them back the woman he'd taken.

I tried to get my head back into my work, but it was useless. I spent the rest of my time playing a damn game on my phone while I waited for Church. It took my mind off things for a short while. Sooner or later, something had to give. Cinder was right about one thing. This job was stressful as fuck, and it wore you down. I wasn't as carefree as I'd been before because I now worried twice as much as I had previously.

My phone chimed with a message from Scratch, one he'd sent to the entire club. *Church in ten.*

I gathered my things, grabbed a fresh beer, and went into Church to wait on everyone. If nothing else, I'd try to give them enough information that they'd leave me in peace a while longer. Last thing I wanted was them trying to peek into my damn windows. Dakota had been awesome about not trying to look out, but I knew it was tempting. I hated having her on lockdown. There were only so many things we could do together to prepare for the baby, not to mention I wanted to get her an appointment with a local doctor.

One day at a time. That's the best I could do for now.

When everyone had filed in, I decided to just drop the bomb on them. At least, the one I could share at the moment.

"There's something you need to know." I scanned the men at the table. "About my true name."

"You've been Charming as long as most of us have known you. We don't care about the name your parents gave you," Stripes said.

"Yeah, well… you might. Especially, you, Stripes. I ran from my past long before I came here. Changed my name years before there was ever a Charming." I blew out a breath. "The name on my birth certificate is Romeo Halden Strayer."

Stripes' brow furrowed. "Strayer?"

I nodded. "Son of Yuri Strayer, of Los Angeles."

Stripes growled and looked away. I knew he was putting the pieces together. The others looked confused as fuck. Didn't blame them. The name wouldn't mean shit to most, if not all the others.

"My father was Bratva," I said. "When I was seventeen, I ran from that life. Didn't want any part of it. Faked my death, created a new identity, and I've never once looked back."

Stripes snarled, much like the large cat he'd been named for. "Why bring this up now?"

"Because Wire decided to resurrect Romeo Strayer. I asked for some help with a personal matter. That was his solution. Not sure I agree with it, but it's too late now. If the Bratva is watching for that name, it won't be long before they come for me. I have no idea what sort of welcome I'd receive. Been too long since I spoke to anyone I knew back then. Could be nothing comes of it. Or they could want my head on a platter."

"Shit," Havoc muttered. "You're fucking Bratva? Seriously?"

I shrugged a shoulder. "By blood? Yes. By choice? Fuck no."

As my brothers started to murmur amongst themselves, and cast me a few dark looks, I had a feeling it was about to be a long day. So much for getting out of Church quickly.

Chapter Seven

Dakota

He'd said Church would only last thirty minutes to an hour. Maybe it would. That still meant he'd be gone until almost one in the afternoon, since he said Church was at noon. I hadn't counted on him leaving this morning, then not returning. If I'd known he wouldn't be back after greeting the new woman and children, I might not have pushed him out the door as quickly as I did. Being alone had never bothered me before. Of course, I'd also had the freedom to come and go as I pleased. Being stuck in the house, unable to even look out the windows, was beyond miserable.

I couldn't call my brother since my phone was now gone. I didn't dare use the house phone. Since Charming had gone to the trouble to get a burner from another state to reach out to Specter, I figured that meant the landline wasn't secure enough. Although my brother was still texting Charming on his regular mobile. I didn't know why. Wouldn't that be just as dangerous as making calls to that phone? None of it made sense to me. Then again, I knew little about technology, or the way my brother operated. He could be using some sort of code to text Charming, one that only the two of them would understand.

While I understood why Charming didn't want me leaving the house, I really hated it. The times he left, I wanted to be by his side. His club had no idea who I was, or that I even existed. Except the prospects, and they could only come by so often before people would get suspicious. As it was, the club had come knocking at the door multiple times. He always stepped outside to greet them and refused to let anyone inside. They had to find it odd.

I opened the Word Search puzzle book he'd gotten for me and tried to focus. I found a few words, then my mind wandered. The baby's room was about as finished as we could make it without being able to leave the house to shop. I refused to furnish everything from the Internet. Which meant I'd started on the rest of the house. Charming had told me to change whatever I wanted. He had blinds over every window, but nothing else. So, I'd ordered some curtains for the bedroom and living room. A valence was now over the kitchen window above the sink. Anything else would have to wait, or I'd have to give up on ever having freedom again.

A knock sounded at the door, and I tensed, staring at it. Someone jiggled the doorknob and knocked again. I held my breath, not daring to move an inch. Who was out there? Weren't they all going to Church? Could it be one of the women or kids? What if they needed help?

"I think it's weird," a woman's voice said.

"Maybe he wants some privacy," another woman said. "I told you it was a bad idea to sneak in while all the guys were occupied. If Charming finds out..."

They knocked again. Were they going to keep trying to get into the house? Why wouldn't they give up? Clearly, they knew Charming wasn't here, which meant they had to think someone else was living in the house with him. He hadn't fooled his club as much as he'd thought.

"You don't think he's shacking up with some woman, do you? Any of the club whores go missing lately?" the first one asked.

My eyes went wide. Why the hell would they think Charming had a club whore in his house? He'd said he hadn't been with those women in a while, and I'd believed him. Did they know something about my husband that I didn't?

No. I wouldn't jump to conclusions. If he'd never had a serious relationship, then why would the ladies think he had a girlfriend in the house? Much less a wife. Oh God. The club wouldn't take this well, would they? Not only had Charming kept me a secret, but we were technically married, and having a baby! I didn't know what would happen if his brothers turned against him. He might be President, but I had a feeling they could still get rid of him. Either by tossing him from the club, or in a more permanent way.

I needed to talk to my brother. Whatever was holding him back, I needed this situation fixed immediately. It wasn't fair to Charming, or to me. At this rate, I worried I'd be stuck inside until it was time to give birth. That would certainly be an interesting conversation to have with the club, or the doctor, for that matter.

The doorknob rattled again. "When did he start locking the house? And all the blinds are closed. He's always had an open door policy."

"Maybe he's going through something right now," the second woman said. "Instead of trying to break into his house, why don't we just ask if he needs help with anything?"

"Fine. I still don't like it. I feel like he's hiding something, or someone. We should go ask Jordan. Havoc knows everything, which means she does too."

I heard them walk away and my stomach cramped. Trouble wasn't just coming for me anymore. It looked like the club was going to come for Charming if he didn't speak up soon about what was going on. I'd not wanted this. When I'd come to him for help, I'd never once thought he'd keep the club in the dark. It wasn't good for any of us.

A few hours passed, and a knot had lodged in my stomach. Every sound had me jumping. I couldn't relax, no matter how hard I tried. My stomach grumbled, but I didn't dare go make lunch. If those women came back, they'd hear me and know someone else was living here.

Mostly, I stared at the clock, wishing the minutes would pass faster. I'd never been the type to rely on a guy. Well, not more than my brother forced me to. Specter had a way about him that made you agree with what he was saying, even if you didn't want to. Which is why he'd paid for my car, covered my health and car insurance, and until I'd run away, he'd put money into my account every month.

Now I wasn't just his little sister. I was also Charming's wife, and soon to be a mother. My life had changed so much in so little time. Sometimes, it felt a little surreal. I'd wake up and wonder if I'd dreamed it all, only to realize this was my new normal. And frankly, it kind of sucked. At least the part where I couldn't enjoy being the President's wife and meet the club, make new friends… leave the damn house.

A sound from the kitchen had me setting aside my book and hurrying in that direction. Just as I crossed the threshold, the door to the backyard swung open, and a man stepped into the house. I pressed my fingers to my mouth so I wouldn't scream. He had on a Devil's Boneyard cut, so I didn't think he'd hurt me. The way he assessed me said he wasn't surprised to find me in Charming's house.

Cinder was stitched on his cut. The man looked to be in his sixties or seventies. While there was a hardness to him, I didn't get a menacing vibe.

"Won't hurt you," he said. "Never thought Charming would get married."

"You know who I am?" I asked, letting my hand fall to my side.

"Know you're his wife. And you're in trouble, so he's decided it's safer if no one knows you're here. I understand where he's coming from. If it were my Meg in trouble, I might be tempted to hide her too."

"Those women who were outside a while ago…"

He smiled. "Clarity is the VP's woman and Janessa was with her. She's with Irish. They're concerned because Charming isn't acting like himself. I'll have a talk with them. Not sure how long he can hold them back. Sooner or later, someone will get nosy enough to get into the house. I'm not the only one with a key. Havoc has one too."

I wasn't sure how I felt about that. Anyone could just walk in? Why hadn't Charming told me? It would have been nice to be prepared for an unexpected visit. Maybe then I wouldn't have been frightened.

"It's nice to see a face other than my own and Charming's. I've never been stuck inside for so long before, and it's making me a little crazy."

"Since I'm aware of your existence, and it seems the prospects are as well, maybe we can work out something with Charming so you can get some conversation with someone other than him. But I already told him, when all this comes out, I'm going to act like I had no fucking clue what was going on. This is his circus. He can deal with the fallout."

I worried at my lip. "How bad will it be?"

"Depends. He's lying to the club, but then, he's been doing that from the start. The fact he came clean about who he truly is might help soften the blow when they find out he's been hiding a wife too."

I pressed a hand to my belly. "A pregnant one. I can't even go see the doctor right now."

Cinder leaned against the side of the fridge. "That could be a problem. You have prenatal vitamins? Any special appointments coming up?"

"I have vitamins. I was supposed to hear the heartbeat, but I had to leave town. I haven't even called my doctor. They can't reach me since they don't have the number here."

"Any idea what's going on with your brother?" he asked. "And yes, I'm aware of who you are. Charming didn't have to tell me. Being old has some advantages, like being smarter than people give you credit for."

Was there anything the man didn't know? I'd thought it might be a problem, Charming keeping me hidden away. He seemed to think he could handle it, but the stress would get to him, eventually. I didn't know how he was balancing everything.

"Specter is in trouble with the Cartel. That's all I know. Something about him killing someone important and the man's wife is now missing. I'm sure my brother took her to keep her safe, but now the Cartel wants her back. They're willing to use me as a bargaining chip."

Cinder hung his head. "Stupid sons of bitches. Those two are going to try fixing this on their own. Or rather, your husband seems to be content to sit on his ass while Specter does fuck all on his end. If you're waiting on either of them to save you, I have a feeling you'll be in this house a long-ass time. That man of yours has connections if he'd only reach out to them."

I had a feeling he meant the Russian Mafia ties I'd recently learned about. I knew why Charming wasn't calling anyone. He'd wanted to remain dead to those people, and because of me, they now knew he was still alive. He worried they'd come for him and put me at even more risk than I already was.

"There's not much I can do. I don't have any skills that would get me out of this," I pointed out. "Charming is just being overly cautious. He doesn't want those men to find me, especially since I'm carrying his child. I can't blame him. None of this is his fault. That lies solely at my brother's feet."

"We can agree on that much."

"If you're here, does that mean Church is over?" I asked.

"It is. Your husband should be here soon. I'm sure he got caught on his way out. The old ladies aren't the only nosy ones around here."

"If the Cartel thinks I'm in Las Vegas getting married, wouldn't it be safe for me to come out of hiding? At least inside the compound?" I asked.

"I would think so, but that's not up to me. Talk to Charming. Let him know you need human interaction, other than just him. Maybe he can work something out. I may not agree completely with how he's handling things, but you're his wife and he's my President. Might have been my title once upon a time, but I stepped down. I don't have the right to say what you can or can't do."

"I'll try talking to him. I don't think it will do any good, though. He's incredibly stubborn."

Cinder laughed. "You got that right. Then again, I think all of us are, in one way or another. There's another thing we have in common. When we claim a woman, we're all in. There's nothing we won't do for our family. Even if you think he's being unreasonable, or an outright jackass, he's doing what he thinks is best. If he lost you, he'd probably fall apart. Wouldn't show it. He's too tough for that. Doesn't mean he wouldn't be a wreck inside."

"I don't plan on going anywhere. Not willingly anyway."

He nodded. "I figured as much. Not too many women would agree to be confined the way you have. Either you're scared shitless, or you're content being with Charming. Not sure I'd go so far as to call it love, since the two of you haven't known each other very long, but I think you could get there. Both of you."

I pulled out a kitchen chair and sat. "You think so? That he'd love me someday?"

Cinder smiled. "Honey, that boy is already falling, if he isn't all the way in love already. He wouldn't go to so much trouble, or worry this much, over someone who didn't matter. And before you ask, it has nothing to do with the baby. Little birdie tells me he's been searching for you, long before you came here."

"He mentioned it to me."

"Give him time. He'll tell you how he feels when he's ready."

I nodded. "I'm used to stubborn alpha men. Charming isn't much different from my brother. I think that's the only reason Specter hasn't thrown a fit. He wasn't overly thrilled that Charming was the father of my baby. Of course, he didn't like the fact I hadn't told him I was pregnant either. He discovered it through insurance paperwork, of all things."

"You'll always be his baby sister, no matter how old you get. Even when your little one arrives, he won't see you any different."

"Well, that's comforting." I shook my head. "Do you want some coffee or tea?"

Cinder moved closer and sat at the table. "Coffee

would be good. Have a feeling your man might need some when he gets home. Saw him down at least two beers during Church, and saw one in his office beforehand."

"Is that not normal? The night we met, I think he had about six or seven."

"Depends. Usually he drinks to let loose, or when he's more stressed than usual. I'm betting it's the latter reason this time."

"Maybe I shouldn't have come here. I'm only causing trouble for him."

"What the fuck did you just say?"

I gasped and turned, seeing Charming in the doorway. "I didn't hear you come in."

"Clearly, or that stupid shit wouldn't have come out of your mouth. Is that what you think? That you're a burden?"

I heard Cinder's chair creak and saw him lean back and fold his arms. Great. It seemed I'd really stepped in it this time, and the ex-President wouldn't help me out.

* * *

Charming

I couldn't believe Dakota thought for one second I would wish her away, or our child. If she hadn't shown up in town and called me, I'd have kept searching for her. Wouldn't have stopped until I had her by my side. Just took me a little too long to realize that's where she belonged. If I'd have been smart, I'd have convinced her to come home with me when we first met. I'd known then she was different.

If Cinder weren't sitting at the table, I'd put her over my damn knee and spank her ass. I clenched and unclenched my fists. Cinder stood. I'd thought maybe he'd read the room and take the fuck off. Nope. Bastard came over and placed a hand on my shoulder.

"She's concerned about you, much like you are about her. Your woman didn't mean that in quite the context you took it. Everyone can see the strain is putting you on edge. Even your brothers and their women, who have no clue what's going on, can tell that things aren't right with you." Cinder patted my back. "You need more of a break from the house, and she needs someone else to talk to."

"That what you want, Dakota? Me to be gone more?" I asked.

She slowly shook her head. "I enjoy spending time with you, Ha… I mean, Charming. But you have things to do, a club that needs you. You can't stay here all day every day, and I need more human interaction."

"Since I already know about her, and so do the prospects, I have a proposal for you," Cinder said. "We can say there's a special project at your house. Super secret, but you'll share when you're ready. I can 'help' and so can the prospects. It will free up more of your time, and keep your woman occupied when you can't be here."

"I don't know how long this will drag on," I admitted. "Specter isn't very forthcoming with how things are progressing. All I know is that I can't lose Dakota. If that means she stays in this house, then so be it."

"I thought you were going to deny any knowledge of me," Dakota said. "You can't do that if the club knows you've been coming here."

Cinder waved her off. "The two of you clearly need more support than you're receiving from Specter. Not a lot I can do without telling more people, so I'll help any way I can. If that means I come visit you for a bit, then that's what I'll do."

I saw the hope shining in Dakota's eyes and knew I wouldn't be able to say no. She'd handled all this surprisingly well. If our roles had been reversed, I'd have most likely been a total dick about it.

"All right, but let's make this look legit, so the club will back off a little. Wire knows about her, so it's possible Shade will figure it out. Might as well tell him. And it gives Dakota another person to talk to." I ran a hand over my head. "The attic could be turned into some extra rooms, in case we need the space later. The prospects could bring in supplies like subflooring and extra insulation. You or Shade could stop by to supervise when I'm not around. Not sure that qualifies for a secret project, but we can say I don't want people in the house during construction."

Cinder nodded. "That could work."

"You'd do all that for me?" Dakota asked.

"And that's my cue," Cinder said. "I'm going to step out back for a few minutes. If you don't come get me, I'll assume the two of you want to be alone."

Once he'd left, I went to Dakota and kneeled in front of her, taking her hands in mine. "Sweetheart, haven't you figured it out yet? There's not a damn thing I wouldn't do for you, as long as it doesn't put you in harm's way. You're my wife, Dakota. My old lady. The mother of my child. Most importantly, you're the woman I think about every single day, even when we were a quick fling. I couldn't get you out of my head."

She pulled her hands from mine and threw her arms around my neck. "I thought about you every day too."

I chuckled. "I also have a confession to make. I didn't delete our video. Watched it every night and jacked off to it."

She gasped and drew back, her cheeks turning pink. "You didn't!"

"I most certainly did. Maybe we can make another one. That way, whenever you're pissed at me, I have plenty of homemade porn featuring my favorite girl. I don't even want to yank one out thinking of anyone but you." I pressed my lips to hers. "In case you haven't figured it out, I'm crazy about you, Dakota. You own me."

"What happens if my brother refuses to give the woman back to the Cartel? They'll never stop looking for me. I can't live like this forever, Halden. It's making me feel like I'm losing my mind, and I've only been in this house for a week. What happens next week? Or next month?"

"One day at a time, sweetheart. I'll try to get in touch with your brother tonight. Hopefully, he has some good news for us. I'll also check with Wire and see if he can tell whether the Cartel took the bait and headed to Las Vegas."

She nodded. "And you can find out if anyone from your past is looking for you."

"Yeah. I should handle that now and not later. I'll tell Cinder to come in and visit with you for a little while before I make a few calls."

She kissed me, holding me close. "Be careful. You might not want to lose me, but I don't want to lose you either. It scares me that the Mafia could be searching for you."

"Always, sweetheart. I have two precious people to come home to every night. Well, technically, one is still hidden inside you, but the two of you are my family. I will fight my way back to you every single time. Doesn't matter what they do to me. I'm coming home at the end of the day."

"Don't make me promises you can't keep."

I kissed her forehead and went to get Cinder. While she poured him a cup of coffee, the ex-President and I shared a look. He gave me a brief nod and I went to the bedroom to make my calls. Although, depending on what Wire had to say, maybe I'd only be making one phone call.

I dialed his number and paced while I waited for the line to connect.

"Are you suddenly psychic?" Wire asked, instead of a typical hello.

"No, why?"

"Just about to call you. I may have stirred up more shit than I realized when I brought back Romeo Strayer. The men after your wife took the bait. They ran to Las Vegas and started searching. Unfortunately, so did a few men from the Bratva based in Los Angeles."

"So they're hunting me," I murmured.

"Not sure yet if it's a bad thing. However, the Cartel ran into them. When they realized the two people they wanted were married to one another, they teamed up to locate you and your wife. There're some texts and emails between a few of them."

"Motherfucker. Wire, this is bad. Like, really fucking bad. If they both come here, I don't have enough manpower to go up against them. It's not just Dakota I need to protect. I have other women and kids who rely on me to keep them safe."

"I know. I'm watching to see what move they make next. So far, they're remaining in Nevada. I didn't leave much of a paper trail for them to follow, so they're spinning their wheels right now. If they have anyone on staff like me, it's only a matter of time before they track you down."

I smiled faintly. "Thought there wasn't anyone like you, except maybe your woman."

"You know what I mean. Besides, there are kids out there wreaking more havoc than I ever did. They're faster, smarter, and by the time they're adults, they could very well be far better than I ever was."

Now there was a horrifying thought. "You run across any, let me know. I'd rather recruit them than end up on the wrong side of their skills, if you know what I mean."

"I do, and I will. Although, the Dixie Reapers and a few other clubs might want a shot at them too."

"As long as they're an ally, I don't care what club they work with."

"I wish I knew what to tell you. I haven't heard from Specter since he asked me to track down his sister. Maybe he can resolve at least one of your issues. As for your father's people… That one's on me. If you need backup, I'll let the club know and we'll send a few people your way." Wire sighed. "It's your call on how you handle things but keeping your woman on lockdown until this is all resolved might not be the way to go. If I tried that with Lavender, I'd probably wake up with my balls locked in a cage. Or worse. My accounts drained."

I snorted. "She loves you and you know it. Things with Dakota are still too new. I walked in tonight listening to her talk about how she should probably leave. She feels bad for bringing trouble here. Honestly, I'd have gone after her if she hadn't come to me on her own. I think she understands that now."

"Wish I had better news. I'll do what I can on my end. If I see movement heading your way, I'll let Venom and Torch know. They're aware you might need assistance and the club is on standby. I'm sure the Devil's Fury and Reckless Kings would help too."

"Let's hope it doesn't come to that." I sat on the edge of the bed. "I'm going to try to reach Specter. I have no idea why he's dragging his damn feet on this. Thanks, Wire."

I disconnected the call and took a moment to gather my thoughts. Pulling out the burner phone, I called Specter. When he didn't answer, I called again. And again. By the fourth time, the fucker finally answered, sounding out of breath.

"What the fuck?" he demanded.

"Hello to you too, brother." He cursed, and I heard rustling. Ah. So that's why he hadn't answered. "If the other side of that bed contains the woman the Cartel wants, and your sister is still a target because you're getting your dick wet, assassin or not, I'm going to nail your ass to the fucking wall. That's my wife and kid in trouble, thanks to you."

"Things are complicated," Specter said.

"Yeah. Sounds like it. Want to tell your sister how *complicated* it is?"

"I need a little more time," he said.

"It's been a week, Specter, since she had to run from her damn home, scared shitless. But this has been going on longer, hasn't it? How long, exactly, since you ran off with the Cartel's woman?"

He sighed. "A month. For the record, she's not the one in my bed. Her husband beat the hell out of her. She was in recovery at a secret medical facility. It will be another few weeks before she's able to walk on her own, maybe longer. I can't hand her over to them, Charming. I'm sorry."

"I don't give a shit if she goes back to them. What I need you to do is pull your head out of your ass, or your dick out of whomever is in your bed and find a way to make the Cartel back off. Or at the very least, get them to stop looking for your sister."

He growled a little. "Wait a fucking minute. You said wife. When the hell did the two of you get married?"

"Wire did his computer shit and married us. Under my real name, which means they can't trace her here yet. It's only a matter of time before my identity comes to light."

"Something tells me I need to know who you really are," he said.

"Romeo Halden Strayer, deceased son of Yuri Strayer, previously of Los Angeles."

"Yuri Strayer," he mumbled. "I know that name."

I waited a moment while he pieced it all together. Then I heard his fist meet the wall and the woman with him shrieked like a damn banshee.

"Motherfucker! You're Goddamn Bratva? What the fuck, Charming?"

"I'm not. Didn't want that life. Which is why I was dead until Wire brought me back to life. He thought it would offer your sister another layer of protection. Now we have the Cartel looking for her, the Bratva searching for me, and they've decided to work together since Dakota and I are married."

"Shit." I heard him pacing. "Fine. I'll figure something out, but I seriously need some time. This situation… I can't go in guns blazing. There's too many people, including some innocents like the lady I saved."

"I need her safe, Specter. I don't care how it's done. Wipe out the entire fucking Cartel if you have to. It's not fair to Dakota. She's an innocent too, in case you forgot."

"I'll call back in a week. It will take me that long, at least, to figure out what I'm going to do. Just try to keep her contained."

I snorted and ended the call. Great. That went absolutely nowhere. The only thing I learned was that Dakota wasn't the only one in trouble. Now I was too. Which meant I needed to talk to the club. Not about Dakota. Not yet. But they needed to know I had trouble coming for me. My past had finally caught up, and I had a feeling it was going to chew me up and spit me out. Or at least try.

Good thing I'd already confessed about my true identity. Otherwise, this would be even worse.

Chapter Eight

Dakota
Three Months Later

I'd noticed a slight bump under my nightgown this morning and couldn't seem to stop rubbing my belly. Thankfully, the morning sickness had stopped, and I'd started putting on weight. At only nineteen weeks, I didn't think I'd be showing yet. The doctor Charming had smuggled in last month had said each pregnancy was different. Some women showed sooner than others, just like some had morning sickness, while others didn't. Sadly, I hadn't been able to hear the heartbeat or see my baby yet. It felt like I was missing out on so much with this pregnancy. What should have been an incredible adventure had been dimmed because of being a prisoner in my own home.

The Bratva were getting closer. Too close. Last Charming had heard, they were heading to Florida. Charming didn't talk about it much, not wanting to stress me out, but I knew that had to mean they'd found him. If they didn't know his current location, why travel all the way here? Which meant the Cartel was on their heels since they'd been working together.

Eventually, Charming and I would have a fight on our hands. Or rather, he would. There wasn't much I could do. Hell, his club still didn't know about me. Well, most didn't. Cinder and Shade could visit me, and same for the prospects. Other than my doctor, I hadn't spoken to another woman in months. And even that visit had been far too brief.

Things needed to change. I felt like I was going to lose my mind. I'd started chewing my nails, twirling my hair, and a few other bad habits. It didn't help that at least once a week someone tried to peek into the house or attempted to come through the front door. The catty comments from the women who came to check on Charming were getting to me. But those weren't as bad as when they talked about setting him up with someone. No one knew he was married, which meant the ladies wanted to see him settled. And apparently the club whores were still attempting to sink their claws into him, even though he hadn't paid them any attention long before I came here. Unless the ladies speaking outside the door were hoping to get a rise out of me. I could tell they suspected Charming was hiding a person in his home, and it was making them feel desperate to solve the riddle.

As badly as he wanted to keep me hidden away, I wasn't certain anymore that it was the right thing to do. Clearly, the Cartel would be coming here. If they suspected I was already at the compound, what would it hurt for me to get out a little? Even just getting to walk outside and feel the sun on my face would be amazing. I didn't care if I went into town. Well, I did, a little. However, I'd take whatever freedom I could get.

Charming came up behind me, wrapping his arms around my waist, and kissing the side of my neck. I leaned into him. I didn't know where I'd be right now if it weren't for him. Even when he frustrated me, he was still my rock. My calm in the storm. And the only reason I'd remained somewhat sane during all this nonsense.

He reached up to cup my breast, giving it a slight squeeze. My pregnancy could either make my breasts so tender they hurt to be touched or made them sensitive enough he could make me come just from rubbing my nipples. I never knew which to expect from one day to the next. Since heat started pooling in my belly, I was going to go with this being one of the better days.

"You're always distracting me with sex," I said. "If you aren't careful, I'll think that's the only reason you want me here."

"Nope. Just an added bonus." He lightly bit my shoulder. "What am I distracting you from now?"

I sighed. "Freedom."

He turned me to face him, tilting my chin up. "Sweetheart, I will give you anything and everything your heart desires. But not if it means you could be in harm's way. You know this. We've been over it, many times."

I nodded. "I know, Halden. I was just thinking, since the Bratva know where you are it means the Cartel is probably coming for me. If my location is no longer a secret, why do I have to stay locked up in the house?"

"How about a compromise?"

"I'm listening," I said.

"We can fix a big dinner tonight. Enough to feed several large men. I'll invite over all the officers and explain the situation. If they can come up with a way for you to move about the compound, without fear a sniper could take you out, or someone could get in and kidnap you, then I'll introduce you to the club and you'll be able to roam the compound."

I pressed my forehead to his chest. "Why do I get the feeling this isn't going to go the way I want it to? They're going to side with you, aren't they?"

"Most likely."

His phone buzzed and he answered, putting it on speaker. "Shade, I'm with Dakota and she can hear this conversation."

"Understood," Shade said. "I'm actually calling about Phantom's family. We've got movement.

Samurai wants to leave Phantom out of this one, take down Mason on our own."

"Make it happen. Send Havoc and Scratch for Mason. We'll meet at the location where we solved Grey's problems."

"Got it, Pres. I'll get everyone moving. Meet you there in twenty."

The call ended and Charming hugged me tight. I hated that he needed to leave, but I understood. Even though I wasn't supposed to know club business, since I'd been stuck in the house for months, he'd confided quite a bit in me. I knew all about Phantom's new family and what they'd suffered, and about the man Shade called Mason.

"Go make him suffer," I said. "Anyone who preys on children deserves a painful death."

"I have a little time before I need to leave. Won't take me but five minutes to reach the location. How about I make you feel good first?"

"Really? You think now is the time for that?" I asked.

"Dakota, I never know when I leave if something will happen to me. I promised I'd always come home to you. Doesn't mean I'll necessarily be in one piece. I want every minute with you to count. If that means I fuck you before I walk out the door, then that's what I'll do."

I reached up and tugged on the beard he'd grown out the last few weeks. "Such a sweet talker. No wonder they call you Charming."

He shook his head. "Are you insinuating, yet again, I'm less than charming?"

"Sometimes." I smiled. "Good thing I like you just the way you are."

He lifted me into his arms and carried me back to

the bedroom. "And I like you with fewer clothes on. Wait. That didn't… I like you all the time. I just prefer you without clothes."

"Nice save."

He eased me onto the bed, then caged me between his arms, leaning over me. "You know how much I care about you, Dakota. I might not always say it, but I do try to show you. I'm lying to my club because I refuse to risk your life, even with the men I trust most in the world. You're everything to me, you and our child. You know that, right?"

I nodded and reached up to place my hand on his cheek. "I know, and I feel the same about you."

He brushed his lips across mine, then deepened the kiss. I wrapped my fingers around the back of his neck, wanting to hold on and never let go. The man was downright lethal. One touch… one kiss… and I went up in flames, eager to do whatever he said. I should have felt pathetic, but honestly, no one had ever turned me on the way he did. It felt like a blessing that I'd found him, and that he wanted to keep me.

So many times these past months I'd wanted to tell him I loved him. Something always held me back. He said he liked me. Cared about me. I had to wonder if he'd ever feel anything stronger. Was I doomed to be in love with a man who couldn't feel the same about me? It was a depressing thought, but I was willing to roll the dice and see where this road took me. I'd rather have a part of Charming's heart than none at all. He'd promised he'd be faithful. As long as he gave me that, and I knew he felt at least a little something for me, then maybe deeper feelings would grow over time.

He lifted off me and started stripping my clothes from my body. I reached for him, easing his cut off his shoulders. He took it from me, folding it and placing it on the dresser. He'd given me a property cut, but I hadn't had a reason to wear it. So it hung in the closet, where it would remain until I could leave the house.

Charming reached behind his neck and grabbed the back of his shirt, tugging it over his head. I sighed, thinking that was one of the sexiest moves I'd ever seen. He made quick work of the rest of his clothes, then dropped to his knees beside the bed. Yanking me closer, he spread my thighs and gave my pussy a lick.

I shrieked and tried to close my legs, but he wouldn't let me.

"No! This is mine. *You're* mine." He glared up at me. "Fight me and I will spank your ass, Dakota."

I gasped, my eyes going wide. "You wouldn't."

"Honey, I've already told you this is the prettiest pussy I've ever seen. Not to mention you taste sweet. Get over the embarrassment. It feels good when I put my mouth on you, doesn't it?"

I nodded, begrudgingly. He was right, though. I felt self-conscious when he was down there. Other than Charming and the doctor, no one had ever seen that part of me. And until him, I certainly hadn't had anyone put their mouth there. It was the one thing I hadn't adjusted to over the months we'd been together.

"I can't help it," I admitted. "It just feels… uncomfortable."

He sighed and came up over my body, pressing me into the mattress. "Then I won't do it anymore. Not until we've been together a little longer, or you tell me you want to try again. I just really love pleasing you, and you come so hard when I lick your pussy."

"I'll get there. Maybe." I gave him a hesitant smile. "Did I ruin the mood?"

"No." He kissed me. "Never."

Charming got up, only to stretch out on his back.

He reached for me, helping me straddle him. Placing his thumb on my clit, he rubbed in small circles until I was so wet I knew I was making a mess of both of us. I braced my hands on his chest and rocked my hips.

"So beautiful," he murmured. He bucked his hips, and I felt his cock against my ass. "Watching you makes me so damn hard."

"I'm close," I said, feeling the pleasure flow through me. He worked my clit faster and I gasped as I came, a cry lodged in my throat.

"Ride me, sweetheart. Get yourself off and let me see you come again. Prettiest sight I've ever seen."

I wrapped my fingers around his cock and lowered myself onto his shaft. I felt the slight burn as he stretched me wide and tipped my head back, enjoying the sensation. He kept working my clit as I moved, lifting nearly all the way off him, then taking him inside me again.

"That's it." His thumb rubbed faster and harder. "Show me how much you love having my cock inside you."

"Halden, I... I can't..." My hips moved faster but it wasn't enough. Even though I'd already had one orgasm, the next remained out of reach. He flipped us and drove into me. "Yes! More! Don't stop."

I clung to him, my nails biting into his shoulders. Sweat slicked his skin as he thrust into me faster. I hooked my legs over his, trying to spread my thighs farther. Charming adjusted, shifting until his cock hit just the right spot.

"Oh, God! Halden! It's too much. I can't... can't..." I screamed, my body bowing as I came, my release soaking the bedding. It only took two more strokes before I felt him filling me up with his cum.

Charming rolled to his side, staying buried

inside me. I cuddled close to him and breathed in his scent.

"Be careful," I murmured. "Come back home to me."

He kissed the top of my head. "I will. I can stay another minute, then I need to go. Can't leave them waiting."

I nodded and held on tighter. This was the part I dreaded. When he left and he wasn't staying inside the compound, I always worried he'd get hurt, or worse... someone would kill him. Not being able to leave probably drove my fear. Even though I wouldn't be able to protect him, knowing I couldn't even go to his side if something happened absolutely gutted me.

He rolled out of bed and I heard him pulling on his clothes. I cracked my eyes open as he walked out of the room.

"Love you, Halden," I whispered. I thought I saw him hesitate, but decided I was wrong when he kept going without saying a word. I only hoped he was right, and he'd be home, safe and sound, soon enough. If anything happened to him, I didn't know how I'd keep going. My world would end.

* * *

Charming

The old barn was actually part of our property now. The club had purchased the land, home, and structure behind our compound. I'd contemplated taking in most of the land, but I liked the buffer between civilians and our fence line. Plus, I had a few ideas for this place. Or rather, for the house. The barn had come in handy twice now.

I eyed the men around me before studying the asshole they'd hauled to the barn. Mason Reynolds IV.

He clearly liked dominating kids because no adult would ever bow to him. The fucker kept whining and blubbering. I'd seen women with bigger balls than this guy.

The barn doors flew open and I turned, seeing Phantom and Drifter walk in.

"Who the hell told you where we were?" I demanded. The entire point of all this had been to handle the matter without Phantom. He had a family now. A wife and three kids who needed him. Samurai had worried about his cousin handling Mason, and I'd agreed.

Shade cleared his throat. "I did. As nice as our gesture was, Phantom needed to be here for this, and Drifter wants a chance to defend his daughter."

"We'll talk later," I said, glaring at the offender. Fucker didn't even have the decency to look repentant.

Phantom and Drifter came closer. We'd strung Mason from the rafters, his toes lightly scraping the ground as he tried to find purchase. Havoc, Scratch, and Stripes had worked him over, bruising his ribs and torso. They'd wanted the man to suffer and we'd been dragging this out. The man had pissed himself twice and a puddle had formed underneath him. I knew everyone wanted a shot at the bastard.

"Know who I am?" Phantom asked.

"The filthy biker who took my precious boy."

I mentally winced. He really shouldn't have said that. Phantom was already protective of his new family. If Mason thought he'd been in pain before, things were about to get a lot worse for him. And the way Drifter eyed the motherfucker, he wanted his pound of flesh too.

Samurai stepped up next to Phantom, rage rolling off him. Most likely, it had triggered the way he'd felt when Heather had been molesting him. I wondered if she'd ever called him that. This had to be a nightmare for Samurai, but he was holding it together.

Stripes strolled up next to Mason. "Wrong answer."

"Tie his feet," Phantom said.

I folded my arms and waited to see what he'd do. I could have forced him from the barn, but it wouldn't have been right. If he felt he needed to do this, then I'd let him. I had no idea what he had planned, but Mason was his, for however long he wanted to torture the asshole.

Magnus brought over a length of rope and tied Mason's ankles together. Mason wriggled like a fish on a hook, his whine taking on a new pitch that hurt my damn ears. Good thing there wasn't anyone else around for miles, except the compound.

"I need two things," Phantom said. "Acid. If it was good enough to hurt Charisma, then he can get a sample. He might not have thrown it on her, but he probably would have if he'd thought of it."

"And the second?" I asked.

"I need my kit. It's in my saddlebags."

Shit. If Phantom wanted that kit, things were about to get ugly. I'd seen his work before. Admired it even. I wasn't sure what his woman would think of all this. How was he going to feel if he tortured this guy, then went home to his wife and kids? Would she condone what was happening?

I had a feeling she wouldn't care that Mason had been killed. It was more of a worry about whether or not she wanted Phantom to do it. We'd clean shit up, and hopefully Mason would never be found. But if he was, and there was any bit of evidence tying him to

Phantom, things could go from bad to worse. I didn't want him locked up, not when Charisma and the kids needed him.

Phantom removed his cut and his shirt, handing both off to Stripes. At least he'd been mindful to try and not carry this rapist's blood home to his family. Fucker might be carrying something for all we knew. The kids had checked out, but who knew where he'd put his dick last. Just the thought of him hurting those kids that way made me want to rip him to shreds with my bare hands.

Cinder gave Phantom a thick rubber glove before handing him some acid. I didn't even ask why he'd brought any, or where he'd gotten it. Some things, I'd learned, I just didn't want to know. With the man's background, he had access to shit even I couldn't get my hands on. Although, acid was probably somewhat easy to locate. Hell, even school labs stocked the shit, or they had when I'd been in high school.

"After hearing what happened to your woman, I figured you'd want the fucker to suffer this way. I made sure we were prepared," Cinder said.

The man might no longer be the President of the club, but he still made sure everyone's needs were met. He'd understood what Phantom would want and made sure it was available. Maybe if I hadn't been so focused on Dakota, I'd have thought of it. Then again, Cinder had been the head of this club for a long-ass time. He had big shoes to fill, and I knew it would take time for me to reach his level.

"If I do this, he won't last long. Drifter, I had them bring the kit in for you. Use whatever you want in there. I'll wait." Phantom stepped back, giving his new father-in-law room to work.

Drifter didn't hesitate. He checked out

Phantom's kit and started by yanking Mason's toenails out. He took his time, making the pain last as long as possible. When he'd removed all ten toenails, he started slicing the man. Small, shallow cuts that I knew would hurt like a bitch. He even cut off an ear. When Mason passed out, like the pussy he was, we threw cold water on him. He jolted back to consciousness, and Drifter went at him again.

The crazed look in his eyes said he'd do this all night, until Mason Reynolds IV breathed his last and wouldn't be able to ever hurt another child again. I wondered if I should step in, but Phantom seemed to have it handled.

"You done?" Phantom asked.

Drifter growled and gave a slight nod. "I'll finish him off after you've done your part. That was my daughter you made deaf! My grandson that you touched. Death is too good for you, but I refuse to leave you breathing. They deserve some closure."

Drifter took a few steps back and the rest of us cleared the area around Mason. None of us wanted that acid anywhere near our skin and clothes. Phantom flung the liquid at Mason, aiming for the bits dangling between his legs. The asshole screamed as the acid hit his cock and balls. Phantom eyed the empty container.

"You know, I think I like this stuff," he said.

Cinder snorted. "You would."

I cocked my head and watched the fight slowly drain from Mason. The acid had been a nice touch. Painful. Brutal, in all honesty. And he hadn't died from it, even though I had no doubt he wanted to. "I think we can arrange to keep some of that on hand. Soon as I research how to store it properly."

"You're both fucking crazy," Cinder muttered.

"Did you forget how you earned your name, old

man?" I asked. If anyone in this club was crazy, it was Cinder. And definitely Havoc and his woman, Jordan. Those two were a match made in hell.

Drifter rubbed his hands together before going back to the kit and selecting another weapon. As much as I wanted to say our club would handle it, the guy had just found out he was a father and grandfather, and Mason had hurt Charisma and the boys. No fucking way I'd not let the man have his revenge. If our roles were reversed, I'd want to make the bastard suffer, I'd need to see the light die in his eyes as I claimed his life.

Drifter was like a kid at Christmas. The gleeful look on his face with every shout of pain would have scared most people. But every man in this barn knew exactly how he felt. We'd all been in that position at one time or another. Blood coated our hands and would never wash off. But sometimes, you had to do something horribly wrong, to make something incredibly right. Like giving Mason Reynolds IV a gruesome death to avenge all the children he'd raped, and the torture he'd heaped on Charisma when she'd tried to intervene.

Mason breathed his last only ten minutes later. I pointed to two prospects standing near the barn doors. "You two. Clean this shit up. Drifter, use the bathroom at the clubhouse. Clean up before you see your daughter and grandkids. You look like you starred in a slasher film."

"Not the first blood my cut has worn. Doubt it will be the last." He wasn't the only one. My own cut had its share of blood stains. Even if you couldn't see them, I knew they were there.

"We sure no one else is coming here?" Phantom asked. "No more like this fucker, or anyone searching for him when he goes missing?"

"Already arranged for it to look like Mason found what he wanted and left the country. Wire is on it. He was happy to help. As to the other thing we discussed before… we found some of the boys, and a little extra." Shade scrolled through something on his phone before showing Phantom. He blinked and seemed confused. "One of Mason's friends seems to like both girls and boys, as long as they don't hit puberty. The little girl you see in the photo is four years old. He'd recently purchased her so he could groom her."

"I think I'm going to be sick," Drifter muttered.

"Me too." Phantom looked at the picture again. "She needs a home."

"Exactly!" Shade grinned like a damn lunatic. I knew he was excited to tell Phantom the news, but damn. The look on his face made me want to take a step back. I couldn't tell if he looked like an evil clown, or a maniacal villain. "Think Nova will share her room while we work on your attic space?"

"She's mine?" Phantom asked, looking dumbstruck. How the fucker hadn't seen that coming, I didn't know. The only thing he'd ever wanted was a family. If there was ever a man meant to be a father, it was Phantom. And now he had three children with a fourth arriving anytime. "I don't understand. Did someone already rescue her?"

"She was closer to the Broken Bastards. Someone is on their way here with her. The others we rescued are pretty damaged, not just physically. Mentally. I'm not sure they'll ever live normal lives." Darkness entered Shade's eyes a moment. "The man who had them has been punished and sent straight to hell. Although the devil may not claim him either. The other kids are going to a special place where they can get the care they need."

"It's not just Shade searching now," I said. This particular subject wasn't just close to Phantom's heart. We all fucking hated child predators and would do anything to take them down. "Wire, Lavender, Wizard, and Outlaw are all doing their part. We'll find as many of the kids as we can. For now, that little princess needs your love and attention. I heard Nova wanted a sister. It seems the man upstairs was listening."

We finished up while Phantom went to share his good news with his family. I felt twitchy as hell, being away from the compound, and knowing not many men had been left behind with Dakota and the other old ladies. If anyone had been waiting and watching, now was the time for them to strike. Heaven help anyone who hurt my wife and unborn child. I'd make Mason's death look like child's play. I wouldn't end them the same day I caught them. No. Those motherfuckers would suffer for days, if not weeks. I'd draw it out as long as possible before finally snuffing out their lives.

"If anyone needs me, call or text. I have something I need to do."

I went outside and got on my bike, heading straight back to the compound. When I approached the gates and saw they were wide open, my heart slammed against my ribs. Where the fuck was the other prospect? I'd left one behind to guard the gate, and now the fucker was gone.

A feeling of dread pooled inside me as I rushed home. I barely got the bike turned off and the stand down before I was rushing into the house, gun drawn, only to draw up short. My wife sat at the table with a man I'd thought I'd never see again. One I'd called my friend a long time ago.

"Anatoly," I said.

His eyebrows lifted. "Do you always greet your friends with your weapon trained on them?"

I tucked the gun into my waistband at the small of my back. "Why are you here and where's my Prospect?"

"The guy from the gate? He's fine. We forced him to show us the way to your house, but he'll be returned to his post now that you're here." He snapped his fingers and one of his men stepped forward. "Lev, see that he's returned to the gates. Unharmed."

The man nodded and left by way of the front door. Where the hell had they put Carlos? I'd left him behind because I trusted him the most. And look where that had gotten me. I needed more manpower, clearly.

"Why are you here?" I asked.

"Isn't it obvious? My long-lost friend is not dead as I'd thought. I wanted to come say hello and meet your pretty bride."

I fisted my hands. "Leave Dakota out of this. You hurt her and…"

He lifted a hand. "I would never. She's your wife, which makes her Bratva. Just. Like. You."

I shook my head. "*Nyet*. I'm no longer part of that world, Anatoly. I died for a reason, so I could walk away and start my life over. I never wanted to follow in my father's footsteps."

"And yet you're here, with your hands every bit as dirty as they were before." He smirked. "I've been looking into you and your club."

"We don't hurt women. We might own a strip club, but those women work there of their own free will and they aren't prostituted. How many brothels does the US-based Bratva own now? How many are in Los Angeles?"

"We provide a service," he said. "Sometimes loose ends must be dealt with. At least we make a profit from it."

Dakota covered her mouth with her hand, looking slightly green.

"When my wife throws up on you, just remember you brought it on yourself," I said. "Anyone in this room, whether it's you or your men, harms one hair on her head, and I will end every last one of you. Understood?"

Anatoly nodded. "It seems you're different from your father, after all. You actually care for your woman. Enough to kill for her. I like it."

He smiled and I wanted to bash in his perfectly white teeth. The fucker knew how to get under my skin. After all these years, he could push my buttons like no one else. Bastard.

"I only came to talk, Charming. That's how you're called now, isn't it? As in Prince Charming?" I nodded. My wife snorted and I narrowed my eyes at her. Anatoly laughed, a loud, booming sound that made Dakota flinch. "It seems your wife doesn't agree with your name. Tell me, Mrs. Strayer. Why is it you don't like the name Charming? Did he *charm* the pants off too many ladies?"

"I don't care what he did before we met," she murmured.

"Then what is it? He doesn't seem like the sort to cheat, so I don't think that's why you made that rather indelicate sound," Anatoly said.

"He's more of a caveman than a prince. That's all. First time we met, he slammed a guy's face into a table." Dakota smiled at me. "That was his version of saving me. The guy had been grabbing me, asking for blow jobs, and being rude in general. Charming stepped in and corrected his behavior."

"He's always talked better with his fists," Anatoly said, fingering the bump on the bridge of his nose. I'd put it there by smashing my fist into his face when we were teenagers.

"Again, why are you here?" I asked, folding my arms over my chest.

Anatoly looked to his men. "Leave us. Wait in the car."

They walked out and once the front door shut, Anatoly relaxed. He loosened his tie, unbuttoned the top of his shirt, and even slouched a little in his seat.

"Christ. It's exhausting sometimes." He smiled. "Good to see you, Romeo. Fucking missed you."

Dakota blinked and looked between the two of us. "Um, I'm really confused."

"Dakota, this is Anatoly. He was my best friend growing up. Anatoly, you've already met my wife."

He nodded. "I did. I'm afraid we scared her a bit when we barged in. Had to put on a good show for the men with me. I'm in charge now, over the Los Angeles area. Showing weakness would only get me killed. I couldn't let anyone know why I wanted to find you."

"I'm still waiting to hear that explanation," I reminded him.

"Right. Look, I've missed my friend. When I heard you were alive, it was surreal. I needed to see you. But more importantly, I think you need me right now." He held my gaze. "The Cartel are after your wife. Her brother pissed off the wrong men, and they won't stop until she's in their possession."

"They'll die trying," I said.

He nodded. "I'm aware. I also noticed she's

expecting. Congratulations. Never took you for the family type. Then again, I thought you'd be the one taking over instead of me. Life never works out quite as we plan for it to."

"Are they close?" Dakota asked.

"Yes. If your brother doesn't return the woman they want, then they'll take you instead. And what they have planned for you…" Anatoly sighed. "Even I could never be that brutal, especially with a woman."

"Halden," she said softly standing and coming to me. I wrapped my arms around her, holding her close, wishing I had the right words to say. I could feel her fear, nearly taste it.

"You don't have enough men here," Anatoly said. "And if we could get inside, then the Cartel wouldn't have an issue breaking in. All we had to do was threaten your guard. With a gun pointed at his head, he opened the gates right up."

"Fuck," I muttered. Looked like Carlos wouldn't be patching in after all. In fact, I'd be replacing his ass soon as I could.

"You need more resources, and I think you might be able to help me find what I need as well." Anatoly leaned forward, bracing his arms on the table. "I can help you keep your family safe. All I need in return… is a wife."

Dakota turned to face him. "Are you crazy?"

He smiled. "Yes. But I'm not insane enough to marry a woman from within my organization. Her father or brothers would only be looking for a way to climb higher in the Bratva. That's not what I want. But a tie to a club like yours… now that would be beneficial for everyone."

"Sorry but we don't have anyone old enough, who isn't already attached." I tightened my hold on

Dakota. "And I'm not promising you any of our daughters. Not mine, and not any of my brothers' kids. You're shit out of luck, Anatoly."

"What about a sister?" Dakota asked.

"Go on," Anatoly said. "I'm listening."

"I haven't been introduced to anyone here, but one of them has to have a sister who's single and of age. It wouldn't be right to force her to marry you. I'd never suggest such a thing. However, a meeting could be arranged. A blind date, so to speak," Dakota said. "Would that be enough for you to help Halden keep me safe?"

Anatoly's gaze softened as he stared at my wife. "Yes. That would be enough. If I didn't need to make it look like I was gaining something from all this, I'd offer my help with no strings. I'm afraid things don't work that way in my world, or in your husband's, for that matter."

"Then we have a deal," I said. "I'll find out who might have a willing sister. Just as soon as I fill them in on everything… and tell them I have a pregnant wife."

Anatoly threw back his head and laughed. "Now that's a conversation I'd love to witness. I have a feeling they're not going to be very happy with you."

He wasn't wrong. My club would be hurt. Angry. Probably would feel betrayed. Too late to change any of that. I'd just have to weather the storm and hope I could earn their trust again. I didn't think they'd vote me out over this, not once they met Dakota and saw her cute little baby bump. Didn't mean they wouldn't give me shit about it for months. And I'd let them.

"Will you stay with Dakota if I call Church to talk to my club? I'll call when I'm ready for her. I don't like the idea of her sitting around the clubhouse, especially since the whores are most likely hovering," I said.

His brow furrowed. "I thought you didn't have prostitutes."

I snickered. "That's what we call the women who spread their legs for any biker. They like to party, get fucked, and a few are hoping to snag themselves a property patch. Don't think it will ever happen, but I don't like the word *never*. Soon as I make that claim, someone will decide a club whore is their destined old lady. I'm not sure I could ever understand accepting someone like that as my one and only, but to each his own. Those women are grasping and devious, so watch your back."

He nodded. "Noted. And yes, I'll help keep her safe and bring her to you when you're ready. The building I passed near the gate? Is that where you'll be?"

"Yeah. Church is down the hall. You'll know it when you see it."

I pulled out my phone and sent out a text to every brother in the club.

Church in ten.

Time to jump feet first into the fire, and hope like hell I didn't get burned.

Chapter Nine

Dakota

I couldn't remember ever being this terrified. After Charming had left, I'd changed my clothes and taken out the property cut he'd given me. I couldn't fasten it, thanks to the baby growing inside me, but wearing it made me feel a little like I had on armor.

I looped my arm through Anatoly's as we entered the clubhouse. I saw Hunter behind the bar and gave him a slight nod, while ignoring the mostly naked women standing nearby. Anatoly led me down the hall and to the double doors at the end. He pushed them open and ushered me inside.

The men glaring at Charming made me want to flee the room, but I forced myself to walk to his side. He stood and laced our fingers together. I hoped he didn't feel me trembling. The anger coming off everyone honestly scared me. He'd said the club would be upset with him for hiding me away, and Cinder had mentioned there being potential issues. Until this very moment, I hadn't considered they might physically harm Charming for what he'd done.

"Please don't hurt him," I murmured, my gaze landing on the one who seemed the most pissed. His cut read *Havoc -- Sgt. at Arms.* He happened to also be the largest man at the table. If he wanted to break Charming in half, I didn't think it would take much effort on his part.

"Shit," someone muttered.

I shifted closer, my cut sliding open more. I heard a gasp and turned to face the nearest man. *Scratch,* according to his cut. And Charming's VP.

"She's pregnant," Scratch said.

I looked up at Charming. "You didn't tell them?"

He shook his head. "Not yet. They were furious when I told them about you. I'd hoped meeting you might cool them off. If that hadn't happened, Anatoly had instructions to get you the hell out of here and somewhere safe."

I eyed the men around the table. "I understand why you're upset. In your position, I'd probably feel like he didn't trust me. He's agonized over this for months. My brother asked him to keep my presence a secret."

"And who the fuck is your brother?" another man asked. *Renegade*. "Last I checked, the Pres is the one in charge of what happens in the club. Not some outsider."

I licked my lips and hoped I wasn't about to make things even worse. "Specter."

"Oh, fuck." I turned to see who'd spoken. I'd need to learn the names sooner or later. Unless they made us leave. Or made *me* leave. *Gator.*

"You're Specter's sister?" Scratch asked.

"Yes. My brother killed someone and took the man's wife with him. She'd been abused. Beaten nearly to death. He can't give her back, but that's what the Cartel wants. If they don't get her, they want me." I looked up at Charming and noticed his jaw was tight with a muscle jumping. "Charming was trying to honor my brother's wishes, while also keeping me safe. If the Cartel gets me, they're going to make me suffer. Most likely, they'll kill me when they're done."

"She shouldn't have that cut," Havoc said. "None of us voted her in. Knocking up some bitch doesn't make her your old lady."

Tears pricked my eyes, but I shrugged the cut off and placed it on the table. His words were harsh, and they hurt. Didn't make them any less true. If a vote was how this typically was handled, then Charming had broken the rules by giving the cut to me. They were angry enough already. I'd gladly give the cut back if it meant they'd stop hating him. I didn't need it.

"Tell them the rest," Cinder said. "They need to know her full name."

"You fucking knew about this?" Havoc asked, his voice full of menace.

Cinder shrugged. "Someone had to watch over her when Charming couldn't be around. She's innocent in all this, Havoc. What did you want me to do? Toss her out of the gates and let the Cartel have her? Let them turn her into a whore, or worse… torture, rape, and kill her? That's not how this club works."

Charming sighed. "Her name is Dakota Strayer. She's my wife."

The room went silent. I was too scared to look at any of them and buried my face against Charming. He tightened his hold on me and I felt his lips brush the top of my head. He leaned down and murmured in my ear. "Everything's all right, sweetheart. They just need time."

I dared to peek at the men in the room. I wasn't so sure I believed him. Especially with the biggest one, Havoc, glaring at him with murder in his eyes. I couldn't hold back my tears and did my best to hide them. Didn't matter. I couldn't stop my body from shaking. Everyone in the room knew I was bawling like a damn baby. Specter would be so disappointed right now.

"When your woman hears you bullied Charming's pregnant wife until she cried, she's going to have your balls," someone said. I thought it might be Gator, but I wasn't certain. "Fucking hell, Havoc."

"I think we need to bring in the old ladies,"

Scratch said. "Or at least a few of them. See how they feel about all this."

"Shit," Havoc said. "Go ahead and call Jordan. You think she's going to be pissed at me? Hell no. It's Charming she'll tear apart for this bullshit. Watch and see."

I tuned them out and felt another presence come up behind me, then heard Anatoly's voice. "Do you want me to take her out of here?"

"Not yet," Charming said. "Let's see what happens. But if the club turns on me, get her somewhere safe. Do whatever it takes to keep her alive and out of the Cartel's hands. *Anything*. Understood?"

"Got it," Anatoly said, sounding resigned.

I heard women's voices and a moment later, the doors were thrown open.

"What the hell?" one of them asked.

"Ladies, meet Charming's wife. Dakota," Scratch said.

"Motherfucker gave her a property cut, without any one of us even knowing she existed," Havoc said.

"Well, that explains why he keeps running home and won't let anyone in his house," one of the ladies said. She came closer and lightly touched my arm. "I'm Clarity. You okay?"

I lifted my head, knowing my cheeks were still wet from my tears and my eyes were probably red and puffy. Clarity narrowed her eyes and looked at the men around the table. "Which one of you bastards made her cry?"

"That would be Havoc," Gator said, grinning at another woman.

The other lady growled and stomped over to Havoc, then leaned down. "I hope you like the color blue, Havoc, because your balls are about to turn that color. It will be a cold day in hell before you touch me. Did you seriously make her cry?"

"And she's pregnant," Gator supplied helpfully, his smile widening.

The woman's eyes narrowed to slits and her fists balled up. "She's pregnant? Do you honestly think Charming would lock her away without reason? What's the entire story?"

"The Cartel is after her," Charming said. "She's Specter's little sister. He pissed them off and now they want to use her in retaliation. I won't let them have her."

The woman straightened. "Of course, you won't! And you shouldn't."

"That's Jordan," Clarity said. "And Meg is the one standing by Cinder. There's more of us, but the others are taking care of the kids."

Jordan's face went so red I worried she might blow. Before I knew what she was doing, she launched herself at Havoc and started swinging.

"You motherfucking asshole! How could you do that? How? Do you have any idea what I'd give…" The fight slowly drained from her. "She's carrying Charming's child, Havoc. A sweet, innocent baby. You scared a pregnant woman. You know damn well what stress can do, especially early in a pregnancy. Is that what you wanted? For her to lose her baby the way we lost ours?"

I gasped, my eyes going wide. My heart hurt for her. I couldn't even imagine the horror of losing a child. Clarity went to Jordan and placed a hand on her shoulder, tugging her off Havoc. The man looked wrecked, and I could tell he hated that he'd upset his woman so much. At least he had a heart buried under all that hatred. I'd wondered.

"I'm going to get rid of the... um, ladies... I think we need to go sit and talk," Meg said. "Let the men sort their crap out on their own."

Meg walked out, and I assumed she meant she was sending the club whores packing. The last thing I wanted was for those women to see me like this. I'd learned enough about them to think they'd consider me weak, which meant they'd try even harder to get into Charming's pants. I couldn't deal with the drama right now.

"Anatoly, stay with Dakota," Charming said. "Don't let her leave your sight."

He nodded. "Of course. I'll protect her like she's my own."

"Who the fuck is this asshole?" Havoc muttered.

"Anatoly is with the Los Angeles Bratva. Actually, he's the head of it," Charming said. "And he's my best friend."

Charming kissed me and smoothed my hair back from my face. I held onto him a moment longer, scared to let go. Anatoly pried me loose and led me from the room. When we reached the main area, those other women were gone, and Meg and Clarity were sitting at a table with three glasses of what looked like sweet tea. I didn't see Jordan anywhere.

"Come visit and tell us how you met Charming," Clarity said. "And don't worry about your man. He'll be fine. The club will get over it, once they have time to think it all through and realize they might have done the exact same thing in his situation."

I hoped they were right. I knew how much the club meant to Charming, and it would kill me to be the reason he lost it all. I'd never let that happen. Whether he liked it or not, I'd leave before his club stripped his colors, or he walked because of me.

"What about Jordan?" I asked, looking around again. "Is she all right?"

Clarity gave me a sad smile. "She will be. It's been quite a while, but she lost her baby. Doctor told her she couldn't have anymore, so she and Havoc adopted. They have one daughter who's their biological child. I sometimes see her watching the new babies with a wistful expression and it breaks my heart. Finding out Havoc could have stressed you to the point you lost your child..."

"She'll rake him over the coals for a while," Meg added. "That was unforgiveable in her eyes, and he knows it."

"Had Jordan been anyone else, things would have gone down a little different," Clarity said. "In front of the club, we show our men respect and obedience. Mostly. Every now and then, something sets one of us off and we unsheathe our claws. Our men make a big production of disciplining us, but at the end of the day, they love us and would do anything to make sure we're safe and happy."

"Now spill it," Meg said, leaning closer. "You and Charming? How did that even happen? I don't recognize you from around town."

"Well, he came into the bar where I was working and decided to rescue me." I told them my story, about running from Specter and the marriage he'd arranged for me, about the handsy guys at the bar and how Charming went all caveman on them, and then I admitted I was in love with the man.

"So you've been hiding this entire time," Meg said. "Alone? I mean, I get it. Charming is scared someone will hurt you. I understand why he didn't want people to find out you were here. The club will get over it, eventually. And my Cinder visited with you?"

I nodded. "He wanted to tell you. I think Charming asked him not to. He worried you might accidentally tell someone else, and then the news would spread. He's even been speaking to my brother on a burner from another state as an extra precaution."

"I still can't get over the fact you're related to Specter. Does he realize Charming is closer to his age than yours?" Clarity asked. "I mean no offense. Scratch is more than twice my age and it's never bothered me. But other people will make comments. Rude ones."

"I've dealt with it too," Meg said. "They think my relationship with Cinder is disgusting. There's over thirty years between us. Closer to forty if I'm being honest. What none of them understands is that men my age and younger hurt me. They raped me. Beat me. Stole me from my family and took me to another country where they used me as a whore for an illegal fighting ring. That man they think is so awful for being with me is the kindest, gentlest guy I've ever known."

Clarity laughed. "Only with you and Tanner. Cinder always intimidated everyone else, except maybe Jordan. That woman isn't afraid of anyone."

Meg nodded. "Which is why it ripped Havoc apart to see he made her cry. She doesn't show emotion often, except anger and occasionally overexuberance. Like a puppy. She has a good heart and protects those she loves fiercely, which is what makes her perfect for Havoc."

"You'll meet the others later," Clarity said. "Janessa is with Irish. Darby and Renegade are together, and his sister Nikki is with Ashes. Josie was the first old lady with the club. She's with Jackal. There's Grey and Samurai, Phantom and Charisma. Samurai and Phantom are cousins, and when you meet

Charisma, she's deaf. You have to speak where she can read your lips."

"Don't forget Alora," Meg said. "You'll love her! She writes these super-steamy romances. She's with Rooster."

"That's a lot of people to remember," I murmured.

Clarity nodded. "It is, and don't worry if you forget names. We won't hold it against you. Especially since there's a slew of kids around here too."

I glanced down the hall toward Church and wondered what was going on behind those closed doors. Anatoly caught my attention and gave me a slight head shake, saying without words that I needed to stay put. I didn't like it, but I'd listen. For now. If I thought they were going to gang up on Charming, well… I made no promises.

"He'll be fine," Meg said. "If Cinder is in his corner, then the others will fall in line. He hurt them by keeping you a secret. Give them a little bit to realize it had nothing to do with his faith in them and everything to do with his feelings for you. Most of them have already fallen in love. They'll get it."

"And the others will learn sooner or later," Clarity said.

I hoped they were right. It would gut me to discover Charming's club had turned against him, all because he wanted to protect me. I knew life wasn't fair, but did it really have to kick a man in the balls? He needed their support now more than ever. Maybe if he told them the Cartel was getting close, they'd rally around him. My fingers were crossed. If push came to shove, I'd have him take me somewhere else. Far from the Devil's Boneyard. Or I'd call Specter and demand he get me out of here. He wouldn't like it, but he'd do it. Besides, my brother owed me. Huge.

* * *

Charming

"Be pissed at me all you want, but don't you dare make Dakota feel like she doesn't belong here." I glared at the men around the table, except Cinder and Shade, who I knew had my back.

"You could have trusted us to keep her safe," Ripper said. "Haven't we proven often enough that we can protect the women and children here?"

"You have, and it had nothing to do with trusting you. I..." I sighed and hung my head a moment. "I'm so out of my element right now. I never wanted an old lady or a family. I'm over fifty and thought I was content to remain a bachelor forever. Until I met Dakota. The day I found out she'd gone missing, I felt terror unlike anything I'd experienced before. I just knew something bad had happened."

"Why didn't you tell us about her before?" Havoc asked. "If she meant so much to you, why did we never hear her name?"

"It was only a fling. At least, that's what we'd agreed to. Two days of fun with no expectations of more."

Scratch leaned back in his chair, making the leather crack. "The extended trip into northern Georgia. You texted that you were taking some time to relax before you came back. You spent it with her."

I nodded. "Yes, I did. And apparently, knocked her up while I was there. I didn't realize she was Specter's sister until I came home. I put things together a little too slow. He's threatened to kick my ass whenever he makes an appearance. If he makes one. Fucker has had months to work this shit out, and he hasn't."

"If anyone could explain Specter's way of thinking, it would be Casper VanHorne. We could call him," Cinder said.

"I could be way off here, but if I were in Specter's shoes and found out my baby sister had married the President of a motorcycle club, I might hang back and see how he resolved the issue of her being in danger." Scratch folded his arms. "Maybe he's not come to help or made a move because he's waiting to see what you do."

I fisted my hands and ground my teeth together. If Dakota had been in trouble this entire time because the motherfucker was testing me, we were going to have words whenever he showed his face. This was my family he was fucking with. Although, as much as he seemed to care about his sister, I had a feeling he'd step in if necessary.

"Well, he's about to get his wish. The Cartel will be here any day now. It's part of what Anatoly came to tell me. We don't have enough manpower to take them on by ourselves, and I'm not sure if we have enough time to get reinforcements here."

"I could call Torch," Cinder offered.

"Wire said the Dixie Reapers were on standby. Go ahead and call. They should have some volunteers ready and waiting," I said.

"Maybe get Scratch to call Beast. If you called Titan, that would get three clubs here, and all of us making calls at the same time would make it happen faster," Cinder said.

"I can reach out to the Broken Bastards," Havoc offered.

"I'll reach out to Outlaw and the Devil's Fury," Shade said.

"Let's do it," I said. "Everyone else sit tight. Once we know how many are coming, I can check with Anatoly and see if he has some men to lend for the fight. We can make a plan afterward."

It took a good thirty minutes to make all the calls and get things set up, and I'd still have to figure out where everyone would stay, but we had more than enough help arriving anywhere from a few hours to half a day. I only hoped they all arrived before the Cartel.

"Reapers are sending Bull, Tempest, and Slayer," Cinder said.

"Outlaw spoke with Badger. The Devil's Fury are sending Dagger, Hot Shot, and Smuggler," Shade said.

Scratch leaned forward and braced his forearms on the table. "Kings are sending Wrangler and Copper. Drifter is already here."

"Broken Bastards said Throttle, Chains, and Discord would head out within the next thirty minutes." Havoc tapped the table. "That's an extra twelve men."

"Titan is sending Smoke, Philly, and Gravel." I scanned the men at the table. "So fifteen plus however many guys from the Bratva. I don't know where we'll house all these people. They'll need a place to sleep at the very least because I have a feeling they'll be here at least a night or maybe even three. The Cartel will most likely hit us hard and fast. They've probably sent someone ahead to scout us, which means our numbers were already reported."

"We'll have the element of surprise when our reinforcements get here," Havoc said.

"And when they realize Anatoly is on our side and not theirs." I smiled. "Sometimes it's good to have friends. Other times, they're a pain in your ass."

"Well, the clubhouse has five empty bedrooms." I shook my head at Havoc. "Six?"

"I had to let Carlos go. I dismissed him on my way into Church. While Anatoly wasn't here for nefarious purposes, Carlos still let him and the other Bratva guys into the compound when they threatened to shoot him. Then he led them straight to my house and my pregnant wife. So we're down to two prospects for the time being."

"You don't think Carlos will team up with the Cartel and give them inside information?" Scratch asked. "Was he pissed about you kicking him out?"

"He looked pretty pathetic. Said he was sorry and knew he'd fucked up. He didn't fight me on it or cuss me out or anything. Just accepted his dismissal gracefully and walked out the gates."

"You going to check with your friend about more allies joining us?" Havoc asked.

"I'll text him." I pulled out my phone and did exactly that. "If I go out there and see Dakota, it will be hard to come back in here. I know Clarity and Meg will be kind to her, but she's had a really rough time. Always scared. Not just for her safety, but she constantly worried when you found out about her that you'd kick me out of the club or do something worse to me."

It only took Anatoly a moment to respond. *Four. I can commit four, including myself.* It wasn't the big number I'd hoped for, but I would take it. That put us at nineteen extra men.

"Bull can stay with us," Scratch offered. "He's family and might enjoy spending time with the kids."

"Drifter can stay with us," Phantom said.

"The little apartments are set up to sleep only one or two adults. We can let the Bratva have them," I said. "Not sure I want them staying in the clubhouse. I'd trust Anatoly, but I don't know the men with him."

"That still leaves thirteen men and six rooms at the clubhouse," Shade said.

"Won't be comfortable, but we can send Hunter out with the truck to pick up a bunch of those camping cots. Not the cheap ones. The kind that hold men over two hundred pounds. Sporting goods store should have some in stock." Havoc looked to me. "What do you think, Pres? One cot per room would let the clubhouse sleep twelve instead of thirteen."

"That's going to be cramped as fuck," Scratch said.

I texted Anatoly again. *Do you have an issue staying at my house and your men sharing an apartment? One might need to sleep on a cot.*

Instead of texting, he called.

"A simple yes or fuck off would have sufficed," I said when I answered.

"I don't want to intrude on you and your bride. Put all four of us in one of the apartments. My righthand man can have the second bed. The other two can each take a cot. Or they can sleep on the floor. Wouldn't be the first time."

"Thanks, Anatoly." I ended the call and conveyed his message to the club. "That means we have two apartments open and four beds, plus the six beds in the clubhouse. All we need are two cots for the Bratva and place three more in each of the other apartments."

Cinder frowned. "I lost count somewhere along the way. I have no idea if that's enough beds or not."

I ran my hands down my face. I was tired as fuck and had a feeling things were just winding up. It was going to be a hellish night. "Have Hunter get at least a dozen cots. If the store doesn't have that many, tell him to wipe them out and hit up the big box stores or the next closest sporting goods place. I'd rather have too many than not enough, and who the hell knows when we might need them again."

"Pres, the club is growing. I know it's not the first time we've talked about it," Scratch said. "But I think it's time we build a little more around here. Our families are expanding. Some of us have kids who will be old enough to start their own lives soon."

"We need a few more apartments. We can add on to what we have already. Add a firepit or something next to the current set, then put three more on the other side of it, each with two bedrooms." I rapped my knuckles on the table. "I also have an idea for the property behind us. I want to lock up the barn so that only club officers have access, with a spare set of keys in my office at the clubhouse for emergencies. But the house… I'd like to set up as a refuge for children who need a fresh start. Like Phantom's kids, and some of Havoc's."

"Damn," Cinder said. "You know we don't get those kids legally. That's a lot of hacking for Shade to tackle."

"Which brings me to another point. Wire said there are some kids out there who are closing in on his skill level. He thinks when they're all grown up, they might surpass him. Scariest fucking thing I've ever heard. But it means there's talent out there we should be recruiting. No offense to Shade, but he's just one man."

Shade leaned back in his seat. "None taken, and I'm intrigued. I may also know of a potential recruit. I've run across them a few times when I was digging through the dark web for intel we needed. Goes by

Lazarus. No fucking clue how old they are much less *where* they are, or their true identity. They're that damn good."

"See what you can find on them, or if they would even be interested in joining our ranks." I looked around the table. "Any objections?"

"Sounds good to me," Scratch said.

"I'm fine with it." Havoc folded his arms. "Some of us are getting too old for this shit. Time to get some younger blood in here."

"If we're taking on new prospects, I may know a guy," Irish said. "Little brother to someone I served with. He's getting out of the military in three weeks. I have a feeling he's going to need a support system."

"Invite him out," I said. "We'll see if he's interested and whether he has what it takes. Anyone else?"

"You care if the guy is missing two legs?" Rebel asked. "He has below the knee prosthetics and sometimes uses a wheelchair around the house. Both lower legs were blown off by an IED. However, he used to ride motorcycles. Last I heard, he'd been talking to a custom shop to make adjustments so he can still ride while wearing his prosthetics. Name's Nick Barker."

"Tell him to stop by, maybe after all this shit is over and done with," I said.

"Can we break for food and beer, Pres?" Gator asked.

"We can do that. I want to check on Dakota anyway and get Hunter out searching for those cots. We'll reconvene in an hour in case anyone wants to go home for a little while." I slammed my fist onto the table. "Church dismissed. Temporarily."

Everyone filed out, and I went to find Dakota.

Clarity and Meg sat with her in the middle of the main room, drinking what looked like sweet tea. I noticed a basket of fries in the center of the table. The moment Dakota saw me, she got up so fast she nearly tripped over her feet. She threw herself into my arms, and I held her tight and breathed in her scent. The fact she trembled slightly told me how concerned she'd been.

"Everything's fine, sweetheart. The club isn't quite so pissed anymore, and I think we're going to cobble together a plan for the Cartel with little trouble. Help is on the way."

"I've been so worried," she said, burying her face against me.

"Promised I'd keep you safe, and that's what I'm going to do. Whatever it takes."

I looked at my club over the top of her head and let every one of them see what she meant to me. The woman in my arms was my entire world. I'd keep her safe, because without her, I'd be a shell of a man. I wasn't sure I'd want to keep going. I didn't know how the pint-sized beauty had come to mean so much to me so soon, but I was grateful to have her in my life. She made every day worth living.

Chapter Ten

Dakota

Charming righted my chair and sat, tugging me onto his lap. With his arm braced around my waist, he held me while I visited with Clarity and Meg a while longer. Jordan came back, looking refreshed and more in control of her emotions. She took the seat next to me and Charming, giving me a smile.

"Sorry about earlier," she said.

"It's all right. I understand." I leaned back against Charming. "Think you'll forgive your husband?"

"Havoc?" she asked. "Eventually. I still can't believe he did that. I'm so angry with him. Are you okay? Everything fine with the baby?"

I nodded. "We're right as rain."

Charming kissed my shoulder. "I'm going to grab some food before we go back into Church. I don't like the thought of you sitting in these hard chairs. Head home and try to rest?"

"Without you?" I turned a little so I could see his face.

"I might be here a while, Dakota."

"We could have movie night at my house," Clarity offered. "I'm sure Phantom won't mind if the boys stay at his house tonight. Although, Charisma might not be too pleased about it."

"I'll call her and ask," Jordan said, pulling out her phone. "Um, I mean I'll text to ask."

She tapped at the screen and set the phone aside while she waited for a response. Charming patted my thigh, and I stood, letting him head over to the bar. He came back with a cold beer.

"I thought you wanted food," I said.

"Ordered a burger. Stripes is putting a bunch on the grill. Someone will bring it to me when it's ready." He pulled me onto his lap again.

"Charisma replied. She said the boys were more than welcome and invited Tanner too. Looks like you're free to join them, Meg. I can't think of a single person who would voluntarily watch Lanie. I'll be sitting this one out since her daddy will be occupied." Jordan shoved her phone back into her pocket. "I'll ask Darby if she wants to drop Fawn and Holt off at my house. Then she could meet Dakota and join you girls for movie night. She doesn't get out enough."

"More like she doesn't want to," Clarity said. "She's glued to Renegade."

"Sam is on the gate tonight," Charming said. "I have Hunter running some errands. With all of us being in Church, there won't be any men around to watch your backs. Be careful."

Jordan rolled her eyes. "You know my house is a mini arsenal. Taggart is mostly grown and knows how to use a gun and carries a knife. If shit goes down, I'll send him over to watch your woman. Chill out, Pres. Everything will be fine."

"Jesus fucking Christ, Jordan. That's like walking into an ER and saying it's quiet. Now shit is bound to go wrong." Charming glared at her.

"I have no idea what that means," I said. "About the ER."

"Hospitals and first responders never want to hear the words 'It's a quiet night' because it jinxes them. The moment someone says it, all hell breaks loose." Meg shrugged a shoulder. "Charming isn't wrong, and Jordan knows better."

"Right." Jordan sighed. "Sorry. You guys are way too superstitious."

"I'll come get you from Scratch's house when we're done," Charming said. "Go straight there and don't leave. Not for any reason at all. I don't care if someone tells you I'm bleeding out. Don't listen to them."

"You sound as paranoid as my brother," I said.

"Speaking of Specter, I need to get him up to speed on our plans," Charming said. "Hop up. I'll make my call while I eat at the bar, then I'll be calling everyone back to Church. Enjoy your time with the old ladies."

I stood and kissed him before he walked off. Before I sat again, Clarity and the others stood. I followed everyone outside and got into Clarity's SUV with her. Meg climbed in back and Jordan waved as she got into her own vehicle and drove off. Charming had mentioned Scratch didn't live far, but I hadn't realized exactly how close they were until now. When she pulled into her driveway, I saw they lived next door. How had that not come up before now? What else didn't I know about my new life?

"Come on," Clarity said. "I have popcorn. We can bake cookies. There's soda, tea, and milk in the fridge. I'm afraid the boys drank the last of the juice this morning."

"What movies do you like?" Meg asked me.

"Almost anything. Well, no gore. Other than that, I'm up for any movie genre," I said.

"Rom Com it is," Clarity said with a laugh. "It's my favorite, and Meg's too. But if you get sick of them, we can switch to something with more action."

"Preferably action flicks with hot men," Meg said. "Cinder might be my one and only, but I'm not blind."

"Amen!" Clarity laughed. "Scratch is perfect for

me, and the only man I'll ever want. Doesn't mean I can't enjoy seeing a shirtless Vin Diesel, or Henry Cavill. And Scratch can't say a damn word. I've noticed him drooling a little when he watches old movies with Marilyn Monroe or Elizabeth Taylor."

"I think she just called him old," Meg mock whispered.

"Did not!" Clarity glared. "Besides, Cinder is older than Scratch."

"You don't find it odd we're all with men who are quite a bit older than us?" I asked. "I mean, it's not exactly the norm, is it?"

"In here? Yes," Meg said. "Out in the world? Not so much. Don't get me wrong. I see age gap couples. Maybe not in our tiny small-minded town, but they're out there."

"The town is coming around," Clarity said. "The charity work the club has done went a long way to making them accept all of us. They no longer think the men are ogres who are going to steal away their children or pump them full of drugs."

Scratch and Clarity's home wasn't quite what I'd pictured. Then again, neither was Charming's. I looked at the family photos on the walls as I followed the ladies into the kitchen. I accepted a glass of milk, knowing it would be good for the baby, and listened as they chatted about the townspeople and the different ways the club had helped over the years.

A chime sounded and I heard a door shut. I tensed and looked around, but Clarity and Meg seemed perfectly at ease. A woman entered the kitchen and smiled when she saw me.

"You must be Dakota. I'm Darby."

"It's nice to meet you. Please don't be offended if I ask your name again at some point. It might take me a few days to get everyone straight in my head. Maybe even a few weeks."

She nodded. "I get it. I felt overwhelmed when Renegade brought me here. My daughter had gotten his attention and led him down an alley. Some men had hurt me and left me for dead near a dumpster."

"Scratch found me outside one of the club businesses. I was trying to sleep in the doorway. He saw I had a small child with me and offered me a safe place to rest, as well as food for both of us. I kept waiting for him to ask for something in return. A blow job. Sex. Anything. He never did." Clarity smiled. "That man is the kindest guy I've ever met. Unless you cross him. Then he's scary as fuck."

"So bad things happened to all of you?" I asked.

"Jordan was in prison. Her shithead brother didn't pick her up when she was released. Havoc and a few of the others found her passed out on the side of the road. She'd tried to walk into town. From what I hear, she shouldn't have been arrested in the first place. Then one of the guards tried to come after her." Clarity sat at the kitchen table and the rest of us did the same.

"Josie is Jackal's woman. She doesn't have a sob story. Not exactly. Her brother is a Dixie Reaper, and Jackal met her at their clubhouse. They went off to have a weekend fling, except he got her pregnant. She never told him, and he found out after his daughter was a toddler." Clarity sipped her drink. "Janessa is with Irish and she's the daughter of a Dixie Reaper. Her story is seriously messed up, but she got an awesome stepmom out of the deal. When her daddy found out she'd been locked up in this hellish asylum, he went after her. Janessa wouldn't leave without Kalani. The woman had sacrificed herself to keep

Janessa safe from the guards."

"Wow," I said. "My brother might be the infamous Specter, and thanks to him, the Cartel wants me, but no one's ever hurt me the way some of you have been harmed. Men actually give me a wide berth unless they're trying to ingratiate themselves with Specter. Never works, but they kept trying anyway."

"Grey and Charisma both have tragic stories. Especially Charisma," Meg murmured.

"Yeah, because yours is just all sunshine and roses," Clarity said. "I don't know how you survived it all, Meg, but I'm glad you did. Although, we all worried Cinder wouldn't pull his head out of his ass in time to claim you. Damn near lost you both because he's so damn stubborn."

"I know. He regrets his actions now. But we're together and that's all that matters. I love him so much." She got a silly smile on her face. "He makes me happier than I've ever been before."

"What's Charming like?" Darby asked. "We've seen two sides of him. The laid-back guy who was just another patched member, and the stoic President of the Devil's Boneyard."

"He's protective. Sweet. Sometimes he's funny. Other times, he acts like a caveman. I guess I haven't seen either version of Charming the rest of you have." I shifted in my seat.

"It's good he's different with you," Clarity said. "All our men are like that. With the club, they're these tough bad asses. When they come home, they're sexy, cuddly teddy bears."

"Movie time!" Meg stood. "We can gossip another day. Anyone up for *Letters to Juliet*? I seriously love that one."

"I'm game," Darby said.

"Anything is fine with me," I said. "I'm not sure I've watched that one."

"Hang around Meg enough and you'll be sick of it within a month," Clarity said. "She watches it at least once a week, when Cinder doesn't have action movies on with shit blowing up every few minutes."

"Must be a guy thing," Darby said. "Renegade is the same way. It's either those or horror movies."

"I don't mind horror," I said. "I prefer the ghostly variety, though, and not icky like *Hostel*. That one just grosses me out."

"Agreed," Darby said. "I'll leave the room if Renegade puts on something like that."

We all went into the living room and found a place to sit while Clarity got the movie going. For the first time in… well, too far back for me to remember, it felt like I had friends. I might have only met these ladies tonight, but already I could see myself forming a friendship with them.

The Cartel might come knocking, but I refused to sit here and cower, worrying about what might happen. I'd enjoy my time with the ladies and have faith Charming would figure everything out. And if my brother didn't get his ass here to lend a hand, I'd never speak to him again.

* * *

Charming

Reinforcements arrived steadily throughout the night and into the morning. We got everyone settled and up to speed. By lunch, Dakota had met all the old ladies from my club, and I'd introduced her to our visiting allies. I kept an eye on her as she mingled with everyone. Her cheeks had more color, and I noticed her eyes were brighter. Until then, I hadn't realized how much of a toll it taken on her being locked up for months.

I curled an arm around her waist, preparing to part ways. Anatoly and I would remain hidden inside the clubhouse. We already had everyone else stationed throughout the compound. Rebel's friend Nick had stopped by and agreed to help watch the other women. We'd divided them, and the children, into two homes. Half were with Clarity and the others were at Phantom's. Nick had gone to Phantom's house, and Sam was with Clarity. Hunter had asked for gate duty, even knowing he'd be knocked out by the Bratva guys. I'd asked them to go easy on him while still making it look real.

"Remember, we'll be close by," I murmured before kissing her. "You're my brave, beautiful wife. I love you, Dakota."

Her eyes went wide. Yeah, probably not the best timing.

"You love me?" she asked.

I nodded. "Yep. Known it for a while now. Just… I guess I worried it was too soon to say anything. I won't let anyone hurt you or our baby. Trust me?"

"With my life," she said.

"Start cleaning this mess and try to look relaxed, or at least not like you're waiting to be attacked. We want their guard down when they enter the building."

"Got it," she said. "And, Charming? I love you too."

I winked before I disappeared down the hall. I'd already heard her say it once, even though I'd kept walking at the time. As much as I'd wanted to stay, I'd had things to do that day. Anatoly hid in one of the bedrooms while I took the hall bathroom. The lights were out in this section to give us better cover. My muscles tensed and my hand gripped my knife. I knew Anatoly had a gun, but he'd said he would use his suppressor. These men were coming for my family. A gun was too impersonal for the task at hand.

It didn't take long for things to start heating up. I heard the Cartel coming through the gates. They were trying to be quiet, but I knew everything about this damn compound, including all the usual sounds. A group of men entering, when all mine were accounted for, wasn't something I couldn't *not* hear.

Muffled voices sounded close to the gate. I heard a brief shout, more voices, then a dragging sound. It meant one of Anatoly's men was dragging Hunter behind the clubhouse, exactly as planned. We'd agreed they'd leave him near the back in the shadows. If Hunter came to, he'd join the fight. But if he didn't, I hoped his current placement would keep him hidden and alive.

Gunfire went off. I tensed at what sounded like a small arsenal being unloaded on my club. As badly as I wanted to jump into the fray, I couldn't. It would leave my wife vulnerable and would ruin the plan. I heart shouts, more gunfire, and a lot of cursing.

The doors at the front of the clubhouse slammed open and Dakota screamed. I smiled, knowing it was nearly time.

More gunshots outside the clubhouse had me grinding my teeth. Especially when I heard Havoc yell out. Something told me he'd just been hit. The fact he was cussing meant he was alive. These fuckers were pissing me off.

Anatoly slipped past me, heading for the main room. I listened as he spoke with the Cartel guys. I opened the door a little farther so I could hear every word.

"Do you think I'm going to let you leave with her when I'm still empty-handed?" Anatoly asked. "*Nyet*. We need her to flush out her husband. The Bratva has unfinished business with Romeo Strayer."

"If he's outside with his club, he's likely dead. My men are armed to the teeth," someone said.

I hoped like fucking hell he was wrong. I didn't want to lose anyone over this. Death happened. It couldn't be avoided, and the Reaper would come for all of us sooner or later. But I'd be damned if the bastard came for me tonight. Not when I had a baby on the way, and a wife who needed me. One I adored, regardless of how little time we'd known one another.

"Let me go!" Dakota demanded. I heard her struggling and hoped she didn't sell it so hard she ended up getting hurt.

The crack of a hand against flesh had me grinding my teeth together. Whoever had just struck my wife was going to suffer. No one touched my woman! My hand tightened on my knife, and I shifted slightly, ready to rush in there the moment Dakota had been removed from the Cartel's clutches. We had a plan. I only hoped it didn't get fucked all to hell.

"I need the woman," Anatoly said. "Until her husband is begging at my feet, she's my leverage. Perhaps your men could search for Strayer to speed things up?"

"We aren't your lap dogs," one of them said.

"And yet, who found Strayer and his wife? That would be *my* men and not yours. You might have gotten us in the right vicinity, but no one else could locate them. You owe me."

"Fine." I heard Dakota gasp and fought the urge to rush out and check on her. I knew Anatoly would keep her safe, or at least alive. He couldn't tip his hand or we'd all die.

A cry from outside the window nearest me made bile rise up in my throat.

"Motherfuckers killed Cobra," Scratch yelled. I knew it was not only a way to tell the club, but he wanted to make sure I knew too. Goddamnit!

"Philly's gone too," Samurai called out.

I squeezed my eyes shut and pushed the pain down. These men had been willing to risk their lives to keep Dakota safe, but hearing they were gone gutted me. It was my job to keep everyone alive and I'd failed.

I heard footsteps moving toward the front of the clubhouse and the soft *pop pop* of Anatoly's gun.

Coming out of hiding, I made my way into the main room. It seemed my friend had taken out two of four men. I hadn't counted on there being so many coming for my wife. Oh, I knew they'd send a lot of men. I just hadn't realized more than one or two would be the ones to try and take her. I'd thought they'd busy themselves with my club outside. It attested to how badly they wanted to fuck over Specter.

"We had a deal!" one of the Cartel men shouted.

"And I'm breaking it." Anatoly smiled. "Gentleman, I believe the lady's husband would like a word with the two of you. But be warned. Keep it a fair fight, or I'll end your lives as easily as I did the other two."

Anatoly backed up, putting Dakota between him and the wall. I gave him a nod and advanced on the two men who'd thought to hurt my wife.

"Did you think I'd let you come for what's mine without there being any repercussions?" I asked. "You assholes thought to hurt my wife, and have been out there trying to slaughter my men. Why did you think you'd walk away from that?"

The one who appeared to be in charge lifted his chin and stared down his nose at me. "Why the Bratva wants you is beyond me. You're nothing but a filthy biker. It's your misfortune to be married to the girl. Her brother owes us a debt. Since he's unwilling to handle it himself, we'll take her instead."

"Wrong," I said. "I'm more than a biker. I was born into the Bratva. I had blood on my hands before I was old enough to grow hair on my chin."

I twirled the knife in my hand, making sure he saw it. His gaze flicked to my hand and back to my face. The smirk gracing his lips unnerved me. Only because it meant the slimy bastard was up to something. He reached into his jacket and before he had a chance to clear a weapon, I threw the knife, embedding the blade in his chest. The fucker's eyes went wide and blood trickled from his mouth. He gasped and stumbled a few steps before going down. I watched as he choked on his own blood, the light fading from his eyes.

The other Cartel man rushed me. Without a weapon left, I had no choice but to fight with my hands. I swung with a right hook and nailed him in the eye. He snarled and advanced again, swiping at me with a blade I hadn't noticed. He managed to slash my upper arm before I landed a jab to his ribs and another to his stomach.

The guy snarled and swung the blade at me. I felt it slice into my chest and hissed at the sting of pain. He grinned like a maniac before roaring and coming at me once more. My foot hit the leg of a chair and I nearly went down. It gave the man just enough of an edge to get the upper hand. His arm pressed against my throat as he took me to the ground.

I slammed my fist into the side of his head once.

Twice. A third time. He backed off again. I managed to break free and stand. The man came at me, trying to take me out at the knees. I kicked out, catching him in the chin with my boot.

He smiled, blood coating his teeth. "Dirty move."

"You'd know all about that, wouldn't you?"

I backed up and he made it all of four steps before Anatoly took him out. A bullet to the head and the man collapsed, bleeding all over my damn floors. I growled, wanting to end the bastard myself. I didn't get a chance to yell at Anatoly. I heard a slow clap from the doorway and glanced that way. My gaze narrowed at the intruder.

"Now you show up? Seriously?" I demanded, glaring at Dakota's older brother.

"Had to make sure Dakota was all right," he said, coming into the clubhouse.

"I'm not speaking to you," she yelled out from behind Anatoly.

Specter's eye twitched. "Really? How old are you, Dakota? Two?"

My wife leaned around Anatoly to stick her tongue out at her brother, proving his point. I bit my lip so I wouldn't laugh. Sometimes she was too damn cute.

"If you wanted me to handle this shit, you should have just said so." I folded my arms and stared at him. "My wife has been hiding for months, waiting for *you* to do something. If you hadn't told me you needed more time, or that you were working on it, I'd have never waited this long. Fucker!"

He smiled. "Welcome to the family."

I opened my mouth to tell him to fuck the hell out, but he came at me so fast I didn't have a chance. His fist connected with my mouth and split my lip. He followed it up with an uppercut to my chin, knocking me off my damn feet.

"Specter!" my wife screamed at her brother, and I heard her rushing toward us.

I snarled at my brother-in-law, shifted to my feet, and launched myself at him. I tackled him to the floor and landed a blow to his nose, breaking it.

"Let them work it out," Anatoly told her, and I hoped like hell he was holding her back.

"Family has each other's back," I said, punching the bastard again. "They keep their women and children safe. Their brothers… Because of you, we lost good men!"

I clipped his jaw with my fist. Specter bucked me off and caught me in the ribs, right where the fucking Cartel guy had hit me. I gasped and had a feeling I'd be bruised all to hell by morning. Specter landed another blow before Anatoly hauled him off me.

"Enough! The two of you are upsetting Dakota."

I groaned as I got to my feet. My woman threw herself at me, and despite the pain, I held her close. She cried, burying her face in my chest. "It's all right, sweetheart. I'm fine," I assured her.

"I'm okay too," Specter said. "In case anyone cared."

"We don't," Anatoly said.

Specter flipped him off. "I'm rethinking your Bratva ties, Charming. I'd hoped you'd tap into them and use your connections to save my sister. If I'd known your friend was such an asshole, I'd have handled the matter myself."

"Why didn't you?" Dakota asked. "Do you have any idea how scared I've been? How awful it was to be locked away like a dirty secret? I couldn't even go to the doctor!"

Specter winced. "Sorry, little sister. That wasn't my intention. I guess you being stuck inside didn't seem all that bad. At least I knew you were safe. I needed to know your husband could take care of you. My life is always going to be filled with danger. Sometimes that's going to spill over to you, and by extension, Charming's club. If he couldn't handle this lot, then I knew he wasn't the right man to stand by your side."

"You don't get a say in who I'm married to," she said. "I thought I made that clear when I ran after you told me about my arranged marriage to one of your associates."

He shrugged. "At least you'd have been protected."

"Dakota is where she belongs," I said. "With me. Next time your shit comes to my doorstep, you get here fast enough to lend a hand. Otherwise, family or not, I'll make you disappear. You aren't my priority."

He gave a nod. "Good. That's the way it should be."

"You staying for dinner?" I asked.

"How can you think about food right now?" Dakota demanded, looking up at me.

"I'm a guy. I got in a fight. Twice. Now I want food and beer." I winked at her. "And other things that require us to be alone."

That and I needed to keep busy. If I thought about the loss of Cobra and Philly, I might fall apart. Cobra had been a friend, and an officer of my club, for more than a decade. Losing him was a pain I'd deal with later. When I was alone. My club needed me to be strong right now, and so did my wife.

Her cheeks turned pink, but she smiled at me. "Love you, Charming."

"Love you too, sweetheart. Think I better get cleaned up."

Anatoly placed a hand on my shoulder. "I'll watch your wife and help get the clubhouse back into order."

"You only lost two men," Specter said, "in case you were wondering. Although one wasn't technically yours. Hades Abyss is down a member. The Cartel has been handled. The ones they didn't kill I took care of on my way in. If there's retaliation later, let me know. You took out two of their bigger players, so they'll need time to regroup. A few of your other men took a bullet, but they'll heal."

Clarity, Jordan, and Janessa rushed into the clubhouse. Each scanned the room and winced. "Damn, Pres. The place is wrecked," Clarity said.

"So is my husband," Jordan muttered.

I looked around and realized she was right. We'd knocked over furniture without me even knowing it. Anatoly started cleaning up and the old ladies went to help. I clapped Specter on the back. "Come on, brother. Let's head to my house. You can use the guest shower to wash up and we'll come back so you can visit with Dakota."

"I'm ordering pizzas," Jordan shouted as we walked outside. I waved my hand so she'd know I heard her.

Checking the area, I saw Hunter back on his feet. It looked like Guardian had taken a bullet to the shoulder. Havoc's shirt had torn from a bullet creasing his side, but the damage seemed minimal. Gator limped by and I saw his thigh had been tied off, his pant leg soaked in blood. All in all, things could have been a lot worse.

My gaze strayed to Cobra and Philly, laid out

side by side. My throat burned and my heart ached. I paused a moment and walked over, kneeling next to Cobra. Someone had shut his eyes, and he looked peaceful.

"Rest easy, brother," I said, my voice sounding like I'd gargled with gravel. "Thank you for protecting our club and my family. You'll never be forgotten."

I glanced at Philly and saw Smoke kneeling next to him. I gave the man a nod and stood. We'd suffered a tragedy, but we'd heal in time. I'd leave Cobra's spot open for a bit. Only seemed right.

Specter grabbed his bag from his vehicle, and we walked to my house. I showed him to the guest bath before heading for the master bedroom. I pulled my shirt over my head and checked my wounds. They'd already started to crust over and didn't seem to need stitches.

I scrubbed quickly and put on clean clothes. When I went back to the hall, Specter had finished, and the bathroom light was out. I found him in the living room, checking out the pictures Dakota had put around the room. We might not have been able to leave the house, but she'd taken a selfie with me every day she'd been here. I'd printed off a few for her and she'd framed them.

"She looks happy," Specter said.

"She is. More so now that she can leave the house."

"Keep it that way. She's the only family I have left, Charming. If anything happens to her, I may lose what's left of my humanity. I've been walking on the dark side for so long. She's been the light in my world since I found out about her."

"She's not all you have," I said. "You have a nephew or niece on the way, and now the Devil's

Boneyard is also part of your family."

He smiled faintly.

I heard a shriek from outside and went to investigate. A petite Asian woman struggled against Magnus.

"Found this one skulking around, Pres," he said, shoving her toward me.

She crumbled at the foot of the steps and stumbled as she tried to stand. Her gaze landed on Specter right before she burst into tears.

"What the fuck?" I asked.

My brother-in-law sighed and pushed me out of the way, going to the woman.

"Cho, what are you doing here?" Specter asked. "I sent you back to your family."

She wiped at the tears streaking her cheeks. "They're gone. All of them."

"What happened?" he asked.

"Fire. It took out half the town. Everyone died."

"Specter, do you want to take her inside?" I asked.

He shook his head. "No. We'll go to the clubhouse. Is there a room we can use while I get to the bottom of this?"

"Sure." I eyed the woman. "But first… How did you know where he was?"

She looked away. Yeah, that one was hiding something. And for whatever reason, Specter hadn't thought to question her. I looked from one to the other, wondering what the hell was going on.

I moved closer, making sure I had her attention. "If you bring trouble here, it won't go well for you."

"Jesus, Charming. Back off." Specter shoved me, but I didn't budge.

"No. Think with your head and not your dick.

She found you here. How? And why is she here? Dakota and our child are finally safe. If she's here to cause problems, I want her gone. Now."

He sighed and ran a hand down his face. "I'll handle it."

"Visit your sister first. Don't just disappear." I walked off, not giving him a chance to say anything else. He might be feared throughout the world, but right now, he was on my turf. I was the king here. Not him.

Fucker better not forget it either.

Epilogue

Dakota
Three Months Later

I ran my hand over my belly and smiled at the technician. A quick glance at my husband was enough to tell me he was still processing. Or maybe he'd turned to stone out of fear. Things had been so crazy since the fight with the Cartel. We'd buried Cobra and the club still mourned his loss. Those who'd been shot had needed time to heal, but everyone seemed all right now. Then there'd been Charming's constant worry about retaliation.

My brother had called last week with the news the Cartel wouldn't be coming for us. It seemed they weren't too fond of the men who'd died at the compound and were willing to look the other way. With all that going on, we'd had to continually reschedule my appointment. This was our first visit having an ultrasound or getting to hear the heartbeat. Except there wasn't one. There were two.

"Twins, Charming. Can you believe it?" I asked. He didn't so much as blink or move. I shook my head, wondering if we'd broken him. I'd already put my clothes back on and I was ready to leave. I wrapped my fingers around his bicep and gave him a tug. "Come on, Daddy. Time to go."

He shivered from head to toe. "Don't call me that. As old as I am, and as young as you are…"

I snickered. "Scared people will get the wrong idea?"

"Yeah."

"Fine. But you know what this means. We need another crib. More clothes. More… everything."

He ran a hand down his face before lacing his

fingers with mine and following me out of the clinic. "Twins."

"On the plus side, they're both boys," I said. "Could have been worse. You could have had two daughters."

"In which case we'd have needed more ammo and not blankets," he mumbled. "Good thing the boys are coming first. They can protect their little sister."

I drew him to a halt. "Halden, are you kidding me right now? I'm going to pop out two babies in a few months and you're already planning to knock me up again?"

He smiled. "First chance I get."

I rolled my eyes. "You're insane. Just wait. All those sleepless nights will make you change your mind. I've heard newborns require a lot of work, and we're going to have two."

"Can't wait," he said, hugging me. His lips brushed mine and I melted against him. "Meeting you was the best thing that ever happened to me."

"Same." I smiled up at him. "You're everything to me. My life would have been so dull if we'd never met. Specter would have kept setting me up with his associates, and I'd have kept running from them. But sooner or later, I might have been lonely enough to give in. I'd have been miserable, though."

"Yeah?" he asked.

I nodded. "Because the only man I'm meant to be with is right here. You're my one and only. My husband. The love of my life. My very own Prince Charming."

He snorted. "You told me I was more caveman than prince."

"Fine. You're my very own Charming Caveman."

He threw back his head and laughed. "Come on, woman. I'll get you a milkshake before we head home."

"Ohh." I rubbed my belly again. "That sounds amazing. Make it a chocolate one and you just might get lucky when we get home."

He swatted my ass. "Honey, I'm lucky every day."

I'd have refuted his statement except I couldn't. The man only had to look at me and I wanted to unzip his pants. It had gotten even worse the last few months. More than once, I'd tracked him down and dragged him home for a few orgasms. The guys in the club laughed their asses off when they saw me coming. Charming had gotten a lot of grief over having a magic dick, but he took their jibes gracefully. Most of the time.

I hadn't seen my brother in months, and he seldom called. I knew something was brewing for him, and I hoped it didn't get him killed. My babies would need their uncle. Of course, Anatoly would be an honorary uncle to them. Even though he was based in Los Angeles, he'd already flown out twice to visit with us. I had a feeling we'd be seeing more of him.

My life wasn't perfect, but whose was? We had ups and downs, and trouble would probably find us again. But we had each other, and the club. A family. Our family.

No. It wasn't perfect. It was messy. But it was full of love and laughter, and that was all that mattered.

Harley Wylde

Harley Wylde is the International Bestselling Author of the Dixie Reapers MC, Devil's Boneyard MC, and Hades Abyss MC series. When Harley's writing, her motto is the hotter the better -- off the charts sex, commanding men, and the women who can't deny them. If you want men who talk dirty, are sexy as hell, and take what they want, then you've come to the right place. She doesn't shy away from the dangers and nastiness in the world, bringing those realities to the pages of her books, but always gives her characters a happily-ever-after and makes sure the bad guys get what they deserve.

The times Harley isn't writing, she's thinking up naughty things to do to her husband, drinking copious amounts of Starbucks, and reading. She loves to read and devours a book a day, sometimes more. She's also fond of TV shows and movies from the 1980's, as well as paranormal shows from the 1990's to today, even though she'd much rather be reading or writing. You can find out more about Harley or enter her monthly giveaway on her website. Be sure to join her newsletter while you're there to learn more about discounts, signing events, and other goodies!

Harley at Changeling: changelingpress.com/harley-wylde-a-196

Changeling Press E-Books

More Sci-Fi, Fantasy, Paranormal, and BDSM adventures available in e-book format for immediate download at ChangelingPress.com -- Werewolves, Vampires, Dragons, Shapeshifters and more -- Erotic Tales from the edge of your imagination.

What are E-Books?

E-books, or electronic books, are books designed to be read in digital format -- on your desktop or laptop computer, notebook, tablet, Smart Phone, or any electronic e-book reader.

Where can I get Changeling Press E-Books?

Changeling Press e-books are available at ChangelingPress.com, Amazon, Apple Books, Barnes & Noble, and Kobo/Walmart.

ChangelingPress.com